For This Week I Thee Wed
by Cheryl St. John

'Are you married?'

Ryan blinked, his warm brown eyes showing confusion over her abrupt change of subject. 'No,' he said finally. 'Is that relevant to the discussion?'

'Perhaps we can negotiate after all,' Francie said.

'Money is not an issue—'

'No, not money. In fact if you agree to this idea, you can keep your money. I'm afraid I've done something—said something—impetuous, and now I don't have any way out of it. Except maybe through you.'

'I don't understand.'

'I told my grandmother that I'd got married.'

'What does that have to do with me?'

'I've been cornered into participating at my ten-year reunion. Nana is expecting me. *And* my husband.' She paused. 'We can make a deal…if you come to Springdale with me as my husband for a week.'

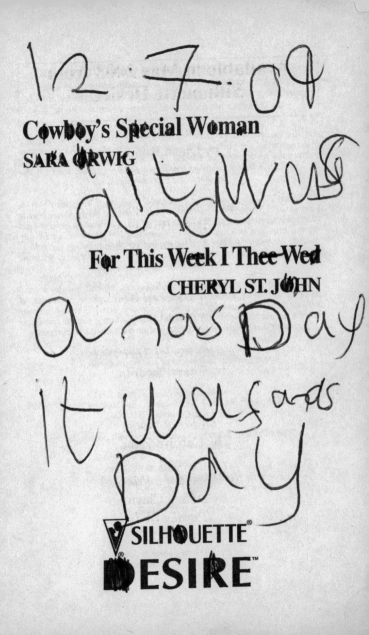

12-7-09

Cowboy's Special Woman
SARA ORWIG

and we

For This Week I Thee Wed
CHERYL ST. JOHN

a nas Day

it was ans

DAY

SILHOUETTE®
DESIRE™

Silhouette, Silhouette Desire and Colophon
are registered trademarks of Harlequin Books S.A.,
used under licence.

First published in Great Britain 2003
Silhouette Books, Eton House, 18-24 Paradise Road,
Richmond, Surrey TW9 1SR

The publisher acknowledges the copyright holders of the
individual works as follows:

Cowboy's Special Woman © Sara Orwig 2002
For This Week I Thee Wed © Cheryl Ludwigs 1999

ISBN 0 373 04865 3

51-0503

Printed and bound in Spain
by Litografia Rosés S.A., Barcelona

COWBOY'S SPECIAL WOMAN
by
Sara Orwig

SARA ORWIG

lives with her husband and children in Oklahoma. She has a patient husband who will take her on research trips anywhere, from big cities to old forts. She is an avid collector of Western history books. With a master's degree in English, Sara writes historical romances, mainstream fiction and contemporary romances. Books are beloved treasures that take Sara to magical worlds, and she loves both reading and writing them.

With thanks to my editors
Joan Marlow Golan and Julie Barrett

One

There weren't many things that could tie him in knots, but fire was one. Jake Reiner held his Harley with a white-knuckled grip and glanced over his shoulder at flames whipping through cedars and oaks. In spite of the hundred-degree August heat and blasts of hot Oklahoma wind, he was chilled by the sight of the fire. He knew he was racing along the dusty road at a dangerous speed, but he had to warn the ranch family who lived at the end of the lane.

In minutes he came roaring up from a dip in the road, took a curve and saw a tall two-story Victorian house ahead. Shade trees surrounded a three-car garage, a brown barn, a bunkhouse, sheds and a corral. A Circle A brand was burned in the wood above the barn door. Inside the fenced yard, a woman stepped around the thick trunk of a giant cottonwood tree. In her hand she held a power saw.

Jake's gaze raked over a figure that made his pulse skip. Cutoffs hugged trim hips and revealed long, shapely legs. Stretching snugly over lush breasts, a T-shirt was tucked into the waistband of the cutoffs. His gaze swept up to her face as he approached. She looked wary. Long, golden hair was in a thick braid that hung down her back to her waist.

Barking a warning, a black-and-tan dog ran around the barn. The woman's head snapped around and she spoke to the dog. Stopping beside her, it continued barking.

Jake slowed and braked, sending up a flurry of dust. As the engine idled, he braced his legs. Then he heard a child's cries. Following the sound, he looked at the cottonwood. Perched on a lower limb was a small girl with a gash on her head and tears streaking her cheeks.

"Mommy!"

"Hold on, Katy," the woman said calmly. Glaring at Jake, she snapped, "What do you want?"

"Can I help?" he asked, getting off the bike, realizing that, between the fire and whatever was happening here, this family had real trouble. At the moment, the child seemed the most urgent problem.

"Why are you here?" the woman asked, her cautious demeanor transforming to anger. As he watched sparks dancing in her blue eyes, he knew he didn't give a reassuring appearance with his shaggy hair, his bike, and his ragged jeans.

"Up by the road your place is on fire."

While her gaze flew past him, the color drained from her face.

"Not now!" she gasped and looked up at the

child. "I have to get Katy free first." She turned away as if she had already forgotten his presence.

Moving closer to the tree and forgetting the stranger, Maggie Langford fought a rising panic. Katy was caught and hurting, and now their place was on fire. A really bad fire would devastate them. She said a small prayer that she could free Katy's foot, which was wedged between a limb and the trunk. As Maggie raised the heavy saw, a hand closed around her wrist and the stranger took the saw from her.

For a split second, with the physical contact, an electric current of awareness zipped through her. When the stranger stepped closer, Katy let out a howl.

"I'll just cut a little more, and then I can break that limb free. You get up there and hold her so she doesn't fall," he said in a deep voice.

"Hang on, Katy, I'm coming up beside you," Maggie said, trying to calm her child.

"This is my little tomboy," she told the stranger. "Katy was climbing and fell. Shh, Katy. It'll be all right. You'll be loose soon," Maggie said.

"Have to watch these trees. They'll just reach out and grab you," the stranger said to Katy with a re-assuring smile that softened his rugged features.

Through tears and the streaks of blood from the head wound, Katy smiled in return.

Maggie caught a limb and pulled herself up, taking hold of her five-year-old. Katy twisted to cling to her.

Maggie looked down at the tall, deeply tanned man. His shaggy black hair hung below the red ban-danna wound around his head. He wore a black T-shirt with the sleeves ripped away, and thick mus-

cles flexed as he sawed the limb. The loud buzz of
the saw was the only sound until he stopped, set
down the saw and glanced up at her with his dark
eyes.

"Ready?"

She nodded. "Hang on to me, Katy," she said,
holding her daughter.

The stranger jumped up, grasped the limb and
hung on it. With a sharp crack the limb split from
the tree, freeing Katy's foot. As agile as a cat, the
stranger landed on his feet and tossed the limb aside.

Katy's arms tightened around Maggie's neck, and
Maggie held her tightly in return, relieved to have
her daughter safe again. Then the stranger reached
up. "Hand her to me."

Maggie passed her daughter down. The stranger
set her gently on the ground and Katy rubbed her
ankle and sniffed. Maggie swung her legs over the
limb to jump down. As she jumped, hands came
around her waist and the stranger caught her. Without thought she put her hands out to grip his arms,
feeling the rock-solid muscles, looking into brown
eyes that bored into her with an electrifying intensity.
The instant her hands had closed on his arms, a current had raced through her. Unable to breathe or look
away, she stared back at him while her heart ham-
mered. He smelled faintly of sweat and aftershave.
The aftershave surprised her. He looked primitive
rather than civilized, yet she knew she was rushing
to judge too swiftly.

He lowered her to the ground and for seconds she
was still caught and held in his compelling gaze.

"Mommy."

Her daughter's voice released her from the spell,

and Maggie stepped back, dropping her hands to her sides. "Thanks again, mister. I have to call 911 and alert them about the fire."

She knelt beside her daughter. "Let me see your ankle, Katy." She was aware that the stranger watched while she checked Katy's bruised and scratched ankle. She moved her daughter's foot gently. "That hurt?"

"No."

"Katy, you should thank the man," Maggie said as she stood.

"Thank you, sir," Katy said politely, sniffing and rubbing her ankle as she tried to stand. Maggie swung her up into her arms.

"My name is Jake Reiner," the stranger said in a voice that stirred a curl of warmth in Maggie. Once more she was riveted by his gaze. With an effort she broke away, turning toward the house. She waved her hand toward the barn. "There's a spigot. You might like a cold drink. I've got a fire to fight. Thanks for alerting me about it. C'mon, Tuffy," she commanded, and the dog trotted at her heels.

She shifted the child and headed for the house as Jake watched, fascinated. Her hips swayed slightly and her cutoffs were short enough to give him a delectable view of long legs. He stood staring at her until the screen door slapped shut behind her.

When he glanced back up the lane to the southwest, Jake saw a plume of gray smoke rising over the treetops, the high wind swirling it away. This ranch family was in deep trouble.

Between the garage and the barn, Jake spotted the faucet and strolled toward it. When he passed the garage and glanced inside, he saw a pickup and a battered flatbed truck that had once been black but had lost most of its paint. Turning the spigot, he splashed cold water over his head. As he ran his fingers through his hair, he looked into the barn that stood open to his left. The barn was filled with a clutter of tack and large trunks. He glanced from the barn to his bike, which held most of his worldly possessions. At least with his wandering lifestyle, he didn't have to mend, repair or care for a lot of things. He bent to take another long drink and splash more water on himself. As he straightened, a pickup barreled up the road and rocked to a stop, sending up a thick plume of red dust. A brown-haired woman jumped out and glanced at Jake.

"Is Maggie inside?" she asked as she ran around the pickup.

When he nodded, she moved faster, sprinting to the house and reaching for the screen door without knocking. In seconds the blonde appeared, unhooked the screen, which Jake assumed had been secured because of his presence. The brunette stepped inside while the blonde came out. He saw the brunette hook the screen and look at him a moment, but then his gaze shifted to the blonde. She hurried toward him, her breasts bouncing with each step.

"Have to get to the fire," she said as she passed him and headed into the garage.

In its dim interior she grabbed a shovel and tossed it into the bed of a pickup where it landed with a clang.

Jake moved into the garage, feeling the coolness when he stepped out of the sunlight. "Can I help?"

"Grab those gunnysacks, wet them down and throw them in the pickup," she ordered while she ran toward the barn. He spotted empty gunnysacks hanging on a hook. Lifting them down, he carried them to the faucet. As soon as they were soaked, he tossed them into the back of the pickup. She threw more shovels into the back.

"Thanks, again, mister."

"Sure," he said, opening the pickup door for her. "And you can call me Jake," he added.

She gave him a quick nod. With another flash of her long legs, she climbed inside. In spite of the fire, the rancher who lived here was a lucky man with a pretty wife and a cute little daughter. Jake was surprised at his sentiments. He valued his freedom enough that he didn't usually view anyone who was married and settled as lucky. He closed the pickup door and turned to go to his bike.

As the pickup raced past him, he waited, letting the dust settle before he followed.

Overhead a gray cloud of smoke spread in the sky and his sympathy for her increased. The south wind was blowing the fire north toward her house. He rounded a bend and smoke rolled over the road, engulfing him. As he drove through it, he held his breath. When the world became a dense gray blur that stung his eyes and burned his throat, panic threatened. He knew the rule: don't drive into smoke. But he had driven into it and now he had to keep going. He could feel the heat of the fire and hear its roar. Then, as he reached the backside of the smoke and fire, he could see again.

Gulping fresh air, he was stunned by the magnitude of the fire that raged out of control, stretching across the land with acres of burning trees and grass. Cars lined the county road as men worked to beat out the flames. Someone had parked a flatbed truck near the firefighters and in the back of the truck were three large orange coolers and a stack of paper cups. Jake wondered how all these people had learned about the fire so quickly, but he assumed word spread fast and neighbors rushed to help out.

Two pumper trucks were driving along the perimeter of the fire, the firemen pouring gushing silver streams of water on the line of flames, but the strong wind was fanning the fire furiously and their effort seemed futile. Accentuated by pops and crackles, the blaze roared while heat waves shimmered in the hot summer air.

Jake spotted the blonde, already in the line of men fighting the fire with shovels and gunnysacks. She was working as hard as any man around her, swinging a gunnysack and beating flames. While dread and sorrow tore at him, Jake parked in the line of pickups.

Jogging back up the road, he spotted a shovel in the bed of a pickup. Grabbing the shovel, Jake fell into line with the volunteers, moving to the edge of the fire to try to smother the bright orange flames while heat buffeted him.

As he inhaled the stinging smoke, his mind jumped back in time. Hating the tormenting memories of that long-ago fire, he dug with fury.

In the flickering orange, he saw himself as a boy, running and looking at a glow in the sky. Deep in the black hours of early morning, coming home across backyards, he had seen pink light the night sky. As he drew nearer to it, the first fear gripped him and then he was racing, bursting around the corner and tearing across the street toward his home that was a roaring blaze lighting up the entire block.

While the raging inferno consumed his house, he tried to run inside and firemen held him back. Over his yelling, he finally heard their shouts. How long did it take him to realize they were telling him his family was dead? Still, all these years later, a knot tightened in Jake's throat. He hated his vulnerability, and thought he had succeeded in keeping his feelings tightly locked away, yet this burning wall of flame brought the horror and hurt back. With the fire dancing in front of him, its flames taunting him, the years vanished and the pain he had felt that night consumed him. Tears streaked his cheeks. Harder and faster he dug as if physical labor could erase the aching memories and the screaming guilt.

A man passed him. "Ease up, son. If you don't slow, we'll be carrying you away. I'm taking water to everyone."

Facing Jake was a tall, brown-haired man in ragged overalls. He held a water cooler and a tin cup.

"You're Jake Reiner, aren't you?"

"Yes, sir. Thanks." Jake filled the cup and drank, not caring that it was a communal cup.

"I'm Ben Alden. I've seen you ride."

"Thanks for the water," Jake said, returning the cup. The man nodded and moved down the line. Jake glanced along the row and saw the blonde talking to the man. She turned back to fight the fire.

Soon it seemed as if he had been fighting fire for hours. As sweat poured off his body, smoke burned his eyes and throat. Around him men yelled, and he could hear the rumble of the pumper trucks over the crackle and roar of the fire.

With his muscles screaming, Jake looked around and saw the blonde talking to Ben Alden again, the man who had carried the water around earlier. The man had his big, work-reddened hands on her shoulders.

Watching the man touch her possessively, Jake had an uncustomary annoyance and couldn't understand his reaction. He didn't even know the woman's name and would never see her again after this morning, but he wished he could push Ben Alden's hands off of her shoulders. Alden was probably her husband. Jake stared at the tall, rawboned man who was much older than she was. His brown hair was streaked with gray. He was solid muscle on big bones. He wore a T-shirt beneath coveralls. Then Jake noticed their profiles, the same straight noses and broad foreheads and he wondered if the man was her father.

Taking a deep breath, Jake returned to digging, throwing dirt on the fire, watching the flames spread with each gust of wind. Now three pumper trucks were working along the backside of the fire, but in spite of everyone's efforts, they weren't bringing the blaze under control. Long ago Jake had shed his shirt and sweat poured off his body. He thought of ice and longed for a cold shower and a cold drink.

The ranch house and other buildings were in view now. Choking and coughing, he felt on fire. His hands were raw, and he had to stop for water. He headed toward the flatbed truck with the water coolers, reaching first to pour a bucket of water over himself.

He spotted the blonde, still struggling to swing a gunnysack and he suspected she must be about to drop from the exertion. He picked up a paper cup and the cooler and walked over to her, catching her arm.

She turned, her face smudged with soot. Her T-shirt was plastered to her body from perspiration. Wordlessly he filled the cup and held it out to her. She looked dazed, and he took her arm to lead her to the pickup.

With shaking hands, she grasped the cup and gulped the water. "Thanks," she said, staring at him while he tilted the cooler and refilled her cup.

"Maybe you should go up to your house and get your little girl out of there and save what you can."

"Shortly after I left, my sister Patsy took Katy and Tuffy, our dog, to her house. She packed some of Katy's things." Maggie looked at the fire. "I'm needed more here."

"We're not going to stop it," Jake said. "Go save some of your clothes and furniture. I'll drive you up there and help. Come on. None of us can stop this inferno unless it rains or the wind changes and those possibilities look unlikely."

When he took her arm, she hesitated. "Come on," he urged. In silence she walked with him. "Which pickup is yours?" he asked.

She stared at him blankly and then looked around, pointing to a black pickup parked in a line of pick-ups. "Keys," he said, holding out his hand.

"I can drive."

"Give me the keys. You can catch your breath."

As she handed over the keys, they walked to the pickup. He drove through a wall of smoke again until they were beyond it.

"Our house," she said softly as they approached her home. "My grandfather built this house."

"Was that your husband you were talking to?"

"No." Her head swung around and she looked at him for a moment as if she had to think back to remember. "He's my father. My husband and I are divorced."

"Sorry."

"I came back home last year to live with my dad when my mother died."

"I don't know your name."

"Maggie Langford."

"I met your dad when he brought me some water. He's Ben Alden," he said and she nodded. Jake pulled to a stop by the back door and climbed out. She was already out and sprinting for the back door.

"Anything in particular I can get for you?"

"Yes. If we can save it, there's some furniture that has been handed down through the generations."

When he followed her inside, all her dazed manner vanished as she began to briskly issue orders.

As he secured the last bit of a second load of scrapbooks, clothing and furniture, Jake glanced over his shoulder and his stomach knotted at the proximity of the blaze. The house, barn and all outbuildings seemed doomed. He heard an engine and when he looked around, the three pumper trucks came down the lane, and her father drove a tractor along the side of the road. Firemen spilled from the trucks and ran to the house with fire retardant blankets to toss over the furniture. In minutes Ben Alden plowed a broad swath on the south side of the house, and then he crossed the road to plow west of the barn and around the other structures.

"You get this pickup out of harm's way. I'll stay and help here," Jake said.

"I want to get some saddles from the barn," she answered. "Thank heaven the horses are out of there!" Jake jogged beside her as she trotted to the barn. When she stopped inside, her brow furrowed. "Dad's stuff…" As her voice trailed away, she looked stricken.

"What do you want out of the barn?" Jake said briskly, knowing they were running out of time. Crackling and roaring, the fire was much closer. The wind was as high as ever and sparks constantly were caught in gusts, flying away to start new blazes.

"Everything," she said quietly. She gave a small shake of her shoulders. "Those saddles," she said, pointing, and Jake ran to get what she asked for. He carried out three saddles and put them in the pickup.

In minutes the blaze approached the barn.

"Get the pickup out of here," Jake shouted to her. "If you don't, you'll lose everything and the pickup, too."

She climbed in and was gone as more men came into view. Jake heard a shout and saw a fireman pointing. He turned and saw the first lick of flame curling on the barn roof. Jake swore, grabbing up a shovel.

Creating a barrier, the drive cut through between the house to the east and the barn, the garage, the bunkhouse and the sheds to the west, so firemen moved to widen the swath of wet, plowed ground between the barn and the house to try to save the house. Maggie's father plowed furrows, riding in widening strips while everyone battled the blaze.

When Jake spotted Maggie back with the firefighters, he worked his way toward her. "You could still get another carload of your belongings out of the house if you want. I'll help."

She shook her head. "No, we'll try to save the house. I'd rather—"

"Maggie, did you get the trunks out of the barn?" her father called, driving the tractor up beside them. Jake glanced at the barn and saw the whole building was burning now.

"No, I got the saddles."

"I'm getting them," her father said, sprinting toward the barn.

"Dad!" Maggie started after him, but Jake grabbed her arm.

"I'll go," he said and raced after her father who had already disappeared inside the barn.

Jake yanked down his bandanna and tied it over his nose. As he ran inside he put an arm up to shield his face, trying to hold his breath and not inhale the thick smoke. All around him, fire roared and he couldn't see through the smoke.

Then a figure loomed up before him. "Take this," Maggie's father shouted and thrust a small trunk at Jake.

"Sir, this building is going to go!"

"Get out!"

Sprinting outside, Jake set down the trunk and ran back toward the burning barn. He spotted a dark silhouette of a man only a few yards inside, but before he reached the open door, he heard a crack like a shotgun blast. A large beam fell.

The beam struck Ben Alden, knocking him down only a few feet from the door.

Two

Running toward the burning barn, Maggie screamed.

"I'll get him," Jake shouted. "You stay out."

Crouching to avoid smoke as much as possible, Jake raced inside. He groped his way until he spotted the figure lying in front of him, a burning beam across his legs. Without hesitation Jake grabbed the beam and shoved it away. He hoisted Maggie's father over his shoulder, moving blindly and praying he was headed toward the door and not deeper into the barn.

As he burst through smoke and into fresh air, he staggered and lowered her father carefully to the ground. While Jake yanked away the bandanna and gulped fresh air, Maggie knelt beside her dad.

"This man needs help," Jake yelled to one of the firefighters who ran toward them.

"Dad! I've called an ambulance."

"Are you all right?" a fireman asked Jake.

"Yeah," he nodded, coughing and still trying to get fresh air into his lungs. He moved back to allow two firemen to help her father.

Maggie thrust a bucket of water into Jake's hands and he poured it over himself, cold water drenching him, a momentary relief from the smoke and heat. "Thank you," she said, earnest blue eyes gazing at him. Her face was smudged with soot and her blond hair had come loose from the braid so that long strands fell freely around her face.

"Sure," he said and then she was gone, back kneeling beside her father while the firemen hovered over him.

With a rumble and a crack, the entire roof of the barn fell, sending flames and sparks shooting high overhead. Firefighters yelled as they worked frantically to keep the flames away from the house. Jake walked to a truck and poured a cup of water, gulping it, aware of hurting and stinging in a dozen different places. His hands felt like raw meat. Wind swirled against him and he lifted his head, realizing that it had shifted slightly.

When he went back to join the firefighters, he heard men talking about the wind, but conversation wasn't needed to tell him the wind was shifting. So far the flames had not crossed the road or flown over the swath of plowed dirt.

He glanced over his shoulder and saw an ambulance with flashing lights. Jake guessed they were getting Maggie's father into the ambulance. He hoped Ben Alden recovered.

The wind shifted, giving renewed energy to Jake

to battle the blaze that was now turning back on it-self.

In another hour they had the blaze under control and the professionals took over to finish the work. On blackened ground lay the smoldering ruins of the barn, the garage and the other outbuildings. Everything was destroyed except the house.

"I think you should let a doctor look at your burns."

When he turned, Maggie stood only a few feet away. She had cleaned up and changed clothes. Now in jeans and a blue shirt, she looked cool and as sexy as ever. She had combed her hair and it hung in a thick braid over her shoulder.

"I'm all right."

"You don't look all right. I'm going to the hospital to see about my dad. Come with me to the emergency and someone will treat your burns."

Half of him wanted to get on his bike and go. The other half was drawn to her soft voice and big blue eyes and the sense that she really cared.

"Sure," he answered, feeling he was making a mistake, yet unable to resist hanging around her a little longer. "I need to move my bike from the road."

"I'll take you to get it." When she jerked her head, he saw she had brought her pickup back to the house. It was still loaded with her belongings.

"If you'd like, I can help you unload first."

She shook her head. "I want to get to town to see my dad."

They walked in silence to the pickup, and he climbed into the passenger side. Sliding behind the wheel, Maggie started the motor. In a few minutes she dropped him off at his bike, turned around and drove back to the house with him trailing behind.

Jake parked his bike, yanked on his black T-shirt and climbed into the pickup. "Want me to drive?"

"No," Maggie answered with amusement. "I'm accustomed to doing things for myself. And your hands look as if it would be painful to drive."

"I don't mind." As they drove away, he glanced out the window. "At least your house is saved."

"Thank heavens! It's bad enough to lose everything else, but our house would have been so much worse. I've been working to turn our home into a bed-and-breakfast. I'd hate to see all my efforts plus our belongings go up in flames like the barn did."

"Aren't you a little far out from any town for a bed-and-breakfast?"

As she shrugged, he shifted slightly in the seat, turning to study her, looking at flawless skin that he knew would be soft.

"I think some city people will enjoy a ranch experience and I can run the bed-and-breakfast while my dad runs the ranch. I'm going to give it a try. We have a big house, and I think I'll succeed."

"Have you always lived here?"

"Except for the two years while I was married. When I went to college, I lived at home and commuted. Where do you live?"

"First one place and then another," he answered. When she glanced at him, he suspected she didn't approve of his vagabond lifestyle.

"Dad said he's seen you in rodeos."

"I'm a saddle bronc rider."

"Dad used to do calf roping, but that was a long time ago. His health isn't as good as it used to be."

"Too bad. This fire is another burden."

"Thanks for stopping to warn us. It would have been worse if you hadn't."

"I don't know. No one could contain it until the wind changed." Jake continued to study her, wondering about her and her life. She was a beautiful woman, and he couldn't imagine her living like she did. "Don't you feel buried out here on your ranch?"

"Buried?"

"Seems like a quiet life."

She flashed him a smile, the first he had received, and it made his pulse jump. She had a dimple in her right cheek and the smile showed in her eyes, animating her face in a quick, enticing flash like the sun coming out from behind a cloud.

"It's a quiet life, and I love it that way. Where's your home now?"

"On my bike."

He received a startled glance and grinned at her. "I don't like a quiet life. I travel."

"Do you work or am I prying?"

"Pry away. I do bronc riding and I train horses. I just quit a job working with horses for a friend of mine near Fort Worth. After a while I get restless and I move on."

"Where's your family?"

"I don't have any."

"You had to have parents."

"They were killed in a fire," he answered, looking out the window and clenching his fists. He had told few people in his adult life about his family and he wondered why he had just told her.

She gave him a searching glance and then returned her attention to the road. "That's why you fought our fire so hard," she said quietly. "Dad and I wondered."

"Why would you wonder? Everyone out there fought hard."

"Not the way you did. You went after it like you wanted to put it out single-handedly." She gave him another searching glance.

"Is your little girl in school?" he asked, not caring about her answer, but wanting to get the conversation away from him and his family and fires.

"Not yet. Katy was just five last week. She'll be in kindergarten when the fall term starts.

"Where did you meet your husband?"

"Bart grew up here and we'd known each other forever. I think we married too young—too young for him, at least, and he didn't like being tied down. Particularly when Katy was born. He was here only a short time after her birth and then he was gone. Just like that, and Katy was without a father. Bart asked for the divorce."

"You can marry again," Jake said, thinking she could if she got off the ranch and met people. "You're young."

"I'm twenty-nine."

"That's young. I'm thirty-five."

"I won't marry again anytime soon," she replied after a moment's thought as if she hadn't considered the possibility before. He looked at her golden hair that looked soft as silk and wondered about her.

"So what are you really like, Maggie Langford? Is it Margaret?"

"It's Margaret and I'm really like the person I am right now. I love home and family."

He had already guessed that from watching her

during the day. He became silent, glancing at her occasionally, amazed someone else hadn't come along and married her and surprised she sounded so happy about her life on the farm.

Taking the highway, they drove into Stillwater, and uneasiness stirred in Jake. He should have hit the road instead of going into town with her. He didn't particularly want to go to the hospital. A shower and a pitcher of ice cold water would make him feel one hundred percent better. He caught a whiff of her perfume, a flower scent that went with her fresh ranch manner, and the enticing, feminine smell drove away all thoughts of leaving. He turned to watch her and found it a very pleasant pastime that made him forget his aches and his hurry to be on his way. What was it about her that drew him? And that first moment they had touched—in her clear, blue eyes he had seen that she had felt something, too.

When they reached the hospital, she told Jake to join her when he was released and then she went to see her father. Jake went to the emergency where a vivacious black-haired nurse treated his cuts and burns.

"You're new around here," she said and for the first time he really noticed her. Her big brown eyes gazed steadily at him while she cleaned a cut.

"Yep. I was driving past and saw the fire and stopped to tell the Aldens."

"Are you staying awhile?"

He glanced at her name tag and saw it was Laurie. "I haven't decided, Laurie. Anything worth staying for?" he asked, unable to resist flirting with her. She gave him a smile.

"We have all sorts of places: bars, honky-tonks, my apartment."

He laughed and looked at her fingers. No wedding or engagement ring. Evidently he could have a date if he wanted one. He thought of Maggie Langford and the thought of asking Laurie out vanished. He shifted restlessly, wishing again that he had his bike with him.

"Sounds interesting," he said, looking at her full lips and still thinking about Maggie. "Do you know if there is anyone around here now who might be going back by Ben Alden's place? I rode in with Maggie, but if I can find a ride, I won't trouble her for a ride home. My bike is at her place."

Laurie moved close against his knees and tilted his chin up to work on a cut on his temple. She paused and looked into his eyes. "If you can wait until I get off, I can take you to the Circle A ranch to get your bike," she said in a sultry voice.

"Thanks. Maybe I'll return later and take you up on that offer, but I need to get going. The fire delayed me today."

She smiled and nodded, and he didn't know if he had softened his refusal enough to keep from hurting her feelings, but he didn't want to take her out. He didn't want to think about why because it had been a long time since he'd had a date with a woman who was fun and pretty. He was ready for a night out, but this wasn't the night.

"I don't know who can take you back. You might ask if Jeff Peterson is still here. He lives out past the Alden place."

"Thanks."

Ten minutes later, Jake asked at the front desk if

anyone named Peterson was still around and was told that Jeff Peterson had left the hospital about five minutes earlier. Jake's only choices were to hitch a ride, wait for Maggie to go home or have a date with Laurie.

He asked for Ben Alden's room and rode the elevator upstairs. When he rapped lightly on the partially closed door and thrust his head into the room, Ben motioned to him. "Come in. I want to thank you. You saved my life." Ben was bandaged and propped up in bed.

Jake shrugged. "Sorry you got hurt and sorry so much of your place burned." Maggie stood across the room from him on the opposite side of her father's bed.

As Jake entered the room, Maggie watched him. He was broad-shouldered, muscular and his presence seemed to electrify the air. There was an earthy sensuality to him, yet she wondered if she thought that because he was in a tight T-shirt, covered with soot, cut and burned instead of dressed in freshly laundered clothes, looking like most other people. She suspected in freshly laundered clothes, he would never look like most other people. His height, rugged features and wild black hair would keep him from blending into a crowd. It was his riveting brown eyes that disturbed her the most. Her gaze slid down over his slim hips. His jeans rode low. She looked up, caught him watching her and blushed at the manner in which she had been studying him.

She was too conscious of his hot-blooded looks, his blunt questions. She tried to shift her thoughts, telling herself he would be out of her life as soon as she took him home tonight. He was going to set off on his bike and she wouldn't ever see him again.

"We'll build back," her father answered Jake. "Thank you for your help."

"You're welcome. How are you feeling?" Jake asked.

"Pretty good, considering," Ben answered, smiling ruefully and raising bandaged hands.

"Pretty good with burns and a broken leg," Maggie remarked dryly. "But you really did save him from being hurt much worse."

"That's good. I'm sorry about your injuries."

"I'll mend. I've mended before. Maggie tells me you've been working with horses."

"Yes, sir. I've been in Texas, working for Jeb Stuart. I'll be in a rodeo in Oklahoma City Labor Day weekend, so I wound my work up with Jeb and hit the road. I was just driving past your place when I saw the fire."

"I thought Jeb Stuart was your biggest rival in saddle bronc riding."

"He is, but he's also my best friend," Jake replied.

"Where are you going from here—except for the rodeo?"

"Dad, maybe that's private," Maggie said, glancing at Jake.

He smiled at her, holding her gaze while he answered. "No, not private at all. I don't have any plans. Just whatever comes along."

"Good. I'm laid up here and will be when I get home. How about coming to work for us until I get on my feet? I need someone badly."

Shocked, Maggie's head whipped around as she

stared at her father. They hadn't discussed hiring Jake Reiner or anyone else. When Jake frowned, she guessed that he didn't want to work for them and relief washed over her. Astounded her father would ask him without consulting her, she wondered if her father was thinking clearly or if the pain pills had muddled his thought processes. Their small bunkhouse for hired help had burned so they had no place for a hired hand to live—not even in the barn. Jake Reiner would have to stay in the house with them. Actually he would be alone in the house with her because Katy was at Patsy's and her father wouldn't be coming home for another day.

"I know you've been more than a help to us so far. A life saver, really, but I can't take care of things for a little while. If you could just stay at the Circle A and work until I'm able to get back to it, I'd make it worth your while. You've got to eat, sleep and work somewhere," he added.

Jake Reiner took a deep breath.

"Dad, Jake probably already had plans."

Her father turned his head to look at her. "Honey, I worry about you and I know I should be home taking care of things. Jake just left a job and he said he's free. We need him sort of on the desperate side." He looked at Jake. "We usually have four or five men working for us, but for one reason or another, we don't have any now. I promise to make working for us worthwhile for you," he repeated.

She looked into Jake's eyes and knew he didn't want to stay. Why didn't he just say so and go!

"Dad—"

He waved his hand. "Let the man get a word in, Maggie. I'll only be laid up for a short time and if it gets too long for you, Jake,'' he said, turning his attention back to Jake, ''we'll find a replacement for you. In the meantime, I could sure use your help.''

Jake was still gazing into Maggie's eyes. Looking into his dark, inscrutable gaze, she held her breath.

''Yes, sir,'' he said quietly.

She closed her eyes and rubbed her temple. What had her father done? She was sure he wasn't thinking clearly. They would need help, but they could find someone who lived in the area and had a house or room they could go back to every night. What was she going to do with Jake Reiner?

''Thanks, Jake,'' Ben said, closing his eyes. ''I can't tell you how relieved that makes me feel. Now I can just worry about rebuilding.''

''Dad, just think about getting well,'' Maggie said. ''I'm staying tonight at the hospital so—''

''No, you're not. I want a quiet night's sleep,'' her father interjected, ''and Imogene is the night nurse. You know she'll take good care of me,'' he added and chuckled.

Maggie knew she wouldn't be needed at the hospital. For the past two years, Imogene Randle had wanted to marry her father. Now, here at the hospital, Imogene had him in her clutches, and Maggie was sure Imogene would be in his room constantly. The past twenty minutes were the longest she had been out of his room since Maggie arrived. Maggie looked at Jake again and met another curious stare. She was going to have to take him home with her and let him stay there.

Her stomach fluttered at the thought. He disturbed her and he was a stranger even though her father knew him from rodeos. Just because the guy won big belt buckles and had lots of money didn't make him safe to take into their house.

She rubbed her earlobe nervously and tried to think what she could do to change the situation. She looked at her father who was breathing deeply with his eyes closed.

"He's asleep. And he's right about Imogene. She'll check on him constantly so I guess we might as well go." Dazed by the swift turn of events, Maggie picked up her purse. "Are you ready to go home?"

The words had a strange ring to them. She knew this wasn't an ordinary man and taking him home with her was not like taking the next half dozen strangers home.

Was she really scared of him or was she scared of her own reactions to him? she wondered.

He nodded and turned to hold the door for her. Neither of them said a word as they rode down in the elevator and headed for her pickup. All the time in her mind, she kept running through the names of every hired hand they'd had or anyone else she could think of she could hire in place of Jake. Surely there was someone, and Jake had looked as if he would jump at the chance to go. Why had he let her father talk him into this?

"I know you don't want to do this. I'm sure I can find someone else," she said as she drove out of the hospital lot.

He twisted in the seat to look at her. They were still in the glow of town lights and she could see him well enough to see the flare of amusement in his eyes.

"You don't want me to work for you, do you?"

"I don't know you."

"Look, if you don't want me there, I'll go."

She shot him a look and then thought about her father. "Let me see if I can hire someone else. You really don't want to work for us, do you?"

"No. It's nothing personal. I had planned to take off work for a short time and travel, but your father needs help. More than you can give him if you're doing the cooking and taking care of your little girl. You see who you can hire. In the meantime, don't worry. I'm a safe, trustworthy person. If you'd like, you can call Jeb Stuart and get references. When we get to your house, I'll give you his number."

"Thanks. It just makes me nervous for you to move into our house when I don't know you," she admitted.

He shrugged. "It's summer. I saw a hammock in your yard—I can sleep there."

"You don't mind?"

"Nope."

She nodded and was silent and wondered what was running through his mind and if he thought that she was the silliest female he had ever encountered. He hadn't wanted to stay and work for them, yet why was he so reluctant to stay? She would call Jeb Stuart when they got home.

"When will your daughter come home?"

"I'll pick her up in the morning. I have two married sisters who live in town. They have kids, too, and all the little cousins are close."

"Nice big family," he said glancing around. "Are there any restaurants between here and your house? It just dawned on me and my stomach that I haven't eaten since last night."

"Sorry. There isn't anything unless we turn around and go back to town, but I have leftovers at home."

"That's good enough. I'd like to take a shower."

"Of course. I'm sorry about your staying in our house—"

"Forget it," he said.

They lapsed into silence again with the rumble of the pickup's engine the only noise. Jake stared into the dark night and felt caught in a trap. The father wanted him to stay, the daughter wanted him to go. And he wanted to go, dammit! Yet when he looked into the old man's eyes and then into hers, out had come an acceptance. He was getting himself tied down when he didn't want to be, in a place he didn't want to be. He was drawn to Maggie Langford and that alone made him uneasy. Most women he met were like the nurse in the emergency—flirtatious, fun and someone he could take or leave. And he always left them.

A broken leg took weeks to mend. Jake had had enough breaks to know. He didn't want to work at Maggie's ranch for weeks. And she sure as hell didn't want him to. If looks could send him flying to Mars, he would be on his way now.

He didn't mind sleeping out in the yard in the hammock. It would probably be cool and comfortable, but it was ridiculous. If he intended to harm her, staying in the yard wouldn't stop him. He was going home to eat with her and shower in her house. He glanced at her again. She was definitely easy to look at. He liked her better in shorts and a T-shirt.

They drove up to the darkened house, and she cut the engine. When he started to get out, he saw her staring at their burned field and the ruins of the garage and the barn.

"Sorry," he said, understanding too well her sense of loss and sobered by the sight of the blackened land that brought back ugly memories for him.

"It happened so fast and took so much. It'll take a long time to get things back to the way they were. Dad was after a trunk of old things that had been his father's."

"That's not as important as his life."

"I know, but he was upset and wanted to save it. I should have had you help me get those trunks out before I ever left the house the first time."

"You did the best you could."

She turned to look at him. "It's been a long day. Sorry if I'm less than hospitable. You've been good to us."

He shrugged. "Forget it." He stepped out and came around to open her door as she opened it. He held it for her and closed it. Getting some fresh clothes from his bike, he caught up with her and walked with her through the gate where she stopped abruptly.

"Oh, my!" Following her gaze, he looked at her family belongings that he had helped her move out of the house earlier. "Our friends must have moved everything back up here in front of the house."

"Where'd you put all this when you left here?"

"Across the road from the fire and friends saw me and helped unload the pickup each time. I thought I'd go back and get it tomorrow."

"I'll move it inside for you."

"Thanks, but not now. I'm exhausted and no rain

is predicted for the rest of the week. We'll do that tomorrow.''

''Sure,'' he said easily as they went inside. She switched on lights in a kitchen that had high ceilings and glass-fronted cabinets. Some appliances were new, and the place looked comfortable with plants, a large walnut table and yellow chintz-covered cushions.

''Do you mind giving me Jeb Stuart's phone number?'' she asked. His gaze drifted down to her full lips and he wondered what it would be like to kiss her. Forget it, he told himself. The lady is definitely off-limits. Yet what was it about her that made him think of long, wet kisses and hot nights? She was Mom and apple pie, wholesome, uninterested in men at this point in her life. He shouldn't give her a second glance or thought. But something happened every time he was around her or she looked at him, something that started his pulse racing. He wondered if the smoke and fire had done something to his senses. If it had, it would be a far less disturbing discovery than to know she could have that effect on him by doing nothing more than looking up at him with those big blue eyes.

When she handed him a pen and a tablet, his fingers brushed hers. He was instantly aware of their fingers touching. Fingers. Nothing except the most casual contact. Except there was nothing casual about the effect on his system. What was it about her?

At the hospital the nurse had blatantly rubbed against him, hip against leg, her body against his shoulder, her soft breast pressing against his back and none of her contacts had done to him what the slightest brush of his fingers against Maggie's did.

Amazement warred with fear in him. No woman had ever caused such an intense reaction. He didn't want this one to.

He scribbled Jeb's number and gave the pen and tablet back.

"C'mon. I'll show you where the bathroom is and where the towels are."

Entranced by the slight sway of her hips and the faint scent of her perfume, he walked behind her through a wide hallway. Large, high-ceilinged rooms were on either side of the hallway. With paneling and beams and mahogany trim, the rooms looked livable and comfortable. The decor was chintz, patterned material and lace. Antiques sat on shelves and tables while pictures decorated the walls. The house held a cozy charm, and he could easily imagine her living in it.

"Your home is nice. This was built by your grandfather?"

"Yes, and then he married grandmother and added on to the house. When it passed to Dad, he built the family room, a bath and another bedroom. I love the old house. I've redecorated a lot of it, getting it ready to be a bed-and-breakfast."

She turned and walked down the hall and he moved beside her. "You'll have strangers in your house when you have a bed-and-breakfast."

"That'll be different," she said, then bit her lip and her cheeks flushed, and his curiosity soared about her answer.

"How'll it be different?"

The pink in her cheeks deepened. "Dad will be home then."

"He might not be here every night. And your

daughter might be gone, too. I don't think that's what you meant when you said it would be different, Maggie,'' he drawled softly, taking her arm lightly. ''How'll it be different?''

He was aware of touching her, holding her arm so lightly because he didn't want to frighten her. And he knew he was treading dangerous ground with his persistent question, yet he couldn't resist. Sparks flew between them that kept the air and his blood sizzling. He wanted to kiss her and he wanted to hear the answer to his question.

She looked up at him, wide-eyed, but in the depths of her eyes was something else, something age-old, a look from a woman to a man, and his pulse jumped.

''You probably have this effect on every woman,'' she said so quietly he had to lean closer to hear her.

''What effect?'' he asked, with his voice getting husky.

She gave a toss of her head and sparks glittered in the depths of her eyes. ''You know good and well what effect you have!'' She turned and waved her hand toward an open bedroom decorated in blue. ''You can have that bedroom to change in. There's a bathroom connected to it and there are towels and wash cloths in the bathroom cabinet. Help yourself. I'll be downstairs.'' Her words were rushed together.

If he wasn't filthy, sweaty, burned and blistered from the fire he would have pursued their conversation, but right now he wanted a shower before he got one inch closer to her and delved into her remarks that set his heart racing.

She hurried to the stairs and turned to look at him. ''Would you like a salad and cold chicken and a baked potato?''

"That sounds great. I'll be down soon."

She nodded and disappeared and he wiped his hot brow as he turned to enter a large bedroom with a bright blue-and-white quilt on the brass bed. In minutes he was in the shower and he wondered if she was talking to Jeb for a reference.

Downstairs, Maggie doodled on the pad while she listened to Jeb Stuart. Then her hand became still and she turned to look at the empty doorway while she listened, and her heart started drumming while her ideas about Jake took another sharp turn.

Three

Maggie listened to the deep voice on the phone tell her how reliable Jake was. Jeb told her in detail how Jake had saved his life in Colombia when they had been in the Airborne and on a rescue mission. Closing her eyes, she could visualize the image again of Jake running into the burning barn and then just minutes later, emerging with her father slung over his shoulder. So he was reliable and a wonderful person and she had insulted him and she was being ridiculous.

"Thank you," she said quietly, only a portion of her uneasiness erased. She replaced the receiver and stared out the window at the blackened field. She didn't want Jake working for them, but it was that disturbing electricity she experienced every time she was around him that worried her. She didn't remember feeling that way around Bart and she had been in love with him and had married him.

She gave a slight shake of her shoulders. She and Jake had already discussed the situation. She would hire someone else, and he would go. He didn't want to be tied down here anyway.

She got out the cold chicken and swiftly set the table, putting potatoes in the microwave oven to bake, then getting out the loaf of homemade bread that was only half eaten. She sliced tomatoes and set them on the table.

"What a picture," Jake drawled, and she spun around. He stood in the doorway with his hair slicked back, giving him an entirely different appearance, revealing his prominent cheekbones more sharply. He had changed to a white T-shirt and wore jeans and his boots, a sight that made her pulse skip.

"Picture?"

"A pretty woman, scrumptious chicken and an old-fashioned kitchen."

"I wouldn't think those would be the things that appeal to you. You sound like you like life in the fast lane."

He shrugged and strolled into the room, dark gaze on her, and a faint smile curving his mouth. "I like all of those things—pretty women, good food—I guess I don't care one way or other about kitchens. Since I haven't eaten for over twenty-four hours now, that food looks like a feast."

"I'll pour water and we'll eat."

As she reached into the cabinet, his hand brushed hers and he took a glass from her. She turned and he was right beside her, brushing against her shoulder. "I'll get the drinks."

"If you look in the back in the bottom of the fridge, you'll probably find a cold beer. Dad has one now and then."

"Thanks, but I don't drink beer." Jake's brow arched. "I surprised you, didn't I?"

As heat flushed her cheeks, she realized she had to stop judging him by his appearance. "You've surprised me all day," she admitted.

"Good," he said in a tone of voice that changed subtly and made her tingle. "Life is interesting when it holds surprises."

"It depends on the surprises. The fire today was one heck of a surprise."

"It was a shock and a bad one. That isn't what I'm talking about, Maggie."

"I'll drink ice water," she said, trying to get back on an impersonal level. Amusement flashed in his dark eyes before he headed to the refrigerator. She wondered if she would ever forget him moving around their house. What was it about him that carried that air of wild recklessness? He hadn't done anything that had been out of line, yet she had the feeling he was not only capable of wildness, but that was his usual mode. She glanced out the window at the big Harley parked outside.

Setting two glasses of water on the table, he held a chair for her and she sat down. "Thanks."

He sat facing her and as she passed the chicken to him, the phone rang. She got up to answer it, motioning him to go ahead.

It was the insurance adjustor, and she made an appointment for the next morning, the first Wednesday in August. She sat down to eat when the phone rang again.

"Go ahead and eat," she said as she answered to talk to a friend.

While she was on the phone, someone drove up and knocked at the back door. Jake opened it for Melody Caldwell, one of Maggie's friends. Maggie saw that Melody carried a large casserole dish.

Maggie watched while Jake flirted with Melody and Melody flirted back. Divorced, Melody lived in town. She and Maggie had known each other since they were five and Maggie knew Melody would be in no hurry to go home. She would be fascinated with Jake.

Maggie hung up. "Hi, Melody. Thanks for the food. I see you two met." She heard an engine and glanced out to see a ranch neighbor drive up. Dressed in jeans and matching Western shirts, looking more like brother and sister than husband and wife with their red hair, Ollie and Pru Morgan climbed out of their truck and crossed the porch with food in hand. Within the hour two more neighbors arrived. After supper, all the friends helped Maggie and Jake move her things back inside the house.

It was half past ten when the last guest left. Maggie was aware of Jake standing beside her on the porch as her neighbors drove away.

"You have a lot of friends."

"I've lived here all my life and so have my parents and my grandparents before them."

Jake sat down on the wooden steps. "It's cool and nice out here now. Sit down a minute."

"I miss Katy being here."

"You just talked to her a little while ago."

"I know. She likes to stay with her cousins, and it's good for them to grow up friends, but I miss her.

Patsy has two girls, Ella who is seven and Tina who is five."

Aware of him only a few feet away, Maggie sat down on the steps. Beside her, he stretched his long legs out in front of him. The night was cool and quiet with only the chirp of crickets and the far-off sound of a bullfrog.

"You have enough food from your friends to last the rest of the week," Jake said.

"They've all been nice."

"Yeah. It's great. What would you like me to do in the morning?"

"I guess you can take over Dad's chores. Because of the drought, he's having to feed the cattle and horses. He checks on their water. We have a stallion, Red Rogue—Dad just calls him Rogue. He's wild so be careful of him. He's penned up by himself in the northeast pasture. Dad is trying to sell him, we have an ad running, but so far, no buyers." She raised her head. "I can smell the burned land."

"Yep, but it won't last long and several of the men said in the seven-day forecast, rain is predicted. First thing you know, it'll all green up again."

"Thank goodness the fire didn't cross the lane and we have our house and trees left in the yard."

While fireflies flitted over the fenced yard, Maggie and Jake sat in an easy silence, and she was amazed he wanted to just sit and enjoy the evening. He was only a few feet from her, and she was very conscious of him.

"You want to have a bed-and-breakfast and you want your little girl to grow up here. What else do you want from life?"

"That's about all. I'm happy here with my dad

and Katy. This is a good life." She glanced around. Jake leaned back on his elbows, almost reclining on the steps with his legs in front of him. He watched her, but she could no longer see the expression in his eyes.

"What do you want, Jake?"

"I want to see parts of the world I haven't already seen. I want to save my money and travel around the world."

"Your life is hard for me to imagine," she said. "I've never been out of Oklahoma."

"No kidding!" She saw a flash of his white teeth. "Maybe one day you should let your sister keep Katy and get on my bike with me and let me take you across the state line to Texas."

She smiled. "Maybe someday I'll go somewhere. Tonight I'm going to bed. I'm exhausted." She stood. "If you'd like, you can sleep upstairs. I'm sorry I wasn't hospitable.

He stood and faced her, shaking his head. "Forget it. That hammock looks inviting, and I like it out here under the stars. I haven't slept outside in a long time. I'll come in and shower in the morning."

"Come get a pillow. You won't need a blanket."

He held the door and they went inside. She left him in the kitchen while she went upstairs and got a sheet and a pillow and brought them back to him. His hands brushed hers as he took the items from her.

"See you in the morning," he drawled. The words should have been a brief parting that she barely noticed, but they weren't. In his husky, soft voice, they were like a caress of his fingers. His eyes held hers extra heartbeats while the silence between them stretched, and she was lost in his gaze.

"Sure," she whispered.

He turned and crossed the room to the door where he paused and glanced over his shoulder at her. "You can lock up. I won't need to come back inside until morning."

She shrugged, embarrassed she had made it so clear that she didn't trust him and didn't want him in her home. "That's all right. We don't always lock up anyway."

"You don't lock your door, Maggie Langford, but you keep your heart locked away," he said, raising an eyebrow. Before she could answer, he was gone, closing the door behind him.

Startled by his statement, she stared at the door. "I need to keep it locked away when you're around," she replied softly. What was it about him that was so blatantly sexy?

She switched off the lights and went upstairs to bed. Before she turned on the lights in her bedroom, she walked to the window. The hammock was below, and she could easily see him stretched out on it. He had shed his T-shirt and boots and wore only his jeans. He lay with his hands behind his head and she wondered if he could see her at the window. She pulled the shade and moved away to turn on a bedside lamp.

She was exhausted, yet she wasn't certain she would sleep. She hated to think of all the work that lay ahead of them, just trying to restore what burned. Thank heavens they had insurance that would carry them through this. But insurance wouldn't replace trees.

She got ready for bed, slipping into an oversize T-shirt. When she switched off the lights and climbed into bed, she was still aware of Jake sleeping down in the yard. He was outside the house, but in her thoughts to a degree that disturbed her.

He flirted a little, but hadn't come on strong, so why was she having this volatile reaction to him? She fell asleep thinking about him.

In the cool night Jake watched the leaves flutter with the breeze. In spite of the smell of charred land, it was cool and peaceful outside. His burns ached and the hammock wasn't particularly comfortable because of blisters and cuts across his back and shoulders, but he was tired and he tried to shut his mind to his aches. Instead he thought about Maggie with her door unlocked, yet she was shut away from the world. She hadn't ever left the state and she didn't date. What was she hiding from? Or maybe it wasn't hiding, but just rooted to this place like the big trees around him.

The thought of always staying in one place sounded like prison to him. She was a beautiful woman and it seemed a waste. He was sure she was a good daughter and a good mother, but she was missing out on a big chunk of life.

He gave a small cynical laugh in the darkness. She was probably thinking just the same about him and feeling he was missing out on life because he didn't have a home and roots and family. She certainly had a lot of friends who had come to her aid. If his bike burned up who would even know? But that's the way he liked to live.

He wondered if he could coax her out dancing one

night. He thought about how skittish she was around him and doubted if he could. What would it be like to kiss her?

"You'll never know, buddy," he said to himself in the dark and looked at the bedroom where he had seen her standing at the window. She was aware of him, he knew that.

Wishing for a bed with cool sheets where he could sleep on his stomach and get the pressure off his blisters and cuts, he shifted and tried to get comfortable.

He watched the leaves flutter and sway and then he was asleep and the next conscious thing he knew was the ring of a phone.

Instantly awake and aware of where he was, he opened his eyes and stared into the darkness. He listened to two more rings and looked up at Maggie's darkened room. Someone was calling her in the middle of the night. Couldn't she hear the phone? He could hear it and he was outside the house.

He started to close his eyes and forget it, but he thought about her little girl. Sprinting to the back door, he half expected to find himself locked out. The door came open and he hit the light switch and crossed the kitchen to answer the phone.

There was a second's pause before a female voice spoke. "You must be Jake. I'm Patsy, Maggie's sister. I need to speak to her."

"I don't know why she didn't answer. I'll go see," he said, wondering what had happened to her.

"She's a very sound sleeper. You'll probably have to wake her, Jake. It's Dad. He's had a heart attack."

"On, damn. Sorry. I'll get her."

Jake swore softly to himself as he put down the

receiver. Maggie and her father had had enough trouble with the fire. They didn't need any more calamities. He took the stairs two at a time and turned toward the room where he had seen her.

Her door was closed, and he knocked and called. "Maggie!"

Nothing.

How soundly did the woman sleep? This was like someone unconscious. He opened the door and stepped inside. "Maggie!"

She was sprawled on the bed, covers kicked away while a ceiling fan slowly revolved. She wore a T-shirt that was high around her thighs and her long legs were bare. As he crossed the room to shake her shoulder, Jake drew a deep breath. She had taken down her braid and long, golden hair spilled over her and the pillow. Swiftly he imagined her without the T-shirt as he touched her shoulder.

She was soft and warm and it was an effort to keep his mind on the emergency. He couldn't resist running his fingers through strands of her hair. It was like silk, sliding over his hand. "Maggie, wake up!" His voice was husky as he shook her more forcefully.

"Maggie!"

"Mmm," she said and rolled over, burying her face in the pillow. Moonlight spilled over her shapely curves. The T-shirt had ridden higher and the lush curve of her bottom clad in a wisp of lace was revealed. Drawing a deep breath, he felt on fire. He turned on a light, saw the bedside phone and shook her shoulder again.

Stirring, she rolled over again and looked up at him, and Jake felt as if something had knocked the breath from his lungs. The long blond hair fell over her shoulders and the T-shirt had molded to her full breasts. Wordlessly he handed her the phone.

Maggie swung her legs over the side of the bed and sat up, shaking the golden cascade of her hair away from her face and tugging down the T-shirt as she held the receiver and listened.

As if snapped out of a dream, she suddenly raised her chin and stood. "I'll be there as quickly as I can," she said solemnly.

As soon as she replaced the receiver, Jake asked, "How is he?"

"Stable."

"Get dressed. I'll drive you to town."

"You don't need to," she said, combing her hands through her hair.

"I don't mind. I'll hang up the phone downstairs. Give me your keys, and I'll bring the pickup to the back gate."

She motioned. "My keys are on the dresser."

As Jake crossed the room to pick them up, he glanced in the mirror and saw her head for her bathroom. The T-shirt covered her bottom, but it clung and he watched the sway of her hips. When he turned and left, he wondered how long it would take him to forget the last few minutes and how she had looked waking up in bed.

In five minutes, dressed in jeans and a blue shirt, her hair tied behind her head with a strip of blue ribbon, she came running out of the house and climbed into the pickup beside him.

"This is his second heart attack," she said tensely.

"How long ago was the other one?"

"Three years ago. I wonder if the fire brought this on."

They lapsed into silence and Jake drove fast, knowing she was worried and wanted to get there as quickly as possible.

At the hospital, he stopped in front and reached across her to open the door. "Go on inside. I'll be up after I park," he said, opening her door.

She slid out and vanished through wide glass doors. He parked and went inside, going to the floor where her father was. He stopped at the nurse's desk and asked about her dad and learned that Ben had had a mild attack and was stable, but he had been moved to intensive care.

For the first time Jake thought about what this would mean for him and realized he might be working longer at their ranch than he had planned. He strolled down the hall and saw Maggie with two other women. He recognized her sister Patsy.

"Maggie, I'll be in the waiting room."

All three women turned to look at him. He could see little resemblance between them except two of them were blond. Patsy was the brunette he had seen at the ranch. Maggie was the tallest.

"Jake, this is my sister Patsy Loomis and my other sister, Olivia Sommersby."

"Hi. Sorry about your father."

They said hello and thanked him for his concern and then he went back to the empty waiting room. Jake sat down, stretched out his legs, and closed his eyes.

The next thing he knew someone was waking him. He came to his feet to face Maggie.

"Sorry. It's after three in the morning. I'm ready to go home now. The doctor said Dad's doing better and since he was right here in the hospital, they realized at once what was happening and could do something for him immediately. The doctor's given me a lot of hope.''

"Good." They fell into step as they walked outside. In the parking lot, Jake took Maggie's arm and led her toward the pickup.

"I guess we got about an hour's sleep before they called." She ran her fingers across her forehead.

"Did your sisters go home?"

"Yes, long before now."

He held the door of the pickup for her and went around to slide behind the wheel. Going home they were silent again and he suspected her nerves were frayed. When they reached the house, he parked at the gate and got out, coming around to open the door. He went inside with her. "Want something cold to drink?" he asked, as if he were the host and she the guest.

She nodded. "Just a glass of tea. I know I won't sleep, but I feel exhausted." She ran her hands over her forehead. "I hope nothing else happens."

Wrung-out and exhausted, Maggie still worried about her father. The doctor had reassured her of the prognosis, but she knew this would change the future. "Dad won't be able to work like he always has," she said, barely aware of Jake as he poured two glasses of iced tea. Jake brought one drink to her and pulled out a kitchen chair. "Come sit down."

With her thoughts still on her father and the changes they would have to make now in the ranch routine, she sat down and sipped the cold drink. Jake pulled another chair from the table. He moved it around to her side. "Turn around in your chair."

He motioned, and she realized he intended to give
her a back rub and the notion was welcome. She
turned her back to him and wondered how he had
gone so fast from a total stranger to someone living
in their house, driving her pickup and now, giving
her a back rub. His hands were strong and steady as
he rubbed her shoulders and moved to her neck, his
hand rotating with just the right amount of pressure
to make her close her eyes. She could feel the tension
leave her body.

"Relax," he said quietly. "You're tense—no surprise. Anybody would be tense after what you went
through today."

"What makes you tense, Jake?" she asked, slanting him a look, curious about him and trying to get
her thoughts off the problems ahead of her.

"Fire, for one thing. Coming out of the chute on
a bucking bronc makes me a little tense."

"And that's probably all," she answered with
amusement. "No cares, no responsibilities, no ties."

"No pain. Look at you now, tied up in knots over
someone you love, frazzled today over the home you
love."

"It's worth it," she said solemnly, taken aback by
his statement. His gaze slid past her, and she knew
he was thinking about someone else or somewhere
else.

"Not when the deep hurts come. Not when people
die," he said solemnly, and she wondered whether
his whole family had perished in the fire, but she
didn't want to ask. He focused on her again, his eyes
searching. "I've told you things today that I haven't
told people who've known me for years. You get to

someone easily, Maggie. You must know lots of secrets."

She turned away. "I could say the same about you, Jake. This morning we were total strangers. Now you're living in my house. Your hands are on me now."

For just an instant, his hands stilled and then he continued. They both were silent and she wondered what ran through his thoughts.

His hand kneaded her back between her shoulder blades, then he began massaging upward and out in slow, steady strokes.

"Now I know why cats purr. This is helping me relax."

"Good," he said, close to her ear. He began to take down her thick braid, the tugs to her scalp sensuous as he pulled gently. Slowly he combed his fingers through the long strands.

"You have beautiful hair," he said softly, and a tingle fluttered in her.

"Thanks." Her curiosity about him was only increasing. "Jake, don't you ever want to have a family of your own? Just someday in the far distant future? Don't you want to ever love and be loved?"

He worked his way across her back and down. "I don't want to be tied down." His voice was harsh, and she sensed he didn't want to talk about losing his family in a fire. "Besides, there's plenty of loving out there. I didn't say I don't like that," he added on a lighter note.

"So there are girlfriends," she said, switching to the present.

"Nope. None at present." This time his voice was lighter and his answer had come quickly.

"Why do I find that incredibly hard to believe?" she asked dryly, and he chuckled.

"No more difficult than for me to believe there are no men in your life."

"Well, there sure aren't any. The most eligible bachelor in this county is Weldon Higgens. He lives next door and doesn't like us at all. You didn't see Weldon fighting that fire today even though it could have burned across our land and onto his."

"Has he ever asked you out?"

"Right after I got divorced and moved back here."

"Did you go out with him?"

She had her eyes closed, lost in the back rub and barely aware of Jake's questions. His hands were working their magic and she was aware of his legs stretched out on either side of her. He was sitting close behind her and his voice was deep and husky in her ears.

"No, I didn't. I don't like the way he looks at me." She paused, realizing what she had just told Jake. "There, I did it again—telling you something I've never told anyone else. You have a way with people, too, Jake." Her voice had slurred, and the tension had left her. She could feel the exhaustion setting in, along with relief that her father had a good prognosis, that the fire was out and that the house hadn't burned.

"The massage feels so good," she said languidly. "I can relax now."

"If you want to go to bed, I'll give you a massage until you go to sleep. I promise to tiptoe out and leave you alone."

Shaking her hair away from her face, she turned

to look at him, amusement tugging at the corners of her mouth. "I think that would be pushing things a bit," she said. "And I don't think I trust you quite that much."

While he gazed at her solemnly, his hands combed through her hair slowly. Drawing a swift breath, she realized it might have been a mistake to turn and face him because awareness, sexual and hot, flared like spontaneous combustion.

They were only inches apart. He sat with his legs spread on either side of her chair, his hands slowly tugging through the long strands of her hair in touches that seemed more intimate than the back rub. His eyes were black pools enveloping her, carrying a midnight magic.

"Ah, Maggie, live a little. Just a little," he coaxed softly, his gaze lowering to her mouth.

Her pulse drummed. Wisdom said move away from him, yet she couldn't move. She was as immobile and steady as everything else about her life. What would it hurt if they kissed? Just one kiss. Her pulse raced because she wanted his kiss. She wanted to do this while she had the chance. This one moment she wanted to break free from the everyday constraints of her routine ranch life.

He looked at her mouth and then into her eyes, and she saw his intent before his gaze slipped to her lips again. When he leaned closer, her heart thudded, and, knowing what she wanted, she slid her hand to the back of his neck. His skin was smooth and warm, coarse strands of hair brushing the back of her hand lightly.

When she touched him, his gaze flew to meet hers again with a questioning stare. She was certain he hadn't expected her to put her hand on the back of his neck. Was she making him bolder?

At the moment she didn't care. She wanted him to kiss her. She wanted to taste and touch and be kissed by this wild, reckless cowboy who was so many things she was not. He was irresistible. Scary. Thrilling.

She closed her eyes and raised her mouth in anticipation.

He leaned closer until his mouth covered hers firmly. With that first touch, desire exploded in her. Moaning softly, she pulled his head closer.

When his tongue slid into her mouth, she was lost in a dizzying spiral of sensation as she kissed him back, her tongue in a delicious duel that made her blood roar.

His hands slid down to her waist and he moved her, lifting her easily off the chair and into his lap. She didn't care. How long—years—since she had been held and kissed by a man?

She had never known a kiss like this that made her toes curl and her heart pound and her blood heat to melted fire.

She moaned again, dimly hearing her own voice, aware of the warmth and textures of him, the soapy clean scent tinged faintly with the scents of salve and antiseptic and his cotton T-shirt. When her hand slid across his shoulder over the ridges and roughness beneath his T-shirt, she remembered his burns and cuts.

"Your back!" she whispered, afraid she had hurt him, startled when she touched his injuries.

He made a sound deep in his throat and tightened his arm around her and stopped any more words, leaning over her and kissing her hard. Sliding her arm around his neck, she forgot his injuries. Desire burned in her, need throbbing with each heartbeat.

Caution and consequences no longer mattered. At the moment she just wanted his kisses and wanted him never to stop. She returned them wildly, passionately, letting go of all else until deeper needs began to burn into her awareness, and she knew she had to stop before passion blazed beyond control.

Dazed by his kisses, aroused by his reactions, she pushed against him. Instantly he raised his head and looked into her eyes.

"Damn, Maggie," he whispered, and he sounded shaken.

She was surprised by his reaction, but she understood it because that was the way she felt. Her world had tilted, changed, and she knew she wasn't going to forget his kisses any faster than she would forget the fire that burned their land and barn.

She was still in his lap, her hands on his chest now. She could feel his racing heart and knew she had stirred him. When she slid off his lap and stood, he came to his feet at once, his hands resting on her waist as he stood close and looked down at her.

"Where do we go from here?" he asked, solemnly, and her heart thudded again.

Four

"We go back to the way we were before," she whispered, knowing she should sound more forceful. "Your life is that hog you ride and mine is this home and family. There's a chasm between us that's enormous. You can't cross over to my side and I can't cross over to yours."

He brushed her cheek with his fingers. "Earnest Maggie. A few kisses won't change our lives."

"Not your life," she said quietly. "I usually get up in another hour—I won't today, but morning will come all too soon. I'm going to bed, Jake. Thanks for taking me to town. You were a help."

"Go on to bed. I'll turn out the lights."

She nodded and left him, feeling his gaze on her as she walked out of the room. His words taunted her, *"A few kisses won't change our lives."* His kiss had been devastating. Was she that lonely and starved for loving? Or was there some special chemistry? The thought that there might be something special in Jake scared her because she suspected that was the truth. She didn't want a man like Jake to sweep into her life with the force of a whirlwind and steal her heart because he would be gone as swiftly as wild storm winds.

She tingled all over from being in his arms. ''Forget him,'' she whispered to herself, glancing over her shoulder. Light spilled from the open kitchen door into the darkened hallway. As she watched, the light went off.

Upstairs in her room, she changed swiftly and switched off the lights in her room. Then she was unable to resist walking to the window. Quietly she raised the shade. He was stretched in the hammock again, his chest and feet bare, and she remembered what it was like to be held tightly in his strong arms against his solid chest.

She turned away and climbed into bed, staring into the darkness while all the events of the day ran through her mind—the first glimpse of the fire, Jake beating at the flames, Jake running into the barn and bringing out her father, visiting her dad in the hospital, sitting on the steps in the cool evening with Jake, being in his arms and kissing him. That set her pulse racing again and she wondered if she would sleep at all.

''Why did you come here, Jake?'' she whispered in the darkness, but then guilt swamped her because he had bravely come to warn them of the fire.

Just keep a distance from him, she decided. And find another hired hand soon.

* * *

The first light of dawn woke Jake. He stretched, seeing the sun was still below the horizon. As he headed for the house, the tempting aroma of coffee and bacon assailed him.

He opened the back door to see Maggie with her back to him at the stove. She wore faded cutoffs, a red T-shirt and sneakers. Her hair was braided and hung down her back. He stood watching her a moment, enjoying the sight of her and remembering the silky feel of her hair over his hands.

"Good morning," he said quietly, fighting the temptation to cross the room and put his arms around her.

Glancing over her shoulder, she flashed a smile at him. "Hey, there. I thought since you didn't get to eat at all yesterday until last night that you might like bacon and eggs for breakfast."

"It's mouthwatering tempting," he drawled, thinking about her instead of breakfast.

Her eyes widened slightly, and that electric current snapped between them. She turned back to cook, but not before he had seen her cheeks flood with pink.

"How can I help?" he asked.

"You can fix the toast, pour the coffee," she answered, glancing over her shoulder at him.

"Sure. I'm going to wash up first," he said, crossing the room and heading for the stairs.

When he returned, he got toast and poured himself a cup of steaming black coffee, all the while intensely aware of her moving around him. Their conversation was light, although he barely thought about what he was saying because he was too conscious of her.

He inhaled, studying her when he thought she was

unaware of his scrutiny. Why was he having this intense reaction to her? He'd been around pretty women all his adult life and had never experienced such electric feelings. Her kiss last night—with another deep intake of breath he stopped that train of thought. What was worrisome, he had been having these feelings even before they had ever kissed.

Over fluffy scrambled eggs and crisp toast, he sat across the table from her and listened to her outline their day. "After I check on Dad, I'll pick up Katy. If they move Dad out of intensive care today, I'll take her to see him. We have to get some things and then I'll be back home. I also have an appointment with the insurance adjustor later today."

"And while you're gone, what do you need done here?"

"The animals need to be checked on first. Besides the pickup, we have an old truck. You can drive it. I'll draw you a map of the ranch. When you get a chance, will you please rebuild the little stretch of fence around our yard?"

"Sure."

"Katy knows to stay inside the fence so I'd like it replaced as quickly as possible. It's scary that the fire got that close to the house. It got part of the fence and the tree where her swing is."

"But that's all. At least your house and the rest of the fence and the trees close to the house are all right."

"I know and I'm grateful."

"Breakfast was delicious. Is this what you eat every morning?" She smiled and his pulse jumped a notch. He fought the impulse to reach across the table and touch the corner of her mouth.

"No, I don't. Dad and Katy need fruit so we have cereal and fruit. Tomorrow morning we'll probably be back to the usual."

"Thanks for cooking something special for me this morning," he said softly and received another wide-eyed look. "I still can't believe you're not dating."

"It's the absolute truth," she said smiling. "What's hard to believe is that you're not."

"Why don't we change that a little? If your dad is all right, let me take you dancing Saturday night."

She shot him a look and then studied her orange juice, running her slender fingers along the glass. As silence stretched between them, he caught her hand in his, running his thumb over her smooth, soft skin.

"I don't think we should," she said.

"Oh, hell, Maggie, it's just an evening out. We're not going to get serious. How much time have you taken for yourself this past year? Not much, I'll bet. It's no big deal. Just think about it and see how your dad is." He pushed back his chair a fraction and stretched out his legs. "Now after feeding and watering your animals, what do you want me to do?"

She caught her lower lip with small, white teeth and his attention focused on her rosy mouth. He wanted to kiss her again. He had said their kiss had been no big deal, but he had been wrong and he knew it.

With his mind more on her than on what she was saying, they went over chores and then she shooed him away as she began to clean the kitchen.

In minutes, outside in warm sunshine, Jake stood looking at Ben's tractor. It was corroded with rust. The engine looked as if it needed a complete overhaul. The dilapidated flatbed truck was in the same condition.

Jake roamed around, finding frayed rope and broken tools. He wondered about Ben's health and if Maggie knew her father had been letting the place go to ruin. The more Jake saw, the more his spirits sank. Maggie needed help and a lot of it.

He could feel his freedom slipping away. He wanted to put a thousand miles between Maggie and him. He didn't want to have such intense feelings for a woman.

He looked at a pile of charred boards from the barn and kicked a board, sending up a puff of soot. "Dammit," he swore.

He climbed into the flatbed truck Maggie had told him to use and looked at the sketch of the ranch she had given him. The horses had been turned out yesterday during the fire and Maggie said he would find them near a pond on the far north section of the ranch, except for the unmanageable stallion that was kept in a fenced pasture to the northeast.

Familiarizing himself with the ranch, he explored the Circle A. Later, as he stood looking at the half-dozen horses, he realized Maggie's dad knew horses and had some very fine animals. Two mares approached him, and he knew they expected to be fed. He talked quietly to them, finally running his hands over a sleek bay. Maggie might want a bed-and-breakfast so her father wouldn't have to work so hard, but right now they had a good start on a horse ranch.

Jake found their cattle and it looked as though all the animals had made it through the fire. That left him with only one more occupant to check on.

He arrived at the fenced-in pasture located on the northeastern part of the ranch. There, Jake stopped the truck and climbed out, easing the door closed. The sorrel was off in the distance, cropping grass and seemingly not interested in Jake. The horse was a magnificent animal and Jake wondered why he was such a hellion.

Moving quietly, Jake opened the gate, then drove into the pasture to the stock tank. Carefully, with an eye on the horse, Jake checked the float in the tank. He glanced at the stallion that stood a couple of hundred yards away with ears now cocked forward.

"You're curious about me, aren't you, Red Rogue?" Jake said quietly, turning his back and walking away to get a rope from the bed of the truck. He glanced over his shoulder at the stallion. The horse had moved closer, but stopped when Jake looked at him. Jake turned his back and started knotting the rope.

By the end of an hour, he knew the stallion was close behind him. Without looking back, Jake stopped working on the rope and walked over to his truck. There, he glanced back to see the horse watching him, only yards away.

"See you tomorrow, Rogue." Jake said quietly, certain the horse wasn't the rogue that Maggie and her father thought he was.

That afternoon while he washed soot off tools, Jake heard the pickup returning. When Maggie parked, Katy and their dog jumped out. Katy looked at Jake and ran toward the house. He watched her pigtails fly, and then his gaze shifted to Maggie who had her arms filled with sacks of groceries. He dropped what he was repairing and wiped his hands on a rag, then hurried to help her.

"How's your dad?" he asked Maggie as he passed her and went to retrieve the remaining bags in the back of the truck.

"Much better," Maggie said, stopping to wait for him. "They've moved him from intensive care and Katy could see him briefly."

"Good," Jake said, catching up with her. He opened the screen door and waited for her to enter. They set down sacks of groceries and Maggie began to put things away.

"I talked to Sheriff Alvarez. The fire was arson. It was deliberately set."

Startled, Jake paused in emptying a sack. "Who do they think did it? It was too far from the highway to have been a tossed cigarette."

"He said it was probably kids. The fire was set by sparklers. With this drought there is a burn ban that covers almost all of the state so anyone shooting any kind of fireworks is in violation of the law. The dry grass caught on fire."

"Kids out with sparklers during the morning?" Jake asked doubtfully.

Maggie moved around the kitchen putting away groceries. "Who else would be out with sparklers?"

Followed by the dog, Katy sidled into the kitchen and when Jake glanced her way, he smiled.

"Hi, Katy. How are you?"

Looking wide-eyed, she scooted near her mother.

"Katy, answer Mr. Reiner," Maggie prodded gently.

"Fine," she said, tugging on Maggie's cutoffs.

When Maggie leaned down, Katy whispered that

she would like a banana. Maggie gave her one, and she dashed outside.

"I must frighten her," Jake said.

"She's just not accustomed to strangers," Maggie replied. "We see the same people all the time. She's shy around most men."

"I saw your stock this morning. You have a fine herd of horses."

Maggie nodded. "That's Dad's doing. He was interested in raising horses, but then he decided he didn't want to."

"I saw Red Rogue. You said you have an ad running to sell him. Cancel it. Let me work with him. I'll either buy him myself or find a buyer."

"Let me tell you about that horse," she said, pausing with a head of lettuce in her hand. "He's a killer. He's never been ridden more than a few minutes and watch out because he'll go for you. He bites, he kicks, and he stomps when the mares are in season. We've had three hired hands who refused to even feed him. Dad doesn't like him, either, and he usually does great with all the animals."

Jake thought about the horse trailing along behind him today. "Just cancel the ad. I think he can be gentled. I might buy him."

Maggie laughed, her dimple showing. "What— and run him along behind your Harley?"

With a flash of white teeth, Jake grinned. "I own some horses and a pickup. I keep them at Jeb Stuart's place."

"Well, you can't want our stallion."

"Yes, I do."

Placing one hand on her hip, she tilted her head

to study him. "Maybe you're as stubborn as that horse. Or maybe you just like a challenge."

"Oh, I like a challenge, Maggie," Jake drawled, his voice dropping meaningfully. She was a threat to his peace of mind, and he knew he was a threat to hers. He was certain he was the kind of man she wouldn't want to get involved with.

Yet even so, he was irresistibly drawn to her. He moved closer to her, placing his hand on her hip. Her blue eyes widened, the color deepening. He rested his other hand against her throat. "Your pulse is racing."

"It doesn't matter. You keep your distance," she whispered, her gaze dropping to his mouth, and his pulse jumped another notch.

"Whatever the lady wants," he said quietly, knowing she was right. His heart pounded, drowning out other noises, and he strode across the kitchen, leaving her to put away the groceries. He had to get out of the kitchen, away from her or she would end up in his arms. And he had a feeling that if he had pulled her into his embrace and kissed her, she would have kissed him back as she had last night.

They were danger and disaster to each other so why couldn't he keep his distance? Why was his pulse roaring and his blood hot as fire? He strode across the yard and saw Katy standing by her burned swing that now was charred ruins on the ground. She was watching him and she looked frightened. He smiled as sweetly as he could. He didn't know anything about little girls. Jeb Stuart, where Jake had recently worked, had a three-year-old, but Jake had hardly ever been around her.

He walked over to Katy and she looked ready to

run. He touched the charred ruins of the swing with his toe. "Did you lose your swing in the fire?"

She nodded.

"Well, I can build you a new swing. We'll have to find another big tree to put it on. Okay?"

She nodded, and he turned to walk away, feeling she was too terrified to talk to him even a little. He glanced over his shoulder once and she was still watching him. He waved and went on his way without looking back again.

Inside the kitchen, Maggie had watched the encounter. She walked to the door. "Stay inside the fence where I can see you, Katy."

Her daughter nodded and Maggie let her gaze shift to watch Jake's long-legged stride, remembering him standing so close with his hand on her hip. She should have moved away, but she couldn't.

Late that night, after she had driven into town to the hospital and Katy was fast asleep in her bed, Maggie sat outside in the cool darkness with Jake, listening to him talk about rodeos and horses and places he'd been. For the second time that day, she thought how she should stay away from him. Do anything to keep space between her and this dangerous man who was moving swiftly into every nook and cranny of her life. But she couldn't.

Jake sat beside her on a lawn chair, his hands on his knees, leaning forward, his voice a deep rumble in the quiet night. "You know about me now, Maggie. What about you?"

Startled out of her deep thoughts, she sighed and said, "Oh, I've led a most ordinary life. Grew up here, married a local boy, had a little girl, divorced and live here now at my dad's. I haven't traveled other places, haven't seen much, but I'm happy here.''

''How long did you say you were married?''

''Two years. My husband said he was chained by marriage, as if every day another rope was tying him to this place until he wouldn't be able to move or think. Since your home is your bike, you must understand that, but I don't. I need roots and history and family.''

''You love, you get hurt,'' Jake said gruffly, and she turned to look at him. He was staring off in the distance with his profile to her, a muscle working in his jaw.

''Who hurt you, Jake? Were you married?''

''No,'' he said, turning to look at her, ''but if you love, sooner or later you'll hurt.''

''It's worth hurting to know love,'' she said, wondering what made Jake so incredibly cynical and hard.

''Did you find a replacement for me today?'' he asked in an obvious attempt to change the subject.

''No, but I've asked around and told people I'm looking. I'm running a small ad in the local paper next week.'' She stood. ''I should go inside.''

At once he came to his feet, catching her around the waist lightly. ''What about Saturday night? Your sister could keep Katy and the doctor told you Ben will be in the hospital at least another week. Go dancing with me.''

Maggie was aware of his hands on her waist, his closeness, the faint scent of his aftershave. She had thought about going out with him Saturday night, knowing she shouldn't, yet part of her wanted to.

Was she being foolishly afraid? She thought of her marriage to a man who couldn't settle and how his leaving had torn her to pieces. Jake was more of a wanderer than Bart was. If she didn't want to risk falling in love with Jake, she shouldn't go out with him. Yet every time a firm no rose to her lips, she found herself unable to utter the word. It had been incredibly long since she had gone out for even a few hours and she couldn't resist the fact that she found Jake exciting.

Exciting the way a wild tiger is exciting. "Jake, I shouldn't leave—"

"Katy will be fine. Your father is in good hands. You and I will have fun. So what's worrying you?"

"Don't act so innocent. You know why I'm hesitating."

"We're not going to fall in love," he said in a voice as warm and soft as melted butter. "I won't break your heart—you won't break mine."

"You sound sure of yourself," she said, annoyed by his confidence. His confidence made her reckless, and she slanted him a look, sliding her hand to the back of his neck. "You're so certain you won't fall in love with me," she said softly. "Maybe you should guard *your* heart." Emboldened by the startled flicker in his dark eyes, she stood on tiptoe and placed her lips softly on his.

In response, his arms tightened around her and he deepened the kiss until she was breathless and her pulse pounding. She broke away, wriggling out of his grasp. "All right, I'll go with you. Only make it a week from Saturday night. I'm still too worried about Dad to go dancing. And I'll guard my heart, Jake. But maybe you should guard your own."

But she wasn't guarding hers. She had just risked another searing kiss that left her breathless, wanting more.

She turned and hurried across the lawn to the house, moving with certainty through the darkened kitchen, knowing every inch of the house she had grown up in.

Later in bed, unable to sleep, she stared into the darkness and wondered who had hurt him so badly.

On Saturday afternoon a week later, Jake was driving a nail into place, rebuilding the rail fence around the yard when he felt as if he was being watched. He glanced around to see Katy nearby. She was sitting on a big red ball, watching him solemnly, and he noticed again what a little miniature she was of her mother with her thickly lashed, big blue eyes and her silky blond hair that hung halfway to her waist.

"Hi," he said.

"Hi, Mr. Reiner," she answered. Several times during the week he had found her nearby, watching him. The first few times, he didn't speak, but went on with what he was doing.

Thursday he had told her hello, and she had mumbled an answer. Last night there had been a sentence or two.

"When will you be through?" she asked.

"I'm about finished. Then I'll start building a new corral. I'll have to build a fence in a big circle so the horses won't get out."

"Are you going to build me a new swing then?"

It was the longest she had ever talked to him, and Jake turned to look at her. He nodded. "Sure thing.

But we have to find a tree to hang the swing in. Will you help me find a tree?''

"Yes," she said, getting up off the ball and grabbing it up to toss it into the air. "We can find a tree now," she said, catching the ball in both arms and looking around. "I can't go where Mommy can't see me. I have to stay in this part of the yard."

"What's Mommy doing?"

"She's trying to decide what to wear tonight. Are you and Mommy going to have a date?"

"Yes, as a matter of fact we are. Is that okay with you?"

She tilted her head to study him. "I guess."

"Tell you what. Tomorrow afternoon we'll get your momma and all three of us will look around for a good tree for your new swing. We need a tall tree with a big strong limb. Want to do that?"

"Yes, sir," she said and turned to run for the house.

He watched her golden hair flying and thought she was cute. Maggie stepped outside, called to her and then looked at Jake. He waved and she waved in return. Mother and daughter disappeared inside the house and he knew Maggie was taking Katy into town soon. He finished the fence and went to get lumber to start rebuilding the corral. He knew he wouldn't see Maggie again until late afternoon.

He couldn't stop thinking about Maggie's final acceptance of their date. She had caught him off guard, surprising him with her answer, surprising him more when she pulled his head down to kiss him. Every time he remembered her kiss, his pulse speeded. From the first few minutes he met her, she had surprised him repeatedly. He wasn't sleeping well at night because he lay awake thinking about her, or he slept, dreaming of her. And he couldn't wait for their date tonight. Maggie in his arms dancing, Maggie to himself all evening. What was she feeling, he wondered. Was she as eager about tonight as he was? Were they both courting disaster as she had warned? He didn't think so. He had always walked away and he was certain she guarded her heart constantly.

With the sun hot and high, it was six o'clock when he put away his tools and quit working on the corral. He headed for the house. He still slept in the hammock, but he had to go inside to clean up. Maggie had given him a bedroom down the hall from hers.

As the screen slapped shut behind him and he stepped into the cool kitchen, his pulse jumped. Maggie stood at the sink with a glass of water in her hand. She looked beautiful and incredibly sexy in tight jeans, boots, a crisp, sleeveless blue cotton shirt. Her hair was drawn and tied with a ribbon behind her head. Fancy silver earrings dangled from her ears and a silver bracelet circled her narrow wrist.

"Wow, lady, you look great," he said quietly.

"Thank you." He could see a faint blush creeping over her beautiful face. "I'm ready to go, but I know you need to clean and change. I'll wait in the family room."

"I'll hurry," he said, wanting every minute possible with her this evening. "Don't go without me."

She smiled and he wished he knew whether her pulse was skittering as much as his was. He would know soon enough.

Five

As she waited, Maggie reminded herself again that she would take the evening the same way Jake would—it was to be a fun time they could forget and walk away from tomorrow. A night of fun memories, but nothing serious. And then Jake walked into the room and all logic went up in smoke while her heart thudded, and she knew she was committing a huge folly.

Wearing a crisp white Western shirt, jeans, boots, and a hand-tooled, leather belt with a silver buckle, Jake looked handsome and sexy. His tight jeans hugged trim hips and his broad shoulders filled out the spotless shirt.

"I'm ready," he said, walking toward her.

"We shouldn't be doing this," she said, looking up at him. He stood close enough for her to catch the spicy scent of his aftershave, see his smooth, clean-shaven jaw. His thickly lashed, dark eyes devoured her, making her drumming pulse accelerate even more.

"But we're going to," he said, taking her arm. "Remember, you're the one who warned me to look after myself. Getting scared now?"

"Let's go before I change my mind."

He held her arm as they went to her pickup. He motioned toward his bike. "Would you rather?"

"No, I'm committing one folly now. I don't want to compound it and commit another."

"Someday, Maggie," he said, holding the door handle, but blocking her way while he touched her cheek with his warm fingers. "Someday I'll get you to let go that reserve. I've seen glimpses of what it's like when you let it slip. One day, it'll go completely."

"Sure, Jake," she answered lightly, too aware of him. Smiling, she held out the keys. "You drive."

He helped her into the pickup and slid behind the wheel. They rode in silence for a time while she looked at her land, the burned and blackened fields, other fields that were turning yellow and drying up from lack of rain.

"You're making progress with the new corral." She finally said, breaking the silence. "Dad will be surprised and pleased."

"I'm trying to get it done before you bring him home."

"It'll be different when he comes back." She sighed. "I need to get my bed-and-breakfast going sooner."

"Hire some help and he can run the place without having to do much physical work."

"I don't want him to worry about it at all," she said, and Jake suddenly felt that he would stay far longer at the Langford place than he had anticipated.

He drove them to a local honky-tonk. As they walked through the rough knotty-pine interior with its dim lighting and raucous noise, people constantly greeted Maggie. The guys looked at her in a manner that made Jake place his arm around her shoulders. Looking around, he saw small tables circling a dance floor with an empty stage at the far end, and booths lining the wall.

"Do you know everyone in the county?" Jake asked after they had been seated with menus placed in front of them.

"I told you. I've lived here all my life. I probably do know everyone around here. I notice you're getting to know quite a few of them yourself. Watch out, Jake, or you'll take root like those big trees in our yard."

"Trying to scare me, Maggie?"

She laughed. "I wonder what scares you. I suspect there's very little."

"Oh, I can get scared," he said. He pulled a menu in front of him. "We'll see if Oklahoma ribs are as good as Texas ribs," Jake said, talking about different dishes and changing the subject.

She wondered what did scare him. Settling down? The thought of marriage? Since he lived on his bike, she suspected commitment of any kind scared him, but she wondered why. What lay beneath his fear of commitment and his declaration that to love is to get hurt? Was it because of the long ago fire that killed his family? She had an idea she would never know.

His dark eyes were inscrutable and he kept a wall around himself.

They were halfway through with heaping plates of barbecued ribs when Jake set down his soda. "A lot of guys here have noticed you, but there's one who's getting downright annoying. He's at the corner table."

She glanced around and looked into the pale, angry gaze of her neighbor, Weldon Higgens. Acknowledging him with a nod, she turned back to Jake and shrugged. "It's our neighbor to the east. We're not friends."

"Well, he's giving you a lot of attention."

"Yes," she said, "and I have no interest in him. Usually he keeps to himself. We had a fence down once and before Dad or any of the hands realized it, two steers wandered onto his land. Weldon killed the steers and told Dad to keep his cattle on his own ranch. No one else around here is like that."

"Want me to tell him to keep his attention to himself."

"No! Ignore him. I certainly can."

"If you can, I can," Jake said, giving her a lopsided smile. "The rest of the attention you're getting seems the normal, garden-variety notice of a good-looking woman, except I'm beginning to think I should have taken you to the next county where every male present doesn't know you. When the dancing starts, I suspect I'm going to have to share you."

She laughed. "There are all sorts of pretty ladies here who will be happy to dance with you."

"I've only seen one."

She smiled, enjoying his compliments and flirting.

"Besides, the looks you're giving other guys will drive them all away."

"I hope so. I don't want to watch you dance off in some other guy's arms. That wasn't the point of this evening."

"What was the point of this evening?" she asked, curious about his answer.

"To be able to hold you close while we dance." He leaned across the table to place his hand on her cheek again. "I want some slow-dancing where we can get up close and personal and I can feel your heartbeat and know that I'm causing your racing pulse."

"There are moments you have a real way with words," she said breathlessly, knowing he had caused another jump in her pulse. "I can't hide what you do to me, and from the very first, that's what's scared me."

Music started, and she remembered the crowd and pulled back, so his hand slid from her face. His eyes were burning with desire. "Rumors will fly all over the county about us and how you're living up at the house with me while Dad is in the hospital."

"I think it's common knowledge that I'm sleeping in the hammock out in the yard," he said with a big grin.

"After tonight no one will believe that."

"Maggie, if people are your friends, they'll want the best for you. The others don't matter."

"I suppose you're right."

"Let's do some boot-scootin'," he said abruptly and stood, taking her hand.

Relieved to break the tension, she went with him to the dance floor.

Musicians had filled the stage and for the next hour, Maggie two-stepped her way around the dance floor while Jake flirted and made her laugh. Between dances he kept his arm around her possessively so no one else would ask her to dance, which suited her fine. As she swept around the room with him, she realized she was having a wonderful time. It was good to dance and it was fun to flirt with him. It was also intoxicating to look into his soulful eyes and see the burning desire in them.

When the song they were dancing to ended, she excused herself to go to the ladies' room. When she returned, her heart missed a beat when she spotted Jake talking to Weldon who stood glowering at Jake with clenched fists.

Jake sauntered away, taking her arm and leading her back onto the dance floor.

"Did you threaten him?"

"I just talked to him a little."

"Jake, he's a neighbor. We have to live next door to him."

"He can stop staring at you like a stalker," he said gruffly. "The next time I see the sheriff, I'm going to tell him."

"Tell him what? Weldon is just staring at me. I told you that he asked me out some when I got divorced. To tell the truth, he gives me the creeps and I didn't want to go out with him so I think he resents that. But that's all."

"Maybe, but he doesn't have to glare at you all evening."

"Well, you don't have to worry about that because he's leaving." She pointed toward the entrance. "There he goes out the door. You ran him off."

"Forget it." Jake smiled at her. "Enjoy the music."

Annoyed she looked at him. "I'm not your responsibility. I can take care of myself."

"I'm sure your dad would have agreed with me."

"Don't bring Dad into this argument. And don't tell him about you and Weldon because I don't want him to get riled up. He's lost his temper with Weldon before and he doesn't need that hassle. Sometimes my Dad has a short fuse as several people around here know. Weldon killed those steers and now he wants to buy our place." Before she could utter another word, Jake spun her around and the argument was forgotten.

The next dance was a slow one and Jake pulled her close, wrapping his arms around her. She held him, aware of his warmth, of his thighs against hers.

They danced until midnight when the last slow dance played. Jake draped his arm across her shoulders as they went into the cool night to climb into the pickup. "Let's go home, Maggie, I want to kiss you good-night."

"I'm ready, Jake. Ready and willing," she said, flirting with him.

His arm tightened around her shoulders. "We're out of here."

Her pulse jumped and she twisted in the seat to study him. At a red light he laced his fingers in hers, and when the light changed, boldly placed her hand on his thigh before putting his hand back on the steering wheel.

Through the smooth denim, she could feel his warmth and feel the muscles in his thigh flex as he drove. It was a personal touch, an implication that she was willing to become more physically intimate with him and she debated whether to take her hand away or not. Yet she liked touching him and maybe she needed a little recklessness in her life.

When they arrived home, Jake opened the door of the pickup for her and lifted her out. For a second, he held her against him, finally letting her slide slowly down his body. Then he wrapped his arm around her and they walked across the yard until they were in the shadows of a tall oak.

"Maggie, I have never known a woman like you," he said, turning to face her.

"That's a stretch, Jake. I'm as ordinary as apple pie." She couldn't believe his words, yet they thrilled her. She knew for certain she hadn't ever met a man like him.

"This isn't ordinary and neither is what it does to me," he whispered. He tightened his arms around her, his gaze going to her mouth.

Her heart thudded, anticipation and excitement climbing. All evening long, she had watched him, wanting to touch him, marveling in the different facets of the man. She mentally reminded herself that she was just having fun as his mouth covered hers. The tip of his tongue began tracing her lips slowly. His tongue lightly stroked hers and ignited a roaring blaze within her.

Maggie clung to him, kissing him in return. He untied the ribbon around her hair and ran his fingers through the long strands. Dimly she was aware when he shifted and caressed her throat with one hand while keeping his other arm tightly around her. His hand slid down the blouse to her buttons.

"Jake—"

"Shh, let me touch you."

She knew he was touching her far more intimately than he realized, touching her heart. And yet, she wanted him to touch her and she wanted to touch him. She had a consuming hunger for this strong cowboy who had roared into her life and brought with him excitement and desire.

He pushed away the cotton blouse and his fingers slipped beneath the wisp of her black lace bra to caress her taut bud. She moaned, the sound lost in their kisses as sensations rocked her and urgency heightened.

Jake was so much more appealing than any other man she had ever known. He was a threat to her heart, but a temptation to her desire. Wanting more of him, knowing this night was unique, she tugged his shirt out of his jeans. She struggled with each button until Jake released her and yanked the half-buttoned shirt over his head and tossed it aside.

Her eyes had adjusted to the night and she could see his well-sculpted muscles. As he unbuckled his belt, she ran her hand across his smooth chest, stroking his flat nipple and then letting her fingers drift lower to his waist.

All thoughts ceased as he peeled away the straps of her lacy bra and cupped her breasts, stroking her nipples with his thumbs and sending shockwaves coursing through her. Momentarily lost, she grasped his waist and closed her eyes. Then he bent his dark head and took her nipple in his mouth, his tongue stroking her, hot and wet and driving away caution.

While he held and kissed her, Jake shook. He wanted her warmth and softness to thaw the cold winter of his dark past. He had half expected her to refuse him and keep herself shut away, yet giving was her nature. She moaned and trembled, her hands in his hair and caressing his chest, which heightened a need that was already raging inside him.

As they kissed, he unfastened and pushed away her jeans. They fell around her legs, caught on her boots. Sitting on a lawn chair, Jake pulled her down into his lap. While she kissed him hungrily and ran her hands over his chest, he yanked off her boots and jeans. He tugged off his own boots and dropped them.

"You're special, Maggie," he whispered.

Cradling her in his arms, he leaned over her, kissing her long and hard, his tongue going deep into her mouth and sliding over hers while his hand slid between her legs to caress her inner thigh.

Silent arguments rose inside her head to stop him now, yet she wanted him. She wanted to take a chance, to know him completely. When his fingers stroked her intimately, reason fled while she cried out and clung to him.

She heard a jangle of keys and then Jake flung his jeans over his shoulder and picked her up, carrying her up the steps and into the house.

"Jake, slow down," she whispered once inside the house before his mouth silenced her sentence. His arms were strong around her, his kisses escalating her need.

He took the stairs easily and walked into her bedroom. He set her on her feet, pulling her against him. Dropping his jeans, he wore only his narrow briefs and his body was lean and hard and marvelous. She ran her hands over his solid muscles, moving her hips against him, wanting him with a desperation she had never known before.

Caution was lost, vanished in desire. She didn't want to reason out how much she wanted or how much she was prepared to give.

Carrying her to the bed, he stood looking down at her and all she could think was how magnificently male he was. He peeled away her lacy black underwear and then he put one knee on the bed. As he leaned to trail kisses along her stomach, she laced her fingers in his hair. He stood and removed his briefs and her breath caught. She reached out to stroke him, sitting up to take him into her mouth and lick him.

He groaned, his fingers winding in her long hair and then he lifted her up to kiss her with such a hunger she thought she would melt.

"Jake—"

He laid her on the bed again, trailing kisses over her while his hand searched between her legs and then he stroked her till she was on the brink of oblivion.

Struggling to keep control over himself, he trailed kisses along her thighs while his hand continued to caress her. "I want to know every beautiful inch of you," he said in a husky voice.

"I can't reach you," she protested, sitting up to pull him to her. He hauled her into his embrace to kiss her and then he released her.

"Lie down, Maggie. I want to know you," he said, lowering her to the bed and rolling her over to trail his hands and mouth over her back and lower, down to her thighs. She raised her head and slanted him a look over her shoulder.

"Jake, you have to let me do the same—"

He was on his knees and looked into her eyes, his gaze blazing with his longing. "Next time, Maggie. You kiss me like this now and I'll explode. You don't know what you do to me."

His words shook her and she rolled over, flinging herself into his arms and kissing him, her need pouring into her kiss.

"Are you protected?" he whispered, and she shook her head. He stepped off the bed, retrieved his jeans and reached in his pocket to produce a small packet. Drinking in the sight of him, she stroked his thigh.

And then he was between her legs, wanting her, ready for her.

She wrapped her legs around him and he slowly filled her, hot and hard. While they moved together, her hands ran over his taut bottom and back that still was healing from the fire. In the far recesses of her mind, beyond sensation, beyond intimacy, she knew she was giving him far more than just her body.

Sweat rolled off Jake as he tried to slow and hold back, trying to make the special moment last, wanting to drive her to complete abandon. He wanted her as he had never wanted a woman before.

"Maggie," he ground out her name before kissing her, feeling her softness enveloping him. She returned his kisses while she was wild beneath him. All her cool reserve was gone as he had wanted. He didn't want their loving to end. She was fire and mystery and fulfillment. Thought fled while physical needs crashed in on him.

Maggie heard Jake say her name. She was lost in a dizzying spiral of ecstasy that wound tighter until a climax burst within her, and she felt his shuddering release.

With labored breathing, he trailed kisses over her temple. Taking her with him, he rolled over, his hand stroking her back while he held her close.

"I told you that you're special, but those words are inadequate," he whispered.

Shaken by his statement, she twisted to look up at him, and her fingers drifted along his jaw. Worry was already tugging at her, but wanting this moment to last, she pushed the nagging thoughts away.

She relished being in his arms. As she stroked his jaw, she turned his face to look into his eyes. "What is it, Jake, that makes you keep part of yourself locked away?"

He ran his fingers through her golden hair, letting silky strands spill slowly over her bare back and shoulders. He pulled her close against his chest where she couldn't see his face and was silent for so long that she wondered whether she had intruded into his private world too much.

"I told you, I lost my family in a fire." Jake's voice was ragged. He stared into the night, feeling Maggie's softness pressed against him, her arms wrapped around him. It was hard to answer her and it hurt badly, yet he knew if there ever was anyone to confide in, it would be Maggie.

"My parents drank, and my dad probably went to bed with a cigarette. The firemen said that the fire started with a burning mattress in my folks' bedroom." While memories assailed Jake, he was only dimly aware of Maggie's fingers that stroked him. Lost in recollections of that terrible night, he had a knot in his throat. "I was fourteen years old and wild and had slipped out of the house so I could go to the pool hall. When it closed, I wanted to just hang out with some of my friends. As I walked home, before I reached our block, I could see the flames. My entire family perished. My parents and my two younger brothers died that night.'' Jake clenched his fists. ''Maggie, I wasn't there to save them. They died because I wasn't there for them.'' The tormenting guilt he had carried all the years since swamped him momentarily, and he was quiet, gritting his teeth while pain stabbed his chest. ''I should have been there.''

She pulled away to look at him. ''Jake, you can't feel guilty about not being home! You might have died with them in the fire if you had been there.''

''I wished I had,'' he said bitterly, closing his eyes. ''I've never talked about this to anyone before,'' he admitted, knowing instinctively that there would be enough sympathy, warmth and understanding in her to trust her with his deepest secrets.

Hurting, he squeezed his eyes closed while she stroked his cheek. ''Jake, you couldn't help what happened.''

''I should have been there for my brothers,'' he argued, remembering the bedroom the two younger brothers shared. ''I could have gotten them out and should have. Damnation, how did we get into this,'' he snapped, annoyed that his dark past had intruded on a night that had been one of the best of his life.

As he rolled over on his back, she raised up on an elbow to look down at him, long strands of her golden hair spilling across his chest.

''We got into it because I asked you to share part

of yourself with me.'' Maggie stroked his shoulder. ''Where did you live after the fire?''

''Foster homes because I was underage, but I ran away a lot. Then I was placed on a boys' ranch and that was my salvation. By the time I was eighteen, I got into rodeos and started winning money. I tried never to look back.''

He turned to face her, his eyes pools of dark brown that were unfathomable. ''If you love someone and they get hurt, you get hurt. I learned that the hard way.''

''Oh, Jake!'' she hugged him, placing her head on his chest and hurting for him. ''Don't blame yourself. Your family wouldn't want you to and they wouldn't want you to go through life without love because of that terrible night.''

He didn't answer and Maggie lay still, listening to his steady heartbeat. This strong, wild man was so tough and so guarded, yet at the same time, he had been kind to her father, so gentle with Katy and the horses, kind to her the night of the fire.

''Jake, love goes beyond physical intimacy.'' She sat up, trailing her fingers over his jaw, down over his throat, marveling at his strong body. ''Why do you like rodeos and all the risks and roughness?''

''It's exciting and when I started, it was the most money I'd ever seen and it gave me a bigger sense of freedom.''

''Have you ever been hurt when you've ridden?''

''Yes, but you mend,'' he said, turning to caress her, his gaze going over her. He swung her down on the bed and leaned over her. ''Ahh, Maggie, I want you again more than before.''

''I didn't know this was possible.''

"Our loving?" he asked, kissing her throat. "'Course it's possible."

"No, the magic between us. You."

His chest expanded with his indrawn breath. "Damn, Maggie, I want you," he whispered and took her words with his mouth.

She wanted tonight to be special for him, yet at the same time, she knew that with every caress, she was heading toward disaster.

He moved over her, trailing kisses over her throat and down to her breasts. He was hard and ready again for her and she wanted him desperately because she suspected this would be the only night of love she would have with him.

This time when they made love, he pulled her on top of him, stroking her breasts while she moved with him until they crashed into exhaustion.

She lay sprawled over him, her golden hair fanned out over both of them. While he combed his fingers through her hair, her pulse slowed to normal.

"Come watch me ride in the Labor Day rodeo in Oklahoma City."

Maggie raised her head to look at him. "All right."

"Ask your Dad and Katy to come with us."

"They both love rodeos so I'm sure they'll want to go."

Jake rolled over so they lay on their sides. "Ah, darlin', I want to stay in this bed all day tomorrow."

"You can't," she said quietly. "When the sun comes up, the witching hour is over. Reality and responsibility return," she said, knowing what lay ahead and refusing to think about it for a few more hours.

"Yeah, well, for a while, you're mine. I want you all for me," he said, sliding off the bed to stand and scoop her into his arms. "We'll shower and come back to bed. All right?"

"Sure thing, cowboy," she drawled, knowing they couldn't shower together without making love again.

It was hours later when he slept with Maggie held tightly in his arms. Exhaustion made her limp, but she was wide-awake, thinking about the night and how foolishly she had rushed into his loving arms and given him everything. He was another man who couldn't settle, the wrong man for her. Yet in so many ways it had seemed right and wonderful. And so much more than anyone else she had ever known. She was in love with him. Jake had stepped in to help where he was needed. He was both strong and gentle. The knowledge that she was the first person in his life to whom he had confided his guilt about his family filled her with a mixture of emotions.

She ran her fingers over his shoulder, feeling his collarbone, sliding her hand down over bulging biceps. She lifted thick, dark strands of his hair off his face. He was a marvel in her life in so many ways, but she knew the day would come when he would say goodbye and leave.

In the morning, they made love again and then after staying in his arms for an hour, she slipped out of bed and grabbed a towel to wrap around herself.

"Don't go," he said. His hands rested behind his head and the sheet covered him below his navel. Each time she looked at his body or into his intense gaze, he took her breath away. Now it was daylight and she could see clearly the bulge of his taut muscles, his smooth tanned skin, and his lean frame.

"I have to go now. I told Patsy I would pick Katy up at church so I'm supposed to meet them there. You can come to church with me."

"Nope. I'll stay here. You could meet them after church and give us one more hour."

She leaned over him. "Forget that. You've worn me to a frazzle as it is."

He swung her down in the bed to kiss her long and hard, until she wriggled against his chest and he raised his head. Both of them were breathless, and desire burned in the depths of his eyes.

"I still want you more every hour," he said gruffly.

Her heart thudded because she wanted him and his words thrilled her. "Don't say I didn't warn you," she said, giving him a saucy answer and stepping out of bed quickly, walking away nude and knowing he was watching.

"Damn, woman," he said behind her and she slanted him a mischievous look, then rushed into the bathroom and quickly closed the door when he jumped out of bed and started toward her. She turned on the shower and ignored his call and the light rap on the door. He finally gave up and she showered and washed her hair. Last night was over, and now it was just a memory.

It would hurt when he left, but she refused to let her feelings for him grow.

She dried and dressed in a sleeveless blue dress, slipping into high-heeled blue pumps. With deft twists, she looped and pinned her hair on top of her head.

When she went downstairs, he was in jeans and had breakfast cooked. He turned to look at her, his gaze sweeping over her and she was conscious this was the first time he had seen her in a dress.

Six

———

"**W**ow, you look better than breakfast," he said, crossing the kitchen to wrap his arms around her and kiss her.

"You look yummy yourself," she said, kissing him and then moving away. "I have to get to town on time, Jake."

He studied her intently, and her heart drummed while she wondered what he was thinking. He merely nodded and turned to dish up bacon and eggs. He had poured orange juice and a glass of milk for himself.

"Want milk?"

"No, thanks." As she ate, she was too aware of him. He constantly touched her, eating little of his breakfast while he flirted with her.

After breakfast, they cleaned the kitchen and in minutes she headed for the door. He opened it for her and then when they went down the porch steps, he draped his arm across her shoulders and raised his face. "East wind—probably rain."

"We're approaching the record for number of days without rain. I hope you're right."

"But you don't think I am," he said, smiling at her. His arm tightened and he stopped her. "You're in plenty of time to get to church. Before Katy and your father are here, come for a ride on my bike with me. We'll just ride up to the main road and back."

"I'm in a dress," she protested.

"So who's to see?"

She stared at him, annoyed, tempted, and finally yielding. "All right, but you better get me back safely."

He framed her face with his hands. "I will always get you back safely."

"Don't promise what you can't deliver," she said, looking into his dark eyes.

"You are irresistible," he whispered, lowering his gaze to her mouth and kissing her.

Instantly, she pressed against him, a moan catching in her throat while her hips moved against him and she trembled. Her intense response set him on fire and he had to fight with himself to avoid picking her up and carrying her back to the house and making love to her. Instead he held her and kissed her and was stunned that each kiss just made him want more of her.

She finally pushed against him and when her eyes opened and met his gaze, his heart thudded. Desire was blatant in their blue depths. Her mouth was red from his kisses, and he wanted her with an ache that surprised him.

Wordlessly he took her hand and led her to his bike. He threw his leg across the seat and sat down, helping her on behind him. She hiked her skirt up and his temperature escalated. He ran his hand along her tanned, smooth leg. "Beautiful."

"C'mon, cowboy, take me for a ride," she whispered in his ear.

He twisted to look at her and saw that mischievous, taunting smile that made him want to throw her down on the ground and kiss every inch of her until she was begging for him. "You know the ride I'd like to take you on."

"Start your engine."

"If you don't think my engine hasn't been revving since you came down to breakfast—"

She laughed. "Let's go, Jake, or I'm going to leave in my pickup."

The roar of the Harley broke the Sunday morning quiet. Jake eased to the road and drove slowly and carefully. He didn't want to frighten her and he liked having her clinging to him while they rode. How he wished he could turn onto the highway and just keep driving with her on through the day until the night.

When they returned, he slowed beside her pickup and she climbed off quickly. "That was an adventure."

"An adventure would be to get on the highway and see where it takes us."

"In the meantime, I'm off to church and I'll bring Katy back with me later," Maggie said as she climbed into the pickup and lowered the window.

He leaned forward, slipped his hand behind her neck and pulled her to him to kiss her one more time. When he released her, she gazed at him solemnly.

"Bye, Jake," she said, and put the pickup in gear. Jake stepped back and watched her drive away. He could still feel her soft lips parting for his kiss, her tongue going into his mouth, her body pressed against him. And all the memories of the night were still with him, yet he sensed that her goodbye had been final in spite of working here or seeing her every day.

She was the woman he would want to travel with him, but he wanted one who didn't need a wedding band, didn't want to settle, and liked the wind in her face on his bike.

Maggie was not that woman. She would want the wedding ring. She would want to stay forever in this part of the country. And he suspected she had little regard for his vagabond ways.

And then there was Katy. He didn't know anything about little girls. He would never want to disrupt Katy's life. Maggie had people who loved and depended on her.

Yet the night had been fabulous. Jake kicked a rock and turned to lock up the house and head for the truck to check on the animals.

Monday night Maggie glanced out the kitchen window and her pulse jumped as Jake parked the pickup and climbed out.

Tuffy ran across the yard and jumped the fence to greet Jake. Maggie watched as Jake hunkered down to pet Tuffy.

"So he won you over, too," Maggie said and walked back to the sink. After a few minutes, she watched Jake sit on the porch steps to pull off dusty boots. Tuffy came up beside him and Jake scratched his ears and she shook her head. "My dad, my dog, me. Next it will be Katy who will love you."

Jake had stripped off his shirt and held it and his boots in his hand when he entered the kitchen, while Tuffy stayed on the porch. Jake was covered with dust, a red bandanna around his head. In spite of his disheveled appearance, she wanted to walk into his arms.

"Where's Katy?" he asked.

"Watching television," Maggie said, jerking her head toward the family room. As he crossed the room toward Maggie, her pulse jumped. Aware how his gaze skimmed over her cutoffs and T-shirt, she inhaled swiftly.

"I'm too dirty to touch you, but I can't walk through this room and miss an opportunity for one quick kiss."

"Jake, if Katy sees us, I'll—" He silenced her with his mouth. Hot desire burst inside her and she returned his kiss, wanting him and knowing she couldn't walk back into his arms.

Shaken, she stepped away. "We need to stop," she whispered.

He studied her. "You don't know how great you look."

"Thanks," she said, feeling as if she were drowning in his compelling gaze.

"I'm going to shower."

She watched him leave the room, looking at his back that was healing fast from the fire. She returned to cooking dinner, her thoughts on Jake.

An hour later, Maggie passed a platter of golden fried chicken to him. He helped himself and set the platter down. "I have a surprise," he said, turning to Katy. "I made a swing for you."

Katy looked up and grinned, her blue eyes sparkling. "Can we hang it in a tree tonight?"

"Wait, Katy, say 'thank you,' before you start asking for more," Maggie said, smiling at her daughter.

"Thank you, Mr. Reiner," Katy said politely. "Can we put it up tonight?"

"Yes. And it would be easier if you called me Jake."

When she looked at her mother questioningly, Maggie nodded. "Jake is fine, Katy."

As soon as they finished eating, Katy ran outside while Jake helped Maggie clear the table. During the afternoon, Maggie had been to see her father. The doctor had said Ben could come home tomorrow because Maggie was there to care for him. Jake knew he wouldn't have her to himself after tonight.

With Katy present, Jake was circumspect, but he wanted to touch Maggie constantly. He stretched out his leg once during supper and brushed her leg lightly. She shot him a look and then they both were trapped, their gazes locked while tension snapped between them.

Now with Katy playing in the yard, he couldn't resist and caught Maggie around the waist, taking dishes out of her hands and kissing her before she could protest. And for a few minutes, she returned his kisses.

Then she pushed away and looked up at him. "Jake, Katy will be right back in here if we don't go outside."

"You're protesting, but your eyes and your pulse

are telling me something else," he drawled in a husky voice.

"Here she comes," Maggie said, and he saw Katy running toward the house, her long blond hair flying out behind her head.

"When are you coming outside?" Katy asked, bursting into the kitchen.

Maggie put dishes in the dishwasher and straightened up. "We'll be out in two minutes."

Satisfied, Katy left and Maggie gave Jake an "I told you so," look before continuing to clean. When they walked outside, Katy ran to join them with Tuffy tagging along behind her.

Katy pointed at an oak. "I know which tree—that one."

"Katy, we need a strong limb that sticks out far enough so that you can swing high. How about this?" he asked, jumping up and grabbing a limb on the oak with both hands.

Smiling, Katy nodded and Jake dropped to the ground. "I'll get the swing."

In a short time he had it ready and lifted Katy onto the seat. "Hang on tight, and I'll swing you."

Soon Maggie and Jake sat in lawn chairs and watched Katy swing. Tuffy sat beside Jake while Jake idly scratched the dog's ears.

"The dog loves you, my child likes you—you have a winning way."

"I hope so," Jake said. "After you get Katy to bed, will you come back out and sit with me?"

She was silent a moment before she nodded. "Yes. I have an intercom on the porch so I can hear if Katy calls me."

Jake's pulse jumped in anticipation. Memories of

Saturday night tantalized him and he wanted to be with her.

They talked until she stood and announced that it was bedtime. Katy smiled shyly at him. "Thanks, Jake, for the swing."

"That's fine, Katy," he said easily and watched mother and daughter walk hand in hand into the house. He sighed in contentment and then wondered if he was getting wrapped in invisible chains that would bind him forever. Could he ride away from here someday as carefree as he always had been?

He ran his fingers through his hair and wondered again why she was so special and what it was about her that made her different from every other woman he had known.

She came back, moving across the yard in the dark with the sureness of a cat. Moonlight spilled over her and his pulse jumped as he stood to meet her. Taking her wrist, he pulled her down in his lap, wrapping his arms around her.

"It's been a thousand years since this morning," he said, kissing her and reaching up with one hand to pull her hair free from her ponytail. In minutes he raised his head. "I'm moving upstairs tonight and giving up the hammock."

Maggie's heart drummed and she wanted another night in his arms. She stroked his muscled chest, tugging his shirt out of his jeans and letting her fingers trail across his bare skin.

"That's fine, Jake. Dad will be home tomorrow night, and if you were still outside, he would insist that you sleep upstairs. I got a lecture about your sleeping in the hammock."

"Serves you right," Jake said, kissing her again,

his hands going beneath her shirt until she pushed him away and scooted quickly off his lap. She pulled another chair close to sit beside him, aware he was watching her intently.

"Let's talk for a while."

"Sure. What about?"

She laughed. "Anything. You're going too fast."

"Okay, Maggie, what's the schedule tomorrow?" he asked, taking her hand.

"I think Dad will get to come home so I'll take Katy with me about eleven o'clock in the morning and if he's released, we'll bring him home."

"Need me?"

"Frankly I think you'll be needed more here at the ranch," she replied, thinking how much she did need him already. She wanted him to be with her, but she gave him the logical answer.

"That's fine," he said easily and stretched out his long legs. "Maggie, when the corral is finished, I want to bring Rogue up here so I can work with him in the evenings."

"You're crazy. Jake, I don't want to risk your getting hurt."

"You won't. I've worked with him daily, and he doesn't give me trouble."

"He doesn't?" she twisted around to look at him. "He doesn't—" Maggie broke off her sentence. "Why am I surprised? Jeb Stuart told me how good you are with horses. Dad's always been good with them, but he couldn't do anything with that one. I don't care if you bring him up here—we have the yard fenced so Katy can't get out and I watch her constantly if she's outside."

"Good thing you don't have a boy—he'd be going over that rail fence."

"Well, I'd be watching and I'd get him right back," she said. "By the way, the last time I was in town, I bought a cellular phone and a pager. I'll have the pager, but I want Dad to carry the phone with him in case he's out and needs help."

"Good idea," Jake said. He reached for her and trailed his fingers back and forth across her nape, stirring tingles in her that made it difficult to focus on conversation.

"Until Dad starts getting out, you can carry the phone with you."

Jake laughed softly. "I've spent a lifetime avoiding phones, clocks, and some of those things that are supposed to help life, but from my viewpoint, simply complicate it. Thanks, anyway. My health is okay."

"If you'd had a phone with you when you spotted the fire, you could have alerted everyone sooner," she replied.

"Point taken. If you want me to carry it, I'll put it in the truck. I'm not putting it in my pocket."

"Why not? Jeans too tight?" she teased.

"You don't like my tight jeans?"

"I love your tight jeans," she drawled and he groaned, stretching out his arm to wrap it around her shoulders. She wriggled away. "Down, fella."

"What do you expect me to do when you flirt like that?"

"Back to our talk. I would feel better if I knew you had the phone with you."

"Sure thing, Maggie," he answered, playing with strands of her hair, and she wondered how long she could resist him.

"I have six interviews set up later this week to hire some men to come work. I had ten replies to my ad." His hand stilled in her hair and then began to slowly comb through the strands again.

"That's good. This place is more than one healthy person can handle."

"I know. We've always had four or five men working for us until last year and things just happened until it got down to Dad only. But we'll go back to the way it was."

They were silent for a few minutes and then Jake asked, "Have your sisters ever traveled?"

"No one in the family has traveled much," she replied. "Tell me more about all the places you've been."

She listened while he talked, enjoying getting to know more about him and sitting close beside him with his hand constantly stroking her hair.

They talked for hours and yet it seemed minutes. Her curiosity never seemed satisfied when it came to him.

"Where were you headed when you stopped to tell me about the fire?" she asked when he had finished with a story.

"Nowhere in particular. I have the rodeo in Oklahoma City coming up so I would have stayed somewhere around there, but I didn't have a specific destination."

"You don't get lonely?"

"Sure, I do," he said, raising her hand and brushing her knuckles slowly with his lips.

She inhaled, knowing each touch increased the need for more of him.

"But when I stay in the same place very long, I get restless."

"Are you restless now?"

"What do you think?" he asked, his fingers tightening slightly on her wrist and he gave a gentle tug. "Come here."

Without thinking, she moved to his lap, and this time when his hands moved beneath her shirt, she didn't stop him for a long time. Finally she wriggled away and stood. He came to his feet at once and rested his hands on her waist.

"Come upstairs with me," Jake said, amazed how badly he wanted her.

"Jake, Saturday night was so very special, but I don't want to fall in love and suffer another big hurt when you leave. And I know you'll leave," she said quietly. "Won't you leave us?"

Pain stabbed him. As he gazed down into her wide blue eyes it was too dark to see her expression, but he could hear the anguish in her voice. And he could hear her determination. He had a feeling that Maggie would stand by what she said without wavering.

Combing her long, silken hair from her face, he let the soft strands slide through his fingers. "Maggie, I can't promise to stay forever."

"I'm not asking you to. I'm just telling you what I have to do."

"Damn, Maggie—not even tonight? This might be the last night before your father comes home."

"Jake, every time we're together, I'm more bound to you. First thing you know, I'll be hopelessly in love with you and suffering another heartbreak."

He framed her face with his hands while agony swamped him. "I don't ever want to hurt you."

"Then we have to say good-night now and each go our separate ways with our memories of a very special time." She stood on tiptoe to brush his cheek with a kiss. "Let me go, Jake. It's what I need."

She hurried toward the house, and he stood watching her, fighting everything in him that wanted to run and pick her up and kiss away her arguments.

"I didn't want to love ever again because it would hurt so badly to lose someone. Hell, I hurt now," he said to himself.

They hadn't known each other long enough for it to hurt this badly to see her walk away. Then again, he thought to himself, where Maggie was concerned, time didn't seem to exist.

He glanced down at Tuffy whose tail thumped against the ground. "What have I gotten myself into, buddy?"

He looked up at her windows. A light shone behind the shades. "I can walk away and I should," he said, as if trying to convince himself. Besides, Maggie had interviews to hire help, and then he wouldn't be needed here, Jake thought. He looked at Tuffy again. "You stay here. I'm going for a ride to see if I can find my way back to my life before I met Maggie."

He jammed his hand into his pocket to find his keys and went to get his bike. In a few minutes the quiet night was shattered with the explosive sound of the big engine roaring to life and then Jake swept away from the house, his dark hair flying out behind him.

Upstairs, Maggie stiffened when she heard the Harley. She slid out of bed and went to the window to raise the shade and watch him speed away. The pain that had been growing all day now threatened to overwhelm her. She could have been in his arms now, loving him, letting him love her.

Hot tears slipped down her cheeks unheeded and she wondered if he was gone forever. "He was going anyway," she whispered, reminding herself. However much it hurts now, it would have hurt worse with another night of loving binding my heart to his. Did he hurt? Did he care? This was the way he lived, she thought.

She straightened her shoulders, wiped her tears away and told herself the hurt would fade. She climbed back into bed and stared into the darkness. It was almost an hour later when she fell into a troubled sleep, only to be awakened by the sound of the Harley. *He's back.* She sighed deeply, feeling better, just knowing that he had returned. Had he just gone for a ride or had he started to leave and come back? Whatever the answer, it wouldn't matter later. The day would come when he would tear out of here and she would never see him again.

The next morning, Maggie learned her father would not be released until Wednesday. By Wednesday morning, Maggie had a dreadful time hanging on to the feeling that she was doing what was best as she and Katy ate breakfast with Jake. He looked incredibly appealing just in jeans and a T-shirt.

After breakfast, Jake stayed in the house to fix a leaky faucet and Katy sat on the floor to watch him work. For half an hour, Maggie worked on the ranch records, but then she put down her pen to go check on Katy. Pausing in the kitchen doorway, Maggie watched Katy play with Jake's leather gloves and ask him questions.

"Is she bothering you?" Maggie asked.

Jake slid out from under the sink and tousled Katy's hair. "No, she's handing me tools. She's a good helper."

"Fine," Maggie said, her gaze running over his long legs and tight jeans and broad chest. She met his gaze and turned abruptly.

Next he went outside to fix the latch on the fence, and Katy asked to go out and watch. Since Maggie had to be in the kitchen anyway where she could watch Katy, she gave her permission. She didn't expect to ask Jake to keep an eye on her child, even though she was certain he would.

Katy tagged after him and sat on the ground watching him. Once he stopped to swing her and he looked at the house and saw Maggie. He said something to Katy and Katy waved. Maggie waved in return and looked at Jake, wanting more than ever to fly into his strong arms.

Katy continued to follow him around until they both returned to the house.

Leaning one shoulder against the jamb, he stood in the doorway with Katy dancing behind him on the porch. "I'm going to work on the corral now. There are no horses in it, and Katy wants to come with me. I promise I won't take my eyes off of her."

Katy paused beside him. "Please, please."

Glancing at her watch, Maggie realized that with Jake watching Katy, she would have a chance to shower and dress to get ready to go get her dad. "All right. It'll be about half an hour and then I'll call you, Katy, to come get your bath."

"Okay."

They left, and Maggie watched them walk across

the yard with Tuffy trailing after them, Jake slowing his long-legged, ground-eating stride for Katy's sake. "Now we've all fallen under your spell, cowboy," Maggie said out loud, wondering how she was going to hang on to logic with Jake constantly around.

Half an hour later, Jake drove another nail into the corral gate. "Katy, you can hand me one of those hinges now. The black things there."

She ran to do as he asked and handed him a hinge.

"Katy!"

As Maggie's call carried across the yard, Jake looked around, his breath catching at the sight of her in a red sundress.

"It's time to stop, Katy," he said, brushing dust off his jeans. "I'll go get Mommy's keys so I can bring the pickup around for her." He headed the same way Katy was going and as she trotted beside him, she slipped her hand into his.

Stunned, Jake looked down at her while his fingers closed around her tiny hand. She smiled up at him, and something inside Jake felt as if it shattered. He inhaled deeply, watching Katy walk with him with her hand in his. He slowed his steps so she would not have to rush. He had known Jeb's kids, but this was the first time he could remember a child placing her hand in his. The trust in Katy's eyes when she had smiled up at him had brought a knot to his throat. Maggie stood watching them and Jake got a grip on his emotions as they neared her. Katy turned loose of him and ran on inside the house.

"If you'll give me your keys, I'll get the pickup for you and bring it to the house."

"Thanks," she said, disappearing and returning to hand him the keys.

Assailed by her perfume, he took her hand. He leaned forward, trying to avoid getting her dusty. "One kiss, Maggie."

He covered her mouth and was lost in her fiery sweetness, aching with longing to have so much more of her. Finally she placed her hands against his chest and pushed.

"Katy will come back and if she sees us kissing, she'll have no end of questions and heaven knows when she will bring it up again."

"Would that be so bad?"

Her eyes were troubled, and she caught her lower lip in her teeth, making him want to kiss her again. "I don't think I want to answer a lot of questions about us. I better go." Turning away, she disappeared inside the house.

He left to get the pickup, but his thoughts jumped back to Katy and what it had been like to hold her tiny hand and see her trust.

As soon as he saw mother and daughter drive away, he left to make his daily rounds. With the drought, it was imperative that the cattle and horses get enough water. When he climbed into the truck, Tuffy jumped inside and sat in the passenger seat, giving him a pleading look.

"All right, you can ride along," Jake said, switching on the engine and driving away.

Along the western border of the ranch, he spotted a fence down and swore. It was the third time since he had started working at Maggie's place that he had found a fallen fence. Last time he'd had to chase down two steers.

There was a fence dividing this quarter of the ranch from the rest and Jake knew there hadn't been any cattle here that could have escaped. He climbed out of the truck and got tools from the back, then went to see what needed to be done while Tuffy trailed at his heels.

"Hellfire." Jake stared at two smashed fence posts and dry grass flattened by tire tracks. Someone had run off the road and smashed the posts. But then he saw another one smashed farther down the road. Vandals? Smashing a few fence posts didn't seem like it would be anyone's idea of fun.

Jake stared at the fence and then began to follow the flattened grass, backtracking across the pasture. Long ago, he had learned to hunt and track animals. As he drove slowly over the Alden land, he swore again. The vehicle had apparently crossed the ranch.

Seven

Jake needed a horse. Swearing, he climbed into the truck, waited for Tuffy to jump inside and then leaned out the open door while he drove slowly alongside the tracks where grass was broken and bent.

In minutes he went back to saddle one of the horses and headed out again on horseback, jamming the cell phone into his pocket.

It took another half hour before he found what he was looking for—a fence cut where the cattle were and six steers were missing. Grass was trampled where someone had loaded the steers into a truck.

Swiftly Jake yanked the cell phone out of his pocket and called the sheriff. As he waited for an answer, he watched the grazing cattle and realized no matter how many men Maggie hired, he wouldn't leave her until they caught whoever was trying to cause her family trouble. Jake talked to the sheriff and then he mended the fence, all the while stewing with anger. Before today, he had replaced three downed fences. Were they an accident or also an act of vandalism? Cattle rustling was certainly no accident. It didn't hit him until he was riding back to the house to meet the sheriff that the fire hadn't been an accident, either.

Midafternoon while Jake worked on the corral, he heard the pickup approaching. He put away his tools and brushed himself off, going to meet Maggie as she drove up to the back gate with her father and Katy.

Dressed in jeans and a cotton Western shirt, Ben was pale and thinner, but he swung his crutches out of the pickup, stood and reached out to shake Ben's hand. "Thanks for all you've done here."

"Glad to do it," Jake answered easily. "I'll get everything from the pickup," he told Maggie as she walked beside her father.

"Grandpa, I have a new swing!" Katy said, pointing to it.

"Good! I'll bet Jake built that for you."

"Yes, sir."

Jake got clothing and a small bag from the back and trailed into the house after them to put things away while Maggie got her father settled. When he'd finished, Jake found Maggie alone in the kitchen.

"Maggie, I need to talk to you," Jake said. "Can you step outside?"

Frowning, she looked past him toward the open door. "As soon as I can, I will."

"I'll be at the corral," he said and left.

He hated that he had to tell her about the rustling.

He went back to work on the corral. In ten minutes he yanked off his T-shirt and rolled a bandanna to tie it around his forehead as sweat poured off his body. It was another twenty minutes before she joined him. She had changed to cutoffs and a T-shirt again, and as he watched her walk toward him, his pulse speeded.

"What is it, Jake?" she asked, moving close enough that he could smell her sweet scent of perfume. "Something wrong?"

"Yes. Your fence was torn down and six steers were taken last night."

"No!" Maggie whipped around to look at the house. "I can't let Dad know. He doesn't need any stress like that."

"Maybe he doesn't have to know right now. I spoke to the sheriff."

Turning, Maggie stared at Jake in surprise that he had taken charge, but she was grateful.

"Maggie, the fire was deliberately set. You've had fences down all over the place and I've had to chase down some steers. Now someone has smashed your fenceposts and driven across the ranch to take your steers. Someone is trying deliberately to cause you trouble."

"Why?" she asked, rubbing her earlobe as she pondered her own question.

"What about that cantankerous neighbor? It has to be someone who doesn't like your family or has a grudge."

"If it's a grudge, Todd Harvey is as good a suspect as anyone." Worries assailed her, foremost how to keep the bad news from getting back to her dad. "I don't know. Suppose it was coincidences?" she said, not wanting to cope with this new concern, yet knowing she was going to have to.

"Who is Todd Harvey?"

She shrugged. "He worked for us. He's from Rayburn—a small town west of here. Dad caught him stealing some tools from us and fired him. Since then he doesn't speak to any of us. He's been in and out of trouble, but he stays in town because he has a girlfriend there, so he's still in the area. Weldon doesn't like us, either, but it's difficult to imagine either one of them doing things like the fire and rustling. Todd doesn't seem like the type to have the energy for it, and Weldon would put too much at risk. He has a thriving ranch. True, he wants to expand and would like to buy part of our land. But what good would rustling six steers do him?"

"It seems likely to me that it's not a random act or a complete stranger," Jake said, resting a hand on her shoulder. "Someone is trying to cause you grief. Sheriff Alvarez said to let him know if you can think of anyone in the area who might have a grudge."

She rubbed her forehead again. "I don't know. Dad can be forceful, but other than the two I told you about, I can't think of anyone immediately. I don't want Dad to know this."

Jake glanced past her at the house and took her hand. "Come here." They walked around on the far side of the big flatbed truck where they weren't in full view of the house and he pulled her into his arms. "I wish I could take away your worries, Maggie," he said softly, and her heart felt squeezed in two. He spoke into her hair while he held her tightly. "I won't leave until we catch who did this."

Joy flared, and she let out a long breath. Jake

would be here a little longer. And it felt so incredibly right to stand in his arms. He was hot, damp from sweat, but she didn't care. His strong arms were a reassurance. She had a friend she could confide in and trust. "Thanks," she whispered.

"I left one other time in my life and when I came back, all those I loved were dead," he said flatly. "I won't run out again and leave someone."

Anguished, she tightened her arms around him and looked up at him. "Jake, don't continue to blame yourself for something you shouldn't have a shred of guilt about! Please, you were only a kid and you had nothing to do with what happened."

The coldness in his eyes frightened her as he shook his head. "I should have been there for them." He framed her face with his hands. "But I can promise that I won't leave you until this is over."

Tears stung her eyes for his hurt, for his staying and for the harsh knowledge that when it was over, he planned to go. He wiped her tears away with his thumbs.

"Don't cry, darlin'," he whispered, sounding as anguished as she felt. "We'll catch whoever it is."

"Jake, I'm not crying about that! I'm thinking about the pain you went through all alone...and I'm thinking about your leaving me," she admitted.

He wrapped her in his arms and crushed her against his heart and she held him tightly, feeling a shudder rack him. She wondered if anyone before had ever tried to comfort him over his loss. She knew he had never let anyone know his feelings about the loss.

When he turned her face up to his, he gazed into her eyes and the longing she saw made her tremble.

Standing on tiptoe, she closed her eyes and brushed her lips across his, taking his full lower lip in her teeth gently and running the tip of her tongue across it. He made a sound deep in his throat and then his mouth opened hers and he kissed her deeply.

In minutes their breathing was ragged and their hearts were pounding. She knew they didn't have any privacy and if she didn't get back to the house, she would have lots of questions. She leaned back. "Jake," she whispered, pushing him away.

She had seen him do all kinds of rough work and never get winded, but now he was gasping for air as if he had run for hours. Sweat beaded his forehead and the look in his brown eyes made her feel as if she were the most desirable woman on earth.

"All right, Maggie," he said hoarsely, stepping back and resting his hands on her shoulders while he appeared to be trying to pull himself together. "You don't know what you do to me, woman."

"It's only half of what you do to me," she said earnestly, thinking about her feelings for him. Her heart and soul were all tied up in a package with physical intimacy and she didn't think he realized it at all.

"Ah, Maggie. Why did fate throw us together?"

"I'm glad it happened," she whispered, and he hugged her again.

They were quiet while he held her and stroked her head for a few minutes and then he released her and moved away, keeping his hands on her shoulders.

"Back to the problem. I've had all morning to think about this. As soon as you hire some help, I can sleep in the daytime and patrol the grounds at night. I can go back to sleeping in the hammock, too.''

"No!'' Her hands rested on his waist and only half her attention was on their conversation. She was acutely aware of his warm flesh, his jeans that rode low on his hips. Too easily, she remembered him without the jeans. ''Don't do that. You sleep in a bed in the house. You could only see one part of the house from the hammock anyway. Besides, surely no one will try to get into the house with all of us there and with you upstairs. Tuffy will be on the porch.''

"Watchdog Tuffy. That dog sleeps as soundly as you do.''

She laughed and leaned back to look up at him. ''I'd rather have you in the house with us than patrolling the grounds at night. I'd feel safer.''

She had meant to step away and go back to the house, but the moment she looked into his eyes, she was trapped.

"I want you so damn badly, Maggie. And I want you more all the time,'' he said in a guttural voice. He bent down to kiss her again, and she was lost in a hunger that was undeniable.

Finally she pushed against him and he released her with his hands still resting on her waist. ''This time I really do have to go. I should check on Dad and Katy. If I think of anyone else who might have a grudge, I'll tell the sheriff, but I'm at a loss now.''

"Promise me you won't worry.''

"I won't while you're here,'' she said and walked away.

As Jake watched her go, he clenched his fists. He wanted her desperately with a need that overwhelmed him. If this was love, it was terrible. Or was the terrible part his emotions warring over whether to let go and love again? The idea terrified him. He remembered Katy slipping her hand into his and the awe it had given him. Mother and daughter. Family. Why did loving someone have to be so damned hard!

Swearing, he walked back to his work and watched Maggie disappear into the house. Images taunted him of her in bed with her silky hair falling over them, her body ivory and pink, soft and full of curves.

He swore again, working with fury, trying to chase all the memories and thoughts out of his mind, yet unable to stop remembering Maggie holding him so tightly and telling him she was crying because he was leaving her.

That afternoon he finished the corral and with expert handling, put Rogue in it. As soon as the gate closed, he watched the horse trot around the area with his ears cocked forward and nostrils flaring.

"It's a new place," Jake told him quietly, "but you'll get used to it and you won't have to stay penned up in here much. I'll be back after supper to see you." The horse stopped across the corral and looked at Jake and pawed the ground.

"See you later," Jake said and headed for the house.

During supper, Jake found himself caught up in the family conversation and enjoying their warmth. Maggie's blue eyes sparkled, and both Katy and Maggie had changed their clothes and looked fresh and cool. Ben was in jeans and a plaid Western shirt and his color looked better.

Ben set down his glass of water and said, "I saw

you brought that stallion up here this evening. Maggie says you want to work with him.''

"Yes, sir.''

"She said she warned you about him. I'd hate to see you get hurt after all you've done for us. That horse is pure trouble and no one can figure out why. I can't sell him, either.''

"I told Maggie, I'll take him, so don't keep searching for a new owner. I'm going to work with him in the evenings.''

"Don't say you weren't warned,'' Ben said. "The corral looks good. I'll walk out there sometime soon and give it a close inspection. Thanks, Jake.''

"You're welcome.''

"I have a crew hired to start rebuilding tomorrow and Maggie has six interviews lined up, so we should get back in shape soon. It would help if we'd get a good rain.''

"I think we will in the next few days,'' Jake said, seeing Maggie frown and he knew she was thinking about someone trying to harm them.

After supper, Jake helped Maggie clean the kitchen while Ben and Katy went out to the backyard. Maggie tried to shoo him away.

"Go on outside and talk to Dad. Katy wants you to swing her and there's only a little left to do here.''

Placing his hands on either side of her on the counter, he hemmed her in. "You know what I'd like to do here.''

"But you can't,'' she said, smiling up at him.

"Your smile could light the darkest place, darlin'.''

"Then I hope it's lighting the dark you carry in your heart, Jake.''

Before he could respond, the door burst open, Katy ran inside, completely oblivious of how close Jake had been standing to her mother. "Jake, will you please come swing me?"

"Sure, Katy, I'll be right out."

She left and he looked back at Maggie, a long solemn look filled with hot desire. Without a word he turned and left. Maggie closed her eyes and sagged against the counter. They were both tearing each other up every time they were together.

She went to work and looked out the window, watching Jake sweep Katy up into her swing and then step behind her to push her. In minutes he was laughing as he pushed Katy. She was laughing, too. "Damn you for charming all of us," Maggie whispered and then immediately felt contrite. "Sorry, Jake," she said aloud, even though he couldn't hear or know. It had been so good to have him here that she couldn't regret having known him.

The news that someone was trying to hurt them was tempered by Jake's strength and help and the knowledge that he was going to stay longer.

Outside, a breeze made the summer evening bearable while shadows lengthened across the mowed lawn. When Katy finally said she wanted to stop swinging, Jake went to sit in a lawn chair beside Ben who smiled at him. "Thanks for all you've done here."

"I was glad to be of help."

Ben reached into his pocket and pulled out a folded bit of paper and handed it to Jake. "Here's your first month's pay."

Jake took the check, opened it and frowned. "Sir,

this is way too much," he said, extending it to Ben. "I work hard, but not that hard. And I haven't been here a full month."

Ben smiled and shook his head, refusing to take the check. "Don't tear it up, son. When I was in a dilemma, you saved us, and I know how much I've let the place run down this year. You gave me peace of mind. How do you think you would have felt in my place with the ranch half burned and Maggie out here alone with a little girl? No, you take the pay. The doctor told me not to argue."

Jake smiled and tucked the check into his pocket, having no intention of cashing it. "Thanks."

"No, we owe you." Ben sighed. "I haven't hired people this year because I couldn't find men I could trust or who really wanted to work. With Maggie and Katy alone at the house, I have to be careful who I hire. It's getting harder to find help."

"If you'd get a horse trainer, you'd have some fine animals here. You have some of the best quarter horse stock I've seen. You could raise quarter horses, and it would be real profitable."

"That's what I started to do, but then I ran out of energy and that stallion was costly and too much trouble."

"He'll come around."

"If he doesn't kill you first," Ben said. Jake heard the screen slap shut behind them and knew Maggie was coming to join them. He stood and turned to watch her, enjoying the sway of her hips and her long bare legs moving gracefully.

"You interested in staying full time?" Ben asked. "Staying to raise those horses and train them?"

With a jolt, Jake looked down at Ben. "Thanks.

I'll be here for a while. Someday, I'll move on, but not soon,'' he replied swiftly, and wondered if Maggie heard him. ''Come sit down and watch the grass grow with us,'' he said as she got closer to them.

She laughed and sat beside Ben. Jake pulled a chair next to her. They talked until Maggie left to get Katy ready for bed and then as fireflies winked over the yard, Katy came running out in pink pajamas.

''Night, Grandpa!'' she said, climbing in his lap and giving him a kiss on the cheek. He hugged her.

''I'm glad to have my baby in my lap tonight and be home with you. I love you, darlin'.''

''I love you, too,'' she said and slipped off his lap to go to Jake, climbing in his lap without hesitation. ''Night, Jake,'' she said cheerfully and kissed his cheek.

He inhaled, hugging her lightly and smelling the clean soapy scent of her, and his heart opened like a flower to the sun. He had a knot in his throat and could barely speak. ''Night, Katy,'' he said.

As soon as he spoke, she was gone, racing barefoot across the lawn to her waiting mother. Jake glanced over his shoulder at Maggie who stood in the porch light. Their gazes met and he wanted her with a hunger that made him ache clear to his soul.

It was late by the time they had all gone inside. Jake changed and went down to work with the stallion. He put two powerful lights in the back of the truck that lit up the corral. Then he picked up a saddle and walked in. Since that first morning Jake had been with the horse every day, and now the stallion ambled slowly toward him.

''Tonight we'll progress a little more,'' Jake said

quietly, turning his back and walking away, knowing the curious horse would follow him. In minutes he had the stallion saddled, which he had done before, but he had never ridden him. He led the horse around the corral, talking to him, and then stopped to run his hands over him. Finally Jake took the reins and eased into the saddle and they moved into a walk. Jake knew better than to let down his guard. He patted the horse's neck. "Easy, easy," he said quietly.

He heard the screen door open and close and glanced into the darkness to see Maggie crossing the yard.

"Will it hurt if I come watch?" she asked.

"Nope. Not as long as you don't come into the corral or make any sudden moves."

She stood quietly, watching him as he rode, then finally dismounted and removed the saddle, bridle, and blanket. He was aware she still watched him and he had to fight the urge to fling down his armload and go to her. Instead he rubbed down the horse, fed and watered him and finally turned off the bright lights to go sit with Maggie and talk. Just having her close was good even if it was torment.

The next day the men arrived to rebuild, starting with the garage, and the place rang with the sound of hammers and power saws. Jake watched the ranch constantly for any new sign of trouble, but the weekend passed without incident. The week was the same until the weekend when they had three days of rain. By the following Wednesday, Jake noticed sprouts of green coming through the blackened earth. Nature was reclaiming its own. Soon, he knew, the blackened land would be gone from sight.

Time was stretching while he fitted more and more into his life on the ranch. The longer he was there, the tighter the tension grew between Maggie and him. They both were on a ragged edge and he knew it.

At night when he couldn't sleep, he paced his room and thought about his feelings for Maggie. The thought of life without her was like a terrible void. Always before, even when he had liked a woman, he had been able to leave without hurting, but the idea of telling Maggie goodbye tore at him. His life didn't seem right without her in it. Yet she would never leave this ranch, and what kind of vagabond life could he offer Maggie and Katy? He had always wanted to move on and he expected that urge to hit him again.

But was he in love with her? She was the best friend he had ever had, closer than Jeb whom he considered to be his closest friend. She was the most desirable woman he had ever known and every kiss made him hunger for more. "I love her," he finally admitted to himself as he stared out the window. The knowledge hurt because there could never be anything lasting to come out of it. She wouldn't leave her home and father. Ask her, he told himself. He wouldn't know until he asked her. He ran his hand through his hair and moved, feeling like a tiger in a cage. The walls were closing in on him and his body ached for her.

With the rain, they had a break in the hot weather. The temperature had dropped from the hundreds to the low nineties. On Saturday afternoon, Maggie stood in front of the mirror studying herself. They were going to Oklahoma City tonight to see Jake ride in a rodeo and afterward they would go eat with his friends, the Stuarts, who had come up from Texas. Maggie was as excited as if she had a date with him, but it wasn't a date. It was a family outing, and she wouldn't be alone with him once.

Her hair hung loose, cascading to her waist. She wore tight jeans, boots and a tan, sleeveless suede blouse that had a band of long fringe that ran from her right shoulder down to her left side at the waist. Filled with anticipation, she shook her hair away from her face and went to find the others. She had already dressed Katy in jeans and a blue blouse and knew Katy and Ben were downstairs.

She opened the door to her bedroom and stopped. Across the hall Jake stood facing her, leaning one hip against the wall.

"How long have you been standing out here?"

"It was worth the wait," he drawled, straightening and crossing the hall to her. He ran his finger along the fringe which crossed her breasts.

"You give a whole new meaning to fringe. I'll never see fringe again without thinking of you tonight. You look good enough to eat," he said softly and leaned down to kiss her. She returned his kiss briefly and then pushed him away.

"We need to go so we can see you do your stuff."

"You know what stuff I'd like to show you."

She smiled at him. "You look delicious yourself, Mr. Cowboy." And he did in a blue western shirt, tight jeans and brown handcrafted lizard boots. The leather belt circling his narrow waist was secured with a big silver belt buckle that proclaimed his winning saddle bronc riding the previous year. Downstairs he put on a black Stetson, and they all climbed into the pickup, Maggie riding in back beside Katy and letting Ben sit in front with Jake.

At the arena they had a box down front. In minutes Jake stood and waved to someone. Maggie turned to see a family of five approaching them. A tall, handsome, dark-haired man carried a little girl and waved in return.

Jake and Ben stood and Jake brushed Jeb's wife's cheek with a kiss, and Maggie faced a tall, slender, pretty redhead with lively green eyes.

Jake shook hands with Jeb before turning around. "Maggie, Ben, Katy, these are my good friends the Stuarts. This is Amanda and Jeb, and he's carrying Emily who is how old now? I think you just had a birthday."

The little girl held up three fingers.

"A big three-year-old girl," Jake said and then hugged the tallest boy. "This is Kevin," he said releasing him and smiling at him before turning to the other boy to give him a quick hug. "And this is four-year-old Brad, who is almost your age Katy."

He turned to Maggie. "This is Maggie Langford, her father Ben Alden and her daughter Katy."

When Jeb took her hand, he smiled. "So how did he turn out—like I told you when we talked on the phone?"

She blushed and smiled, glancing at Jake. "Yes."

"Ignore him, Maggie," Amanda said.

Jeb set Emily on her feet and in a minute all the children were together while the men clustered and talked and Maggie chatted with Amanda. In a short time, Maggie felt as if she had known Amanda far longer than only the evening.

The men left for their event, Ben going with them to talk to friends who were riding.

"I keep trying to talk Jeb out of riding, but he loves it," Amanda said. "The kids love it. They think it's great."

"I guess I've grown up watching rodeos and my dad ride. I used to barrel race, so it's always been part of my life."

She could see the curiosity in Amanda's eyes. "I've never seen Jake look at anyone the way he looks at you, and I never thought I'd see that happen."

Maggie blushed and looked away.

"I'm sorry if I intruded."

"Oh, no. It's just that there can't be much that ever comes of what we feel. He's got his life, and I have mine."

"That's what I thought one time, too," Amanda said, laughing. "Jake didn't approve of me when I first knew Jeb."

Startled, Maggie stared at Amanda. "I can't imagine that. Jake is so nice."

"He's protective of Jeb and he thought I'd hurt him. It doesn't matter any longer because Jake and I are friends now."

Maggie wondered again about Jake's past. So much of it was a dark shadow to her. She looked toward the chutes as the announcer's voice called the next event.

In the working part of the arena, while Ben stopped to talk to two old cronies, Jeb and Jake strolled ahead to look at their horses.

"I never thought I'd see the day," Jeb said.

Jake's head whipped around. "What?"

"You in love," Jeb said, with a flash of white teeth as he grinned at his friend.

Jake didn't answer. "Hell yes," he finally ground out.

Jeb sobered immediately. "So what's the problem?"

"What kind of life can I offer a woman?"

"A damn fine one if you want to."

"Wandering from pillar to post," Jake replied in a cynical tone.

"What's wrong with staying where you are now? Her dad seems to like you."

"He does. But you know I can't settle. Maggie has roots to the center of the earth. She's never even been out of Oklahoma."

"You might settle. Stranger things have happened," Jeb drawled. "Look at my marriage."

He turned to shake hands with a friend and in minutes the conversation was forgotten as Jake got ready to ride.

Jeb was the first one out of the chute, and Maggie watched, cheering and clapping his performance. A cowboy from New Mexico rode next and then Jake came flying out of the chute on a bucking roan and Maggie forgot everything else happening around her as she watched him stay with his horse. The roan was stiff-legged, leaping and twisting, Jake swinging his legs with one hand held high and she drew a breath, thinking how wild he could be, courting danger and risk, yet so tender and gentle. This wild cowboy took her breath and she knew he already had her heart.

When the buzzer sounded, the audience roared. Jake slowed and climbed into the saddle behind one of the cowboys who rode out to assist him. Then Jake dropped to the ground and left the arena.

When the tally was over, Jake beat Jeb by a point with Jake taking first place and Jeb second.

"He said Jake always beats him," Amanda stated with a smile. When the men returned, Amanda stood to brush Jeb's cheek with a kiss.

"I can't beat him," Jeb grumbled good-naturedly and sat down, pulling Emily into his lap while the other children were enthralled with a cowboy pouring out of a chute on a wild bull.

As soon as the rodeo was over, they all went to eat ice cream together. Afterward, the Stuarts told everyone farewell. Jake, Maggie, Ben and Katy watched them climb into a van and drive away.

"I can see why he's your best friend," Maggie said. "They're very nice."

"So are you," Jake said quietly in a low voice while Ben and Katy were climbing into the pickup.

Earlier, they had checked into a hotel in the city, Maggie and Katy sharing a room, Ben next to them and Jake down the hall. Now as they drove back to the hotel, Maggie rode in silence while Ben and Jake talked about riders and animals. She looked at the bright lights and traffic and knew the evening was coming to an end. She turned to watch Jake, seeing only part of his profile as he drove. His hat was pushed to the back of his head and his hair was thick and shiny black and she wanted to reach out and touch him. Katy's head lolled against Maggie's arm, and she saw her daughter was already fast asleep. Ben twisted around to look at Maggie.

"Honey, I'll sleep in the room with Katy. You

never get out, and Jake hasn't, either. You two go dancing or catch a late show.''

"Dad!" Maggie cried, embarrassed and chagrined. "Jake may not want to go dancing—"

"Oh, yes, Jake does," Jake interrupted quickly, grinning at Ben. "And I know just the place. Thanks, Ben. C'mon, Maggie, go with me."

She threw up her hands, yet in seconds her pulse was skittering at the thought of being alone with Jake, even for only the ride in the pickup. "I'm outnumbered here," she said good-naturedly and caught Jake's look in the rearview mirror that stole her breath.

Eight

At the hotel, Maggie got Katy tucked into bed.
"Dad, I have the cell phone and I have your number
and you have mine. If you need anything—"

"I'll call, honey. Go have a good time. Katy's
asleep and we'll be fine. I'm not the sound sleeper
you are, and Katy knows how to wake someone up
when she wants something. Don't worry. Just go
have fun for a little while."

"Thanks," Maggie said, smiling. Jake had carried
Katy to bed and stood in the doorway waiting. As
the door closed behind them, Maggie heard the lock
turn. Jake draped his arm across her shoulders and
walked to the pickup to open the door.

As he started the truck, she twisted slightly to look
at him. "Did you and Dad plan this ahead of time?"

"Honestly, no. I'm as surprised as you, but I'm a
hell of a lot happier about it. You almost refused."

She laughed. "I didn't think you should be pushed into taking me out."

"That really took some pushing. Come on, Maggie, let's have a good time." He hit the accelerator and they drove several miles to a large building with a well-lit asphalt lot filled with cars.

"The music is good here and there aren't many fights. 'Course if you'd go back to my hotel room—"

"Let's go dance," she said, climbing out of the pickup. He came around to walk close beside her, his arm around her waist.

"How do you know all these places?" she asked.

"That's one of the things that goes along with being single, riding in a lot of rodeos and riding my bike all over this part of the country."

"For a cowboy who doesn't drink beer, that's rather astounding. What's worse, I know you haven't gone alone to any of these places."

"You don't know any such thing," he replied with great innocence. But then his voice lowered, and his expression became solemn. "I swear I have never gone to one with a woman who sets me on fire with just one blue-eyed glance or keeps me from sleeping for a month or has me tied in knots all the time."

She stopped and looked up at him. "I do that to you?"

"Damn straight. That is the unvarnished truth. Or let me say it another way," he said, stepping close, pulling her into his embrace and settling his mouth on hers. Her heart thudded while dreams and lonely moments vanished and she hungrily devoured reality, kissing him in return. His demanding kiss left no doubt that she was desired. She could feel him shudder as she arched her hips against him. Holding him with one arm around his narrow waist, she wound her other hand in his thick hair. She kissed him long and thoroughly and knew they had to stop or leave. When someone whistled and a man cheered, she pushed against Jake's chest. Two laughing couples passed them and climbed into a pickup to race out of the lot.

"Come on, darlin', before I do something out here in public that will embarrass us," Jake said, taking her hand to head inside.

For the next two hours, she was in his arms or dancing fast with him, watching him and feeling excitement build to a fever pitch.

They danced until two and drove back to the hotel. On their floor, they got off the elevator near Jake's room, which was at the far end of the hall from Maggie's and Ben's. Jake took out his key. "I have pop. Come in and have a drink and talk to me for a while. It's early."

"It's not going to make things between us easier."

"Maybe not, but come on. It'll make things a hell of a lot better."

She entered his room that was almost identical to hers with two large beds, a television, chairs, and tables. He tossed the key down, switched off the overhead light so the only light was one spilling from the bathroom and pulled her into his arms.

"Maggie, give me a couple more hours of memories."

She couldn't protest. All the pent-up desire exploded in her. And she saw her hunger mirrored in his dark eyes as his gaze went to her mouth and he leaned down to kiss her. Her lips opened to taste and take his strength one more time and the instant their tongues touched, the fire in her blazed hotter. He turned so he leaned against the door and fitted her up against him. When she felt his manhood straining against his jeans, she knew he wanted her as much as she wanted him.

As Jake walked her back toward the closest bed, they shed their clothing. He ripped away the covers and they fell together on the bed. Maggie couldn't get enough of him, wanting him to let go and love and trust and not be afraid to sink some roots into living. Rediscovering his magnificent body, she slid her hands over him.

His hands and lips were everywhere as if he had never known a woman before and she trembled, aching for him, letting go completely.

With shaking hands, he yanked a packet from his jeans pocket. A few moments later he moved between her legs and entered her, taking her hard and fast and with a hunger that made her pulse roar. "I love you," she cried out, wanting him desperately.

"Ah, Maggie," he said, and then his mouth covered hers, ending words.

Warmth burst through her as she climaxed while he shuddered and moved spasmodically with his release. They held each other and finally slowed to lie quietly. He rolled over, keeping her close against him.

"Ah, darlin'. Stay with me for a couple of hours. Then I'll get you to your place."

"How can I resist you?" she said.

"You resist too damn easily," he said gruffly. "You don't know what I've been through night upon night."

"Oh, yes, I do know, Jake," she answered solemnly. "You're breaking my heart to pieces."

He cupped her face with his hand. "I never, ever meant to hurt you."

"I know. I didn't want to hurt you."

He pulled her close and they were silent for a long time.

"The next time," he said, breaking the silence, "will be for you, long, slow loving until you're crying out for me." Just his words in his deep, husky voice made her stir with desire and as he started kissing her throat, she shifted to turn his face up to kiss him.

True to his word, the loving was long and slow and it was half-past four when he walked her to her door, followed her inside for one last kiss and then went back to his room. As she closed the door behind him, she had a feeling she was really telling him goodbye this time.

The next week it rained for two days. Afterward, they had warm sunny days that brought out more green across the land. Jake walked out of the new barn that was now complete. It was the second week of September now, and Ben seemed to be regaining his strength daily. No more trouble had happened, so maybe it had been a case of strange coincidences.

It didn't matter because Jake knew he wasn't ready to move on yet. He glanced at the house before climbing into the pickup.

Since the night of the rodeo he was one big ache, wanting Maggie and thinking about her to the point of distraction when he worked. He was doing dumb things because his mind wandered, but he couldn't stop thinking about her. Without seeing his surroundings, he drove across the rolling land past trees that were beginning to show the first yellow leaves of fall.

He slowed and stopped beside an antiquated windmill that needed repairs and got out tools to go to work. Before he left, he intended to replace the windmill by plumbing the stock tank, but for now, he would fix the structure. He wondered if Ben had hung on to the windmill out of sentiment or simply out of neglect.

Midafternoon Jake wiped sweat from his brow and sat in the pickup to rest a minute. "I love her and I want her with me," he said to no one. Go ahead and ask her and let her make the decision, he argued with himself. Each time, he knew what her answer would be. She wouldn't leave her home.

Jake rolled possibilities around in his thoughts. Tomorrow he had to go into town for some wire and spark plugs for the truck. He would look at rings. He realized he might be the sole owner of the ring for a long time to come.

"Dammit!" he swore and hauled himself out of the truck to resume his work.

Out of a stand of scrub oaks Tuffy came bounding toward him, and Jake leaned down to scratch the dog's ears. "Where've you been, fella? You're a long way from home. If I could sit around at home and let her pet me, believe me, I wouldn't be out here."

Tuffy's tail thumped as he sat at Jake's feet. "I suppose you want a ride home. Well, you'll have to wait until I finish repairing this windmill."

It turned out to be the following week, mid-September, before Jake got into town. After running errands, he went to a jewelry store and found a ring he liked. He wondered what he would do with it when she refused to take it. In the quiet of the store, he stood staring at a two-carat solitaire and was lost in memories of Maggie in his arms, gazing up at him with her eyes filled with desire.

"That's a beautiful diamond," the clerk said.

"Yes, it is. I'd like to think about it," Jake replied gruffly, knowing it had never taken him this long in his life to buy anything. The clerk moved a discreet distance away and waited patiently.

Jake turned the stone, catching glints of dazzling light. Was he delaying because he was sure Maggie would refuse—or because he was uncertain of himself? As fast as he asked himself the question, he knew he was deeply in love. How had she gotten past all his defenses so easily?

He swore under his breath and caught the clerk's eye.

The man returned. "Yes, sir?"

"This is the ring I want and I have a string here that I put around her finger, so maybe you can tell the size from this."

"Yes, sir. That's a beautiful choice, and I'm sure she'll be thrilled with it."

Jake wasn't sure at all. While the clerk wrote up the ticket and put away the ring, Jake remembered sitting in the family room with Maggie late one night last week. After Katy and Ben had gone to bed, Jake and Maggie had watched a movie, although neither one had seen half the movie because they talked all the way through it. While they talked, he had pulled a string from his pocket that he had put there earlier and looped it around her finger, tying it.

"What are you doing?" she asked, laughing, her dimple showing.

"Tying you to me," he said, looking into her eyes and her laughter vanished.

He slipped the string off her finger and tucked it away. He wondered whether he was off with his hasty and poor measurement, but he thought he'd be close enough.

"We'll have that ready a week from tomorrow, sir," the clerk said when he returned.

Jake finished the transaction and finally left the store, not feeling much better than he had when he went in.

Tuesday night a week later, Maggie showered and changed for bed. She had sat on the lawn until three talking to Jake, and she was too aware he was just down the hall, yards away yet light years from her.

Sleep was impossible because all she wanted was to be in his arms. Each day she knew he was slipping away more from her. If only he could let go of old hurts. Every time she had that thought, she knew that even if he did open his heart and love her, he wouldn't settle down. The day would come when he would have to move on and she and Katy could not go with him.

Moving restlessly to the window, Maggie looked down at the empty hammock and remembered that first night Jake had been with them. Now they had a new barn, garage and corral, and she was head-over-heels in love with a vagabond cowboy.

She sank down on a rocker and put her arms on

the windowsill, resting her head in her hands while she finally let loose a watershed of tears that she'd locked away for a long time.

When she was through, she wiped her eyes and began rocking, wondering if the hurt would even stop in this lifetime. She didn't know how much time passed when a movement in the yard caught her eye. She stiffened as a dark shadow drifted toward the garage.

Someone was walking around the garage and she didn't think it was Jake. The new hands she had hired all lived in town and went home at night. Anger shook her that someone might be trying to cause them more trouble.

Furious and determined to catch whoever it was, she ran across the room, yanking on her cutoffs and pulling a T-shirt over her head. Jamming her feet into sneakers, she raced downstairs where she stopped at the hall closet to get her father's shotgun from a high shelf.

Dashing across the porch, she stepped over a sleeping Tuffy. As she hurried across the yard, she slowed to move with more care. All she could think about was someone starting another fire and she couldn't bear for her father to have to go through another big disaster.

Looking at the darkened garage, she slowed and listened. Crickets chirped and there were faint rustlings. Then metal clinked against metal.

Maggie crept forward cautiously, going around the side of the garage. Shocked, she stared at the dark silhouette of a man who was leaning under the hood of the pickup.

*   *   *

Restless, unable to sleep, Jake stood at the upstairs window. He paced the room and moved back to the window, looking out at the dark night when a movement of white caught his eye. He frowned when he recognized Maggie's long hair, pale in the night. Then he spotted the silhouette of a gun in her hand.

"Dammit!" He yanked on jeans and ran. He didn't know what or who she was after, but she had no business going out alone.

Terrified for her safety, he took the stairs two at a time and ran out the back door, wanting to shout her name, but afraid he might make a dangerous situation worse.

He caught sight of her ahead of him and then she disappeared around the corner of the garage. Stretching out his legs, he ran headlong after her.

Nine

Maggie raised the shotgun and pointed it at the man who was leaning under the hood of the pickup. "Move away from the truck with your hands in the air," she snapped. Her heart pounded with fury that someone was trying to do them more harm.

The man straightened, turning toward her. Then he lunged at her, hitting the shotgun and knocking her down. Sharp pain stabbed her side and arm.

Yelling, Maggie scrambled to her feet. While she tried to find the shotgun, she heard her assailant running away.

Approaching her rapidly, footsteps pounded behind her. Her heart thudded with fear that there might be two intruders until she recognized Jake's dark silhouette.

"Call the sheriff!" he yelled as he dashed past her, racing after the man.

She yanked up the shotgun and turned to hurry back to the house.

With shaking hands she dialed 911 on a cordless phone and told the dispatcher about the intruder. "Whoever comes, please ask them to keep the sirens off. My father is back from the hospital—"

"Maggie, this is Ida Holmes. They won't turn on sirens. Tell me what happened."

"Thanks, Ida," Maggie said and tried to relay everything as it had happened. While they talked, she walked outside, peering into the darkness, wondering how long it would take the sheriff to send someone out.

She was worried about Jake's safety, and she began to feel stings and aches from her fall.

It seemed like eternity until she saw flashing lights through the trees. The cars pulled up in front of the house and the sheriff got out and closed his door quietly.

"Where is he now?" Ty Alvarez asked her as three men climbed out of the other car.

"We were by the pickup and he knocked me down and ran," Maggie replied. "Jake took off after him," she said, pointing the direction she had last seen them. "I ran back here and called you."

"Stay here and keep the house locked up," the sheriff said and motioned to the men. With guns drawn, all four fanned out, and she was even more afraid for Jake's safety. She worried that Jake would mistake a lawman for the intruder. Or that they would mistake Jake for her assailant.

Except for the back door, the house was locked. She went inside and returned her father's shotgun to its place on a high shelf in the closet, far out of reach of Katy. Switching off the downstairs lights, she went to the backyard, sitting on a lawn chair in the darkness, mulling about what had happened and hoping they caught the man.

The intruder was tall. She knew that much, but nothing else. She didn't have time to see his face so she couldn't give the sheriff a good description.

Her hip hurt where she had fallen, and her ribs ached where he had tackled her. Her elbow stung, but she didn't care. She tugged her earlobe and worried, wishing the men would return, wanting to see Jake safely home. She glanced back at the house, thankful her father and Katy were sleeping through all this. Staring into the darkness, she tugged her ear nervously. Where were they?

When she saw figures moving out of the darkness, she had to curb the urge to run to them. The moment she spotted Jake's tall silhouette, her heart thudded with relief.

As she walked toward the police cars, she realized they had caught someone.

Curious and angry, she was relieved to see that Jake was all right.

Jake hurried over to her and slid his arm around her waist. His cheek was scraped, he had a cut on his shoulder and he was smudged with dirt. She inhaled, wanting to touch him.

"Are you all right?" Jake asked.

"Yes," she answered.

As one of the lawmen turned on his headlights, she glanced around, looking into the angry gaze of her neighbor.

"Weldon!"

Covered with cuts, welts and dirt, with a swollen

mouth and one eye swollen shut, Weldon Higgens stood glaring at her.

Besides his injuries, Weldon's T-shirt was ripped and bloodstained. She wondered if Jake had done all that to him. She blinked at the hate she could see in his expression. Stunned, she could only stare at him in amazement. "Why?" she whispered, but no one answered.

Lawmen hauled him away to put him into the back of a car while Sheriff Alvarez walked over to her. "Jake got Weldon to confess that he's the one who has been causing all the trouble around here."

"The fire?" she asked, horrified that it was deliberately set by someone they knew.

Ty Alvarez nodded grimly. "When Higgens gets out of jail—and I hope that's a long time from now—he'll have to move out of these parts. No one will want him around. That fire threatened all of us and could have cost lives."

"Why did he want to harm us?" Maggie repeated, surprised and mystified.

"I intend to find out all about it," the sheriff said, glancing in Weldon's direction. He turned back to Maggie. "I'll send someone out to get a statement from you, Maggie."

"Thanks for coming so quickly."

Suddenly he grinned. "Bet it didn't seem quick at the time."

"No, it didn't."

"You said he knocked you down. How badly are you hurt?"

"Nothing serious."

He nodded. "Thanks, Jake." Ty climbed into the other car and both cars turned, driving away.

The moment their taillights were going down the road, Maggie turned to Jake. "You're hurt."

"I'm all right. What about you?"

"My ribs hurt and my elbow and my hip."

"Let's have a look," he said, striding toward the house. "Where's the shotgun?"

"I put it on the top shelf in the hall closet."

He stopped and looked down at her, holding her shoulders. "Maggie, Uncle Sam trained me for combat. There should never be a next time, but if there is, will you come get me instead of running after the guy yourself?"

Astounded, she stared at him. But her surprise was quickly replaced by annoyance. "Jake, next time you may be in another state. I didn't think. I reacted. I wanted to stop whoever it was and keep them from doing something else that would hurt my dad."

"If I'm here," Jake said evenly, "will you come get me?"

"I'll try to remember that you asked," she said with a lift of her chin.

"Come on."

She fell into step beside him. "Why? Why would Weldon do those things to us?"

"He confessed to me. Your bed-and-breakfast."

Her mouth dropped open. "Why the bed-and-breakfast? I don't even have one yet. That's just plans in the future."

"He was afraid of people coming out here and ruining his privacy and ranch life and trespassing on his place. Also, I think he's angry you wouldn't go out with him."

"Oh, my word," she said, rubbing her forehead,

shivering and suddenly aware of the dark night and aware of her vulnerability when she went after him.

"Yeah. Come on. Let's look at your injuries." Jake put his hand across her shoulders and walked up the steps with her. At the top she turned to look at the new buildings and corral, and the dead, leafless trees across the lane.

"How could he hate enough to do something so terrible? Dad could have died in the barn if you hadn't been here to get him."

"When it comes to hate, no one can figure out the way some people's minds work. It's over, Maggie. Higgens is going to jail and then he'll be smart to leave this county."

Jake locked up and they went upstairs to his room. As soon as he switched the light and looked at her, he swore. "Damn him. I'd like to hit him again. Do you have any bandages?"

She studied her scraped and bloody elbow. "I'll be right back." She left and in minutes returned, holding antiseptic, gauze, bandages and tape. As soon as Jake shed his boots and shirt, she looked at a cut across his shoulder.

"You're hurt, too."

"Only a scratch. Let's go into the bathroom."

He led her into the high-ceilinged bathroom with its footed tub and lacy curtains. She washed her arm and then Jake dried it gently and sat on the edge of the tub, pulling her between his legs to bandage her scrapes. As he applied antiseptic, she inhaled swiftly. It stung and she bit her lip.

"Just be glad you aren't hurt worse," Jake said darkly. "It could have been a lot worse you know."

She looked down at him. "Are you trying to scare me?"

His dark eyes were fiery. "Do you know what a scare you gave me?"

Her heart skipped a beat. "Did I?" she asked, suddenly interested in how concerned he was over her welfare.

"Damn straight you did," he snapped, wrapping gauze around her arm. "Hold this, Maggie."

"How did you know I was outside?" she asked, placing her finger on the gauze until he could put tape on it.

"I saw you out my window."

"Couldn't sleep?"

"No, I couldn't sleep," he replied slowly.

"Well, neither could I. That's why I saw someone out in the yard." When he met her gaze again, she drew a sharp breath at the smoldering fires in his eyes. Their gazes locked and her heart drummed and finally he looked down at her arm. "That's finished. Let me look at your ribs."

"Jake—" she said, but he had already tugged up her T-shirt just below her breasts and, with the seeming clinical detachment of a doctor, was feeling her ribs.

"Ouch!"

"Sorry. Does it hurt to breathe?"

"No, but I don't want to cough."

"I don't think you have any broken ribs, but you've probably bruised them. Same with your hip."

She yanked down her T-shirt. "Thanks, Dr. Reiner."

Standing, he framed her face and looked at her

with an intensity that sobered her. "I mean it, Maggie. When I'm here, don't go chasing someone."

"I don't think it'll ever come up again. They've arrested Weldon."

"You're not giving me the reassurance I want."

"Jake," she said, becoming annoyed with him again. "The next time something happens—and I hope that's never—you could be ten states away."

"But if I'm here, Maggie—"

"All right. If you're here, I'll let you know."

"Lord, woman, I can't tell you what that did to me," he said, enveloping her in a gentle embrace and it was good to be in his arms. He was careful of her ribs, holding her lightly.

"The best thing for bruises like that is steamy water. Come on, I'll show you." He tugged off her shirt before she could protest.

"Jake, no—"

"Yes. You'll feel one hundred percent better. I've hurt my ribs enough to know." All the time he talked, he was twisting free buttons on her jeans, shedding his own and in seconds, she forgot her arguments as he stepped into the shower and pulled her in with him.

Hot water hit them and she looked up at him, slanting him a look. "What you do to me—" she whispered and stood on tiptoe to kiss him.

For the next hour she forgot her scrapes and aches as they loved and Jake was careful of her ribs, yet setting her on fire with his caresses and kisses.

Later, as she lay in his arms, she glanced at the clock. "It's after four in the morning!"

"There's still time before everyone stirs."

She slid out of bed. "No. I'm going to my room,"

she said, swinging her hair away from her face and gathering her clothes, getting dressed swiftly. She turned to find Jake with his head propped on his hand, watching her. Shedding a soft glow in the bedroom, a light still burned in the bathroom, and she blushed.

"Don't stare."

"You're beautiful, Maggie," he said hoarsely. "I wish you'd come back here."

"No. I have to go."

He was out of bed and past her, blocking her way at the door. "I want a kiss."

She stared at him and then wrapped her arms around his neck, standing on tiptoe and placing her mouth on his to kiss him with all the longing and passion she had. She wanted to melt him, to do to him half of what he did to her. Even more, she wanted to win his heart and love as he had won hers so easily.

Jake's arms tightened around her waist and his hand slid over her bottom, pulling her up hard against him while he kissed her in return. Her heart thudded and in minutes she pushed away because if she didn't, she would be back in bed with him.

"I'm going," she whispered and fled, hurrying barefoot down the hall to her room where she closed the door behind her without looking back.

In bed, she thought about the night, still stunned about their neighbor, but forgetting him as she thought about Jake and their lovemaking. How much longer would Jake stay with them?

"I love you," she whispered, feeling hot tears sting her eyes. She had fallen in love with a man who would never love in return. She hurt for herself and she hurt for him because he was shutting himself into a lonely life.

She rolled over and pounded the bed with her fist. "Jake!" she cried against the pillow, knowing all sound was muffled.

She slept fitfully to wake early. Worrying about breaking the news to her father about Weldon, she dressed and went downstairs to cook breakfast.

In the kitchen Jake had coffee brewing and orange juice poured. He stood by the stove, stirring a steaming pot. Her gaze ran over his jeans and T-shirt, his hair shaggy, black. She wanted to cross the room and walk into his arms. Instead, she reminded herself to keep a distance between them.

"Good morning. What're you cooking?" she asked as she crossed the room to look at the stove.

"Oatmeal for everyone. I hope everyone eats all this."

"They will. Thanks."

"Think the news will upset your dad?"

"I don't know."

"What will upset your dad?" Ben asked, entering the room and Maggie smiled at him as he carefully crossed the kitchen on his crutches.

"You talk about how soundly I sleep—last night you slept right through a lot of excitement," she said.

"Is that right? 'Morning, Jake. What're you cooking?"

"Oatmeal and it's ready. Sit down and I'll serve."

In minutes all three were seated and Ben lowered his glass of orange juice. "All right. What did I sleep through?"

"There was someone in the yard. Jake went after the intruder," Maggie said, skipping the fact that she had gone after him first and aware Jake was studying her. "I called Ty Alvarez and they caught him. It was Weldon, Dad."

As he dropped his spoon and swore, Maggie reached over to touch his hand. "Now don't get excited. The police have him and he'll be charged. Weldon Higgens isn't worth you getting your blood pressure up."

"Don't fuss over me, Maggie. I'm not going to injure myself swearing about Higgens. He set the fire?"

"He confessed everything to me when I had him pinned down," Jake answered. "He didn't want a bed-and-breakfast drawing a crowd out here and running down the value of his ranch."

"Sonofagun!" Ben snapped. "Weldon! I never did like him very much, but I didn't think he was downright evil."

Jake looked at Ben. "I also don't think Higgens was happy that Maggie wouldn't go out with him," Jake added.

Ben snorted derisively. "I didn't think he was so damn dumb, either. Now he'll be in jail instead of running that ranch he thinks so much about. Well, damn. Why didn't you wake me?" he asked Maggie.

"I didn't see the point. You're hearing about it now, and why get you up?"

"I can't believe I slept through the sheriff coming out here. What was Higgens up to last night anyway?"

"I don't know," Maggie said. "He was under the hood of the pickup—"

"I told Alvarez about that," Jake said, smoothly interrupting her. "He's coming out here to look at the pickup this morning. Until he does, we can't drive it. That may be part of their case.''

"I forgot all about the pickup," Maggie said.

"I didn't," Jake replied. "I want to hang around here until the sheriff gets here. In the meantime, I need to ask you about moving some things from the shed to the barn," Jake said to Ben.

"After breakfast we'll go look."

They talked about Weldon and then the conversation changed until breakfast was over. Then he and Ben walked out toward the barn. As he did, Jake glanced over his shoulder and looked into Maggie's eyes. He paused for an instant, taking one last long look at her. She was in jeans and a sleeveless blue shirt with her hair braided. She looked as fresh and rested as if she had been undisturbed all night. All he was thinking about was Maggie in the pale light of the bedroom in the early hours of the morning when she was naked, in his arms and raising her mouth eagerly for his.

"See you," he said, unable to keep the huskiness out of his voice.

Hurrying, he caught up with Ben. "Ben, where do you keep your shotgun?" he asked, already knowing the answer.

"It's in the hall closet on the top shelf where Katy can't possibly get to it. She can't climb on a chair and reach up there. She's never in there, anyway, because there's nothing in the closet of hers." Ben glanced his way. "How'd you know I have a shotgun?"

"Maggie saw Weldon first and she got your gun and went after him. I happened to see her going across the yard and took off after her."

"Oh, hell. Maggie just acts. I'm sure she was trying to protect me from getting upset or getting into something that might hurt me. Dammit! I hate being feeble!"

"You're getting stronger every day," Jake said. "If anything ever happens again, I asked her to get me, but I was wondering if you could find another place for your gun."

"There's a high shelf in the closet in my bedroom. I'll put it there. Katy's never in my closet and she couldn't get up there, either. Just to be on the safe side, I guess I'll unload it."

"It'll be safer that way. Maybe now you won't have any more bad incidents."

"That bastard. What could he expect to gain?"

"He was trying to drive you folks out. Alvarez said Higgens is finished in these parts because when he does get out of jail, no one will welcome him around here."

"Thanks, Jake, for coming to the rescue again."

"On another subject," Jake said. "I'd like to ask Maggie out Saturday night."

"Go right ahead. I'm well enough to stay with Katy and if Maggie is worried about her, she can take Katy in to spend the night with her cousins. I'll be fine. Better yet, Patsy has been wanting me to come stay with them for a few days. I'll take Katy Saturday, and we'll stay at Patsy's house. Then Maggie won't have to worry about either one of us."

"Thanks, Ben," Jake said and wondered how long before he would have a chance to ask Maggie about Saturday.

"Jake, when Ty comes out to look at the pickup, I wish you'd get me."

"Sure," Jake said.

An hour later both men stood watching while Ty looked beneath the hood of the pickup. His deputy was underneath the front end. Jake wanted to join them, but knew he'd be in the way.

"He cut the brake lines," Ty said, straightening. "We've got another stiff charge to add to the ones he already has."

"With no brakes, we all could have been killed," Ben said in a cold, deadly voice while Jake swore quietly. All he could think about was Maggie driving the pickup, which she did constantly. Maggie and Katy. He wished he could hit Weldon Higgens again.

"Damn," Jake said, glancing at the house. "Maggie will want to know."

"You go tell her," Ben said. "Ty, what's he charged with?"

While Ty read the list of charges, Jake headed toward the house, trying to bank his rage at Weldon Higgens. Jake dreaded telling Maggie. Even though the ordeal was over, he suspected the news would shock and worry her.

He found her braiding Katy's hair and he stood in the doorway, watching mother and daughter. Katy's pink room with stuffed bears and fancy dolls made Jake feel out of place. Looking like a big doll herself, Katy perched on a chair, so her mother could braid her hair.

"What's going on in here?" he asked.

"I'm getting my hair fixed like Mommy's," Katy said, smiling at him and he smiled in return, feeling all his anger vanish. What was it with these two females that with just a look they could make him feel

better? Their smiles and big blue eyes seemed to hold
sunshine.

"Come see my dolly," Katy said. "She has her
hair like mine and Mommy's, too. Mommy braided
it this morning." She held up a doll and he entered
the room, taking the small doll in his hands.

"Your dolly's very pretty, Katy, but not as pretty
as you and your Mommy," he said. Maggie wrinkled
her nose at him.

Maggie finished and Katy jumped down. "Can I
go out with Grandpa?"

Maggie went to the window and raised it to call
to her father. "Can Katy come outside with you?"

She turned back and nodded to Katy. "You stay
right with Grandpa."

"Yes, ma'am. Can I take my dolly?"

"Yes, you may," Maggie said and watched Katy
scamper out of the room. When she turned to the
window, Jake sauntered over to stand beside her. In
a few minutes he saw Ben take Katy's hand.

"You must be here for a reason," Maggie said,
facing Jake and moving away from the window.

"I am. It doesn't matter now, Maggie, because
they have Weldon locked up, but he cut the brake
lines in the pickup. Whoever drove the pickup next,
when the brake fluid leaked out, would have had the
brakes go completely."

As she paled, Jake swore. "Damn him. Don't let
it scare you or worry you now. He's history."

"I suppose you're right," she said, anger snapping
in her blue eyes. "Thanks for telling me and thank
goodness you caught him."

He ran his finger along her collar. "Ben's putting
his shotgun up in his closet."

"You got Dad to do that!" she exclaimed in exasperation, placing her hand on her hip. "Jake Reiner! You have no business meddling in my life when you probably won't even be around here a year from now."

"Well, maybe and maybe not," he drawled. "But right now I'm here, so I might do a little meddling, darlin'," he said, reaching for her and sliding his arms around her waist. "How are your ribs today? Plenty sore, I'd imagine."

"That's right."

"But not too sore to go out to dinner with me Saturday night. Ben is going to Patsy's this weekend and he said he would take Katy with him."

"You've already worked this all out, haven't you? And I'm the last to know."

"Well, that's because we needed to work out a few details before I could ask you. Otherwise, you'd have to say no because you'd have to stay home to watch Katy. Go to dinner with me, Maggie."

"How can I refuse?" she said, smiling at him.

He kissed her until she pushed him away. "I know where kisses with you end, and we can't go back to bed now. Now scoot."

"Yes, ma'am. About six o'clock Saturday night. Let's get an early start," he said, eagerness making him smile.

As she nodded, he caressed her throat, feeling her pulse race. "I excite you, Maggie," he said, his voice dropping and his temperature climbing. "But not half as much as you excite me."

She inhaled swiftly, and her eyes darkened as they did in moments of passion. He wanted to pull her back into his arms, but he knew he needed to get to work.

Late that night for the first time, after he had put Rogue through his paces, Jake dismounted, opened the corral gate and rode the horse down the lane toward the county road. He was conscious of the horse, but his mind kept wandering to the ring he had tucked away in a drawer in his bedroom.

He didn't expect Maggie to say yes, but if she did, was he absolutely certain that's what he wanted? How would they live? Going from pillar to post and taking Katy with them? Could he be heartless enough to ask her to ever leave Ben? Jake couldn't imagine staying on the Circle A ranch the rest of his life. Or could he? All he knew with certainty was that he had to ask Maggie to marry him and he wanted her desperately.

Saturday night Jake showered and dressed swiftly in a white Western shirt and crisp jeans, too aware that Maggie was just down the hall and Ben and Katy had gone to town. He had Maggie all to himself now. He was half inclined to chuck his plans for the evening, go down the hall and take her to bed and give her the ring later tonight.

Yet he wanted to take her out. He had made elaborate plans to try to do something she would remember and something that would please her.

He opened his drawer and removed the ring box, raising the dark blue lid and staring at the dazzling diamond set against white satin. He couldn't summon an ounce of eagerness because he was unsure of her reaction. He removed the ring, wrapped it in a bit of tissue and jammed it into his pocket, wondering if he would even give it to her tonight.

Her door stood open and he hurried downstairs to find her in the kitchen, talking on the phone to Katy. Pausing in the doorway, he let his gaze drift over her appreciatively. She was in a red dress and all he wanted to do was go peel her out of it. It was made of some kind of material that clung to her curves. Sleeveless, the dress left her slender arms bare and it was short, leaving a good portion of very shapely legs showing. She wore high-heeled red pumps and she looked sexy and delectable. Watching him, she replaced the receiver.

"Hi, handsome," she drawled seductively as she hung up the phone, making his pulse accelerate another notch. His throat closed up while the world vanished. All he knew was Maggie was too far away from him. He crossed the kitchen to her to wrap his arms around her.

"Lady, I want you," he said, his voice a husky rasp.

Ten

Jake leaned down to kiss her, his arms tightening around her waist. While Maggie's heart thudded, she wrapped her arms around him, feeling his warmth through the crisp cotton shirt that was a dazzling white against his dark-skinned handsomeness.

She opened her mouth to him, taking his scalding kisses that promised so much more. As his fingers dug into her shoulder, he leaned over her, one hand sliding over her bottom and pulling her up against him. He wasn't hiding how badly he wanted her. His desire and his kisses made her tremble and melt into his arms. She wanted him as urgently, kissing him hungrily and taking what he was offering of himself.

He straightened to look down at her. As fire blazed in his eyes, she slid her hands across his broad shoulders, moving to the buttons of his shirt, wanting to get closer to him and have all barriers gone. When he caught her hands, she looked up in surprise.

"We're going to take time tonight, Maggie. I want to savor you and the evening with you. We haven't had too many times out together and we need some more memories."

She ran her fingers across his chest. "I don't mind not going out."

He inhaled, causing his chest to expand while his gaze burned into her. "I'm trying, Maggie, to make this a night for you to remember. Help me out here."

"Whatever you want, Jake," she said, thrilled by his words and excited, knowing they would come home and make love the rest of the night. She turned to head to the door and he caught her wrist, spinning her around into his arms to kiss her hungrily as if he would devour her right here and now. As she wrapped her arms around his neck and clung to him, her pulse raced. When he ground his hips against her, she felt his manhood and knew he wanted her. He raised his head. "This is what I want. You, Maggie, naked in my arms, your softness taking me and shutting out the world."

His voice was a breathless rasp, and he kissed her again before he released her. "If we're going, we better get the hell gone. Another minute of your kisses and we won't leave this house."

She looked at him, debating, knowing he had plans for them, yet wanting to love all night long. "C'mon, cowboy. Show me what you have planned. And bring me home early."

He groaned. "Early wasn't part of it, but we'll do what we can."

While he kept her hand on his knee, he drove to the Stillwater airport.

"There's a restaurant here?" Maggie asked, staring at the planes and runway.

"Nope. I've chartered a plane and a pilot to fly you out of Oklahoma."

"Do Dad and Patsy know where to find me?"

"Of course, they do."

Maggie felt a mixture of reactions, turning to him and smiling. "Where are you taking me?"

"As close as I can get in one evening to an ocean. I've chartered a small jet and a pilot to fly us to Houston where we'll rent a car. We'll eat in Galveston on the Gulf. It'll be black as midnight, but you'll see the Gulf and you will finally have been outside of Oklahoma."

She leaned forward to throw her arms around his neck. "Jake, thank you! For my first trip out of state, I'm glad you're with me. But we won't have much time tonight at home."

"We'll do the best we can with what we have," he said, grinning at her, but she had a scary premonition that they were running out of time together.

Everything was a wonder to her and as the small jet lost altitude, coming in to land, she gazed at the twinkling lights of Houston. Unable to sit still and talking nonstop to Jake, she knew this was old stuff to him. Yet he kept grinning and seemed pleased that she was thrilled by all of it.

"Jake, it's just gorgeous." She turned to kiss him, long and deeply, wrapping one arm around his neck to hold him close. She pulled away. "I'll never forget this night!"

"I hope not, Maggie," he replied solemnly, and her heart turned over.

In a rental car they drove to Galveston, and she was so excited, she was still fidgety and talking constantly. "I'm being silly, I know, but this is exciting."

"I'm glad," he said, sounding pleased. In Galveston they drove along the highway next to the seawall and she could see whitecaps as the waves rolled in. As she listened to breakers splash against the seawall, she inhaled the fresh air. "Oh, Jake! I can't believe we're here!"

"We're here, Maggie." He stopped in the parking lot of a restaurant. Neon light played over him when he turned to face her. "I'll give you a choice. I've made reservations here for us for a candlelight dinner and then I planned a walk on the beach. Or we can get something in Houston to take on the plane. It might not be as fancy, but it'll be hotter than if we get something here and take it back."

"Let's get something in Houston."

"Good enough. C'mon. I have to cancel some reservations."

In minutes he drove them to a stretch of sandy beach. The water was rough and even though it stretched away in inky blackness, she was thrilled. She could see occasional white caps near the shore and they walked hand in hand while she inhaled deeply. "Jake, I love this."

He laughed. "You can't see a damn thing."

"I don't care. I know it's there and I can see a little glimmer."

"We could spend the night here and you could see

it at dawn. That's the best. The tide will be going out and there'll be shells.''

She shook her head. "This is enough for now. I want to go home with you tonight.''

"Come here," he said in a husky voice and pulled her to him to kiss her. He was warm while the cool wind coming off the water tugged at her hair and she held him tightly until he released her.

"Thanks, Jake, for giving me this night.''

"Sure." He took her hand. "Take your shoes off and we'll wade out," he said as he sat in the sand and yanked off his boots. He rolled up his jeans several inches.

"Is it safe to wade at night?''

"It's shallow here and this isn't jellyfish season or they'd be all over the beach. C'mon, just a little ways. I'll keep you safe.''

She knew he would. Kicking off her shoes, she waded out with him. While cold water swirled around her ankles, she thought about where the water would go, exotic places so far away. She listened to the splash as waves came in and loved every moment. Inhaling deeply, she wanted to store up all the memories she could: the smell and feel of the Gulf waters, the grainy sand squishing between her toes, Jake's warm fingers laced through hers, his kisses still warm on her lips.

"Jake, I love this!" she told him again, turning to kiss him while they stood with water swirling around their ankles. "I wish I could bottle some up and take it home and keep it forever.''

He laughed. "It's just sea water, Maggie.''

"It's special because it's the first time I've seen it

and I'm here with you. Those are two reasons to want to keep a bit of memories forever.''

"Ah, lady, what you do to me," he said, pulling her to him to kiss her again.

Finally they waded out and returned to the car. Jake drove to the other side of the island so Maggie could see the shrimp boats. Before they left Galveston, Jake phoned ahead and ordered steak dinners and they ate on the plane while she watched the lights of Houston fade behind them.

It was long after midnight when they locked the door behind them at home. The moment Jake turned, she moved close, wrapping her arms around him. "Tonight has been wonderful, but this is the best part," she whispered. "And I've been waiting since we left here earlier."

He inhaled and leaned down to kiss her, wrapping his strong arms around her as his mouth opened hers and his tongue played with hers.

"I've waited too long tonight, darlin'."

Their breathing was ragged when he picked her up and carried her upstairs to her room and kicked the door closed behind him. He set her on her feet to turn her around and slowly tug the zipper of her dress down, trailing kisses over her back.

Cool air spilled over her shoulders while his kisses were warm and tantalizing, stirring fiery tingles in their wake. She turned to tug at his belt, sliding it away and reaching up to unfasten his shirt.

As he pushed her dress away, it fell around her ankles, and he inhaled deeply. His hands cupped her breasts while his thumbs circled her nipples. Maggie moaned with pleasure, her body responding to him.

The evening had been a wonder; now it became even more important.

"Ah, Maggie, you're beautiful," he whispered. He released the catch to her bra and shoved it away, bending to take her nipple in his mouth and stroke the taut bud with his tongue.

Shaking with urgency, she pushed off his shirt and attempted to unbutton his jeans. In minutes they had shed clothes and Jake picked her up to carry her to bed.

He sat down, cradling her in his arms while he kissed her. When he raised his head, she stroked his jaw, feeling the faintest stubble. "I love you, Jake." Whether wise or foolish, for better or for worse, she loved him with all her heart. Without answering her, he kissed her hard, driving thought from her mind while she clung to his lean, powerful body and shook with need. She wanted all of him, wanting to take him into her softness, wanting his strength, wanting for even a few moments to feel that he was hers.

Jake shifted, laying her on the bed and moving over her to trail kisses from her throat to her breast while he caressed her. She moaned, her hands moving over him. As he kissed her, he watched her. Her long hair was fanned out on the pillow with a few strands lying on her shoulders.

"You're beautiful," he repeated, thinking he would never tire of looking at her. She was breathtakingly beautiful. She had just told him she loved him, and he felt awed and humbled that he had won her love. And the last thing he ever wanted to do in any way was hurt her.

And now, some things in the world he was seeing through her eyes. He had been to the Gulf too many times to count in his life, but until tonight, it had never seemed special. It was sea water, wide and open with sandy beaches and a small island town and seaport. But tonight the beach and water had been touched by magic, the magic of Maggie's delight. And now, for the next few hours, she was his and he was intoxicated with her. He wanted to drive her beyond the brink of control. For this night he wanted to make her his, because for the first time in his life, he was truly and deeply in love.

He trailed kisses along her inner thigh and then moved intimately between her legs, until she was thrashing wildly and tugging at him. "Jake, please. I want you!"

He struggled to maintain his control, waiting as long as he could before he slowly lowered himself into her. As she enveloped him, he cried her name while his control vanished.

Maggie held Jake, trailing her arms down his smooth back and over his firm buttocks, feeling the rough hairs on the backs of his muscled thighs. He was solid planes, hard where she was soft, fascinating to her.

"Maggie, my love!" he cried, and her hips rose, meeting his. Clinging to him, she moved with him, but his words were ecstasy to her. *My love!* She relished those two words. He did love her.

Joy heightened every sensation and the moment was etched in her heart and memory. Conscious thoughts spun away as her urgency grew.

"Jake," she cried, moving wildly with him, her pulse drowning out sounds. She cried out, arching her back, bursting with release and feeling him shudder with his own earth-shaking climax.

They both sagged, slowing and trying to regain their breath.

Jake showered light kisses on her forehead and cheek and the corner of her mouth, shifting beside her and turning her into his arms to hold her close. Listening to his heart slow, she stroked his back that was damp with sweat.

"I love you," she said softly, knowing that no matter what tomorrow might bring, she would love him forever.

"Darlin'," he whispered, kissing her lightly. His hands moved over her. "I feel like it's been a thousand years since I held you like this."

She leaned back to look at him, placing her palm on his cheek. "Thanks for tonight. It was special in every way."

"I want to make it more special," he whispered, brushing a kiss on her forehead. He slipped out of bed and picked her up, carrying her to the shower. They showered and made love again and lay in the dim light talking until Jake slid out of bed and walked over to find his jeans.

"I have a surprise," he said as he dug in his pocket.

"Oh?" Maggie sat up against pillows and pulled the sheet high under her arms.

Jake slid beneath the sheet and scooted over to sit by her, his knee against her hip. He looked solemn and she wondered what the surprise was. One fist was clenched and she studied him, unable to discern any hint from his expression.

"Open your hand. I have something I want to give you."

She held out her hand, still mystified, wondering

if he had gotten her a necklace because there were few things small enough to fit in his fist. Yet he seemed far too solemn and now, as he stared at her, she was puzzled. "What is it?" she asked, smiling at him.

"I love you, Maggie." With a surge of joy, she watched as he took her hand in his and opened his fist. A sparkling diamond tumbled into her palm. "Will you marry me?" he asked.

Stunned, she looked up at him. "You want to get married?" she whispered. Her first reaction was pure joy. She took the ring and slipped it onto her finger and threw her arms around his neck. "Oh, Jake!" She kissed him and his arm went around her waist, hauling her into his arms as he kissed her hungrily.

He released her and looked down at her solemnly and her heart thudded because he was too somber. She sat up, tugging the sheet up tightly under her arms while she looked at the ring and then at him. And then reason began to assail her, and she knew why he looked so solemn. Dread started as a tiny icicle of fear and then mushroomed into a coldness that turned her entire heart to ice.

"There are some questions and things to discuss before I can give you an answer," she said.

"I thought there would be," he said. In that moment she knew that he wanted her to marry him, but he didn't want to change his vagabond lifestyle.

"Jake, I have to think of Katy and Dad and the ranch. It's not just me."

"I know that."

She looked at the ring on her finger. Even in the dim light, the diamond sparkled, catching and giving off tiny lights, yet not enough sparkle to chase away the shadows. "If we marry, would you settle here?"

As he drew a deep breath, his gaze met hers and he shook his head. "Maggie, I can't promise that."

"How can you want to marry then?" she cried. "You want Katy and me to ride across the country on your bike? Jake, she'll start kindergarten this year and then she'll be in school." Something inside Maggie shattered, and a dull pain started.

"Maggie, for now I'm happy here, but I can't promise that I won't have to move on to something else someday. I can't promise that I'll take root here like you have. Kids move and change schools and I can stop moving as much, but to promise to stay forever—I just can't do it," he said.

"You know I can't leave my dad now."

"I know and I'm not asking you to now. I'm just being honest enough to tell you that I can't promise to stay here forever."

"Dad's health isn't good, but it isn't terrible, either. He could live for years, and it wouldn't be any easier to leave five years from now than now. Probably harder to leave. Katy would have her friends. If you love us, why can't you stay?"

He moved impatiently and a muscle worked in his jaw. "There just comes a time when I have to keep moving. I get so damned restless and penned in."

"And scared to love," she said softly. "When you really begin to care, I'll bet that's when you move on."

"I don't know about that." He reached out, sliding his hand behind her curtain of hair. "I just know that I love you and I want you in my life." He leaned forward and kissed her long and hard, but all the time she kissed him back, she knew it was impossible. Hot tears stung and she tasted their salt.

"Ah, Maggie, dammit," he whispered, wiping away her tears with his thumbs. "I don't want to hurt you. But you don't want me to give you all kinds of promises I can't keep."

"No, I don't." She wrapped her arm around his neck and kissed him and he pulled her down into his embrace, rolling her onto her back and moving over her.

"I love you so damned much," he whispered and kissed her.

But not enough to stay with me, she thought. She kissed him, wanting him with the same hungry desperation she had felt earlier in the evening, knowing she was losing him even as she loved him.

They made love far into the early hours of morning and then slept in each other's arms. When she stirred, Jake was gone and she showered and dressed to go searching for him. She found him in the kitchen with breakfast cooked.

They ate scrambled eggs and toast and talked, but there was a somber knowledge that hung in the air and had changed their relationship.

After breakfast, she sat facing him across the table. Feeling as if she were tearing her heart out and giving it to him, she slowly pulled the ring off her finger. When she held out the ring, she looked into his eyes. "Here, Jake. I can't take your ring. This is my home, and I have to stay here with my family."

"Maggie, I'd never take you away from them forever. We could come back."

She shook her head. "No. I can't do that to Dad. Would you really want me to leave him?"

Jake stared at her. "I guess that's why I've known all along what your answer would have to be, but I love you so much it hurts. I had to ask you."

She closed her eyes in pain and fought tears, wanting to avoid crying again in front of him.

When she opened her eyes and stood, he came around the table swiftly to reach for her, but she stepped back. "Have you ever thought that if you loved someone, life might be different? You might not feel that urge to keep moving?"

"I don't know. I just don't feel that I can promise I'll change."

"And I can't promise anything, either," she whispered and spun around to leave the room. Knowing their weekend was over, she raced upstairs, tears blurring her path. So much was over. She heard the back door and guessed he had gone outside.

In her room she went to the window and watched his long stride eat up the ground as he headed toward the barn and disappeared inside.

She touched her ring finger where Jake's diamond had rested so briefly. "I love you now and I always will no matter where you are or what you do," she whispered, knowing that if he left, she couldn't stop loving him. Nor could she ever take up Jake's way of living.

Two hours later Maggie left for church. Jake watched her drive away and swore under his breath. He had put the ring away in a small knapsack in the bottom of a drawer in his bedroom. He didn't want to think about the future. Always before, tomorrows had taken care of themselves, and he hadn't given much thought to the rest of his life. Now he didn't want to think about the future without Maggie.

He hurt and he suspected the hurt was just starting and was something he would have to live with for a long time.

He mounted Rogue, knowing that he would have to concentrate on the horse and that it would take his mind from the early hours of the morning and the woman he loved.

It was a week later when Maggie came down for breakfast and found Jake already sipping black coffee and orange juice. A bowl of strawberries was on the table.

"Thanks for cooking breakfast," she said, her pulse accelerating at the sight of him in jeans, a T-shirt and his black boots. He had been avoiding her more and more lately, just as she had tried to stay away from being alone with him. He stood and gazed at her solemnly. One look into his eyes and she knew something was wrong.

"I've been wanting to talk to you," he said quietly.

As Maggie's heart lurched, she was filled with dread.

Eleven

He came across the room and with each step closer, her heartbeat speeded up. Stopping only a foot away, he placed his hands on her shoulders. "I love you, Maggie. I love Katy and Ben and this place, but seeing you every day and wanting you in my arms and my bed, knowing I can't have—that's hell."

"Oh, Jake," she whispered, thinking if he loved all of them, there was a simple solution.

"I've never stayed anywhere long. Never once in my whole life. My folks moved a lot and even when I was a kid, I was a roamer. I'm going because this is bad for both of us."

Closing her eyes, she felt enveloped in pain. She always knew he would go, but she didn't know how badly it would hurt. She opened her eyes, wrapped her arms around his neck and stood on tiptoe, pulling his head down and placing her mouth on his to kiss him with all the pent-up longing she had been suffering this past week.

His arm banded her waist and he crushed her against his chest while he kissed her as if it were the last kiss he would ever have.

She tasted salty tears and didn't care. She loved him desperately and wanted him. She stepped back. "If you love me and you love my family, why can't you stay?"

"This hurts every day, Maggie. I want you as my wife."

"You know why I can't marry you. It doesn't have to be this way." Hurting, she stepped back. "Go on, then. Jake, you're running from the guilt you have over your brothers and parents dying when you didn't die with them, but you didn't have one thing to do with the fire or their deaths."

"I'm not running from that!" he snapped. "And I might have saved them if I'd been there."

"Jake, life is full of 'ifs,' but the truth is that you weren't there. You're running from guilt over something you shouldn't feel guilty about."

"Like hell."

"Go on. Just go," she said, hurting for herself and for both of them. He was a wonderful man and he shouldn't lead a solitary life because of something that wasn't his fault.

"I want to tell Katy and Ben goodbye."

"Then do it without me. I'll say goodbye now." They stared at each other, each caught in an impasse that she knew was unresolvable as long as he felt the way he did. "Can't you see what you're doing to yourself, and it's so needless. Let go of guilt. Let go

of the past and live life fully. When you get to the
point where you do, you run.''

"Maggie, you're wrong.''

"Goodbye, Jake,'' she said, leaving the room in a
rush. She yanked up her jacket and went out to get
into the pickup. Ben would take care of Katy and
Jake would stay until they both woke up. For once,
Maggie was going to give herself some time and
space and privacy. She drove away without looking
back, hurting and wondering if the pain would ever
ease.

When she returned two hours later, Ben met her
at the back door and stepped outside, closing the door
behind him.

"We told Jake goodbye.''

"Daddy, he asked me to marry him, but he
couldn't promise to stay here. I can't leave—it isn't
you. I can't have that kind of life for Katy.''

Ben stepped forward and wrapped his arms around
her. "Ah, Maggie, I'm sorry. I guess I shouldn't have
ever asked him to work for us.''

"No. I'm glad he did. I love him, but I couldn't
live the way he does.'' She held her father, glad for
his comfort, knowing she was right, yet hurting in a
way she had never hurt before.

She moved away. "I'm all right. What about
Katy?''

"She's in there crying her eyes out because she
loves him. He's become a father to her, but children
adapt. By afternoon she'll be all right. I told her I'd
take her to town to see the latest Disney release.''

"Thanks,'' Maggie said, smiling at him. "I don't
know what I'd do without you.''

"And I don't know what I'd do without you. I'm

sorry, honey. I wouldn't want you to stay just for me, but I can see where Katy fits into the equation and gives you reason to say no. Maggie, maybe he'll come back.''

She shook her head. "No, he won't. He's been this way all his life and he's thirty-five years old. He isn't going to change now. I'll recover.''

Ben draped his arm across her shoulders. "I'm sure you will. I wonder if Jake will.''

When they went inside, Maggie had to reassure Katy and comfort her when all she wanted to do was cry right along with her daughter. She hurt and she missed Jake.

That night she didn't sleep, crying until there were no tears left, wondering if he was hurting, too, or just going on with his life as he had done times before.

Jake sat in a dark motel room in Kansas. He had crossed the state line and he didn't know or care where he was. For the first time since he was fourteen, he bought a six-pack of beer. He slammed down two bottles and threw the rest in the trash. Sitting at the window, he stared at the empty swimming pool and hurt more than he had ever hurt in his life. He stared at still blue water, but all he could see were blue eyes filled with love.

Was she right? Was he running away from guilt that he shouldn't be suffering?

How hard would it be to let go of the past? Was he running again as he had that night—running away from his family and consequently losing all of them. Now he was running again and he was losing a family that could be his if he would just let them.

"Maggie," he whispered hoarsely into the darkness. "I love you. I want you."

He swore and stood up, pacing the dark room and then he stuffed his billfold into his pocket and looked at himself in the mirror. "Who are you?" he asked his reflection, wondering who he was and what he was doing.

He picked up his keys and went out, locking the motel room behind him. He had already paid his bill. Climbing onto his bike, he revved the engine, shattering the stillness of the crisp fall night. He didn't care. He turned the bike and drove out of the motel lot, heading for the highway and turning south.

It was four in the morning when Maggie heard the roar of the Harley. Her heart thudded and excitement shook her as she ran for the door and raced down the stairs and went outside.

When Jake drove up to the back gate, she thought she would faint from joy. Was he a dream? She ran toward him as he vaulted the fence and ran to grab her up in his strong arms, swinging her around and kissing her hard enough that she knew he was no dream. He was flesh and blood, and her heart thudded.

While he still held her off the ground, she raised her head and framed his face with her hands. "Why are you here?"

"You might have been right. To hell with the past. I can't live without you, Maggie."

"Oh, Jake," she said, melting. Joy bubbled in her as she kissed him and clung to him tightly.

"You're my special woman, darlin'," he said. "Marry me, Maggie. I'll stay. I'll take root here like you and Ben and these damn trees. In a few years you won't be able to get me ten miles from here. Will you marry me?''

''Yes! Oh, yes! I love you!'' she answered while she laughed and cried at the same time. ''Jake, I love you,'' she said and kissed him, barely aware that he had swung her up into his arms and was carrying her toward the barn.

''Come on, darlin'. We have some lovin' to catch up on,'' he whispered as he showered kisses over her face.

Epilogue

As his boot heels scraped the bare floor, Jake moved close to the hospital bed. Over an hour earlier, on the second day of April, a year after their fall wedding, he had helped as Maggie gave birth to a seven pound boy. Now Katy was with them and Maggie held the sleeping infant, wrapped in a blue blanket, in the crook of her arm.

Sitting down beside Maggie, Jake lifted Katy onto his lap. With a sparkle in her eyes and her hair spilling over her shoulders and blue gown, Maggie had never looked more beautiful to him. As his arm tightened around Katy, he looked at his new son, his little daughter and his radiant wife. A knot thickened Jake's throat while tears filled his eyes. "Darlin', you've given me a family."

"Jake," Maggie said softly, reaching for him, sliding her arm around his neck and pulling him closer, hugging Katy and careful of the baby at the same time.

He kept one arm around Katy and the new baby, Matthew, while he held Maggie with his other arm. "Darlin', I love all three of you. I can't tell you how much."

"I love you," she whispered, stroking his head, and he realized how blessed he was with this wonderful family that he had been given.

"Knock, knock," came a deep voice, and Jake straightened, trying to get control of his emotions and wiping his eyes as he turned to look into the gaze of his friend, Jeb Stuart.

"I'll come back later," Jeb said, backing up and closing the door behind him.

"Hey!" Jake jumped up and Katy followed him into the hall where he saw Jeb and the rest of the Stuarts.

"Come in," Jake said, shaking hands with Jeb and turning to hug Amanda.

"How's Maggie and the new baby?" Jeb asked as Jake hugged each of the Stuart children.

"They're both doing great. Come see him."

When Jake knocked lightly on the door before putting his head inside, Maggie smiled. "Tell everyone to come in," she said, looking at her handsome husband as Jake led the way. He wore his hair shorter now, but he still had that streak of wildness that showed in his rugged features and his lively dark eyes. All five Stuarts followed him into the room and Maggie greeted them and showed them the new baby.

"We've named him Matt for Jake's youngest brother," Maggie said, smiling at Jake.

"He's beautiful," Amanda exclaimed.

"Boys aren't beautiful," Jeb teased and she gave him a haughty look.

"Baby boys are," she said, leaning over the bed.

"You may hold him if you want," Maggie said.

Amanda carefully took the sleeping baby into her arms. She stepped back and said, "We brought Matthew a present."

Both boys set a large box beside the bed.

"Katy, why don't you unwrap it," Jake said. Grinning, Katy began to peel away ribbon and paper until she finally stepped back to look at a large box.

"It's a swing!" Katy exclaimed in delight, her small fingers sliding over the picture on the box. "Can we open it?"

Thanking the Stuarts, Jake laughed and took the box from her. "It might be better to open it at home where I can set it up for Matt."

"Katy, here's something for you," Amanda said and Emily held out another present, which Katy unwrapped swiftly, tossing aside colorful paper.

"A book!" She held up a book and ran her fingers over the title, reading it aloud.

"What do you say, Katy?" Maggie prompted.

"Thank you," she said, grinning at the Stuarts. "Let's read it," she told Emily and the two girls hurried across the room to a sofa to sit with their heads together, Katy slowly reading to Emily.

By ten o'clock that night, Patsy had taken Katy home with her and Ben had gone back to Patsy's. The Stuarts had left and all the other visitors were gone. Jake was sleeping on the sofa in Maggie's room and he sat on the bed beside her, holding her hand and smiling at her.

"Oh, Jake! It's so wonderful!" She held out her arms and he leaned forward to gather her gently into his embrace. Maggie held him, feeling his heart beat against hers. When she looked at the sleeping infant in the nearby crib, joy brought tears to her eyes. "I'm the luckiest person in the world."

"Sorry, darlin', that person is me," Jake said gruffly, holding her close. Maggie closed her eyes, knowing Jake's roaming was over and he would stay in her arms for the rest of their lives.

*   *   *   *   *

FOR THIS WEEK I THEE WED
by
Cheryl St. John

Dear Reader,

Opposites really do attract!

After twenty-seven years of marriage, my husband and I have learned to laugh about our differences and to celebrate the very precious and few things we do have in common.

Jay is a man of punctuality—gets up at the same time every morning, goes to bed at the same time every night. He plans his day according to the clock and abhors being late.

I've been known to: forget my children at school, forget the man was coming to install cable before the big game, lose track of what day it is, wonder how old I am…well, you get the picture. The best thing about writing is that I can work according to my impulsive nature.

This amusing contrast is probably why I had such a ball creating Francie and Ryan, two people who couldn't be more different, yet who are inexplicably drawn to each other. I hope you enjoy reading their story even more than I enjoyed writing it!
VIVE LA DIFFÉRENCE!

Cheryl St. John

1

ONCE AGAIN HER impetuosity had landed her in a jam. Francie Karr-Taylor rifled through a stack of papers on her gigantic wooden desk and picked up the letter for the tenth time that morning. Last week she'd placed the irksome missive on the edge just so, in case her cat took a notion to jump up on the desk and accidentally knock the reminder into the wastebasket. He hadn't.

She'd used the envelope postmarked Springdale, Illinois, as a coaster for the better part of a week, but the return address still remained legible.

No, the letter was still here and she hadn't forgotten about the impulsive promise she'd made, so she guessed she was going to have to give the reunion committee a call. The letter requesting she be the photographer for Springdale's tenth class reunion had arrived months ago, and rashly she'd agreed to participate.

What had she been thinking? She'd known then, just as she knew now, that she wasn't going to be able to attend the class reunion. She was going to have surgery that weekend. Or something else was going to come up. A debilitating sickness maybe. Or perhaps even a death: her own would be convenient.

The intercom buzzed her that someone was downstairs, and she walked distractedly to the panel, the wrinkled letter in her hand. "Yeah?"

"Miss Karr-Taylor, it's Ryan MacNair. I'd like to speak with you for a few minutes, please."

"Who?"

He repeated his name and added, "We spoke a few weeks ago. About the brooch you had appraised? You told me to call back at a more convenient time."

"Oh." She glanced around the cluttered loft where she worked, barely noting the photographs hung on every wall, or even the wet ones drying on a line strung from the bathroom that doubled as a darkroom to the door that led to her sleeping area. The place wasn't going to suddenly become neat and organized, and the time never got more convenient, so she might as well let him in. "Come on up."

She jabbed the button that unlocked the security door and sauntered back to her desk.

How hard could it be to fake her own death? She'd seen it done on TV plenty of times. She could assume a new identity and move her studio to Peoria under a different name.

Francie flopped into her chair and grimaced at her own thoughts. No. Nana needed someone to check up on her every few weeks and make sure the care center was doing a good job. Deserting her dear fragile grandmother was out of the question. It had distressed the old woman enough just thinking Francie wasn't married yet. What a selfish thought. Self-preserving and really clever—but selfish.

How on earth, then, was she going to get out of

this bothersome class reunion? What was she going to tell her grandmother? Nana was the only person in the world she was close to. The only person whose opinion mattered. But Nana didn't agree with Francie's decision to choose a career over a marriage and children. A few months ago, to alleviate the old woman's worry over her being alone, Francie'd told her she'd gotten married.

To a *rich* man.

To a rich man *with kids*.

To a rich *handsome* man with kids.

Holy criminey, how was she going to get out of this one?

A knock sounded on the door.

Francie crossed to open it.

"Hi, Miss Karr-Taylor—"

"Francie."

"Francie. Thank you for seeing me."

She swung the door open wide and ushered the tall dark-haired man in the tailored navy blue suit into her studio. "Would you like a soft drink? The coffee isn't any good anymore."

"No, thank you."

"Well..." She wandered back to her chair and sank into the comfortable cushion, her gaze immediately landing on the letter that still lay on her desk. Darn cat. Darn Nana for thinking a woman couldn't be fulfilled with her career.

"I have an offer for you," MacNair said. He moved a stack of manila envelopes from the seat of the chair opposite her desk to an available spot on the floor and plucked the crease at the knee of his trousers as he sat. "Are you moving out?"

"No, why?"

"Uh, no reason. Do you recall why I'm here?"

Absorbed in her predicament, Francie tapped a fingernail against the edge of the desk. The reunion was less than two weeks away now, and she still hadn't figured out what she was going to do.

"Francie?"

"What? Oh. No, I guess I've forgotten what it was you wanted to see me about."

"The brooch you had appraised at Grambs and Sons last month."

"Right. It was in a box of old junk that I bought at an auction. I thought the stuff would make a great still life. Black and white. Maybe a pair of gloves. Kind of draping out of an old jewelry chest with a piece of old lace beneath it."

"I put the word out to all the jewelers that I was looking for that particular piece," he said. "Grambs called me after you'd been in. That brooch rightfully belongs to my daughter. It's her legacy."

She'd found the perfect pair of old lace gloves. What had she done with them? "Uh-huh."

"It belonged to my grandmother on my father's side. Unfortunately my grandfather's will was contested, and the jewelry went to one of my aunts who only wanted what she could get out of everything. She wouldn't even let my father buy the pieces he wanted, just to be spiteful. I can't even remember why she started the feud with my father. I'm not even sure she does."

"She sounds lovely." Francie picked up a pen and doodled on the letter.

He blinked at her. "She sold it all, and we've been trying to find the pieces to buy them back. My father had intended for that brooch to remain in the family."

Francie's attention drifted to Peyton Armbruster's scrawled signature on the page, and Francie knew she couldn't stall any longer. She either had to come clean…or come up with a husband.

"The brooch was appraised at five hundred dollars," MacNair said. "Miss Karr-Taylor, I'll double that offer."

At his concerned tone, Francie glanced up into his grave features, and finally his words sank into her dilemma-drugged brain. He was as intense about this silly old brooch as she was about taking a husband to the reunion.

For the first time she took a good hard look at Ryan MacNair. His dark hair, bearing a distinguishing widow's peak, was neatly styled and brushed back from a square-jawed face. Dark brows were divided by a V of anxiety that didn't diminish his well-bred features. *He was handsome.*

He had a nice straight nose and an interesting mouth that could probably slide into a knockout smile if he'd loosen his collar and tie and give himself a little air.

His navy suit and cranberry silk tie were of the best quality and taste, and he wore them with ease and panache. *He was rich.* Not her type—if she had a type—but wouldn't he impress the control tops right off the women back in Springdale? She imagined Nana looking him up and down.

"You wanted to use the brooch in some photographs," he said. "Have you done that?"

"Are you married?"

He blinked, his warm brown eyes showing confusion over the abrupt change of subject. "I'm divorced," he said finally. "Is that relevant to the discussion?"

Actually a discussion took two people, but she spared him that reminder, and let the wheels in her mind whirl with possibilities. "I'm just beginning to sympathize with your situation, Mr...."

"MacNair."

"Mr. MacNair. I'd certainly feel bad if something of my grandmother's was sold off against my wishes."

He nodded, his brow still furrowed. "Then you'll sell it to me?"

"You want this brooch pretty badly, don't you? It means a lot to you. And your father."

His carefully guarded expression didn't change. "Yes."

"So, my decision carries a lot of weight."

"It does," he admitted, though his aggravated expression showed his reluctance to do so.

Francie smoothed the letter, refolded it and placed it inside the stained and warped envelope. "Perhaps we can negotiate after all."

"Money is not the issue here. The brooch has sentimental value. Five thousand."

"No. Not more money," she said with a flick of

her hand. "In fact, if you agree to this idea, you can keep your money."

His frown deepened. "What idea?"

"I'm in a bind myself. I'm afraid I've done something—said something—*impetuous,* and now I don't have any way out of it. Except maybe through you."

"I don't understand."

"I told my grandmother that I'd gotten married."

"And that's a problem?"

"It wasn't true. It's not true."

"You told her you were married?"

She nodded.

"But you're not married. And you weren't married."

"Right."

"Then why did you tell her that?"

The question was so simple. The answer was so complicated. "Because I'm not."

He stared at her.

"It's a long, boring story," she supplied. "Maybe sometime we'll go over the details, but for now I'll just say I had my reasons."

"So you lied. And now this lie is causing you a problem."

"Oh, yeah." She stood and walked restlessly to the row of windows and gazed, unseeing, down on the street.

"What does that have to do with me?"

She turned back. "I've been cornered into participating in the tenth reunion celebration in my hometown. Nana is expecting me. *And* she's expecting me to bring a husband."

With a wary expression, he waited for her to speak. "You can have the brooch…"

He leaned forward in the chair, waiting for the other shoe to drop.

"…if you come to Springdale with me as my husband for a week."

He stood. "I suspected you were going to say that, but I didn't believe you would. That's the most absurd thing I've ever heard."

"Well, hey, it was worth a try." She gave a half-hearted wave. Shoulders slumped, she hugged her upper arms and turned back to the window. "I saw something about escort services on *Dateline* the other night. Do we have any of those around here?"

Ryan studied her small frame in profile against the window, her words sinking in and shocking him once again. "You can't go to one of those places!"

"Why not?"

"You don't know anything about them. You could place yourself in serious danger."

"I am in some serious danger, here, Mac."

He straightened his shoulders at the flip nickname. "You're simply in an embarrassing situation because you lied. You have only yourself to blame."

"I'm not blaming anyone. I'm trying to come up with a solution."

"Why don't you tell your grandmother the truth?"

She turned back, a hint of irritation in her blue eyes. "Because she'd only make my life miserable until I *really* found someone to marry, and I'm not willing to do that. I guess we don't have anything more to talk about."

"What about the brooch? An arrangement? I'm sure we can come up with something—"

"Those were the terms, Mac. If you want the pin, you need to pose as my husband. It's only one week out of your whole life. If that's too much of a sacrifice, well…"

"Lady, I've never heard anything so unprofessional and unethical in my life. Real people just don't go around doing these kinds of things. That only happens in the movies."

"Sure they do. Negotiations take place on Capitol Hill every day."

"Honest negotiations."

"*You* think."

He didn't know if it was her irreverent attitude or the fact that she held him over a barrel that irked him. Ryan reflected back on the only heirloom he had to hand down to his daughter and held himself in check. His grandfather had had that piece of jewelry made for his grandmother as a wedding present.

He intended for Alanna to have that brooch, and had been sick over its loss for the past year. When Ryan had received the call from the appraiser and learned that the piece of jewelry had fallen into the hands of a young woman, he'd decided to appeal to her sense of fairness.

How could he ever have imagined that the woman would be a zany, flippant photographer with more nerve than sense? She didn't operate on his wavelength. He didn't think she operated on anyone's wavelength but her own.

"Bartering was the first type of selling around," she added. "Our country was founded with trades."

Artists. He'd dealt with his share in his position at the museum. He could deal with this one.

But a week in Springdale pretending to be her husband? The demand was preposterous. Outrageous.

It was also his only option.

"I don't have anyone to take care of my children for an entire week." It was as good of an excuse an any, and it was the truth.

She inched toward him like a dog sniffing a steak. "Children?"

"Yes. I've never left them for that long. I keep my business trips to just a day or two. My housekeeper fills in during that time, but—"

"How old are they?" she asked, circling him. "Girls? Boys?"

"Twelve and nine. A girl and a boy."

She stepped close, her blue eyes lit with a determined fire he didn't trust. "That's perfect. They can come along!"

"What do you mean?"

"I need kids, too! Oh, this is great. Now I won't have to do something drastic."

"What? What could be more drastic than this scheme you've concocted?"

"I'll make the plane reservations, don't worry about that."

"Hold it. I can't just pull up and take off for a week. I have a job. My children have school."

"A week out won't hurt them." She perched on the edge of her desk, sending a stack of papers sliding across the top and onto the floor, and grinned a naughty grin. "This is great."

"Now wait a minute," he said, stopping her gush of pleasure with an upraised palm. He leaned down to collect the papers she'd knocked off and shuffle them into a semineat pile. "I never said I'd do this. I can't just take a week off to play some game of house. And I can't subject my children to it, either." He tried to find a place to lay the papers, and finally shoved them into her hands. "What kind of father would drag his children along and ask them to participate in something so dishonest?"

Carelessly she dropped the stack of papers on the already laden desktop behind her. "A father who wants my brooch?"

Her irritating confidence got under his skin. "I can't ask my kids to lie. I've always taught them honesty."

"I guess we could say they're at boarding school."

Ryan's mind had remained three steps behind hers since this meeting had begun. He gave himself a mental shake. "What about the logic of all this? What did you tell your grandmother that your husband's name was? Who would I be expected to be?"

"I don't think I actually gave you a name. I told her I go by Karr-Taylor because that's the name I've established in my career. Plenty of women don't take their husbands' names. Don't tell me you're a chauvinist."

Ryan blinked. "No! I'm not—what does being a chauvinist have to do with it, anyway? It would never work."

The woman was enough to drive a sane man nuts.

Hopping off the desk, she sat in her chair, rifled though the papers and books and produced a Rolodex. "Fine. You know the way out."

She flipped index cards, pulling a few out and setting them aside.

"What are you doing?"

"Finding someone else to do it. I don't know why I didn't think of this before. Of course they may not have kids. We'll use the boarding school story."

Ryan stood watching her peruse the cards with a pencil between her teeth. His logical mind grappled with what was happening. She had no intention of selling him the brooch unless he went along.

He had an ultimatum.

He could walk out and disappoint his father and his daughter.

Or he could grit his teeth and go along with her outrageous mandate for one week. One week. How difficult would that be?

He could get the time off. He'd gone over his planner just that morning and knew what lay ahead. The next few weeks were going to involve intensive cleaning and painting in preparation for the summer and fall exhibits, and he could afford to take the time off. There was only a week of school left before summer vacation, and then what? He had no one to care for his daughter and son for a week.

He had been promising to take them on a vacation and teach Alex to swim. He never got enough time with them.

What would he tell them?

The truth. He'd never done anything less.

They would see how important this was—he'd have to stress that he didn't condone the masquerade, but that he'd had no choice—and they'd understand. His daughter had lost so much already. She wasn't going to lose her legacy if he could help it.

Francie had picked up the receiver and was dialing.

He took a step forward. "Is there a pool in Spring-dale?"

"There's one in the hotel, I think."

"All right," he said.

She paused and glanced up. "All right?"

"All right," he repeated. "I'll do it."

A delighted grin spread across her features, and she slid the receiver back into place. "The kids, too?"

He nodded grimly.

"All right!"

"When exactly is this...event?"

She gave him the dates. "It'll be fun, Mac. You'll see. We'll wow 'em."

"My name is Ryan."

"Right. I'll make the flight arrangements and call you with the itinerary. What are the kids' names?"

"Alanna and Alex."

"Good choices. We won't have to change them."

"I'm so glad you approve."

"We'll leave a day early," she went on, apparently oblivious to his sarcasm, "because we need clothes for the oldies dance, and there are some great consignment and thrift stores in Springdale."

"Oldies dance?"

"Yeah, you know...bobby socks, bell bottoms,

ducktails. The theme is a mixture of fifties, sixties and seventies. The Partridge Family, Frankie and Annette, styles like those. You'd make a great Ricky Nelson. Who do you think I could be? Shelley Fabares, maybe?''

A disturbing knot of indigestion settled in Ryan's stomach. A week with this woman. One solid week. But it was one week versus his daughter's legacy.

He hoped he had the stamina to live through it.

2

A BATTERED SUITCASE in each hand, the strap of a travel-worn camera case slung across her chest like an ammo belt, Francie hurried through O'Hare airport toward the agreed meeting place. Ryan MacNair, dressed in sand-colored summer trousers and a neatly pressed linen sport shirt, waited impatiently beside two dark-haired children.

"You're late," he stated, a look of displeasure creasing his brow.

She dropped her mismatched suitcases on a nearby cart. "Well, White Rabbit, I had to take Stanley to a friend's."

He ignored her jest, moving her cases from the stranger's cart, and placing them on top of his steel gray leather luggage. "Stanley?"

She adjusted her purse and camera bag on her shoulder. "My cat."

"You knew you'd have to do that two weeks ago, couldn't you have left a little earlier?"

She looked up at him. "What's the big deal? We're not late. The plane doesn't leave for another twenty-five minutes."

"That's cutting it close. We still have to check our luggage and find our seats."

"Okay, okay, don't pop a blood vessel, Mac. Are you going to introduce me to our children?"

He set his mouth in a straight line and nodded at the kids beside him. "This is Alex."

"Hi," the boy said. He had neatly trimmed hair and wore an outfit much like his father's. He resembled MacNair, except that his eyes were a friendly gray-blue.

"Hi, Alex." Francie stuck out her hand and he placed his small one into it for a shake.

"And Alanna," MacNair added.

"Hi, Alanna." Francie reached forward again, but the dark-haired girl deliberately kept both hands on the handles of the designer carryon she held.

Her assessing eyes, the same deep brown as her father's, swept Francie from head to foot. "I'm really going to have to use my acting skills," she said with a sidelong smirk. "No mother of mine would be caught dead in those clothes."

Francie glanced down at the lightweight slacks and top she'd bought for the trip, then pretended to study the area leading to the terminals. "Do the fashion police have a checkpoint set up again? Darn!"

Alanna glanced uncertainly in the direction Francie had indicated, then back, her eyes narrowing suspiciously.

"Let's check our bags." MacNair ended the strained moment and gestured to an attendant who wheeled the cart toward the baggage check.

The line moved quickly, and they hurried down the corridor, through the metal detectors, and had only a five-minute wait before boarding their plane. MacNair gave Francie the window seat and sat on the aisle, directly across from his children.

"What's there to *do* at this Springdale place, anyway?" Alanna asked.

"We'll be staying at a nice hotel," Francie offered, leaning in front of MacNair to speak to his daughter. "You guys'll find stuff to do. We'll go thrift store shopping tomorrow, getting ready for the dance."

Alanna's nose almost skimmed the ceiling of the plane. "*Thrift stores?* What does that mean?"

At the stiffening of MacNair's posture, Francie realized she'd pressed her thigh against his and that if she turned her face slightly, her eyes would be level with his mouth. She recognized the expensive spicy scent of his soap.

She deliberately focused on the conversation with his daughter. "You know, consignment shops, Salvation Army, stuff like that."

The girl gaped. "You don't mean *used* clothing? That's disgusting! You won't actually *wear* someone's old clothes, will you?"

Alex watched the verbal exchange as though he had a front row seat at Wimbledon.

"I don't know where else we'd find outfits for the dance," Francie said, vividly conscious of the man scrutinizing her at close range. "I doubt your dad has anything in his closet left over from his high school days in the seventies." She turned, and sure enough, his sensuous-looking mouth was mere inches away. "Do you?"

"Junior high," he stated, his lips softly forming the words.

"Really." An enveloping warmth cloaked her, and she quickly settled back in her seat. "Hard to imagine."

"What is?"

"Well, I'm trying to picture you stuffing other guys into lockers and hiding Playmates under your mattress."

"I never did those things."

"No kidding." She pretended surprise and cast him another glance. "You belonged to the German club and were class valedictorian."

"Do you think you know everything?"

"Which part's wrong?"

He averted his face. "It was the chess club."

"Well, see? I know more about you already." She grinned and leaned forward slightly, this time careful not to touch him.

"I think I'm going to be sick," Alanna said.

Alarm crossed MacNair's face. He turned toward his daughter. "Are you air sick?"

"I think it was either the thrift store talk or the fact that you and I are having a conversation," Francie said for his ears alone. She reached into the pocket on the seat ahead of her, found the blue bag and tossed it across the aisle.

Alex caught it with a grin and handed it to his sister.

She gave Francie a haughty stare, stuffed the bag into the pocket ahead of her and turned her gaze out the window.

MacNair looked relieved that it had been a false alarm.

"You know she really is perfect," Francie said, settling back. "Those snooty looks are great." Feeling MacNair's gaze again, she turned. "What?"

He simply shook his head and pulled a folder and a laptop computer from his briefcase.

She studied his profile surreptitiously, noting his classic good looks and impeccable grooming. He could easily be the Armani poster boy.

He plucked a pair of gold-rimmed glasses from inside his case and slid them on. They did nothing to diminish his refined good looks. In fact they added a touch of sophistication. "Do you wear those often?"

"When I read. Is my vision going to be a problem?"

"No. I, uh, just wondered. You look very nice in them. Wear them all the time if you like."

"Well, now that I have your permission to wear my glasses, I feel so much better. Does this shirt meet your approval?"

Her gaze skittered across his broad chest in the lightweight shirt. "It does."

He opened the Franklin planner she'd suspected he carried, and turned his attention back to his work.

Francie closed her eyes. She'd stayed up too late, packing and trying to find mates for earrings, and she could use a nap before they arrived in Springdale. She wanted to be rested tomorrow when she saw the look on Nana's face. Ryan MacNair was a major coup on her part. A self-satisfied smile turned up the corners of her lips. Her old high school acquaintances would be pretty impressed themselves. She couldn't wait.

"I almost forgot."

She opened her eyes. "What?"

He slid a minute white envelope from his pocket and shook something shiny into his palm, then extended it.

Francie stared at the modest gold band. "What's this?"

"Your grandmother will think it's odd if you aren't wearing a wedding ring. I guessed at the size."

Still she stared. "Where did you get it?"

"I bought it."

"You bought me a wedding ring?"

"Just put the thing on your finger. Gold is a good investment."

Hesitantly Francie took the ring from his palm and slipped it on her finger. It went on easily.

Ryan turned back to his blinking cursor, as if dismissing her. This time when she closed her eyes, all she could think of was the weight of the gold band on her finger. She should have thought of it herself. Maybe MacNair wasn't as unimaginative as she'd thought. Nah, he couldn't be.

She smiled a satisfied smile and relaxed. She really couldn't wait.

RYAN STOOD NEAR a pillar with Alanna and Alex while Francie handled the room registration with her credit card. From the expression on the desk clerk's face, Ryan could tell he wasn't the only one who wondered if it would be more gratifying to kiss her or place her on a plane headed for a distant country.

Why had the thought of kissing her entered his

head? She must have him more rattled than he thought. He buried that image deep.

Minutes later she hurried toward them, her shoulder-length dark blond hair swaying and her pert energy drawing admiring glances. He had to pull his gaze from her curvy figure to pay attention to her chatter about the registration process. She doled out three plastic card keys. "Room 512," she said.

Ryan gestured to a bellboy standing nearby and gave him the room number.

"We could've gotten the luggage ourselves, couldn't we?" she asked, leaning into him again, and Ryan didn't know a woman who felt softer in all the right places.

"That's what the bellhops are here for." He led them to an elevator, and stood a safe distance from her.

"Seems kind of silly, paying them to carry our suitcases when we're perfectly capable," she said with a shrug.

Alanna rolled her eyes.

"Francie! That's you, isn't it?"

Ryan turned at the cry. A pencil-thin young woman with a man and boy in tow, hurried toward the elevators. Her hair was cut in a sleek short bob that made her neck appear all the scrawnier.

"Peyton," Francie said, and Ryan couldn't tell if the look on her face was dread or pleasure. "I've been looking forward to seeing you."

The woman she'd called Peyton stopped a foot from Francie and leaned into a mock embrace, kissing the air by her cheek. "Donald, come see Francie. And we get to meet the husband we've heard about."

She turned and cast an assessing glance on Ryan's hair and clothing. One penciled eyebrow rose. *"Well…!"*

Her stocky husband stepped forward and extended a fleshy hand. "Don Armbruster."

"Ryan MacNair." He adjusted his briefcase and shook the man's hand.

"And this is Donald Junior," Peyton said, gesturing to the chubby boy of about ten or eleven just as the bell dinged and the elevator doors whooshed open.

The two families stepped into the elevator and the doors slid shut. The atmosphere grew claustrophobic.

"These are *our* children," Francie announced proudly. "Alanna and Alex."

Peyton gave them the once-over. "How old are they?"

Francie's gaze flew to Ryan's as if trying to recall the information. "Uhh."

Alanna, never one to appreciate being talked about as though she weren't present, piped up and saved her. "I'm twelve. My brother's nine."

"These are *your* children, then," Peyton said to Ryan.

"Yes," Francie said quickly. "But they're like my own. Aren't you, dears?"

Alex accepted the arm that Francie threw around his shoulders and gazed up with mingled surprise and pleasure on his face.

"When are we going to shop for my new bathing

suit, Mom?'' Alanna asked in a syrupy sweet voice. ''I want to try out the pool right away.''

''We'll go shopping as soon as we're settled into our room,'' Francie replied without blinking an eye. ''That is if Daddy's not too tired.''

Still keeping a hold on Alex, she slid her arm around Ryan's waist and leaned into him, this time, her breast pressing against his chest. Their thin layers of clothing weren't enough to prevent his body from taking notice at the same time his brain grappled with her words. *Daddy?*

''You're not too tired, are you, *Daddy?*'' his daughter asked, downright devilment lacing her words. She'd never called him Daddy in her entire life.

Ryan focused on ignoring Francie's warm curves pressed along his side. ''No, *Pumpkin,* I can't wait to shop with you girls.''

Alex looked from his sister to his father and back up at the woman enfolding them in a hug, a look of total puzzlement on his young face.

''Isn't that sweet?'' Peyton asked. She looked from Francie to Ryan and her gaze slid assessingly across his features. ''I don't believe I've heard what you do, Ryan.''

''Executive arts administrator for the Shepperd Museum in Chicago,'' Francie replied for him, and to his ears it sounded like boasting.

Peyton's green eyes narrowed as though she were calculating how much he earned at a job like that. ''Donald's a financial analyst with the Daily Corporation.''

"Is that a local company?" he asked, turning to Donald, and praying for the salvation of reaching their floor. In order to look at the man, he had to turn his head, placing Francie's fresh-smelling hair directly beneath his nose. The scent, combined with the pressure of her supple body, stirred his long-dormant hormones to life.

"His office is local," Peyton answered for him, "but the company is international. Donald has an M.B.A. and a law degree."

The bell rang, saving him from hearing any further bragging, and Ryan ushered Francie and the children from the elevator.

"We'll see you soon," Peyton threatened, waggling long red-tipped fingers.

Alanna and Alex hurried ahead, searching for the room number.

Ryan moved away from Francie as quickly as possible. He shook his head helplessly. "This whole thing is already out of hand. I can't imagine why I agreed to this."

"Because you love me," she replied with a teasing grin. "Remember?"

"Do you need to play this thing to the hilt in front of your friends? I thought this was all for your grandmother."

"This is a small town," she replied more seriously. "Nana has already told the nurses and the nurses have spread the news around. That's how my 'friends' heard it. It has to look real."

"It sounded like someone should have been keep-

ing score while you two sparred over whose husband
was more prosperous.''

Francie waved an unconcerned hand at him. His
daughter had the room unlocked, and she and Alex
were inspecting the television and the balcony.

''You guys did just great back there,'' Francie said,
including all three in her praise.

Alanna perched on the edge of one of the double
beds. ''Let's go get my bathing suit.''

''That was a slick one,'' Francie said, admitting
she'd been duped. The look on Peyton's face when
she'd sized up MacNair had been worth a dozen bathing suits, but she didn't plan to tell the girl that. Not
for the first time, Alanna's confident words didn't
meld with the way she hunched her shoulders forward, and Francie thought it a curious posture for a
girl so slim and lovely.

''As soon as the luggage comes, we'll hang up our
clothes and head out. Lunch first, then shopping.
How's that sound?''

''Yeah, how's that sound, *Daddy?*'' Alanna asked.

MacNair frowned at Francie. ''I can't wait.''

ALANNA HADN'T allowed her near the dressing room
door, so Francie had no idea how the suit she'd forked
over eighty bucks for looked on the girl. She appeared
with a faded T-shirt covering the suit, and the four of
them grabbed towels and took off for the elevator.

Beneath an enormous skylight, tables and chairs
surrounded the pool area, a small restaurant advertis-
ing drinks and the hours for breakfast and lunch. On

two sides and above, hotel rooms opened onto balconies.

Alanna immediately perched on the edge of the pool, dangling her legs in the water. Alex sat several feet away. MacNair kicked off his deck shoes and walked toward the board. He looked as good in modest trunks as he did in a three-piece suit. Nah. Better.

He had a handsome amount of dark hair on his well-formed chest and legs, and a nice flat stomach. Francie kept her perusal covert, and observed his impressive dive into the deep end. He swam to the edge and came up beside his son.

She removed her terry robe and thongs and met his eyes as she approached the edge. He slicked his hair back and watched, undeniable attraction revealed in his dark eyes. She was no Cindy Crawford, but she knew she had an adequate shape. She plunged into the water.

"Coming?" she called to Alanna.

The girl glanced self-consciously at a couple of other swimmers with a toddler at the opposite end, and slipped into the water without removing the T-shirt.

Francie cast MacNair an inquisitive glance, but he'd swam to where Alex sat, and was encouraging him to leave the side.

"Wanna race?" Francie asked Alanna.

The girl shrugged.

Francie left her and swam several laps.

Reluctantly Alanna joined her and kept up.

Finally Francie paused in about four feet of water

to catch her breath. Ryan was holding Alex in the water.

"Look, Francie," Alex said. "I can stick my head under."

He proceeded to demonstrate.

She laughed. "Don't you get water up your nose?"

He laughed. "Nah. Ya just gotta blow out. My dad's showing me."

"Ask your dad if he can stand on his head underwater."

"Can you, Dad?"

To Francie's amazement, MacNair accepted the challenge. He left Alex on the side and dipped under, his feet appearing above the surface for an impressive length of time. He somersaulted and came up sputtering.

Francie had to laugh aloud at the man. This certainly wasn't the same guy who'd appeared at her door so serious and stuffy. Right now he didn't act like the uptight man who resented her infringing on his time and had seemed so wholeheartedly disapproving of her.

"That's cool, Dad!" Alex cried.

"Want to try it?"

Alex shook his head.

"Okay, we'll practice your back float, then."

Alanna swam over and encouraged her brother.

Francie stood watching him with his kids for a few minutes, puzzling over the difference in the man. The revelation came to her immediately: His love for his children loosened him up and made him seem more human.

Her attention became distracted by two women entering the pool area in long brightly colored caftans. They carried frosted drinks to a nearby table.

With a little start of surprise, Francie recognized Becka Crow and Shari Donegan. Before the women had a chance to see she'd discovered their arrival, Francie quickly sliced through the few feet of water separating them, and slipped her arm around Mac-Nair's shoulders from behind.

Sleek skin slid against Ryan's legs and shoulders, and those soft, ample breasts, covered by a thin layer of spandex, pressed into his back. He'd already been unable to ignore the fact that Francie had a soft, round figure, unlike women who thought anemically skinny was stylish. As a man he appreciated that.

He immediately experienced more difficulty breathing than he had after a full thirty seconds on his head underwater. "I have a fun idea," she said near his ear, loud enough for Alanna and Alex to hear, yet sending a shiver across his shoulders. "Let's play war!"

"How do you do that?" Alex asked.

"You get on Alanna's shoulders. I get on your dad's shoulders and we try to knock each other off."

"You can't knock me off," Alex said, terror in his eyes. "I can't swim yet."

"That doesn't sound very fair, anyway," Alanna complained. "I think Alex should get on your shoulders and I should get on Dad's."

"We'll switch off," Francie agreed. "And I promise I won't knock you off, Alex. You can take your best shots at me. Go under,'' Francie said to Ryan, ''so I can get on.''

At her insistent pressure on his arms, he sank under the water. She slid onto his shoulders, her sleek legs hanging down his chest, and he stood.

He grasped her supple calves to keep her balanced.

Alanna and Alex had to go to the side, and ended up with Alex squealing and Alanna screaming for him to let go of her hair.

Ryan couldn't help a laugh.

Alex did his best to knock Francie from her roost, but Ryan had no trouble keeping his footing. Alanna insisted they trade partners.

They played the game that way for a while, and finally, Alanna begged to stop.

''You're the best,'' Francie whispered in his ear, sliding her water-slick body alongside his, and flattening her palm against his chest in an intimate caress.

His physical reaction to her nearness was immediate and potent. He placed his hand on her wrist as if to pull it away, but the pleading look in her blue eyes halted him. She blinked, water dripping from her lashes.

Over her shoulder, a movement and a bright flash of color caught his eye. Two women watched them intently. Realization dawned. His gaze skittered back to hers. ''Friends of yours?''

''Becka and Shari,'' she said softly.

Unnerved, he didn't know why her acting out her part should insult him. That's what they were here for. This whole thing was a charade.

If she wanted a performance, he'd give her one. "Let's give them the whole show, then."

Impulsively he hooked his arm around her waist and pulled her flush against him. Her eyes opened wide in surprise, but she came along easily, both arms draping over his shoulders.

Her skin glowed with the same health and vitality that oozed from her personality. Though her eyes were wide and filled with doubt, her lips parted ever so slightly, and Ryan dipped his head and kissed them full on—a healthy, this-is-just-a-promise-for-later kiss that he should have known better than to initiate.

Because she kissed him back. And she was good at it. Too good. There wasn't enough fabric or space between them to keep his response a secret, and he released her. Her craziness was rubbing off. That was the kiss he'd thought of giving her earlier, and under any other circumstances he'd have had enough sense to keep it just a fleeting thought.

Francie loosened her arms from his neck and drifted back a couple of feet in the water, staring…her heart pounding.

They'd had an eyeful, old Becka and Shari. She fully expected to see steam rise off the water. Old Mac could kiss, she'd say that for him.

When her thoughts came into focus, she looked over to see Alanna and Alex staring, Alex's expression amused, Alanna's horrified.

"Are you hungry?" Ryan asked them, as though they hadn't just witnessed their father soundly kiss a near stranger.

They nodded.

"Let's go before we sprout gills." He hoisted himself on the edge and walked away, water sluicing down his muscular body. The kids scrambled out behind him, both glancing back at Francie.

Still slightly dazed, Francie swam to a ladder and climbed out. MacNair held a towel out to her. She stepped forward and hesitated, wondering if he planned to continue the charade, and not knowing how she'd keep her cool if he did. She hadn't expected that kiss to feel so real, or for either of their reactions to be so intense.

But he turned his attention to helping Alex find his vinyl thongs and saved her the worry.

Alanna fixed her with a frigid glare, and Francie knew whatever points she'd gained in the pool play, she'd lost when she and the girl's father had locked lips. She gave her a tentative smile, and Alanna cut her stare away abruptly.

After they'd dried, donned their robes and headed for the exit, she reached for Ryan's arm.

"We don't have to pretend when nobody's watching," he said, drawing back from her touch.

Francie glanced over to see the table where the women had been sitting empty. She shouldn't have felt disappointed or shut out. This was only a charade.

Ryan MacNair didn't have to touch her or even be nice to her when they were alone. The touchy-feely game they'd played in the pool had been for the benefit of their observers, and for no other reason. That kiss had meant nothing to him. To either one of them.

That fact gave her small comfort.

Unexpectedly Francie found herself hoping they'd find themselves watched a lot over the next week, *and* she found herself not giving a hoot why she wished it.

3

"THAT WAS THE worst pizza I've ever had," Alanna complained as they let themselves back into the room after a late supper.

"There are only three pizza places in town," Francie apologized. "That's the one we went to when I was in school."

"I think they're still using the same batch of dough for the crust." Alanna flopped herself on one of the beds.

"I thought it was good," Alex said.

Francie smiled at the boy. He was so eager to get along and see everyone happy, it made Francie feel bad to see how hard he tried only to have his sister complain about everything.

"We'll try the buffet in the hotel dining room tomorrow, how's that?" Ryan asked.

Alanna shrugged. "Whatever."

"Sure," Alex agreed. He opened a cabinet, found the remote and flicked on the television. "Cool! We have cable!"

Immediately Ryan crossed to the cabinet, found a cable guide and thumbed through it. "Don't change any channels until I come back." He went into the bathroom and closed the door.

Francie watched him with puzzlement. It was fine if the man liked to read in the bathroom, but why had he instructed Alex not to change channels?

"He's calling the desk to see if there are any bad channels," Alex explained with a grin as he settled cross-legged on the other bed nearest the bathroom.

"Bad channels," Francie repeated.

"Hel-lo!" Alanna said, snottily. "R-rated? Stuff us kids aren't supposed to see?"

"Oh." Francie went to one of her bags and unpacked her toiletries.

Ryan returned. "Okay, Alex. Go ahead."

Alex grinned at Francie and flipped through channels. She returned his amused smile, went into the bathroom, washed and moisturized her face and brushed her teeth.

When she returned, the family had settled, Alex and Ryan on one bed, Alanna on the other, watching a movie with a dog and cat finding their way home. She made herself comfortable on the other side of the bed where Alanna sat.

"Wait a minute," the girl said a few minutes later. "I'm not going to sleep with *her.*"

Ryan looked over, staring at his daughter. "Honey, there isn't—"

"No! I don't want to sleep with her."

"There's no other place for you to sleep," her father reasoned.

"I don't care. I don't like her, and I'm not going to sleep with her. You shouldn't try to make me."

"Maybe they have rollaways," Francie said. She picked up the phone near the bed and dialed the desk.

A minute later, she rested the receiver back in its cradle. "They're all rented out already. We should have called earlier. They'll call us if they get one returned."

"This wasn't my idea," Alanna continued. "Let her sleep on the floor."

Ryan's face actually reddened, and he avoided Francie's gaze. "You're being rude, Alanna. There's no reason why this arrangement can't work out. We—"

"No," Francie interrupted. "She's right. She shouldn't have to sleep with me if she feels so strongly about it. I'll sleep on the floor tonight. I saw some extra blankets in the closet. I can make a pad."

"If anyone sleeps on the floor, it will be Alanna," Ryan said firmly, no room for more argument in his tone. "*You* can sleep on the floor, miss."

"Fine." Her dark eyes shot daggers at Francie. "Just as long as I don't have to be next to her."

"I can sleep on the floor, Dad," Alex offered.

"No. Alanna will."

That was that.

They watched the rest of the movie, Alex laughing from time to time, Alanna shooting Francie a frosty glare every time she knew her dad wasn't looking.

When the movie was over, Ryan announced bedtime, then flicked to a news channel and lowered the volume. Alex used the bathroom and snuggled right down. "Night, Francie."

"Night, hon," she said softly. She made Alanna's pallet on the floor and gave her the extra pillow off the bed while the girl was in the bathroom. Alanna returned in a long T-shirt nightie, deliberately rearranged everything Francie had just done and laid down with her face turned away.

Francie used the bathroom to change into her T-shirt and the shorts she'd decided to wear since she had to cross in front of Ryan to get back to her bed. She slid under the covers and halfheartedly watched the news. Her eyelids grew heavy. Packing and flying had zapped her energy.

"Will the lamp disturb you?" Ryan asked softly, glancing at her over the top of his glasses.

He'd opened his laptop and briefcase while she'd been in the bathroom, and sat with his back propped against the headboard.

"No."

"Do you have a schedule for the week? I'd like to enter the times on my calendar."

"Yeah, they sent me one. It's in my bag somewhere. I'll find it for you in the morning."

He looked as if he wanted to say something else. Though Alex appeared soundly asleep, Alanna might still be listening, so Ryan turned back to whatever he'd been doing.

So far Alanna was the only wrench in the works. And yet, she'd put on a perfect performance in front of Peyton that morning. Francie could only hope that she'd contain her surliness to the room, as she had until now.

She hoped, too, that Alanna's obvious contempt for the whole situation wasn't going to change Ryan's mind about going through with this week. They were here now, and he'd given his word.

But they'd only made it through the first day.

RYAN SURVEYED THE double sink and counter in the bathroom with dismay. His shaving kit sat in one corner, the kids' toothbrushes and toothpaste beside it, while Francie's paraphernalia had been strung from one side to the other with the same haphazard carelessness that characterized her reasoning.

There were cleansers and toners, a bag of makeup, a bag of sample-size toiletries, a blow-dryer, brushes, combs, hair bands and cologne. He made a spot for his razor and shaving cream and proceeded to shave.

The shower stall looked the same: a sleek purple razor, shampoo and conditioner, body cleanser, and a loofah sponge. Her scent hung everywhere, that exotic, erotic smell he'd noticed from the first time he'd been close to her. Shaking his head, he unwrapped the hotel soap and showered.

Dried and dressed, he found the family waiting for him. "Can we have breakfast in the hotel, Dad?" Alex asked. "They have a place by the pool. Me and Alanna just went and saw it."

He raised a brow at Francie, and she gave him an agreeable nod. She wore a pair of belted white shorts with a peach-colored cotton shirt tucked into them, and a pair of clunky suede sandals. The feminine scents from her shower still lingered in the room. One side of her freshly washed and dried hair had been tucked behind her ear, and the other swept across her cheek as she grabbed her purse and camera case from the unmade bed. She could have passed for a teenager.

The car rental agency was just across the street from the hotel, so after breakfast by the pool they walked.

"Francie!" the man at the counter cried, when he saw her. She pulled her sunglasses up on her head and walked to the counter. "Digger?"

"Nobody calls me Digger anymore." He laughed.

"Uhh," she said, as though she had to think about it. "Tom, is it?"

He grinned. "Yeah. It's great to see you! This week is going to be so much fun."

"I'm looking forward to it. I reserved a car."

"This your husband?"

Francie turned and gestured for Ryan to step forward. "Yes, this is Ryan MacNair. Tom Wallace."

Ryan shook the man's hand. "Tom."

"Okay, let me find you on the computer. Do you have a confirmation number?"

"Yes." She opened her purse and dug through the contents. Ryan watched, wondering how she managed to find anything in the disorganized jumble. "It's here somewhere."

He and Tom exchanged a look over her head. Alanna rolled her eyes and took a seat on a plastic chair. Alex found a gum machine and asked for change. Ryan handed him a coin.

"Here it is." She produced the familiar envelope stained with coffee rings.

"Okay." Tom pulled up her account and asked for their driver's licenses. They each placed one on the counter, and Francie turned to Ryan, a look of alarm on her face.

He frowned a question at her.

She rolled her eyes and turned to watch Tom. He took her license first, entered the data into the computer and then picked up Ryan's. "She doesn't use your name?" he asked with a raised brow.

"I'd already made a name for myself with my photography business," she replied quickly, as though she'd been anticipating the question. "It was a business decision."

She looked pleased with her quick reply, and Ryan noticed she draped the hand with the wedding ring over the top of her purse.

"You don't have the same address, either?" Tom asked.

Her gaze flew to Ryan's, and he held his passive expression. This was her show. Let her write the lines.

"We, uh, we just moved," she said. "He hasn't had his license renewed yet."

"New house?" the man asked.

"Yes," Ryan said.

"Condo," she replied at the same time.

Tom glanced from one to the other. "A house or a condo?"

"Well, it's a condo, but it's so spacious, it's like a house," she said.

"I've always wondered," Tom said. "Do you have to do your own lawn work on those condo deals?"

"Ask her," Ryan replied.

She stabbed him with a glare, then smiled at the man behind the counter. "He doesn't have to, but he likes to so much that the groundskeeper lets him help."

Tom offered insurance and took Francie's credit card. She signed the receipt. "You can come over and do mine if you like taking care of lawns so well."

"I don't think I'll have time," Ryan replied as if he thought it was a clever joke.

Tom handed Ryan the keys. "Stall ninety-one on the east side of the lot. Don't forget to fill it with gas before you bring it back, otherwise they charge you an arm and a leg. We're meeting for drinks at Quigley's at eight tonight. Can you come?"

"We'll sure try," Ryan replied. "Thanks." He held the door for Francie and his children to file past.

They located the rental car and Francie directed as Ryan drove to the Thrift Store.

"This place smells," Alanna complained as soon as they set foot inside. Dramatically she pulled the neck of her shirt up and covered her nose and mouth.

"Now, we have to decide on our characters," Francie told Ryan. "Look! Here are love beads. Who would have worn love beads?" She held up a strand of multicolored beads she'd spotted on a jewelry rack. "This is going to be more difficult than I thought. Alex, get us a shopping cart, will you, sweetie?"

His son ran obligingly to bring back a wobbly cart, and presented it to Francie as if it were a gift. She smiled and thanked him, and his features nearly glowed. Ryan recognized his need for a woman's attention. He'd been so small when his mother had abandoned him, and Mrs. Nelson was kind and efficient, but she was hardly a warm, nurturing replacement for a mother.

He hoped it hadn't been a terrible mistake bringing

his son on this trip. A week with Francie wasn't going to fill the gap in the child's life, and growing attached to her could be detrimental when the agreement was fulfilled.

"Check this out." Francie laughed, showing him an orange flowered synthetic shirt with a long, pointed collar.

"That's awful," he replied.

"Yes, but it's Greg Brady all the way."

"Who?"

"'The Brady Bunch,' Dad," Alex piped up.

"We could find a pair of bell-bottoms and some round-toed shoes, and you'd be all set. You could wear a curly wig to look like a 'fro."

"No wig," he replied firmly.

"We could be the Brady parents and Alanna and Alex could pick two of the kids."

"There aren't enough of us for the kids," Alex said, getting into the spirit.

She agreed and moved on through the racks. "You're right. Not macho enough for you, Mac. This could take most of the week just deciding on our costumes."

Ryan and Alanna exchanged a look of dread.

She stopped in her tracks. "But then..."

"What?" Alex asked.

"There's always the *Grease* theme."

"What's that?"

"The play the high school drama class is presenting. It's a movie, too. You've seen it, Ryan."

Forty minutes later, they exited the store with three bags of clothing, jewelry and shoes.

"I'm not wearing those stinky clothes," Alanna said.

"We'll wash them all," Francie said. "They'll smell just like your own clothes. I have to drop this leather jacket off at the cleaners."

"I think I have that smell in my head," she complained.

"I think it was in your head to start with," Francie said under her breath, but Ryan caught it, and so did Alanna, because she snorted and flung herself into the car.

Alanna's temperament didn't improve as the morning progressed. His daughter was never easy to get along with, but this petulant side was one Ryan hadn't seen with such prevalence before now. Yes, Francie was irritating, but Ryan was making the best of the week for Alanna's sake, and she could certainly try harder to do the same. He'd talk to her later when they had a few minutes alone.

For now, Francie had taken the keys from his hand and slipped behind the steering wheel. She pulled out of the parking lot and into traffic. If she drove the way she did everything else, they were in big trouble.

She talked to Alex over her shoulder. She changed lanes as if they were in the Indy 500.

"Do we have air bags?" Alanna asked from the back.

Ryan turned enough to assure himself both offspring had their seat belts buckled.

They pulled up in front of a spacious well-manicured lawn, and she parked, scraping the bumper on the concrete stopper and backing up.

"Bring me here to mow, did you?"

She grinned. "No. This is where Nana is. I brought you here to meet her." They got out of the car. "Remember, kids, it's important that we make a good impression and play convincing parts for my grandmother. This is all for her."

"No," Alanna argued. "This is all for me and my great-grandma's brooch."

"That's right," Ryan told her. "And in order to get that brooch, we have to go along with this."

"If she was a decent person, she'd have given it to us," she said with a sneer in Francie's direction.

"Excuse us for a minute, please," he said to Francie, and took his daughter by the hand.

He led her to the shade of an ancient weeping willow near the curb. "Alanna, she didn't have to agree to give it to us at all. But she did. And we want it, so we're going through with this. Is that understood?"

She looked away and answered quietly, "Yes, sir."

"Now, I expect your behavior and your attitude to improve immediately."

"I don't like her, Dad. I don't want to be around her."

"You don't have to like her. I can't make you like her. But you do have to be civil. That means polite. This is our vacation…can we please not have it ruined?"

"This isn't a real vacation. Other kids' parents take them to Disneyland."

Her words stabbed him with guilt. He studied the daughter he loved so much and who was slipping away from him. He had only himself to blame. "I'm sorry. I know this isn't your idea of fun, and I will do better in the future. For now this is the week we have to spend, so let's not make each other miserable.''

''Why do we have to spend it with her?''

''You know why. We agreed to treat this as a vacation knowing we'd get Great-Grandma's brooch for you at the end. And we're going to make the best of it. Understood?''

She nodded.

''Now, show this grandmother of Francie's what a lovely girl you are, okay? For me?''

''Okay.''

He hugged her. She pulled away, and they joined Francie and Alex, already engaged in a conversation with two white-haired men seated on the cement bench beside a fountain. One of them pointed at Ryan and Alanna with his cane. ''This your daddy now?''

''That's him,'' Alex said with pride.

''Well, no wonder you're such a fine lookin' young fella. Your daddy is, too. Is he a hard worker? I worked in a mill most of my life. Was a farmhand when I was your age. Are you Duane Sweeney's boy?''

''No, sir,'' Ryan replied.

''Raised turkeys, he did.''

''Ah.''

''Come on,'' Francie whispered, and waved goodbye to the men.

It took a while for Francie to track down her grandmother. The white-haired woman was sitting in the shade of a long side porch in a wheelchair.

"Nana!" Francie cried, and knelt to give her a hug.

"Francesca?" she asked, reaching for her hand and looking into her face.

Francesca? Ryan had to grin. Francie suited her much better.

"Francesca, you look so pretty." She fingered Francie's hair.

"Look, Nana, you get to meet my husband and our kids."

Francie's grandmother cast faded blue eyes his direction. Her skin was a mass of wrinkles, and her frame feeble-looking, but her eyes were bright. "Jim? I finally get to meet you. Francesca told me all about you."

Jim? Francie took on a startled expression, met his eyes with a shrug, then looked back.

"Pleased to meet you, ma'am." He crouched so he'd be eye level with her, and extended a hand.

She took it in her papery-dry one, and patted his fingers.

"So, you're the one, huh?" Her alert gaze inspected his face as though she could read all there was to know of him.

"Yes, ma'am."

"She said you were handsome. And rich." She cackled, and the laugh surprised him. "I can see you're handsome. What about the rich part?"

"I make a good living, Mrs...." He looked up at Francie, surprised to see a blush staining her cheeks.

"Taylor," Francie supplied.

"Mrs. Taylor."

"None of that crap. Call me Nana. That's what Francesca calls me."

"All right, Nana."

"Here are Alanna and Alex," Francie said, taking Alex's hand and stepping forward with him.

"You look like your daddy," Nana said to him. "'Cept your eyes. Whose eyes did you get?"

"My mama's," he replied.

"She abandoned us," Alanna said bluntly, and humiliation clawed its way up Ryan's cheeks. "She left us when we were babies."

He'd only told Francie that he was divorced. He hadn't told her the sordid details. He didn't meet her eyes.

"Some people ain't cut out to be parents," Nana said. "Too bad God don't see that ahead o' time and keep 'em from havin' young ones, ain't it?"

"I'm very grateful for my children," Ryan replied automatically. "I'm glad their mother had them."

Nana's eyes narrowed. She gave him the once-over and a grin creased her aged features. "I think I like you, Jim."

"Nana, his name is Ryan. Ryan MacNair."

"You told me you married a Jim."

"You must have gotten it mixed up."

"I don't get mixed up. I'm old, not stupid."

"Does this chair go fast?" Alex asked, looking the wheelchair over.

"When I can get someone to push me," she replied. "Push me, Jim," she said. "Don't ever have nobody to push me where I want to go."

"Where would you like to go?" he asked.

"To the garden. And down by the fountain. Did you see any ducks down there?"

"I did," Alex said.

Nana's eyes twinkled at Alex. "Hop on," she said, patting her lap.

He looked up at his dad.

Ryan looked at Francie, and she nodded.

"Okay, but only down to the fountain. We don't want you putting Nana's legs to sleep."

Ryan pushed the wheelchair, balking at Alex's cries to go faster. Alanna followed without speaking.

At the sound of a high-speed shutter, Ryan glanced to find Francie snapping away with a state-of-the-art Nikon. "*That's* the camera you carry in that beaten-up case?"

She zoomed in for a close-up of his face as they passed beneath the shade of a tree, then lowered the camera. "There's nothing wrong with this case. It's been a lot of places with me. It's sort of an old friend."

"It was her daddy's," Nana supplied.

She'd never mentioned her parents. Ryan wondered if they were dead. He and Francie sat on the concrete bench surrounding the fountain, Nana's wheelchair between them. Alex balanced on a short fence nearby and Alanna found a spot in the shade.

Francie took pictures.

"I wanna put my feet in," Nana announced.

"In the water?" Francie asked.

"'Course in the water. Take my shoes off."

Ryan glanced at Francie and then around them. How would they handle this?

Immediately Francie placed the camera in the bag and knelt to remove her grandmother's shoes.

"Francie, you can't do that," he objected.

"Why not?"

"What if someone sees?"

"Her feet? So what?"

"Well, it—it might not be good for her. She might catch cold."

"It's seventy-five degrees, in case you haven't noticed."

Their gazes locked.

"She's an old lady," she whispered. "She has few pleasures left, and I aim to see that she gets this small one." She set the last shoe and sock aside, and stood from her crouched position. She was barely bigger than the old woman.

"Move aside," he ordered.

She looked at him, then obliged. He gathered Nana up effortlessly and turned to sit her on the concrete, her feet dangling in the water.

She sighed and laughed out loud. "I do like you, Jim."

He sat beside her. "I like you, too, Nana."

"You got a grandma?" she asked.

"Had a wonderful one," he replied.

"What about your mother?"

"She's gone, too."

"No wonder you needed a woman in your life. Francesca's a whole lotta woman in a small package."

He'd noticed.

"Look, kids!" she called. "There's goldfish nibbling at my toes!"

"Can I do it, too, Dad?" Alex asked, excitedly.

Francie slipped off her sandals, helped Alex with his Nikes, and the two of them sat side by side on the other side of Nana, giggling as the fish brushed against their feet. The gold band on Francie's finger glittered in the sunlight and the sight sent an odd sensation pinging through his chest.

"Come on, Jim," Nana said with a cackling laugh. "Put your feet in the water."

"Come on, Dad, it's cool!"

Ryan glanced from the old woman to his son, and finally allowed his gaze to light on Francie. Her lips held a smile, and her blue eyes a dare.

He slid off his leather sandals, rolled up his pant legs and lowered one foot into the cool water. "You didn't say it was cold."

"Ain't cold," Nana declared. "It's refreshin'."

Ryan grinned and plunged the other foot in. He turned and observed his daughter, her haughty facade keeping her from enjoying their company, or the day, or this week away from home. But from time to time, she glanced over, and once he thought he saw her hide a smile. Maybe this week was going to do her more good than harm, after all.

Maybe it was going to do them all some good.

4

"ARE YOU SURE it's okay?" Francie asked as they closed the door and headed for the elevator.

"Alanna's twelve years old. She's very responsible. They'll watch TV for a while and fall asleep."

She glanced back. "I left the number for Quigley's near the phone."

"They won't call. They'll be just fine."

"We can call them after an hour and make sure everything's okay," she suggested.

"If you want to," he agreed and ushered her into the elevator.

Francie studied his closely shaven jaw while he watched the numbers above the doors. They'd just spent two days and one night together, and she knew little more about him than she had before. Except what the kids had revealed.

"Your wife abandoned Alanna and Alex?" she asked hesitantly.

A muscle in his firm jaw twitched. "We're not friends," he said pointedly.

"You're right. Sorry." With a stab of hurt his suitably chastising words shouldn't have caused, she glanced up at the numbers he watched so intently.

Silence stretched between them. She would have to

be more careful not to cross any boundaries that bent his nose out of joint. He didn't have to discuss his life with her. He didn't owe her anything. What he was doing this week was enough.

They walked to the car, and Francie pulled the key from her purse.

"Allow me." He plucked it from her fingers.

"Do you have a problem with my driving?"

"The less stress, the better, all right?" He unlocked the doors and drove in silence. At a stoplight he asked, "This the street?"

"Yes. It's just behind that sign there."

He parked the car and glanced at her.

"It's going to be just fine," she assured him. "These people have no way of knowing we're not exactly what we say we are."

"I'll take my cues from you," he replied.

They got out of the car and entered the dimly lit lounge. Francie smoothed her wraparound jungle print skirt, a fluttering of nerves in her stomach, and swept a glance across the interior. It was show time. They had to make these people believe they were married. Where had the assurance she'd just exhibited for Ryan flown?

"There they are," she said, spotting a few familiar faces. She took his hand and led him forward. Several voices called greetings. Becka Crow and Peyton Armbruster were seated together chatting, and Peyton scooted over to make room to pull in two chairs.

"Have you met Francie's husband?" Peyton asked Becka.

"Not yet," the young woman replied.

"Everyone, this is Ryan," Francie said.

A chorus of voices welcomed him.

"Newlyweds," a female drawled. "Isn't that precious?"

Francie turned on a smile for Shari Donegan.

"When were you married?" she asked.

"Six months ago," Ryan said at the same time Francie came up with a reply.

"Valentine's Day," she answered.

They glanced at each other, but apparently the others didn't notice February had only been five months ago.

"Valentine's Day! How romantic," Shari said. "Whose idea was that?"

Wisely Francie bit her lip this time. Ryan must have done the same because a blatant silence followed. Finally she turned to look at him.

"It was my idea," he said, meeting her gaze steadily. "She thinks she has all the good ideas, but I have my share, too."

"Yes, you do," she agreed.

"We were beginning to wonder if Francie would ever find a husband," Peyton said.

Anger warmed Francie's cheeks. "Apparently everyone else has been more concerned about my marital status than I have. I have a fulfilling career and I support myself nicely. What do I need a husband for?"

The stares she garnered revealed she'd just stuck her foot in her mouth. She glanced around for a waitress.

"Apparently Ryan showed you something you

need a husband for,'' Becka said, joining the conversation with a suggestive tone.

The others laughed.

''You don't need a husband for that, either,'' Francie said quickly.

Becka's husband, J.J., chuckled.

''Was your biological clock ticking?'' Peyton asked with a grin.

Francie frowned at her. ''No! I'm not going to have children.''

The others exchanged glances.

Becka giggled. ''Remember, guys, this is Francie. If she had a biological clock, it would be set for another time zone.''

Laughter rose around them.

Ryan didn't appeared amused. He straightened in his chair. ''What Francie means is Alanna and Alex are a handful. In a few more years they'll be grown, and we'll have all our time just for each other. That's why we decided not to have more kids.''

He looped his arm around her shoulder, and something inside her warmed at his quick defense. He'd behaved just like a real loving husband would have.

A waitress arrived. ''What can I get you?''

''A Coke, please,'' Francie said.

Ryan named a prized Chicago beer.

''Sorry. Don't have it.''

''Killian's Red then,'' he said, and the waitress left.

''So, you were married before?'' Peyton asked, leaning toward Ryan.

''I've been divorced for almost eight years,'' he replied.

"Goodness, you must have been Chicago's most eligible bachelor when Francie caught you."

"I don't know about that."

"Oh, you're modest. Where did you do your graduate work?"

"Stanford for an M.B.A. and an art history."

"A double masters?" Peyton asked with both brows raised, probably sorry she'd asked now.

He nodded.

"Have you given Francie exposure?" Peyton asked. "As a local artist, I mean?"

"That's a good idea." Thoughtfully he turned to Francie. "Come to think of it, I've seen some of your photographs displayed around the city. How come we've never done a show at the museum?"

"I tried to interest the museum in my old Chicago photos last year and didn't reach first base," she said. "Didn't fit in with the ancient artifacts themes, or something."

"Your photos would be perfect for the bicentennial celebration coming up this fall. We can work out an offer. Give my office a call when we get back. We'll set up a show."

The surrounding silence grew deafening. The jukebox played a song for the third time. Francie glanced up quickly.

"You have to call his office for an appointment?" Becka asked, voicing the question on all their faces.

Francie's cheeks warmed again. She faced the women, but cuddled into Ryan's side. "As if work is on my mind when this sexy guy comes home. If you had to compete with his job for his attention, would you talk business when he finally got there?''

The men snickered.

Ryan leaned down and placed a gentle kiss on her lips, then drew her snugly to his side. Her lips tingled from the unexpected contact. Against her shoulder, his heart beat steadily. The waitress brought their drinks, and Ryan paid.

It was the first time he'd paid for anything on this trip, since she felt responsible, so she planned to pay him back later.

He took a drink of the Irish beer without pouring it into the glass the waitress had brought. Don Armbruster leaned across the table, and started a conversation. Francie sat in the shelter of Ryan's arm, recognizing the oddity of the scene. No man had ever held her so possessively in public. No man had ever kissed her so purposefully. She wouldn't have allowed it. But Ryan was playing his part as her husband. And for some bizarre reason, she was almost enjoying it.

She imagined the possibility of a man who loved her enough to come to her defense, a man who found it natural to express his tender feelings with a kiss. As the others talked, she glanced from one face to the next. Envy tinged the faces of the women. She gave each of them a self-satisfied smile.

They thought she was in the first bloom of new love, probably imagined her and Ryan having hot sex once or twice a night. They'd all been married for years, and no doubt the initial flame had faded to an ember. She glanced at balding, squatty Don Armbruster and tried to picture him and pencil-neck Peyton locked in a passionate clinch. A giggled escaped her. She covered her mouth with her hand. "I should go call the kids now."

"Got change, honey?"

She stood. "Yes, I do, sweetie. Will you miss me?"

"You know I will." He slid his warm hand up the back of her thigh in a suggestive caress. Francie's heart skipped one beat too many, and her breath stuck in her throat. "Hurry back," he said huskily.

Oh, he was playing this game to the hilt. She hadn't thought he had it in him. Or was he deliberately taunting her when he knew she couldn't do anything about it or risk exposing the truth to their audience?

"You know I will," she repeated, using his words as suggestively as he had. With one hand on his shoulder, she leaned down. Recognition flared in his dark eyes. His lips parted slightly in anticipation, and he met her mouth with his. He raised a hand to her neck and kissed her back as if they were lovers!

His lips were warm and pliant and tasted yeasty. The tips of their tongues touched, but his remained impassive, as though he were waiting...hoping... Heat curled right through Francie's chest and slipped lower.

Her mind registered the catcalls on either side of them, and she came to her senses and pulled away.

He gave her a smile that the others would see as a sexual implication. She would herself, if she didn't know better. It was deviltry, pure and simple.

Heart hammering, she made her way to a phone in the hallway near the rest rooms. She'd have to check her face after this call. She couldn't have any lipstick remaining, and her cheeks were probably as flushed as a case of hives.

It took her a couple of minutes to sort through the paper clips and coins on the bottom of her purse and come up with correct change.

She dialed and the phone rang twice.

"Hello?"

The woman's voice startled Francie. "Oh! I'm sorry, I must have the wrong number."

"No, no," the heavily accented voice replied. "Are you seeking the MacNairs?"

"Yes. Who *is* this?"

"This is Señora Miguel from housekeeping. I am attending young master MacNair until his parents can be located."

"What? Where is his sister? Put Alanna on, please."

"Miss Alanna is not here. The staff is searching for her now."

Francie listened to a couple more disjointed sentences before slamming down the receiver and running back to the table.

"We have to go!"

"What's wrong?" Ryan asked, setting down his beer.

"Alanna's not there. Alex said she's been missing since he went to the bathroom shortly after we left. He got scared and called the desk. They have a housekeeper with him until we get there."

Ryan stood. "Why didn't they call us? We left the number."

She shook her head. "I don't know."

The others settled up their tabs and rose to leave, too.

Ryan drove the rental as fast as he dared, his heart thudding, and his mind conjuring up images he couldn't let himself dwell on.

"It's going to be all right," Francie said to him. "This is just some mistake, and we're going to find her. She'll probably be back when we get there."

"I know, I know," he said, his voice unsteady. "You just hear such awful things. I mean, on the news every day."

"This is nothing like that," she reassured him. "There is a simple explanation."

He parked with a screech of tires, and they ran from the car to the hotel. They arrived at the desk out of breath. "I'm Ryan MacNair," he said. "What's going on?"

The young man standing behind the counter turned to exit a door and appeared in the lobby with them in seconds. "Your son called the desk earlier. He said your daughter was not in the room, and that he didn't know where she'd gone. We think he waited about an hour before he called. He thought she'd gone to the pool and would be back soon, but then, I guess he went looking for her himself and couldn't find her.

"I went and searched your room first, myself, thinking she might be playing a prank on her brother. We've had every available person searching the hotel and the surrounding streets since then. They meet back here every fifteen minutes for a check in. So far nothing."

Ryan ran a hand through his always impeccable hair, setting the waves in disarray. "I guess I need to see my son."

Francie thanked the assistant manager and followed.

The elevator took forever to arrive. Once inside, they stared at each other. He cut his glance toward the door and flexed his fingers impatiently. Finally the elevator reached their floor. Ryan was out the door and down the hall before she could catch her breath.

He had his plastic key out and the door open without waiting for her. She arrived to see Alex get up from the bed and run to his father. "I'm s-sorry, Dad. I didn't know what to do. I d-don't know what happened to her."

Ryan sat on the end of a bed and took Alex in his lap. He stroked his dark hair. "It's all right, son. Everything's going to be all right. Can you tell me exactly what happened?"

The tearful story sounded just as the manager had relayed it. Alex had gone into the bathroom and returned to find Alanna missing. He'd searched the room for her, thinking she was teasing, and then he'd become worried. After a while, he'd grown scared and ventured down to the pool area.

After that he'd come back and called the desk.

"Why didn't you call us?" Ryan asked.

"I forgot about that number," Alex wailed. "I picked up the phone and the man at the counter answered."

Ryan patted his back. "That's all right. You did just fine, and we're here now."

The dark-haired housekeeper stood. "I will help the others now. We will find your *niña*."

"Thank you," Francie said to her. The woman let herself out quietly.

"I have to go help, too," Ryan said, grimly.

Francie understood it was harder to wait here and do nothing. "Alex and I will stay together and wait for her to return."

"You didn't do anything wrong," Ryan said carefully, looking his son in the eye. "It was very smart of you to call the desk and ask for help." He got up and left the room.

Francie glanced at the clock and noted that it was after ten-thirty. She pulled back the covers on Ryan and Alex's bed, sat, and patted the mattress. "Come lie down. I'll sit with you."

"I'm scared," he sniffled.

"It's okay to be scared," she told him.

He padded to the bed and crawled between the sheets. Francie tucked him in and snuggled on top of the covers beside him. He seemed so small and helpless. What an enormous responsibility children were. She'd always known she wasn't cut out to be a mother, just as her parents weren't cut out to be parents. She had her career, and she hadn't time nor energy to maintain the physical and emotional well-being of another human being.

"When I was little, I had a dog for when I was scared," he said.

"A real dog or a stuffed dog?"

"A stuffed dog. But he was as good as a real dog."

"I bet he was. Where is he now?"

"Home. I don't take him with me places anymore. That's for babies."

"Well, you're sure not a baby."

"I cried."

"Everybody cries sometimes, Alex."

"They do?"

"Sure."

"When did you cry?"

Francie remembered only too well what it was like to be an alone and frightened child. "I cried when my mother left me."

"Your mother left you, too?"

She'd known he would grasp her story. It was something she had never shared with anyone else, but Alex was different. "My mother and my father left me."

"Both of them? Why'd they do that?"

"Oh," she said, brushing his hair back from his forehead. "They had careers. They were photojournalists."

"What's that?"

"They took pictures for newspapers and magazines. They were out of the country a lot. It was hard for them to keep me with them. So they left me with Nana."

"How old were you?"

"I was ready to start junior high. That was a problem, too. They never stayed in one place long enough for me to go to school."

"But you love Nana, don't you?"

"I love her very much. She took care of me and loved me and gave me a home. That's why I took her name. My parents' name was Karr, but I added Taylor onto it, because she was my real parent.

"But I'd only seen her a few times when my parents left me with her. I'd been moved from place to place and stayed with too many people to ever become attached to anyone."

"I don't remember my mother leaving," Alex said.

"Do you wish you could remember her?"

"Sometimes. Sometimes I hate her."

"It's okay to be mad at her," she told him. "But don't stay mad at her. You'll only hurt yourself."

"That's what my dad says."

"Well, listen to your dad. He's a smart guy."

"I know."

He snuggled closer. "I get mad at Alanna, too, but I love her. I don't want anything bad to happen to her."

"I know you love her," she said softly.

In seconds he was sound asleep.

Francie paced the floor for another half hour until she heard a commotion in the hall. She hurried out, closing the door behind her so Alex wouldn't be awakened.

Alanna's voice carried down the corridor, and relief swept through Francie as if it were a warm current. Ryan had his daughter by the arm. A few of the people who'd been at Quigley's followed them, including Becka and Shari, their husbands, and Tom Wallace from the rental place.

"Oh, thank God," Francie said, hurrying forward. "Why on earth you would pull such a fool stunt and scare me half to death is more than I'll ever understand," Ryan said angrily.

At the passion in his tone, Francie stopped her forward motion.

"Look at all these people you've put out," he went on. "The entire hotel staff has been searching for you."

"I don't care!" she shouted. "I told you I didn't want to come here. This hotel stinks! I didn't want to come because of *her!* You never spend any time with me, and when we finally go somewhere, it's to a stupid reunion in a stupid little town, all because of her!" Tears streamed down Alanna's cheeks, and the hurt and anger in her voice made it shake. "And that *stupid* woman has spoiled everything! *Everything!* I hate her!"

Ryan glanced up and saw Francie standing outside the room. He looked back at the half-dozen hotel patrons and staff who had heard Alanna's outburst. Francie noted Becka's and Shari's aghast expressions, and the embarrassment on the faces of the men.

Francie forced her feet into action. She walked right past Alanna and Ryan without a word, and stopped in front of the others. "Thank you, everyone, for your concern. We appreciate your help."

"We'll see you tomorrow, Francie," Shari said.

Subdued good-nights sounded, and the group moved to the elevator. She didn't even want to speculate as to what they were whispering about.

Francie walked back past Ryan and Alanna and stopped with her hand on the doorknob. "Do you have your key?"

Ryan moved behind her. Without saying a word about her locking herself out, he unlocked the door and ushered her in. She went into the bathroom, washed her face and returned. "I'll be down by the pool for a while."

"Francie—" he began.

"You two need some time alone together. Please wake up Alex and tell him his sister's safe."

A stricken look crossed Alanna's face. Francie knew she wasn't afraid of her father. He was angry, but he was a kind and gentle man. Alanna must have just realized the panic she had inflicted on her brother.

Without a backward glance, Francie left the MacNair family to themselves.

5

AN HOUR LATER, sitting at one of the small tables near the pool, Francie swirled the melting ice in her Coke and contemplated going back to the room. She'd watched couples and families returning to the rooms above, those whose doors opened onto the balconies.

It seemed everyone was paired off and grouped together. The entire civilized population moved in twos and fours and fives. She'd always considered herself self-sufficient, never lonely. Not until now, anyway. It was this town and the people she'd gone to school with and her grandmother that were making her feel this way. They'd pointed her out as an oddity for as long as she could remember.

Oh, Nana didn't mean to. She had good intentions. She just thought every woman should have a husband whether or not she needed or wanted one.

And the dating fiascoes... Idly Francie stopped the straw with her index finger and dribbled watery cola back into the glass. She'd tried her best to put those high school dates out of her mind. Rarely had she clicked with a guy, and if she had, something had come up to spoil the relationship.

Like Ted Chapman. Their interests had been fairly well matched, and he hadn't minded Nana's constant checks on their whereabouts; he'd even tolerated Francie's passion to take pictures everywhere they went.

The iguana had been the end of that.

Francie'd bought it at a carnival. She planned to place it in the neighbor kids' sandbox and take photos. Ted had hated it and refused to allow it in his car. She'd walked, the iguana tucked under her arm.

The pictures hadn't been outstanding. Nana hated it, too, so Francie'd sold the lizard to a pet store. Ted had never called again.

Whatever had made her think of that? She needed to get some sleep. She'd forgotten the room key again, and Ryan and the kids might be sleeping. Maybe she could get an extra one at the desk. The entire hotel staff knew her by now; ID wouldn't be a problem.

The window where she'd purchased her soft drink had closed, and the lights in the small restaurant turned out one by one. A lone swimmer, an older gentleman, sliced through the water.

"Francie?"

"Oh!" She jerked her arm back at the touch, and cola shot out of the straw across Ryan's shirtfront. Recognizing him, Francie stood. "Oh, I'm sorry. You startled me."

"It's all right." He accepted the damp napkin she offered and dabbed at the spots ineffectually. "You've been gone a long time."

"You needed time with your daughter."

He gestured for her to sit again, and she did.

"Are they both okay?"

"Yes. They're fine. She's in deep trouble, but she's asleep now." He sat in the chair opposite her and placed his forearms on the table. He watched the man swimming for a few minutes. "I'm sorry about the things she said—especially in front of everyone."

"You don't have to apologize for her."

"She will apologize, too."

"Don't make her do that, Ryan. She hates me enough already."

He tipped his head as though he were uncomfortable with her words or the situation. In the glow of the soft lights that lit the pool, she studied his handsome features.

"It's okay," she reiterated. "You can't force her to like someone she doesn't want to."

He fixed his dark eyes on her face. "Her rudeness is unacceptable."

"She has enough to deal with at this age without me adding to her problems," she said.

"She added to her own problems," he said. "She should not have left Alex alone in that room. She knows that." His tired eyes and grim mouth revealed the extent of his exhaustion.

"Where was she?" she asked.

"She hid in one of the conference rooms in the dark."

"She did it for attention, you know."

"That's the wrong way to get attention."

"Kids don't think about that." She shifted in her chair. "They're hurting and they just do things. Her resentment of me and the time I've taken from your family is justified." Francie glanced away and then back. "I do things without thinking them all the way through, too, so I know how ideas seem good at first, then get kind of out of hand."

"You're defending her."

She gave him a crooked smile and placed her hand on his. "Yeah. Don't punish her on my account, okay?"

He glanced at her hand on his. She pulled it away self-consciously.

"Okay," he said finally.

She smiled.

The lone swimmer splashed out of the water. They glanced up as he dried off and left.

Silence stretched between them.

"Their mother just left," he said. "Packed up and took off."

The subject surprised her. Especially after his re-action that afternoon when she'd questioned him about Alex's comments. "You were right earlier. You don't have to tell me."

"I know I don't. But it's part of who Alanna is. And why she does some of the things she does."

Francie nodded her understanding. "You had no warning that your wife was going to leave?"

"I knew she was unhappy. She did okay with Alanna when she was a baby. Left her with sitters a lot. Alex was an accident, and she was unhappy from the minute she knew he was on the way. She was in such denial, I couldn't even get her to the doctor until she was five months along. She slept all the time while she was pregnant." He wadded the napkin into a tiny ball.

"I thought it was just her condition, you know, that she'd get over it. But she got more and more depressed."

Francie listened without saying anything, hearing the frustration he tried to keep from his tone.

"She became self-absorbed," he said. "They needed her, but she didn't want to do anything or go anywhere. I insisted she see a doctor, and she was better for a while as long as she took her medication. But she didn't want to take it, and she'd slide back into her melancholy."

"That must have been awful," she sympathized.

"I came home one day to find her gone. She hadn't even called the sitter. Alex had lain in his bed all day, wet and crying. I found Alanna in our bed. She must have cried herself to sleep. She wasn't even three yet."

"Oh, Ryan, that's awful," Francie said, blinking back tears and swallowing a lump in her throat. She knew his intent in telling her hadn't been to gain her pity.

"I was used to taking care of them with the help of sitters by then," he said. "When I realized she wasn't coming home, I hired a live-in nanny. Her name was Chris, and she loved the kids. She stayed with us until she got married a few years ago. Since the kids were older, I just hired a housekeeper."

"It's fortunate you could afford to hire help."

"Fortunate?" he said, looking up with a frown.

"I wasn't making light of your situation. I just meant that a good many men wouldn't have had the means to keep the children with them, and do as well as you did for them. A lot of men wouldn't have wanted to try without a woman to do most of it.''

"I did the best I could," he said.

"I know that. You've done a great job with them."

He raised a brow.

"I mean it. All teenagers act like that. Worse."

"I guess." He shrugged, and leaned back, glancing across the now deserted pool. "I don't know why I told you all that. It's not something I talk about."

"It helps me understand the kids better," she said.

His dark eyes came back to her face. "And why would you want to understand them?"

"Well…" She looked at her hands. "I don't. But now I'll know to be wary of Alanna when we're in public situations."

His gaze warmed her, and she refused to look up. She should have known better than to take an interest in hearing about his wife. She didn't need this man to become a real person to her. He was just a means to get her through the week and keep Nana happy. If she were to think of him in any other manner, she would have to wonder what kind of a woman would walk out on this guy.

He was the perfect catch Nana had believed she'd needed.

And she would have to wonder how hard all this was on him.

Once again she'd been impulsive, and once again, she was seeing repercussions. When would she learn? She caught herself twisting the wedding band on her finger and dropped her hands self-consciously.

"Don't you think we'd better head back?" he asked after several minutes.

She stood, and together they walked down a corridor to the elevator. The deserted lobby provided no distractions, so they watched the numbers above the door. The elevator arrived, and he ushered her in.

Francie glanced at his spotted shirtfront, then at his face. The image of kissing him so boldly at Quigley's that evening rose up in her mind and amazed her, embarrassed her. In front of her old classmates and as long as it was a performance, they'd both been daring and uninhibited. Alone and confined like this, they awkwardly avoided each other's eyes.

The elevator stopped, and they walked to the room. Ryan inserted his card. The image of doing this with him under different circumstances flashed before her. She couldn't help wondering what it would be like to stay in a hotel room with Ryan MacNair…without his children along…with a different plan in mind.

Cheeks uncomfortably warm, she entered ahead of him and hurried about her nightly routine. She glanced at both of the kids in the dark, Alex settled in the bed, Alanna on the floor. Unexpected tears came to her eyes at the reminder of how much the insecure girl resented her.

Francie climbed into bed and listened to the sounds of Ryan turning off the bathroom light and getting into bed. Even if the entire population were paired off, she could still be herself. Francie Karr-Taylor was satisfied with her life just the way it was. Wasn't she?

"It said on that poster that today was a roller-skating party!" Alex shouted.

"Is that right?" Ryan's deep velvet voice interrupted Francie's sleep. "I still haven't seen the schedule."

She rolled over to see him being bounced awake as Alex jumped enthusiastically on their bed.

"Sit down, Alex," he commanded gently.

The boy sat by aiming his feet in the air and dropping on his behind. Ryan grunted with the impact of seventy pounds of child against his hip.

Alex discovered Francie awake and bounded from their bed to hers. "You're awake!"

"It's not easy to sleep through your morning calisthenics," his father said. Francie avoided looking at his bare chest and shoulders above the sheet.

"When are we gonna roller-skate?" the boy asked, his gray-blue eyes wide with excitement.

"That's not until tonight," she replied. "I have the schedule in my purse. I think it's at six-thirty. I thought I'd visit Nana today. You guys can do whatever you'd like."

"I want to visit Nana, too!" Alex cried. "We can go, too, can't we, Dad?"

Ryan sat up and scratched his head, and Francie stifled a giggle at his tousled head of hair. "What would you like to do, Alanna?" he asked.

Francie turned to see the girl sitting in one of the wing chairs, her knees up under her nightgown. She shrugged. "We can go see her if Alex wants to."

Her guilt over frightening Alex the night before was apparent in her congenial reply.

"We could do a little shopping this morning," Francie suggested, hoping to catch Alanna's interest and lighten the mood that had been created the night before.

Alanna met her eyes, but replied only, "Whatever."

They took turns showering and dressing, ate breakfast by the pool again and again Ryan insisted on driving. Francie directed him to the mall.

"Alanna and I will meet you back here in an hour," she said.

Alanna's expression revealed displeasure, but she said nothing.

Ryan glanced from one to the other and nodded.

"Come on, Dad. Let's go to the baseball card shop." Alex grabbed his father's hand and dragged him away.

Alanna gazed down the mall as though she were bored already.

"Anything special you want?" Francie asked. "A haircut? A dress?"

Alanna shook her head.

"Well, let's just look then." She led her into a department store. Alanna didn't want to try the perfumes or sample the lotions. They passed the purses and the girl said, "You should get one of those, so you're not always hunting through your purse, holding everyone up."

Francie glanced at the organizer she'd pointed to. "That's a good idea."

After a few minutes, she selected one and wrote a check for it. They remained at the counter where Francie dumped out the contents of her old purse and stored them neatly in the compartmentalized bag.

A photo wallet lay flopped open to a picture of two adults and a toddler.

"Who's that?" Alanna asked.

Francie glanced at it. "My parents and me."

"Are they dead?"

"They are now."

"Alex told me what you said about them."

"It's not a secret."

"Did you ever think they didn't love you?"

The question caught Francie off guard, but it had seemed sincere. "Sometimes. Nana said they loved me. But I wondered why they didn't love me enough to keep me with them."

"Parents are supposed to take care of you," Alanna said.

Francie had finished loading her purse, and tossed the old one into a wastebasket behind the counter. "Yes, they are. So I guess it makes a kid wonder if there's something wrong with them if their parents run out, huh?"

Alanna still held the miniature album. She closed it and handed it to Francie. "It wasn't your fault," the girl said. "The problem was theirs."

The adult-sounding comment brought Francie's brow up.

"That's what the counselors told me," Alanna said with a dismissive shrug.

"They were right." Francie led her toward the clothing. "But it doesn't make up for the years that I didn't have a parent like everyone else."

Alanna gave her a noncommittal shrug.

Francie found the lingerie department. "I need a few things here. How about you?"

Alanna glanced around in dismay, her cheeks reddening.

Francie had finally figured out that Alanna's slouching posture was caused by embarrassment over her developing body. The girl's father obviously hadn't thought to consider her maturing figure when he'd bought her school clothes.

Francie sought out the salesperson, a friendly gray-haired woman who smelled of expensive powdery perfume. "Will you measure us and bring us a few bras to try on?" she asked.

Alanna looked at her with shock written plainly across her face. "You'll never see this lady again," Francie whispered.

The woman led them into separate dressing rooms.

Twenty-five minutes later, Alanna joined her, her face flushed beet red, but her posture straighter. "I can't believe you made me do that."

"I don't think seven bras apiece is too many," Francie said. "Do you?"

Alanna rolled her eyes and followed Francie toward the shoes.

NANA WAS OVERJOYED to see the children again. This time they joined her in the day room, where the residents gathered to watch television and play games. The room had a wall of windows and sliding doors, giving it an open and airy feeling. Francie opened the box of chocolates she and Alanna had purchased, and the confection enticed several visitors, including nurses, past their table. Nana licked chocolate from her fingers and grinned with delight.

Alex had immediately climbed into Nana's lap. She hugged him soundly and showed him how to see what kind of center the candy had by poking a hole in the bottom of the chocolate.

"Tell me how you met my granddaughter, Jim."

Ryan glanced at Francie in immediate dismay.

She shrugged.

"Well, I—I had asked all of the jewelers in the Chicago area to notify me if they bought or appraised a certain piece of jewelry I was looking for." He explained about his grandmother's brooch. "Your granddaughter acquired the piece at an auction and had it appraised. I sought her out to buy the piece for Alanna."

Nana patted Ryan's hand. "That's a lovely story. And when you saw her, did you know you loved her right away?"

Ryan glanced from Nana's weathered face to Francie's ivory-complexioned one. "I knew she was unlike anyone I'd ever met before."

Nana cackled. "That's the truth, isn't it? How'd you convince her to give up her single life she values so much?"

"I'm irresistible," he replied.

Even Francie had to laugh at that one.

"Let's go see the ducks," Alex suggested.

"Push us, Jim," Nana directed.

"Is Alex getting too heavy for you?" he asked.

"I'll tell him when he is," she replied in her no-nonsense tone.

Ryan, getting used to responding to his new name, glanced at Alanna, but she didn't seem jealous of the attention Nana bestowed on the boy. In fact she carried herself a little straighter today for some odd reason. And he didn't think it was the new pair of shoes. She seemed less angry, or perhaps what he was seeing was repentance; in any case the lack of hostility came as a relief.

After a lengthy walk, they wheeled Nana to her room. The facility and the old woman's surroundings were impressive. This home must cost a pretty penny, and he wondered how much of the cost Francie provided. It was obvious that the old woman meant everything to her.

Alex had taken to her from the start, and seeing the two of them together pleased and worried Ryan at the same time. Alex knew this was a show. After this week he wouldn't see Francie's grandmother again.

That, too, was one of those things Francie had spoken of that had seemed like a good idea at the time. Now, all the details he hadn't considered were cropping up.

Alex was starved for the attention of these two women. But growing attached to either one of them would only cause heartache later on. Watching his son with Francie and her grandmother had a painful effect on Ryan's chest. The sight pointed out vividly how much the boy had missed having a woman around to spoil and coddle and love him. It pointed out, too, how sadly lacking all their lives were.

And he was partly to blame for it. He worked long

hours and had depended on Chris, and then Mrs. Nelson, to meet the kids' needs. He'd had to provide for them, though. His job granted enough for them to live comfortably and have things many other children didn't have.

"Who are these pictures of, Nana?" Alex asked, looking over the woman's possessions.

"Those are my children."

"Who are your children?"

"Francesca's father was my child. I have another son, too."

"Oh." Alex studied the photographs. "Where is he?"

"He lives in Anchorage. He's a professor."

"Is that far?"

"Yes, it's far," Alanna said. "It's in Alaska."

"Oh. Does he come here?"

"Not very often. He calls me sometimes. Francesca is the one who comes to visit me."

Ryan listened with half an ear. He had been trying to fool himself, but something about this week and these women made him take a long, hard look at reality. Time at home with his children had always pointed out the glaring absence of their mother. It had been more painful to stay at home with them than to work long hours.

He was as much at fault for deserting them as their mother had been.

6

I'LL JUST WATCH," Ryan said, trying to edge his way to the tables behind a waist-high barrier around the skating-rink floor.

"No, Dad, you gotta skate with us," Alex cried, pulling on his arm. "It won't be fun without you."

Guilt over his revelation that afternoon still ate at him. He could probably count on one hand the number of times in the last year he'd done things with his kids. And this was supposed to be their vacation time. So what if he made a fool of himself? "All right."

Alex whooped and ran ahead to the rental counter. Alanna followed more sedately. But Francie. Francie had a grin on her face and a spring in her step that he didn't like one bit.

Skates rented and laced, Francie and his children rolled across the carpet toward the highly polished floor. As a body, they turned and looked back at him expectantly.

"Dad?" Alanna said.

Hanging on to the table, he stood.

"You've *never* done this before?" Francie asked.

He shook his head and reached for the wall, making his way slowly, awkwardly, toward the opening into the room that yawned, in his imagination, as wide and incomprehensible as a black hole.

"Not exactly a chess club activity, eh, Mac?"

He ignored her. Many of her classmates and their families had arrived and were rolling around the rink like pros. At least nobody was paying any attention to his clumsy progress.

"I'll stand here and watch a minute," he said.

"Okay. We'll come back for ya." Alex and his sister and Francie moved into the flow of skaters. Francie skated as fearlessly and purposefully as she did everything else, weaving in and out of the crowd, turning to take pictures of Alex and Alanna behind her. She skated forward, backward, without a care or a pause.

She rolled past Ryan, a smile on her pretty face, her soft-looking hair flying behind, the ever-present camera strap around her neck. Alex passed next, and Alanna followed. After several times around they returned, smiles lighting their faces. "Okay, come on."

"Maybe I'd better stay up here on the carpet," he said, already shaky on his feet.

"Come on, you'll get the hang of it," Francie coaxed.

Hanging onto the wall, he sidestepped his way to the floor. Several skaters whooshed by, and he let them pass before venturing farther.

"Take my hand," Francie offered.

He raised a brow.

"Come on. Trust me."

"I've seen your driving, remember?"

She was a dangerous person to trust, he knew, but

clinging to any tenuous lifeline seemed imperative at this moment. He grasped her hand.

"We'll just stay here close to the wall for a while," she promised.

"Thank you." His feet wanted to go in different directions, rolling back and forth in a seesaw motion. "This is harder than it looks."

"You have to work your skates," she said, "don't let them work you. Walk into it, like this."

"I think I should stay on the carpet."

"You can't skate on the carpet. Now take a few sliding strides forward."

He did as she instructed and made a little progress.

"There you go—confidence is the key."

He was skating now, away from the wall, but still clinging to her hand. They made it halfway around the rink before he lost his balance and had to grab the wall.

"You're doing great," she said.

"Look, Dad!" Alex came up from behind and skated past, a wide grin splitting his face.

Ryan gained a little momentum, getting into the flow of the skaters with Francie's help. "You can let go now," he said.

She did.

They made another half turn around the rink. Now it felt as if he was going way too fast. "How do you stop?" he called.

"You slow down and then use the toe stop," she called. "But don't try it until—"

He tipped his toe forward and the rubber stopped his foot cold. The rest of his body propelled forward, and he splatted on the wooden floor with a resounding *thwack.*

"Of course, that's another way to stop." Francie glided to a stop beside him. "You all right?"

"I'm just fine," he said, sitting up. His palms stung and his teeth felt numb.

"Oh, you've skinned your chin," she said, sympathetically.

"I'm lucky I didn't break my leg and an arm and loose my teeth," he grumbled.

Alanna and Alex each skated to a smooth stop beside him. "Awesome landing, Dad!" Alex cried.

"Are you all right?" Alanna asked.

"Did everybody in the place see it?" he asked, now crawling to the wall.

"No, not everyone," Francie denied.

He kneaded his palm. "Did you get a picture in case someone missed it?"

"It *was* pretty loud," Alex argued, and Francie cast a wide-eyed look meant to stifle him. "But I don't think everybody saw it," he added quickly.

"No, there might have been *someone* in the bathroom," Ryan said dryly.

Alanna giggled, and he looked up in surprise.

"Sorry, Dad. I couldn't help it. I've just never seen you so…so…" At a loss for words, she shrugged.

He brushed his palms together.

Laughter erupted. Ryan glanced toward the tables on the other side of the barrier where Don Armbruster, Becka, J.J. and Shari sat like a row of judges and held up napkins with numbers from zero to nine scribbled on them.

"Very funny," he muttered. "Does Armbruster have a pair of skates on?"

"Dad?" Alanna said.

"What?"

"You'll never have to see these people again after this week."

He glanced up to see her grinning, a look of pure enjoyment on her young face. What was a little humiliation compared to giving his children the joy they deserved? "That's true enough, I guess."

She and Francie exchanged a look he didn't comprehend.

Hoping to regain at least a small measure of dignity, he got to his feet and stood against the wall.

"Let me get a washie out of my bag for your chin," Francie said. "I know right where they are." She skated off and returned in a flash to dab his chin. "Does it hurt?"

"Not much. You really did know where it was."

"You have to get back on the horse that threw you, you know," she said, her blue eyes wide and serious.

"Come on, Alex, they got free hot dogs over here!" Donald Armbruster Junior called to Alex, and Alex skated toward the refreshment stand.

Francie and Alanna urged Ryan back into the flow of skaters, and by the time they were ready for a break, he was skating on his own and proud of himself for only falling down two more times.

They joined the other adults at the tables and watched the kids for a while. Ryan removed his skates and, grateful for the solid footing, bought a round of colas.

"Hi, Francie." A slender man with thinning fair hair and a toothy smile greeted her.

"Ted. I hadn't seen you yet. Did you just get in town?"

"Yeah. I'm living in Rockford. Drove over for the rest of the week."

Francie seemed almost reserved when she spoke to the man, not like her gregarious manner with everyone else, arousing Ryan's curiosity.

"Ted, this is my husband, Ryan MacNair. Ryan, Ted Chapman."

"Hi, Ted." Ryan shook his hand.

Peyton spotted them and came over to stand beside their table, too. "Hello, Ted, how are you? Is Marian with you?"

"I'm divorced," he said simply.

"Oh," she said, clucking sadly. "There are just so many domestic problems everywhere you turn. So many dysfunctional families." She looked right at Francie, the implication plain. She patted Ryan's arm. "Hang in there, darling."

She moved off, leaving Francie glaring.

Ryan took her hand and rubbed his thumb across the backs of her fingers. She closed her eyes, briefly, then gave him a smile.

"Still taking pictures?" Ted asked Francie.

She nodded.

"Taken any good iguana shots lately?"

"No, not lately."

Shari Donegan discovered Ted and drew him into a conversation with her and Becka's husband.

"Iguana shots?" Ryan asked later, as they got into the car and buckled their seat belts.

She gave him a quick version of the lizard story. Francie must have seemed as odd to Ted back then as she had to Ryan the first time he'd met her.

"Dad?" his daughter said softly from the back seat.

"What, Alanna?"

"You and Francie can meet the others tonight. I will stay with Alex. You can trust me."

Her words touched his father's heart. "I do trust you, Alanna. Thank you for the offer. Would you like to go, Francie?"

She looked over at him in surprise. "Actually I wouldn't. Why don't we take the kids to a movie?"

She no longer seemed so odd to him. He understood that she felt out of place with her old classmates. The only reason she'd come to Springdale was to ease her grandmother's worries by convincing everyone she was happily married. "I'd like that," he said.

And he discovered he meant it.

THE KIDS TALKED them into a late swim after the movie. Francie cut through the water vigorously. She'd be exhausted when they got back to the room. She'd been enjoying her swim immensely when the Armbrusters showed up, followed by several other families.

"Hey, Alex," Donald Junior called. "I got some Gummi Bears!"

Alex climbed the ladder and joined Donald at a table.

"Dad, there's a show I wanted to see tonight. Is it okay if I go up to the room and watch it?" Alanna asked.

"Let me walk you up," he said.

Francie was talking with Becka when Ryan returned and slipped into the water beside her. "Did you get her settled?" she asked.

"She's fine. She was just tired."

"Girls that age need time alone," Francie said.

"You mean it's not unusual for her to want to spend so much time alone in her room?"

"Not at all," Becka agreed.

From behind, Ryan placed his arms around Francie's waist and pulled her back against him in the water. "Stay here," he whispered.

Her bare back brushed the hair on his chest, and the backs of her legs came against his thighs. Enough was enough when it came to this showing off business, but something kept her where he'd pulled her.

Becka pushed away and swam off, as if leaving them to their private cuddle.

"I know that man," he said into her ear, and a shiver of pleasure ran across her shoulder.

"What man?"

"That one. Up there."

She glanced up and caught sight of the man in dark trousers and a sport shirt letting himself into one of the rooms on the balcony above.

"Of all the places to run into someone I know," he muttered.

"How fast can you grow a beard?"

"I've never grown one."

"It was a joke, Mac. Who is he?"

"He's a historian. Owns an enormous Abe Lincoln collection." His low voice rumbled in his chest against her back. "We've had it on display at the museum."

"What's he doing here?" she asked rhetorically.

"Making my life more insane," he replied.

"He didn't see you."

"No." The man had gone in and closed the door. "Let's go."

She swam to the side with him, and they got out and towel-dried. He held her terry-cloth robe open for her to slip into. Francie caught Shari's expression as she watched them leave. She smiled a satisfied smile and waved.

Ryan got Alex and they took the elevator to their room, another day put to bed.

THE FOLLOWING EVENING was Springdale High School's production of *Grease*. The couples met for dinner preceding the event, filling a banquet room in a local restaurant.

The salad dressing passed while Ryan visited the rest room with Alex.

"What kind does Ryan like?" Lisa Richards asked from the chair on the opposite side of Ryan's empty one. She held the tray, ready to spoon dressing and pass it on.

"Uh." Francie racked her brain for what kind of

dressing she'd seen him order if any, and couldn't remember.

Lisa waited.

Her husband and, farther down, the Armbrusters waited.

Francie glanced in the direction of the rest rooms, praying he'd be coming.

She glanced at Alanna, but the girl deliberately kept her eyes on her own plate and offered no help.

"He'll eat anything—except blue cheese," she added, just in case he hated it.

Shrugging, Lisa spooned something on Ryan's salad and passed the tray.

On the other side of the table Alanna chose dressing for Alex and spared Francie that decision. "Thanks a lot, girlfriend," Francie said barely loud enough for Alanna to hear.

"Making me buy underwear didn't make you my friend," she said with her usual haughty flair.

Francie had thought they'd made a little progress, but obviously she'd been fooling herself. Alanna didn't like her, and she had no intention of trying. Francie could handle that.

Ryan and Alex finally returned.

"All this has to be costing quite a bit," Ryan said softly from beside her. "You've been paying for meals and activities, not to mention the hotel and the plane fare." He reached inside his jacket and withdrew a slip of paper.

She cut her tomato slice. "What's that?"

"A list of the meals and expenses. Some of them I'm not sure of because you've taken care of everything. I know you bought Alanna something at the mall, because I saw the bags, but she won't say.''

"It was part of the deal, remember? I'm getting what I wanted.'' She took the paper from his fingers and wadded it into a ball.

He gave her a puzzled look, but something more lurked behind those dark eyes.

"What?'' she asked.

"*Are* you getting what you wanted?'' he asked.

She had no idea what he was getting at. "Is this really the time and place for this discussion?''

"Let me pay for dinner this time. My kids have been having a good time.''

Oh, yeah, Alanna was having the time of her life. "What about you?''

"What do you mean?''

"Have you been miserable?''

"You shouldn't have to pay for all the entertainment is what I'm saying.''

"No, Mac, what you're doing is avoiding the question.''

"Is this really the time and place for this discussion?'' he asked, using her own words in retaliation.

Francie couldn't help a grin. "You're not such a stuffed shirt, after all, you know that?''

"And you're—never mind.''

"No. Go ahead.''

"You're the ditzy blonde I suspected was in there all along.''

"Thank you.''

"You're welcome.''

He took a bite of his salad. "What is this?''

"Looks like Thousand Island."

"My favorite."

"Really?"

"No. I like blue cheese."

"Figures. They were in a hurry, and I didn't know your preference."

"So, where do you live in Chicago?" Lisa asked from Ryan's other side.

Peyton's long neck stretched as she strained to hear his reply.

He glanced at Francie, and she quickly stuffed a bite of salad into her mouth and gestured for him to reply.

"One of the North Shore suburbs," he replied. "Winnetka. It's on the lake."

Even Francie's eyes widened. The area he indicated was one of pricey estates with private beaches.

"Wasn't the house they filmed in *Home Alone* in Winnetka?" Lisa's husband, Robert asked. "I only know that because my brother lives in Lincoln Park, and he mentioned it."

Ryan didn't seem to know, but Alanna confirmed Robert's question.

"So, how long does it take you to get to work?" Shari asked from the other side of the table, and Francie hadn't even realized she was listening.

She placed a tomato slice into her mouth and chewed slowly.

"About thirty-five minutes taking Lake Shore Drive," Ryan replied. "But the drive along the lake is so pretty that even in traffic, we don't mind."

Francie leaned into him to whisper, "Do you have

a map in your pocket, too? You could show them that.''

He ignored her jibe.

''I thought your studio was in your home,'' Shari said. ''That's what I'd heard, anyway.''

''Oh, it is,'' Francie said, finally having to answer. ''I drive into the city for business. And, of course, for pleasure.''

''What's your favorite restaurant?'' Lisa asked. ''We'll have to try it out when we visit Robert's brother.''

''The 95th,'' Francie replied. She'd never been there, but she'd seen the advertisements for the plush, glass-enclosed restaurant lounge at the top of the Hancock Building.

''They have the best Thousand Island dressing,'' Ryan commented from beside her.

Francie covered her lips with her napkin to hide a smile.

''Take your kids to the zoo, too,'' Alanna piped up, and Lisa showed interest. ''There's all kinds of animals and paddleboats to rent. *Daddy* takes us all the time.''

A disturbed look crossed Ryan's face. ''I was thinking we could go when we get back home,'' he said to his daughter.

Doubt clouded her features as if she were asking, ''For real?''

''Would you like that, Alanna?''

A blush tinged her cheeks. ''Yes.''

''It's a date then,'' he said, and Francie heard the promise in his tone.

Alanna glanced at Alex, and then gave her father a hesitant smile.

By theater time, Alanna and Alex had bonded with the other children and sat in a cluster near the front.

"Alanna seems to have found a friend," Francie commented, watching her chatter with a girl about the same age.

"Looks that way," Ryan replied.

They had about a twenty-minute wait until the production began.

"You don't think she'll say anything, do you?" Francie asked, leaning to whisper. "I mean about us. Something that could get back to that girl's parents?"

"I don't think so. I made it clear to them that the secret must be kept in order to keep the bargain. She doesn't have anything of her mother's. The brooch is important to her, even as young as she is. Maybe more so because Nikki left her."

"Was that her name?"

He nodded. A few minutes later, he said, "I think I owe you."

"You paid for dinner."

"No, not that. For this week. For opening my eyes. I was hiding in my work, avoiding my kids without knowing it or realizing why. It hurts to know that part of Alanna's fantasy in this game we're playing includes trips to the zoo. It's a normal family thing, but she had to make it up."

"You've never taken her?"

He shook his head regretfully. "No. She went with her school once."

"You'll fix that," Francie said.

He turned his attention to the curtained stage.

His stuffy workaholic demeanor was a cover-up for a lot of pain and uncertainty. Underneath that Armani suit beat the heart of a loving father and a man with as many hopes and dreams as the next guy. The thought of how he'd been hurt disturbed Francie in a way she wouldn't have expected.

Once again, Francie regretted peeling back the layers and discovering the man beneath them. She couldn't afford for Ryan MacNair to become a real person to her. He was a means to pacify and please her grandmother, and nothing more.

The lights dimmed, and anticipatory silence filled the theater. The scent of his unique aftershave drifted to her. His warmth emanated along her side. Her gaze dropped to his hand on his knee in the darkness, and for some unexplainable reason her heart tripped a little faster.

Yes, he was a real man. A handsome, rich, complicated man whose presence rocked her already precarious thinking. But he wasn't for her. The kind of life that involved a family wasn't for her. She'd made her decision years ago, a decision to absorb herself in her career. She'd risked a lot and given up too much to change her way of thinking now.

She was not the wife and mother type.

And until now that had never bothered her.

7

FRANCIE LOVED THE high schoolers' rendition of *Grease*. She clapped and cheered, and praised each one of the performers during the refreshment time in the gym afterward.

"*This* is where you went to high school?" Alanna said, looking around with a lack of appreciation. She'd appeared wearing a vivid fire engine red shade of lipstick and enough mascara to fill all the cracks along Interstate 94.

Francie glanced around the small gymnasium that had once seemed so huge and intimidating during basketball games and Friday night sock hops. "This is it."

"Where did you get that makeup, Alanna?" her father asked, in a horrified tone.

"Some of us girls put it on in the bathroom," she replied.

"You shouldn't use other people's cosmetics."

Francie gave Alanna a knowing girl look, and rolled her eyes.

"Besides, it makes you look like a hooker," he added.

"What's a hooker?" Alex asked, just coming up beside Francie.

"Never mind," Ryan said. "But you don't need to look like one, Alanna."

"You treat me like a baby, Dad," Alanna said, her cheeks turning pink. She glanced around. "I'm old enough to wear makeup."

"No, you're not old enough to wear makeup. You're twelve."

"Maybe if your lipstick was a soft shade of pink. That would be pretty," Francie said to Alanna, and to Ryan, "And then you wouldn't mind, so much, would you? I have some in my bag."

Alanna turned on her. "I don't need your help. I can talk to my father without you butting in, can't I? You're not my mother."

"I'll handle this," Ryan said to Francie, his tone soft but stern enough to let her know she'd been dismissed.

Alex slipped his hand into Francie's, whether for his own comfort or for hers, she didn't know. She grasped it gratefully. Unexpected tears smarted behind her eyes, and she blinked, turning away, castigating herself for getting involved in the father-daughter encounter. Their argument was none of her business.

But she hated to see Alanna embarrassed when her self-esteem was so obviously fragile. She led Alex to the punch table and the teenager standing behind the bowl filled a clear plastic cup for each of them.

"It was a cool show, wasn't it?" Alex asked.

She nodded. "I liked it a lot."

"Maybe someday I can be in a play like that."

"You can if you want to."

"Will you come watch me?"

Francie's guard had been temporarily lowered, and his earnest young gaze zinged an arrow to her heart. It was the first mention anyone had made of a relationship continuing after this week. Their understanding had been that this would be their one and only time together, and when the week was over, they'd gratefully go their separate ways as though they'd never met.

Francie studied Alex's solemn young face, his narrow chin and the sprinkling of freckles across his nose.

That would be impossible.

"When that time comes, and you still want me there, you ask your father. If it's all right with him, I'll come."

"Cool!" he said and grinned. "Maybe Nana can come, too."

Tears sprang to her eyes again. Nana would not be around when Alex reached high school. Francie would have enough trouble facing that when the time came. "Maybe," she said.

The crowd dispersed a few minutes later, and the somber foursome walked to the rental car. Alex was the only one who spoke as they rode to the hotel, his enthusiasm over the play still high.

"I'll be up later," Francie said, leaving them at the elevator. She bought a blended drink at the window and sat beside the pool, nursing it and her bruised feelings.

If this was what parenthood was all about, she was better off than she'd even dreamed. Why had Nana ever wished this on her? Being self-reliant was better than being stuck with an egotistical man and mouthy children.

No, thank you. Her career decision suited her just fine. Nobody told her what to do. No one demanded her time and attention. She and Stanley got along just fine together. Stanley only required feeding and litter box changing. He didn't wear clothes to grow out of and he never smarted off.

Lisa and Robert and a few others had left early and were using the pool. Idly Francie watched the couple. They'd separated themselves from the rest and were nestled in the shallow end of the pool, speaking with their heads together.

After a few minutes, they called good-night and walked up the stairs to the balcony above, Robert's arm around her shoulders.

No show. The real thing.

The statistics were more convincing, however. Considering Peyton and Becka and Ted Chapman, as well as being on the fringes of the MacNair family, convinced her she'd chosen right.

A week of marriage was long enough for her, thank you very much.

The hour grew late, and Francie had grown tired. She waited for the elevator. It arrived, and the doors opened. She faced a surprised Ryan, who was just preparing to step out.

She entered, and he stepped back in.

She leaned around him to press the button, and noted he'd removed the suit jacket and tie and unbuttoned the top two buttons of his shirt. He still smelled great.

"You all right?" he asked.

"Fine. Why wouldn't I be?"

"I'm sorry about earlier. I was terse with you."

"You were perfectly right. How you discipline your daughter is none of my business."

"I wasn't disciplining her."

"Okay. You were criticizing her."

"I wasn't criticizing her. I'm her father. She's twelve years old."

"As you've pointed out to all of us."

His exasperation was evident in his tense posture. He gestured with one hand. "Look, it's tough being a parent, cut me a little slack, will you?"

She crossed her arms and leaned back into the wide metal handrail. "Sure. All you need."

"Francie." He stepped forward and cupped her elbows.

She raised a hand instinctively, and placed her fingertips against his shirtfront. It was warm, and beneath it his heart beat steadily. "I was wrong. You *are* a stuffed shirt. You're uptight and rigid with yourself and with your kids, and you don't know how to cut loose."

"I skated," he said defensively.

She raised one eyebrow. "What you did can't really be called skating." At his wounded look, she cut him the slack he'd requested. "Okay, you skated," she agreed. She took her hand from his chest and tapped her temple. "But up here, Mac, your inhibitions are more than social restraint."

"So, I don't blab my every thought like you do—"

"I don't!"

"You do."

"You're just repressed."

"Oh, and what is the cause of this psychological repression, Dr. Francesca? Is it Freudian? Jungian perhaps? Maybe if I wasn't sexually frustrated, I'd pull out all the stops and run wild."

"Shut up."

He did. For about ten seconds. The elevator came to a stop, and behind Ryan the doors opened. "I said I was sorry," he tried again.

"Yes, you did. Now move out of the way." She tried to step around him, but he blocked her. In the brief glimpse she had of the hallway, she spotted Becka Crow carrying an ice bucket.

"I forgive you," she said.

His expression smoothed out.

She stepped against him, wrapped her arms around his neck and kissed him with a groan, as though she couldn't wait until they got to their room.

He caught her around the waist, and balanced them, his response more shock than passion.

That changed in a heartbeat. She sensed the joining of their lips change to a mutual exploration. His taste created a hunger for more.

He wrapped one arm across her back and drew her flush against him. She slanted her head, and aligned their mouths more perfectly. His tongue dipped out to test her inner lip, surprising her with the warm tactile sensation. She inhaled sharply, breathing him in, using every sense she possessed to enjoy this kiss, forgetting Becka in the hallway, forgetting everything but the confusion he created in her head and her heart.

He pulled back slightly, pleasure and apprehension dueling for prominence in his dark eyes. She placed a hand on each side of his strong neck and caressed the warm flesh. The hand on her back slid a little lower.

"What are you doing?" he asked, his voice a low grate.

She remembered what she'd been doing. "Forgiving you," she replied against his lips. "Isn't this how married people make up?"

Behind him the elevator doors closed again, but the compartment didn't move. The isolation wrapped around them like a sleek, tantalizing secret.

Becka could no longer see them. Francie didn't have to continue the kiss for her benefit. But when Ryan's head moved toward hers and his lips descended again, Becka was nowhere in Francie's thoughts.

For a repressed fellow, Ryan sure kissed like there was no tomorrow. His unrestrained kisses made the earth move, and she clutched his shoulders to keep from falling. The glorious pressure of his lips sent a tingling through her body, and she pressed herself more closely against him.

"Francie," he groaned against her lips, not quite an endearment, not really resistance. And he shifted her to the back wall of the elevator, and braced his arms on either side of her head, his forearms against the interior as though he needed the steadying support.

His teeth found her ear and nibbled it at the same time she threaded the fingers of one hand through his hair. His breath in her ear created havoc with her senses. Her fingers and toes felt numb.

He kissed her ear, her neck, her jaw, her cheek…and paused at her lips.

Their eyes met for the briefest of moments, and she read the unfettered desire in the depths of his. She was flattered that he desired her, frightened that she felt the same.

He kissed her again, openmouthed this time, a possessive, mind-drugging sort of kiss that stole her breath and her sense and swept her mind free of all thought except him and this enticing embrace.

Ryan pressed her against the wall, the wide handrail arching her hips toward him. He feathered his hands down her sides and back up.

His touch gave Francie a jolt of pleasure and excitement that nearly buckled her knees.

A sound broke through her passion-dazed senses. She paused and listened. Clapping—as in applause. A few giggles thrown in.

Francie grasped Ryan's upper arms and pushed him away. His eyes registered confusion, and finally comprehension. He ran a hand through his hair and turned to look over his shoulder at the crowd outside the elevator.

They'd returned to the first floor lobby, and the doors stood open. Several of the reunion attendees, in wet bathing suits and robes, applauded them.

"*That* was a perfect ten, MacNair," Robert Richards announced.

"Lucky for you he kisses better than he skates, eh, Francie?" someone else kidded.

Another couple, hotel guests Francie had never seen before, stared in abashment.

"Shall we wait for the next elevator?" one of the men asked, a grin on his face.

"No," Ryan said, and gestured for the group to enter.

They did so, still tittering.

Francie stared straight ahead, her heart pounding, embarrassment spreading tingling fire across her cheeks.

A few of the passengers disembarked a floor ahead of theirs. The elevator arrived on five, and they got out amidst a few good-natured jibes.

The doors closed. Francie walked several feet before leaning her forehead against the wall.

He stood behind her, but she tasted him on her lips, smelled him on her skin and her clothing.

"You all right?" he asked.

"I'm all right. I've been kissed before." *Not like that. Goodness, not like that!* She had been rude. She didn't mean to be, words just came out that way. "I'm sorry," she said. "I'm just embarrassed."

"You've even kissed *me* before," he said.

"I know, but that was for show," she said, still not turning to look at him. "Becka was in the hall when we reached our floor."

"I might have known you weren't just a forgiving soul."

"No, no," she said hastily. "It didn't end up that way."

"What did it end up like?"

"You know…you were there."

He chuckled.

She turned around. "You're laughing!"

"You're funny. I confess! You're really funny."

"I wasn't trying to be."

"That's when you're the funniest."

His hair stood in finger-combed waves, and his shirt had been pulled from the waistband of his trousers. He had a five-o'clock shadow, the sight of which made her cheeks tingle. His arresting mouth drew her attention. Her heart dipped and her legs lost strength again. "Have you had enough laughs for one night, Mac?"

His gaze traveled her face and hair as hers had his. "We're both tired," he said.

Tired, she thought. But wide-awake. "I'll be visiting my grandmother tomorrow," she said. "You're welcome to come or not, whichever you prefer."

"I'll do what the kids want to do," he replied. He dug in his pocket and came out with the plastic card for the door. He paused, just before inserting it into the slot. "Good night, Francie. Sweet dreams."

She met his eyes. "Good night."

THEY SPENT THE morning with Nana, who asked Francie to play the piano for her in the dayroom.

"Oh, Nana, you know I'm not very good," Francie objected. "Those lessons were years and years ago, and I haven't practiced since."

"Alanna can play," Alex announced.

All eyes turned to the girl.

"You can play?" Nana asked, a smile creasing her already wrinkled features.

Alanna nodded.

"You don't have to," Francie assured her, not wanting to pressure or humiliate her.

"I like to play," Alanna said simply.

She went to the upright piano, and they gathered chairs nearby. Alanna discovered sheet music in the bench, but nothing familiar. She tried a few of the hymns and the old songs. The piano was in tune and in good condition.

"Do your practice pieces," her father suggested. "You don't need music for those."

She began a piece Francie vaguely remembered hearing before. "What is it?" she asked.

"Mozart," Ryan replied.

The notes flowed in fluid progression, some played lightly, others with intensity and concentration. Other residents came to sit and listen. A few of the nurses wandered in.

"How long has she been playing?" Francie asked quietly.

"Since she was five."

"She's wonderful."

He nodded. "She has a gift."

Nana watched and listened with rapt pleasure, her face glowing.

The piece trailed off and everyone in the dayroom applauded. Alanna nodded to her audience, and smiled brightly, a smile Francie had never seen her wear before, and she led right into another composition.

Francie glanced over at Ryan midway through and noticed the sheen glistening in his eyes.

"I've missed a lot of her recitals," he said thickly. "Or I've been late."

She wanted to reach over and take his hand, but she didn't. She couldn't. They weren't friends. They weren't anything. Not even after that kiss last night.

"I'll be at all of them from now on, and I'll be early," he said, and she knew it was a promise he made to himself, one that he would keep.

She admired his devotion to his children. He'd done something commendable, made more of a commitment than many parents ever did. What kind of person had his wife been to leave him? Francie couldn't bring herself to think too harshly of her. Perhaps she'd been like Francie, just not cut out for children and marriage and the whole commitment thing, and she'd realized it too late.

Thank God Francie had known from early in her life that she was not parent material. She hadn't messed up anybody's life or walked out on any children. She'd never left a child thinking they were unloved and unwanted.

Oh, but she might have. She might have if placed in the same set of circumstances.

Alanna's song ended. Francie joined the others in applauding her.

"I'm tired, Francesca," her grandmother said.

"I'll take you to your room, so you can rest." Francie excused them and wheeled Nana to her room and helped her into bed.

"Jim's a good man," Nana said softly.

Francie nodded.

"He loves those kids so much," she said with a smile. "It just does my heart good to see such a good father."

"Mine, too," Francie admitted.

"He loves you very much, too," Nana said, her eyes twinkling. "I see it in his eyes every time he looks at you." Francie tucked the spread around her. "Don't be so afraid, Francesca," she said.

"I'm not afraid, Nana," she denied.

"Yes, you are. You're afraid to love him too much. But you can't love anybody too much. Especially not him. And not his kids."

Flustered, Francie kissed her cheek.

"Remember that."

"I will." She gave her a smile and located the MacNairs waiting for her by the fountain.

"Is Nana all right?" Alex asked.

"She's fine. Just tired."

Satisfied, he took her hand and they strolled to the car.

Francie pondered her grandmother's words. Ryan didn't love her. Nana was seeing what she believed to be true. He desired Francie; she had no doubts about that, but he couldn't love her. She was a career woman with no time for emotional investments.

She smiled, remembering Nana thinking she was afraid to love "Jim" too much. She didn't love him at all, and she didn't plan to. As appealing as being with him was, as heady and liberating as his kisses were, she had no plans that included loving Ryan MacNair.

"I'll drive, okay?" he asked. He wore his sunglasses, preventing her from seeing amusement if it danced in his eyes as she suspected.

She shrugged, and got in on the passenger side, allowing only a momentary glance at his features. She placed her right hand over her left in her lap, hiding the gold ring. No, no plans whatsoever that included feelings for this man. Why then, did she repeatedly need to remind herself?

RYAN HADN'T WALKED or thought straight since their encounter in the elevator the night before. Looking at the surface, he and Francie had nothing in common. They were as opposite as two people could be. But if he hadn't spent these last days with her, he'd never have known the lack of truth in that superficial assessment.

She'd drawn him out of his safe habitat, away from the distractions that kept him from seeing exactly what he was doing to himself and to his children by thinking all he had to provide for them was a nice house and good schools and designer clothing.

He watched Francie help Alex with his slicked-back pompadour for the dance, and once again recognized the boy's hunger for love and attention. He gave Francie bashful smiles and complimented her on her slinky black pants, leather jacket and high heels.

"You look just like Sandy!" Alex cried, meaning Olivia Newton-John's character in the movie they'd had to rent twice and Alex had watched again that morning. "Do I really look like Danny Zuko?"

"You're a T-Bird if I ever saw one," Francie said

and gave him a hug. "And look at your sister, she's a regular Pink Lady."

Alanna grinned, pleased as punch with this present situation because she got to wear as much makeup as she wanted. This was, after all, a costume dance. She twirled around, and her poodle skirt flared in a circle.

Alex grinned at his dad. "Dad, you have to try to look tougher if you're gonna be a Scorpion."

"I'll try to get into character," Ryan replied. "Will I have to beat anyone up?"

"Not unless that Chapman guy tries to put the moves on Francie again," Alanna said with a smirk. "She's supposed to be your wife, after all."

"Ted Chapman?" he asked. "What did he do?"

"She's exaggerating," Francie said. "He just stood a little close after the play last night."

"Tell him he blew his chance when he freaked out over the iguana," he said, and realized his vernacular sounded like something Francie or Alanna would say.

Francie burst into laughter. "Did you say that?"

"I said it." He grinned. "Can't be too 'stuffed' in this shirt."

She perused the form-fitting black T-shirt she'd cut the sleeves from, and gave him an appreciative wink. "Guess not. Seems you're loosening up, Mac. So don't plan to tell me you can't dance."

"I can dance."

"He goes to fund-raisers all the time," Alanna said. "They have dinners and orchestras."

Francie shot him an amused glance. "Not *that* kind of dancing."

"Dancing like in *Grease,* Dad," Alex said and demonstrated a twist.

"You won't get me doing that, so forget whatever you're thinking right now," Ryan stated adamantly.

Francie loaded a new roll of film into her camera, smiling to herself.

She glanced around, checking the lighting and the most interesting visual aspects of the enormous room. Springdale High School's gymnasium had been transformed into a bygone era, using the sets from the play and hundreds of balloons.

A cash bar had been set up in the cafeteria window, punch and snacks on tables along the walls.

"They must have worked all day at this," she said aloud.

Ryan leaned his head back to observe the multicolored balloons suspended from ceiling beams. "Be glad you're the reunion photographer and not the cleanup committee."

"Tom Wallace and I were talking. We're going to ask the old yearbook committee to put together an album using the pictures I've taken and articles written by several of us."

"You've been enjoying yourself, haven't you?"

She glanced over. "I guess I have. And I guess I'm surprised."

"Why is that?"

"I'm sure it's been obvious to you that these weren't exactly my best friends."

"Who were your best friends?"

She shrugged. "Didn't have any."

"Why not?"

"Springdale was even smaller back then. It's a close-knit sort of town. When I came to live with Nana, I was an outsider."

Not many had arrived yet, so they had their choice of tables. Ryan selected one and Francie placed her scuffed camera case on it. "So that changed?" he asked.

"No." She seated herself and glanced around. "I stayed an outsider. But I've never been a wallflower, so they had to deal with me."

He leaned against the edge of the table.

"I think that's why I love taking photographs so much," she said thoughtfully. "That's when it became important to me."

"Why?"

"Well…" She wanted to express it to him, and wasn't sure how. "I love taking photographs of all kinds of things, but I especially love the shots of people. I love to capture and study their faces. Candid shots are the best. The subjects seem like friends later."

She wasn't doing a very good job. He probably thought she was nuts.

"There's nothing judgmental about a picture," he said.

She smiled. He understood better than she thought.

"They're safe," he said. "You can't hurt them and they can't hurt you."

She looked away.

"Sort of like working all the time was safe for me."

She looked back at him, not liking what she'd revealed to both of them.

"Francie! Oh, my gosh, that's darling!" Becka cried, examining Francie's outfit, and ending the conversation that had grown far too serious. "You're a perfect Sandy!"

She and J.J. were hippies, with their hair crimped, bare feet and threadbare bell-bottoms.

J.J. let out a hoot, and they all turned to observe the Armbrusters' arrival. Don had dyed and slicked his hair, pasted on sideburns and wore a white glittery Elvis suit that emphasized his short legs and neck; a wide gold belt was lashed around the girth of his belly.

Peyton, his extreme opposite, had outfitted herself in a dark beehive wig that made her appear six feet tall and six inches wide. Her black eyeliner was the tip-off that she was supposed to be Priscilla. Francie stifled the giggles that welled up in her throat.

J.J. didn't hold his amusement back, however, and Becka slammed her elbow into his ribs.

Tom Wallace and his wife showed up as Sonny and Cher. Francie had a ball snapping posed and candid photos of each arrival.

The band appeared, and the music began, a combination of fifties, sixties and seventies hits that had the crowd cheering and dancing wildly.

Sometime later, Francie found Ryan still at the table with Lisa and Robert.

"Out of film?" Ryan asked.

"Never. Came for you."

"Don't you think Danny'll be jealous?"

She grinned, placed her camera on the table and took his hand. "You're cutting loose more every day, Mac."

"Don't be surprised if I waltz."

"Don't worry, I won't."

She pulled him onto the dance floor just as the music changed and "Blue Moon" echoed from the speakers.

They exchanged a glance and he took her into his arms quite naturally. Francie raised one arm behind his neck, and he held her other hand. He led gracefully, the heat of their bodies touching where her jacket gaped in the front.

This closeness did something wacky to her pulse. Though he worked hard at being standoffish, Ryan was one of the most intense men she'd ever known. If he ever focused all that fiery drive and energy on her alone, she'd probably melt into a puddle.

Francie glanced at the other couples, some with partners other than their spouses, others actually dancing in intimate embraces. What would it feel like if she'd danced with him a hundred times? What if he really was her husband? Would the excitement of being this close to him have worn off?

"Do you think it's possible to keep the romance alive in a marriage?" she asked.

"Why do you ask?"

"Have you seen how some of them have been looking at us this week? They think we're newly wed and hot for each other, and they're envious."

He glanced over and spotted Tom Wallace and his

wife locked in an embrace. "Some of them seem to have done it."

"Some," she agreed, remembering Lisa and Robert leaving the pool the other night. "But what about the others, like Peyton?"

"Peyton married Don for his degrees and his job potential, not the chemistry between them."

"You're right. And Becka and J.J. got married directly out of high school. She had a baby that very summer, and I assume that was their reason for marrying."

"Must have been chemistry there to start with."

She shrugged. "Hormones don't make a marriage."

"You can't analyze a half a dozen marriages and come up with sound statistics," he said.

"Why not?"

"There are more than a few reasons for marrying, and hundreds more why marriages don't work out. If two people are committed, they can keep the fires burning."

She shook her head. "I've seen too many people sorry for the choices they've made."

"Are you talking about your own parents?"

"Maybe."

"Or maybe you were thinking about my marriage."

She shrugged again, noncommittally.

Gratefully the music changed, and along with it the mood. Francie kept Ryan on the dance floor, and he held his own among the throng of nostalgic dancers.

Francie had a ball.

Ryan MacNair had turned out to be a good sport. She'd never in a million years have imagined he had it in him to join the celebration, even participating in the contests and the partner-switching games.

By the end of the evening, she realized he'd not only kept his word by coming to the reunion and all its various activities, but he'd shown everyone that Francie Karr-Taylor had made a great choice in a husband and that they were a match unequaled.

Any reports that got back to Nana would be glowing ones. She owed Nana's present peace of mind to him.

Alanna and Alex fell asleep in the car on the drive to the hotel. "Where did you and Nana live?" Ryan asked.

"Want me to show you?"

"Sure."

She directed him to the neighborhood where Nana's old house stood, and they pulled up in front.

"Who lives there now?"

"I don't know the people." She pointed to the basketball hoop above the garage door. "They obviously have kids."

"Would you like to see the inside again?"

She shook her head. "I'm sure they've remodeled and changed things. I like to remember it the way it was."

They studied the house for a few minutes longer, and then Ryan drove to the hotel.

HE HAD TROUBLE sleeping that night. The more he was around Francie, the more sense she made, and that was scary. Yes, she had a chameleonlike nature, and could adapt to situations seemingly effortlessly. Her fabrications were like self-preservation skills she had created.

Yet he knew she'd never lied to him. When he asked her a question, he got a straightforward answer. Seeing her day after day in real situations, she was not at all like he'd thought at first. She loved her grandmother above anything else and had concocted this scheme to placate her.

Finally Ryan got out of bed, hoping a shower would relax him. He stood under the warm water, letting it buffet the muscles of his neck and shoulders, and entertained thoughts of seeing Francie after this week was over. In a million years, he'd never have imagined himself being drawn to her, enjoying her company, but he admitted to himself now that he liked being with her. Her humor and her zest for life was contagious. She made him feel younger somehow, almost as though life had passed him by until she'd pointed it out to him.

Ryan dried, momentarily studying his reflection in the foggy mirror. What did she see when she looked at him? A stuffy businessman grown old before his time? He didn't know how or when he'd come to this point, but he knew he wanted to change the direction he'd been headed. Finally he stretched back out on the bed and drifted into a restless sleep.

Francie awakened them early. She'd gone to the lobby for coffee, juice and rolls, and opened the drapes, allowing bright sunshine to spill across the beds and Alanna's pallet.

"Good morning, MacNairs!" she called.

Ryan opened one eye and blinked at the red digits on the clock radio. Behind him, Alex bounced to his usual morning attention with a flurry of covers and bedsprings.

"This had better be important," Alanna said, sitting up groggily.

"It is. Here, have your juice and coffee to wake up." Francie poured and served.

"Wow, breakfast in bed," Alex said cheerfully. "Cool!"

Alanna went into the bathroom and returned to sit in one of the chairs.

"I have something for you," Francie said finally.

Ryan hadn't lost all his good sense yet, because he remained skeptical of her ideas and offerings. "What is it?"

"It's for Alanna, actually, but it will mean a lot to you, too." She went to her organizer and pulled out a gaily wrapped little box.

Alanna took it from her without a change in her sullen expression.

"Go ahead," Francie urged. "Open it."

Alanna glanced at her dad, who nodded. She sat down her juice and used both hands to untie the ribbon and peel back the foil wrapping paper.

She revealed a silver box.

Francie gestured for her to continue.

Alanna glanced at Ryan again before taking the lid from the box. His daughter stared at the contents with a blank expression. "What does this mean?" she asked finally.

"What is it?" he asked.

Alanna left her chair to come over to the bed and show him the contents.

Nestled on a bed of cotton lay the gold-and-garnet brooch he hadn't seen for years; his grandmother's brooch.

8

RYAN LOOKED AT her in confusion. Her smile seemed a little strained, or maybe he read uncertainty in the tightness around her mouth. "What does this mean?"

She backed up to the edge of her unmade bed and sat. "It's a gift. For Alanna. For all of you. It was really unfair of me to ask you to go along with this. It was selfish. I wish I'd just given you the brooch in the first place."

Ryan didn't know what to say. Alanna wore a stunned expression, and Alex looked confused.

"It was unkind of me to use up your vacation time together." Francie stood and jerked up the bedcovers, found a pair of earrings on the nightstand and placed them in her ears without looking at him. "You still have this weekend." She went to her suitcase, withdrew folded papers and carried them back.

He looked at the plane tickets she handed him.

"But there's still the picnic," Alex said, jumping up to retrieve the schedule. "And the thing on Sunday." Disappointment laced his tone, and the almost panicked look on his face gave Ryan a sick feeling in his stomach.

"I can tell everyone that one of you kids got sick.

Or that you had other plans for the weekend already. I'll think of something.''

"I've no doubt you could think of something.'' Ryan studied the tickets. But why go? Why quit now?

"Thanks for everything this week,'' she continued briskly. "I'm sorry I made you do this.'' She grabbed her bag, and paused before Alex as though she wanted to say more, as if she'd like to scoop him into her arms. But she walked to the door, her posture straight. "Enjoy your weekend together. Please.''

Ryan stared at the door, then at his children's faces. Alex looked ready to cry.

Francie closed the door behind her, regretting so many things she didn't know where or who to start apologizing to. She'd made the decision during the night to give them the brooch as an offering of repentance. The MacNair family could still salvage a couple of days together.

Feeling good about this decision, yet sick at heart at the thought of them leaving and her not seeing them again, she bought coffee and sat by the pool. She'd give them an hour. That way she wouldn't have to witness their departure. All through the night she'd struggled with not only her conscience, but in making a decision on the kindest and easiest way to end this for everybody's sakes.

She'd been awake when Ryan had climbed from bed and taken a shower. He'd been right to remain protective of his children. He'd been right about nearly everything. Maybe he'd even been right that she should never have lied to Nana about a husband. Maybe. But thinking it was so lent Nana a peace and comfort that made her remaining days easier. Francie didn't regret that.

She only regretted she'd involved a truly good man and his children in her scheme. And she'd known she needed to bring it to an end before anyone was truly hurt. Giving Alanna the brooch was the honorable thing to do, the thing she should have done first.

Belatedly she noticed the gold band she still wore. She would return it when she got back to Chicago.

After only thirty minutes, hurried footsteps sounded behind her. A small hand fell on her shoulder, and she glanced up at Alex.

"Alex! Is everything all right?" He'd come to say goodbye, no doubt, something she'd hoped to avoid.

Alanna and Ryan appeared behind him, and they seated themselves at the table.

Francie glanced at each of them. "Are you going?"

"We're going," Ryan said.

The dull ache in her stomach intensified. Why hadn't they just gone on without a big scene?

"To the picnic!" Alex added.

Butterflies fluttered in her chest. She hadn't even wanted to hope. "You're staying?"

"We discussed it as a family," Ryan said. "And we all agreed to stay."

Francie let her surprised glance slide to Alanna. *She* had wanted to stay? The girl made no comment. Francie gave her a timorous smile.

"We made a list of pros and cons," Ryan said and unfolded a slip of paper.

"Oh, and I can't guess whose idea that was," she said in a wry tone.

He grinned and stuffed it back into his pocket.

"Let's get our breakfast here, Dad." With a nod, Alex indicated the restaurant a few feet away.

"You had the rolls Francie brought for breakfast."

"Then let's call this brunch," the boy said.

Ryan pulled out his wallet. "Go ahead and get something."

"Coming?" Alex said to his sister.

Together the two entered the restaurant.

Ryan moved to sit in the chair at Francie's right, and leaned his elbows on the table. "We didn't do something wrong here, did we?"

She tipped her head to study him. His deep brown eyes were filled with uncertainty and concern.

"By staying?" he clarified. "Did you want us to go?"

Had she wanted them to go? It might have been easier to break it off sooner rather than later. Surprisingly enough, she enjoyed Ryan's company. Alex, of course, was lovable and fun to be with. And even though Alanna merely tolerated her and cracked scathing remarks, Francie didn't mind having her around.

No, she hadn't really wanted them to leave. The thought of having their company for the picnic and baccalaureate gave her profound pleasure. Her mock family unit had lent her security during this week's activities. She'd felt more accepted and more a part of things than she ever had in the past. And she didn't resent that fact as she should.

"No, I didn't really want you to go," she admitted honestly, hating the little catch in her voice. "I wanted to be fair to you, though. I got to feeling guilty about the time I'd taken you away from your kids.''

His intense expression relaxed, and he flattened his hands on the tabletop. Francie couldn't help noticing his long fingers, the dusting of dark hair on their backs. ''It's not like that. This week has shown me the importance of spending time with my children. I have you to thank for that.''

She shook her head, still not looking up.

His hand moved toward her, and her heart skipped a foolish beat. Reaching across the tabletop, he took her hand. ''It's true.''

Francie looked down at his thumb as it brushed back and forth across the backs of her fingers, grazing the wedding band with each sweep. Warmth shot along her arm and created a soft fluttering in her chest. She studied his ringless fingers and his gold watch, rather than raise her gaze to his. ''Have you changed your mind about what a demented idea this was?'' she asked.

''No. I still think it's nuts.''

She looked up then, and grinned. ''Alanna really voted to stay for the weekend?''

Tiny lines fanned out from the corners of his eyes in his grin. ''She did.''

''And there were a lot more pros than cons on the list?''

''There were.''

Spending the rest of the weekend together was a reckless thing to do, considering the way she was feeling about his touch on her hand. But for some insane reason, she didn't want to get off this emotionally crazy roller-coaster ride just yet.

"Hi, guys." Lisa sat a tray on Francie's other side and seated herself. Robert appeared next. Ryan and Francie exchanged a look of regret that their privacy had been interrupted, and morning greetings were exchanged.

Alex and Alanna returned with their food, and Ryan released Francie's hand to help Alex get settled.

"Ryan MacNair!" a male voice called behind Francie.

Ryan glanced up, and his expression alerted Francie to a problem. She turned as the man approached their table.

Ryan stood and extended his hand. "Ralph."

The shorter man shook it. "Do you have business in Springdale?"

"No, I'm here purely for pleasure."

The man's gaze darted from Francie to Lisa and Robert.

Francie recognized the man Ryan had spotted on the balcony before pulling her back against him in the pool. The historian with the Abe Lincoln collection.

"It's my wife's tenth class reunion," Ryan said, and Francie's hearing stuck on his use of the word "wife." "This is Francie," he said, "and these are my children, Alanna and Alex. These are our friends, the Richardses. This is Ralph Hanscom, a professor from the University of Illinois."

Lisa and Robert nodded and went about their meal.

"I didn't realize you were married," Ralph said. "You must keep her all to yourself."

"I guess the subject never came up in our business dealings," Ryan replied. "Are you married?"

"Oh, yes. I have a grandson who is two years old."

"No!" Ryan said.

Francie raised her cup of cold coffee to hide her smile. Ryan had just lied every bit as effectively as she had from the beginning. But he'd adroitly managed to turn the topic of conversation. Ralph proudly showed photos from his wallet, and Ryan studied them appreciatively.

Finally, the man wished them goodbye and headed up the stairs.

Ryan, Francie, Alanna and Alex all exchanged a knowing look, but no one said anything in front of the Richardses.

After everyone had finished eating and started their separate ways, Francie asked, "Will Mr. Hanscom's thinking you're married be a problem after this?"

"I don't think so. I rarely see him. And only for business. I don't know why he'd mention it to anyone, and if he did, what difference would it make?"

"I didn't plan to mess up your life." She slowed down as they neared the door to the room.

"You haven't messed up anything." He slowed his pace to stay beside her.

"Dad, do you have change for the pop machine?" Alanna asked.

"You just ate."

"But now I'm thirsty."

Ryan dug into his pocket. Both kids stopped with him.

Francie went on ahead, finding her key and entering the room just as the phone rang. She grabbed it. "Hello?"

"I—I was calling for Ryan MacNair," the male voice said. "Do I have the wrong room?"

It sounded like the man they'd just seen by the pool. She hoped he wouldn't cause a problem for Ryan. "No, this is the right room. Hold on just a minute."

"Who's this?" the voice asked.

"This is his wife, hang on." She laid the receiver down and went to see if Ryan was coming.

He and the kids had almost reached the room.

"Someone's on the phone for you. Sounds like that guy we just saw by the pool."

He picked up the receiver. "Hello? Hello?" A few seconds later he hung it up. "No one there. That's odd."

She shrugged. "If it was important, they'll call back."

THE WEATHER COULDN'T have cooperated more. The sun shone brightly, yet it wouldn't be too hot to enjoy the day and the games. The picnic committee had gone whole hog just as every other committee had. There were games and contests planned for all ages, plenty of food and drinks on the way, and picnic tables and lawn chairs ready.

"There had better be real bathrooms," Alanna said as soon as they arrived at the park.

Ryan glanced at Francie. "I'm not sure," she said. "I haven't been here for years."

"If they're those awful stinky ones, you'll have to

drive me back to town to go.'' Alanna got out of the car and looked around.

The ride to the park had taken twenty-five minutes. Ryan's brows lowered into a thunderous frown.

''If they're outhouses, I'll drive you to that convenience shop we saw on the highway,'' Francie offered quickly, hooking the strap of her camera case around her neck. ''That was only about ten miles back.''

Alanna looked at Francie in surprise, but said nothing. She glanced from her to her father and nodded.

A van pulled into the gravel parking lot, and a couple of Alanna's new friends jumped out and ran to greet her. They carried a bulging bag and a CD case.

''I'll see you later.'' Alanna waved to her dad and walked toward a shade tree with the girls.

''S'pose that bag was full of makeup?'' Ryan asked.

Francie grinned. ''Seems likely.''

''She wasn't always this difficult.'' He didn't know if he meant it as an excuse or as an apology. ''I guess I'm to blame for much of her attitude.''

The breeze tossed Francie's silky-looking hair. She threaded it away from her face with her fingers and replied, ''Don't be too hard on yourself. You've done the best you knew how.''

''Is it too late?'' The question was directed more toward himself than to her. Could spending more time with Alanna make up for the past?

''It's not too late,'' she said, and surprised him by touching his arm. ''She needed your attention, and you're giving it to her. Give her a little time now. She'll learn that you're there for her.''

They strolled across the grass. Alex took Ryan's hand and then Francie's, forming a link between them. He beamed his engaging smile at both. How could Ryan have missed Alex's hunger for a woman's attention? What could he have done if he had?

Holding the ever-present camera to her waist, Francie leaned down to say something to his son, and when she straightened and smiled at Ryan, his heart constricted. How had he not recognized his own need for a woman's companionship? No, not just any woman.

He returned her smile. *Francie.*

What kind of a chance did they have of continuing their relationship once they returned to Chicago? Would she want to see the kids? Would she care to see him? She seemed to have changed her outlook on the situation since their first meetings. She now appeared to regret inconveniencing them. He believed the circumstances had changed for her as much as they had for him. And the physical attraction was mutual. But would she wish to pursue this oddly entangled association?

Perhaps she just needed a little persuading.

Francie's graduating class had been fertile. Children of all sizes and shapes lined up for the races and games. Babies napped in playpens in the shade. Ryan had never attended functions geared to families as this was, and he regretted missing that.

Caterers carried in lunch, trays of chicken and tubs of potato salad and slaws. Those who lived in Springdale provided blankets and tablecloths for out-of-towners, and Francie spread a borrowed quilt in the shade for the MacNair family.

The kids ate quickly and raced off to play.

"Francie?" Ryan said.

Instinctively she prepared herself for what he was going to say and looked over at him.

"Is there a chance we could continue this...after we go back to Chicago?"

She took note of the seriousness in his dark eyes. "You don't mean keep pretending we're married."

"No."

As long as he'd said nothing she'd been able to pretend that there was nothing going on past a few impulsive kisses. "Trust me on this one, Mac, I'm not your type."

"What's my type?"

"You need somebody stable and dependable. Conservative and, well, you know, committed. Someone willing to dedicate herself to you and your kids."

"I didn't propose."

Heat climbed her neck and reached her cheeks. "So you just want to sleep with me when we get back home?"

"No. I mean...we don't have to make a commitment right away."

"But eventually. Sooner or later you'd want a commitment."

He shrugged.

"You would. It's the natural order of things, and it's who you are. It's what you should expect. But I'm not the one to expect it from."

He looked away, allowing her to study the sun dappling his perfect features through the leaves. That first day he'd come to her loft she'd never have imagined seeing through his impeccable demeanor to the vulnerable man inside.

"There are some things you just can't organize into a tidy little plan," she said.

"Then, could we just take it one day at a time?" he asked.

"We can," she agreed. "As long as you understand."

"That you would never want to marry me."

"That I couldn't."

"It's a lot to expect, asking a woman to take on a man with a ready-made family. But that's who I am, too."

"I know that." And that's why she would never set them up to let them down. He'd already had one unsuitable wife. He didn't need another. And knowing that, Francie couldn't let him think she might be any different.

The afternoon progressed, and more than once Francie heard her Nana's words. *"Don't be so afraid, Francesca... You can't love anybody too much... remember that."*

No, a person couldn't love too much. But they could love too little.

She and Alex stood along the sidelines in the sun while Ryan and Alanna took third place in a three-legged race. Ryan had had to convince his daughter to participate, but she'd quickly caught the competitive spirit and had accepted the plastic trophy with the same smile an Olympic athlete wore when she accepted her gold medal.

Alex asked Francie to be his partner for the boat-building match. She balked, knowing her skills were woefully inadequate, but Ryan's encouraging nod and Alex's pleading gray eyes won her over.

Lisa and Robert, the contest hosts, had laid out a variety of tools and supplies. No one could leave the area while building their boat. Only materials within the cordoned-off area could be used, and they had one hour.

Francie and Alex chose balsa wood and fast-drying glue for the base of their ship and dowels for the masts. Francie perused the selection of materials for sails and knew they hadn't created their boat heavy enough to hold the added weight.

"We need something heavy in the bottom to keep the whole thing from capsizing," she said, looking their project over thoughtfully.

"Rocks?" Alex asked.

"They are within the roped-off area, aren't they?" They grinned and Alex nonchalantly found a couple of smooth flat stones they could easily glue into the bottom.

"Now the sails," she said. "This stuff is all too heavy."

"Leaves?" he suggested, glancing around.

"Not sturdy enough. We need something practically weightless. Like cotton."

They glanced at each other's clothing.

Francie smiled immediately.

"What?" Alex asked.

She slipped her hand inside the neck of her shirt and pulled a shoulder pad loose from its Velcro mooring.

Alex giggled.

Francie ripped the cotton material away from the pad and discovered it was a suitable shape and size to make two sails.

With fifteen minutes left to spare, they picked glue from their fingers and kept their model hidden between them.

When the big moment arrived, the Richardses inspected and labeled the boats, and the launch was announced. Alex impatiently awaited their turn, watching as other crafts sank or capsized or traveled a few precarious yards in the swiftly moving creek.

At last their turn came. They traded hopeful looks. Francie nodded at Alex to do the honor. He removed his shoes and socks and waded out into the creek until the water reached his knees. Settling the little boat on the current, he released it.

Their masterpiece listed to one side and then righted itself to the collective groan of the onlookers. And then the current caught the vessel and carried it swiftly downstream. It hit a protruding stick once, spun in a circle and continued on its way.

The crowd cheered. Alex climbed the bank and ran alongside, following the boat until it reached a curve and neatly snagged in an outcropping of rocks.

Francie had never seen a bigger smile than the one on his face when he returned for his plastic trophy, carrying the water-darkened boat. She hugged him until he squealed.

Ryan enveloped Francie in an embrace that caught her by surprise and took her breath away. "Thank you."

She blinked back tears of happiness.

"I hope you don't mind," he said. "I took a few pictures."

She accepted her camera now, having forgotten it when she'd been elected to assist Alex. She never forgot her camera. She blinked. "You knew how to use it?"

"I've taken a few shots in my day. Did you mind?"

She shook her head. "Of course not. Alex, let's get a picture of you with the winning boat."

"Can we get a trophy case, Dad?" Alex asked, holding up the craft and grinning ear to ear.

Ryan smiled at his son's enthusiasm. "We'll see."

"They're just plastic," Alanna said. "They don't even have our names on them."

"I know that."

Francie snapped his photograph. "You can find someplace special to keep it, Alex."

"Will you help me find a place?" He stared up at her with wide questioning eyes.

Francie touched his cheek in a loving gesture. Here it was again. His desire to carry their bond past this week, past this game of pretend, and into the reality beyond. She caught Alanna's wistful expression before she masked it with practiced aloofness.

She met Ryan's eyes. He, too, had asked for an extension on their time together. He seemed to be waiting for her reply to his son to see if it was more satisfactory than her answer for him.

"Yes, Alex," she said finally. "I'll come help you find a special place for it."

Alex hugged her around the waist, and Ryan lifted his chin in acknowledgment. *I've only committed to this one thing,* she tried to tell him with her eyes. *I can't promise more than I know I have to give.*

She turned then to see Peyton studying them with an odd expression. Francie gave her a hesitant smile and the woman acknowledged it with a quick wave before turning away. What had that look been about? What had they said that Peyton might have overheard? Nothing incriminating, certainly.

Much later, another meal was laid out, this time barbecue sandwiches and chips and pickles. Watermelons were sliced and served, and near dark, several ice-cream makers were put into use, and Springdale's reunited class and their families ate their fill of homemade ice cream.

The grand finale of the evening came after full dark. A local expert put on a magnificent fireworks display.

Francie sat on the quilt with the MacNairs, full of ice cream, full of the most unexpected sense of completion she'd ever experienced. Alex's head lay in her lap, the boat still within his reach on the blanket. From time to time he touched it, ran a finger over the crude balsa wood structure as though it were an expensive treasure.

Alanna and her friends sat within sight and hearing on a blanket of their own. She seemed relaxed and sure of herself with the girls, and Francie loved seeing her that way.

Ryan moved until their hips met and stretched his much longer legs alongside hers. She moved the minuscule distance it took to incline her shoulder back against his, and leaned into his warmth and strength and his ever-present wonderful smell.

A myriad of starbursts exploded in the night sky above, and he wedged his nose behind her ear, along her neck. Delicious shivers raced down her arm and across her breasts. His breath gusted warm and soft at her ear. His lips opened against the column of her neck.

Pleasure washed through her in a wave of sensation. She wanted to turn and touch him, run her hand over his handsome face, his strong neck, his wide shoulders and hard chest. She wanted to open herself to his kisses, to forget time and place and the impossibility of their desire ever going anywhere. She wanted to toss caution in the creek like a stone and lose herself in the man. *Ryan.*

Instead she watched fireworks burst in the heavens while sensation throbbed in her body, and reminded herself what she wanted out of life, what she needed.

Francie Karr-Taylor had never cared about pleasing anyone but her grandmother. Since reaching adulthood she'd never had to depend on anyone to meet her needs. She wasn't accountable to anyone but herself. And she liked it that way. If she forgot a plan or blew an assignment, she let only herself down. If she wanted to change her life at any time, or in any way, she had the freedom to do so. There was no one to hurt. No one to let down or leave behind.

Against her back, Ryan's heart beat wild and strong, the heart of a man with wants and hopes and needs like those she'd denied for so long. And for the first time, she wished she had more to give.

9

RETURNING TO THE room late that night, the blinking light on the phone alerted them to a message. Alanna readied herself for bed and Ryan tucked Alex in.

Francie called the desk.

"Mr. MacNair is to phone his father in room 417 immediately," the woman on the other end of the line said.

"Room 417?" Francie asked, then said over her shoulder, "Ryan, do you know where to call your father?"

"If he's not at home, I have no idea," he replied.

"Where would that room be?" she asked the desk clerk. "Is there a phone number?"

"It's in the hotel," the voice replied. "You just dial eight and then the room number."

"In *this* hotel?" Her mind grappled with the thought for a moment. "All right. Thank you."

She hung up. "He's here. In this hotel."

"My father is where?" His brow wrinkled in puzzlement. "Here? What on earth would he be doing in Springdale?" He turned out the light over Alex's head and perched on Francie's bed to pick up the phone. After punching in the numbers, he waited.

Francie went about gathering her nightclothes, curious, but trying not to be nosy.

"Dad? Where are you? What are you doing here?" A lengthy pause. Ryan glanced at Francie. "That was you?" Another long pause. "I think we'd better talk. I'll be down in a few minutes."

He hung up the receiver.

Francie wadded the nightshirt she held and waited impatiently.

Finally he looked at her. "That was him you talked to on the phone this morning. The one who called asking for me."

"Is something wrong?"

"No. Yes. He called my office. My secretary told him I'd taken a vacation and gave him this number. I never take a vacation, so he found that unusual. Add to that the fact that you mentioned you were my wife when he called the room."

"Oh, boy."

"He didn't recognize your voice, didn't think I'd been seeing anyone seriously and so he wondered if we'd come here to meet..." His voice trailed off.

"What?" she asked. "Who?"

"Well, he was confused, and the thought that entered his mind was that the children's mother had somehow contacted us, and that we were meeting her. That idea upset him."

"I can see why," she thought aloud. She wanted to kick herself. She'd thought the voice on the phone had been Ryan's acquaintance they'd just seen near the pool. Now she'd gotten Ryan's father involved and left Ryan to do all the explaining.

"So he flew here today? Oh, my goodness. What will you say to him?"

"I'll just tell him," he replied simply.

"The truth?"

He stood and checked his pocket for the room key. "Why is the truth always the farthest thing from your mind?"

Chastised, she glanced over to see Alanna facing away from them on her pallet. Francie doubted she'd fallen asleep already, especially with this conversation going on. "Would you like me to do it?"

"Do what?"

"Explain to him? I'm the one who started this mess."

His dark-eyed gaze took in her face and hair. "You know, maybe he would understand better if he actually met you."

"I'll come with you then."

He nodded.

Francie freshened up before joining Ryan in the hall. They stood waiting for the elevator, watching the numbers, and she couldn't help remembering the kisses they'd shared within its confines. They entered the car and she knew he was reminded, too. He glanced at her once, then stared straight ahead, a muscle in his cheek jumping. The elevator took them down a floor, and they located the correct room.

Ryan knocked and the door opened immediately.

The tall gentleman, dressed in trousers and a belted wine red robe, did a double take at Francie's presence. Immediately he recovered his manners and invited them both into the suite.

"Dad, this is Francie Karr-Taylor. Francie, my father, Stuart MacNair."

"How do you do, Mr. MacNair?"

"Miss—is it Miss Karr-Taylor?"

"Call me Francie."

He accepted the hand she offered. "Please. Have a seat."

Thus Ryan's formality and gentility, she thought kindly, sitting in the chair he'd offered. Ryan's heritage. He and the still-handsome older man were strikingly similar in features and height, as well as mannerisms. Ryan waited until his father took the other chair, then seated himself on the sofa.

"Mr. MacNair, I asked Ryan to let me come along so I could explain this whole mess. I'm so sorry for any confusion or worry I may have caused you by what I said on the phone this morning. I feel so bad that you flew all this way after talking to me. I thought you were someone we'd just seen by the pool, an acquaintance of Ryan's from Chicago. He's a historian who collects Abraham Lincoln artifacts...do you know him?"

"I don't believe so." Stuart glanced at Ryan, then back at Francie.

"Well, we'd just seen this guy, and I thought he was calling Ryan about something. If I'd known it was you, I'd never have said I was Ryan's wife."

Amusement twitched at one side of Ryan's mouth, but he remained silent.

The silver-haired gentleman showed less tolerance for her explanation. "And it would have been...

normal for you to tell this historian person that you were my son's wife?''

"Yes. Well, Ryan had just introduced me that way. You see, we were with a group of my friends by the pool, and this fellow showed up, and Ryan didn't really have much choice.''

"No choice but to say you were his wife.''

"Right. Because my old classmates were there. They think we're married.''

Stuart MacNair looked decidedly confused. "My son's private life is none of my business. If he registers into hotels with...*friends,* I don't need to know about it. I was only concerned when I didn't know whether or not you were someone who would try to hurt him or the children in some way.''

"We're not friends,'' she said before his words sank in, then stopped. He thought they had registered as married so as not to raise eyebrows at the hotel? He thought they were having an affair! "Wait. It's not like that at all,'' she tried to explain. "The children are in the room with us.''

The elderly gentleman's eyebrows climbed his forehead at that bit of information. "My grandchildren are here?''

"Yes, but we're not...'' She raised a hand in a helpless gesture. "We're not...''

"Sleeping together,'' Ryan finished for her.

She felt herself blush to the roots of her hair, and she dropped her hand to her lap. "That's right. We just want people to *think* we're sleeping together.''

Stuart blinked as though he'd been abducted by

aliens and set down in a place he didn't recognize. He turned to his son. "You understand this?"

"Perfectly."

Francie realized she was sinking fast. "We're just pretending to be married for my grandmother's sake."

Ryan wore a composed expression and sat listening to her explanation. Francie glared at him suddenly. "Jump in here, anytime, Mac."

"You're doing just fine." He leaned back in smug repose and crossed one ankle over his bare knee.

At that action, Stuart seemed to take note of Ryan's grass-stained shirt and shorts. "Whatever have you been doing?"

"Oh. Fell during a three-legged race." He rubbed at a smudge on his knee. "Got third place, though."

"So you see," Francie continued, ignoring the interruption, "we really don't even know each other. But Nana's crazy about Jim and the kids, and pleased as punch with the whole situation. She thinks I'm settled down and happy."

She launched into an explanation about Nana's concerns for her marital status, the reunion invitation and how happy the children made Nana each time they visited.

"Alanna and Alex are well?" Stuart asked.

Ryan nodded. "Perfectly all right."

A niggle of exasperation tugged at Francie. Was this man even paying attention? She went on determinedly, at last mentioning the brooch.

"You have the brooch?" Stuart asked, as though

finally hearing something he understood. "My mother's brooch? Where is it?"

Ryan spoke up. "It's in the hotel safe now, Dad. Francie gave it to Alanna this morning. We voted to stay and finish the weekend anyway."

News of the piece of jewelry seemed to have softened the senior MacNair's opinion of her. Even his body language became less defensive, and he turned to her. "Thank you for giving my granddaughter the brooch, Miss Karr-Taylor. That piece means a lot to our family."

"I understand that," she replied. "I should have just given it to Ryan in the first place, but I was panicked over how I was going to pull off this week and still have Nana thinking I was happily married. I probably didn't use my best judgment."

"In selecting my son to carry out your deceitful plan, you mean?" He puffed out his chest.

"No, no, Ryan was perfect. He *is* perfect. I meant I didn't use good judgment in blackmailing him."

Ryan chuckled this time.

Stuart scowled.

"It wasn't blackmail," Ryan said, coming to her defense. "It was bartering. People do it all the time, remember?"

Had she actually used that argument to convince him to go along with her scheme? Once again, her impetuous nature had sprung her headlong into a predicament. Would she never learn? She caught herself twisting the wedding band and laced her fingers to keep them still.

"Francie is no threat to me or the children," Ryan

assured his father. "In fact she's been good for us. I'm sorry you had to come all this way to find that out. You could have waited to speak with me. Or I would have called you back."

"I probably wouldn't have believed you without seeing for myself. Without seeing *her* for myself."

Indignation brought a frown to Francie's brow. What was that supposed to mean?

"This is not like you," Stuart said, and she knew he meant *she* was not like the company Ryan normally kept.

Ryan rested his elbows on his knees and flattened his palms together. "It's not like I have been the past several years. I've been so absorbed in business that I haven't taken time to see how much Alanna and Alex needed me with them. That's all changed."

He took a long minute to look his father over, measuringly, and cast Francie a look she didn't quite understand.

An uncomfortable silence fell over the room.

Finally Francie stood. "I'll go. You two probably want some privacy."

"I'll be right up," Ryan said, and stood to hand her the key.

She nodded. "Good night, Mr. MacNair."

"Good night, Francie. If that *is* your name."

His sarcasm stung. She made her way to their room, knowing she'd embarrassed Ryan in front of his father, and knowing every bit of the damage done had been her fault. She could only hope that in trying to smooth it over she hadn't made it worse.

Alanna was sitting on the side of Francie's bed when she let herself in. "Was the old man mad?"

"He was worried."

"Did he ask about me and Alex?"

"Yes. He was pleased you had the brooch."

"Were you afraid of him?"

Francie studied the girl's features in the light that slipped through a crack in the drapes. Her skin was pink and flushed as though she'd recently scrubbed it hard. "No, Alanna. Why would I be? He's a perfect gentleman. Just like your father."

"Is he coming down here?"

Francie shook her head.

Alanna smoothed the hem of her nightshirt over her knees, visibly relaxing. "Did you tell him anything about me?"

Francie didn't understand. "What's to tell?"

"Nothing," Alanna said hastily. "I just wondered."

"You can see him tomorrow."

Alanna nodded and fell silent.

Francie located the nightshirt she'd taken out earlier.

"Thanks for being Alex's partner today," Alanna said. "That meant a lot to him."

Though the girl obviously didn't like to show it, she was sensitive to Alex's needs. She treated him like any big sister would, acting put out with him, but Francie had observed her protectiveness.

Her "thank you" came as a shock. Was Francie only imagining that a tiny window of communication was being opened here? "It meant a lot to me, too."

In the darkness, Alanna brushed her fingers over the bedspread.

"Thanks for being your dad's partner," Francie said. "That meant a lot to him."

The girl seemed to stiffen in the crack of light. "It's not your place to thank me. He's my dad."

That figurative window slammed and locked tightly. It had been fitting for Alanna to thank Francie, since Francie was an outsider. But not vice versa. The girl never missed an opportunity to point out that Francie was not really a part of their family.

"Thanks for pointing that out." Tiredly Francie padded into the bathroom and changed her clothes. By then Ryan tapped at the door, and she let him in. Alanna had gone back to her pallet and now lay silent, though she couldn't have been asleep.

Francie wanted to apologize to Ryan for his embarrassment. She wanted to know what Stuart had said after she'd left. Impetuously she took his hand, led him into the bathroom and closed the door. "What happened?"

"Thank you."

"For what?"

"I got a good hard look at where I was heading and I didn't like it," he replied, closing his hands over her upper arms.

Francie sensed a change in Ryan, a change that had something to do with the new light in his eyes and the spirited tone in his voice. "What are you talking about?"

"I'm talking about my father. I love him. But I

don't want to be him—buttoned up…reserved…
indifferent. You saved me.''

"*I* did?''

He nodded, stepping so close, she backed against
the counter and reached to steady herself, knocking a
comb to the floor. "Well, good. But, I meant what
happened after I left?''

He threaded the fingers of one hand into the hair
at her temple. "I assured him everything was fine. I
told him we'd meet him for breakfast in the morning.''

"You did?'' Her heart fluttered at the touch of his
fingertips against her scalp and hair.

He nodded.

This intense closeness and his electrifying touch
caught her off guard. She'd pulled him into the bathroom in her impatience to know what had been said.
She hadn't thought about the fact that she'd changed
into her nightshirt, or what Ryan would think. Or how
their confined closeness would feel. "What are you
doing?''

"Getting ready to kiss you.''

His words sent a thrill of anticipation along her
nerve endings. "With no one watching, I might think
you're doing it because you like it.''

He brought his face closer to hers. "You might.''

She read the purpose in his dark eyes. "Kissing me
in here, like this, would be a reckless thing to do.''

His lips came within a hairbreadth of hers. He
raised his other hand and his fingers brushed her jaw.
"Not well considered or advised, you mean.''

Eager anticipation scattered her thoughts. "That's what I mean."

"I haven't done many reckless things…you'll have to let me know how I do." He touched his lips to hers, and if she'd had any resistance it fled in the wake of the sensation.

The ardent kiss awakened wants and longings she hadn't known she'd harbored. Self-reliant Francie needed Ryan MacNair. A feverish desire to have more, be more, feel more, flared to life, and she clung to his shoulders, raising herself fully into the experience, wondering all the while where her sense had flown to.

Through the fabric of his shirt, his skin was warm, the muscle beneath firm. Touching him like this, not by accident or for show, was heady in its own right. The fact that she'd closed them alone in the tiny space of the bathroom and that she was wearing nothing but her nightshirt and flimsy panties added a tantalizing electricity.

He plowed his fingers into her hair on either side of her head and held her still, availing her mouth to the onslaught of his lips. His head slanted, his urgency a living breathing force that made her senses reel and her skin tingle.

There was nothing cautious in the way he kissed her, none of his studious careful manner. Francie ran her palms down his strong back, grabbed fistfuls of his shirt and clung.

Ryan pressed closer, until she was sitting on the counter, her face raised above his, him standing in the V of her thighs. Behind her, bottles tipped and clanked and she dimly recognized the bristles of her hairbrush dimpling her backside. She leaned sideways and reached to dislodge it. Ryan moved with her, but their lips parted.

His breath ragged, he traced a path along her jaw with his lips, scattering goose bumps along her limbs. "How am I doing?"

She stopped the journey of his mouth by cupping his jaw and raising his face back to hers. "You get an *A* in reckless kissing, Mac."

She kissed him this time, spurred on by the flames of desire he'd ignited. Their breathing grew harsh and irregular, the sound magnified in the stillness of the enclosed space.

Ryan ran his hands down her sides and cupped her hips. She enjoyed that primal sensation until it wasn't enough. Grasping his wrists, she pulled his hands up to cover her breasts through her cotton nightshirt. He made a groaning noise in his throat.

"What are we doing?" she said against his mouth.

He kneaded her flesh gently. "We're doing what we've been thinking about doing for days."

"Did you think it would feel this good?"

"I didn't think anything felt this good."

"Oh, Ryan, I think we'd better stop."

"Okay."

"No, I mean really."

"Okay, you stop first."

His gentle tugs had her quivering. She closed her eyes and sought his lips once more.

His tongue drew hers this time, and she leaned into

the stirring pressure of his hands and the limitless allure of his sensual mouth.

The situation had grown way out of hand. "Okay," she said, drawing air. "We'll both stop at the same time."

"Okay," he said again, the word and his hands not in accord.

"Now," she said. "Stop."

She leaned away and caught her balance with one hand on the counter where she sat.

He raised both palms and took a step back.

They stared at each other.

Her lips were pink and swollen, her skin flushed.

His dark eyes held heavy-lidded desire.

Francie modestly tugged her nightshirt over her thighs and forced herself to look away from his face, willing her heart rate back to normal. "So, what did he say?"

"Who?"

"Your father."

"He, um. He just asked me if I'd lost my mind."

"And what did you say?"

"I said I didn't think so. But then that was before this."

"And then what?"

"And then I just reiterated what I'd said about wanting to change from the way I was before."

"And what did he say?"

"He said he liked me fine that way."

"And—"

"And I said I didn't. There. Geesh. You wanted to

give us privacy, now you want to know everything that was said."

She slid from the vanity counter, careful not to touch him. "I just thought he'd feel free to speak if I wasn't there. Or maybe you would. I don't know."

"I said everything I had to say while you were there."

"He thinks I'm a complete and total idiot."

"He thinks you're a little odd. We're all odd. Odd is relative."

She absorbed that one without comment, and edged around him to the door. "We'd better get some sleep."

"Somewhere," he said, stopping her with his palm against the door, "hidden inside that Francie who would've called an escort service to get a husband for a week…"

She didn't look up to meet his eyes.

"Would you have?"

She tilted her head. "Probably."

"…is a Francie who's very afraid to take chances."

She turned her back to him. "I'm not afraid."

"Yes you are."

"I'm not."

"Mmm-hmm. In there is a Francie in a stuffed shirt. Oh, it's probably red silk with matching pumps, but it's a stuffed shirt."

Finally she met his intent gaze in the mirror. "What are you talking about?"

"You're afraid to take a chance on me. On us."

He wasn't touching her anywhere now, but her

heart beat as fast as it had moments ago when he'd been kissing her senseless. "Relationships aren't about chances."

"It's *all* about taking chances," he insisted. "You have this hang-up because your parents left you. You're afraid you'll be like them and not be able to stick with a commitment."

"A child is a little more than a commitment, Ryan."

"Of course it is. But that fear keeps you from letting go."

"You really don't know me well enough to make that analysis. You don't know what my life has been like before I met you."

"Yes, I do."

She stared at him in the mirror, his eyes dark and more piercing than she was comfortable with. The heat from his body penetrated the back of her nightshirt.

"You live a free and easy life with nothing more entangling than a cat you can drop off at the cat sitter's—"

"Cat sitter's?"

"—because you're not willing to take the risk of really getting involved."

"You're a fine one to talk."

"I don't take chances with my kids or with business affairs. Yes, I was married once and it ended horribly. But I certainly don't think every woman is like Nikki. I don't think you're like her."

Ryan spoke that disclosure softly, his warm breath touching her neck and sending a shiver along her spine. She saw nothing but the blur of their combined reflection. The earnestness in his handsome expression tore away a little more of the restraint his words had eroded and that their sensual attraction had begun.

"Okay, you're right," she said, her voice not sounding at all like her own. "I'm afraid."

He said nothing.

"I've worked hard at making a name for myself and earning a reputation. I chose to go after what I wanted with my career, and I didn't let anything get in the way of that."

"And you think seeing me, maybe caring about me would get in the way of that?"

"I don't know." She passed a hand over her eyes and tried to put her feelings into words. "I'm not willing to give up my freedom."

"Freedom to do what?"

"Whatever I want."

"See other men?"

"No. It's not that."

"Francie, you can have a career, too. Lots of families make it work, find a balance. There's no reason why you can't have both. Trust yourself."

Hope swelled inside her, but she feared giving in to it. She wanted to turn around and fold herself against him, but she held back, and the self-denial left an ache in her chest.

"If being with me takes something away from you," he said softly, "then it's wrong. A relationship should add, not take away. You can have both. You

can have it all. Your parents made a bad choice. That
doesn't mean you have to.''

"Maybe it was the right choice for them.''

"Maybe it was the right choice for you, too. You
had Nana, didn't you? She loves you as much as any
parent could.''

Yes, she'd had Nana. No one could ask for a more
loving, more caring person to raise them. Francie lowered her gaze to the littered vanity and blinked back
tears.

He moved away from the door, bent to pick up a
comb and a can of mousse from the floor and returned
them to the disarray on the counter. "Think about it,
Francie.''

She nodded, reaching for the doorknob. She would
do little else but think about it. Would he press her?
"We have a big day ahead of us.''

"Will we be picking up Nana?''

She scrambled to collect her thoughts. "How about
after breakfast?''

"All right. 'Night.''

She fled from the confined space and scrambled
into her bed, her whole body still tingling from the
kisses and touches they'd shared, her mind numb
from his suggestions. She had to be nuts for even
thinking of continuing a relationship with Ryan. Why
was it the whole family commitment thing she'd
scoffed at for so long didn't seem quite so stifling any
longer?

But even Ryan had allowed his career to over-
shadow his relationship with his children, and she
knew how much he loved Alanna and Alex. If some-

one as steady and dependable as he couldn't juggle both acts, she didn't have a prayer.

That was an unfair assessment, she knew. Ryan had allowed his job to occupy his time to deaden the hurt of his wife's abandonment. And when he'd realized what his behavior was doing to his children, he'd chosen to correct that mistake immediately. But she knew only too well that his regret and change was not indicative of most career parents.

Hers had never come back for her. Never cared that she needed them.

Francie buried her head and refused to listen to Ryan climb into bed with his son. If she thought about him lying only four feet away from her she'd never rest.

Perhaps Stuart would discourage him from continuing to see her, anyway. Maybe in a week or so this whole infatuation would be blown over and behind them.

Maybe she'd better wait to make any decisions until she didn't have the feel of him on her skin and his taste on her lips.

Sure, and maybe it would rain pigs from the sky tomorrow.

The night was long.

10

SHE WAS AVOIDING him like a bad case of hives. All morning as they prepared to leave, she remained polite, but distant. Since checkout time came before the service would end, they packed so their bags could be loaded into the car.

They'd all dressed for the morning's event, planning to leave out casual attire for the plane ride. Ryan and Alex wore lightweight suits. Alanna had brought an ivory dress with a matching midriff jacket. Francie exited the bathroom in a short red dress that nearly stopped Ryan's heart.

The garment was cut straight and plain, not fancy at all, but the way it accentuated her curvy figure and bared her arms and legs kicked his hormones into overdrive.

She'd twisted her hair up into a gold clip in the back, with a few straight tendrils hanging against her neck and cheek, giving her an allover alluring appeal. She caught him staring, and he tried to smile appreciatively, rather than as lecherously as he felt. "Did that dress come with a warning label?"

It took her a second to figure out what he meant, and then she smiled. She handed Alanna a small silky-looking mauve bag, and they spoke with their heads together for a few moments. Alanna followed Francie into the bathroom and the door closed.

Ryan zipped his other suits into his garment bag, refusing to ponder the vagarious nature of women. Especially those two.

Alex sat beside his suitcase and the box that held his carefully packed prize-winning boat, and watched his father with forlorn gray eyes.

"Something wrong, son?"

"No."

Ryan made a neat stack of his luggage beside Alex's. "You sad about this being the last day of our vacation?"

"Kinda."

Ryan sat on the end of the bed he'd straightened and faced Alex. "I made a promise. We'll be taking more vacations together. I'm not going to forget that promise. The way we've done it in the past is not going to be the way it is from here on. We're making a fresh start."

An engaging grin showed off new teeth that still seemed too big for the gaps left by Alex's baby teeth and gave Ryan the bittersweet sensation he got whenever he thought of his children growing older. "Do you think we could go to Disney World?"

"Is that where you want to go?"

Alex nodded.

"If Alanna is agreeable, it sounds good to me."

"Alanna wants to go, too."

"Then I guess we go to Disney World."

Alex got up and stepped closer until he was resting against his dad's knee. "Thanks, Dad."

Ryan opened his thighs and pulled his son back into his lap, dismissing the fact that he wore one of his best suits and that it would probably wrinkle.

Alex reclined against his chest. "Dad?"

"What?"

"Can Francie come with us?"

He'd known the question was coming. Tightening his arm around Alex, he replied, "I'd be happy to have Francie come with us. But we have to remember she has her photography business and a life of her own. Her going would depend on whether or not the time we choose is good for her, and if she wants to come along."

"I bet she will. Francie likes to do fun stuff."

"We'll have to see."

The bathroom door opened and Francie and Alanna emerged, looking toward Ryan and Alex expectantly.

"You two ready?" Ryan asked.

With wide eyes, Francie stood a little behind Alanna. She bobbed her head to one side a couple of times. What on earth was wrong with the woman?

Now her mouth moved, too. She was trying to say something, but no sound was coming out. She kept her hand on Alanna's shoulder, only her face showing any movement.

"You look nice, Alanna," Alex remarked.

Alanna's expectant gaze locked on her father.

Ryan got worried.

Francie rolled her eyes. She'd been trying to tell

him something. He was supposed to do something. Say something. Notice something.

He looked hard at Alanna, trying to see what Alex had seen. She looked lovely, her skin a clean youthful pink. She was his beautiful Alanna.

What was he supposed to notice?

Perhaps she looked a little older, her eyes a little more defined, her lips shiny. Cosmetics? Yes, she was wearing makeup. But this time the effect was natural and becoming.

"You look nice, honey," he said. "Did you try some new makeup?"

His daughter's expectant face broke into a pleased smile. She nodded. "Francie bought it for me."

"It looks nice."

"You really think so?" she asked. "You aren't going to say I'm too young?"

"No. I'm not going to say that. Not as long as it looks this nice."

Alanna smiled.

Francie smiled.

Ryan released a sigh of relief.

Alex piped up, "We're gonna go to Disney World, and Francie, you can come, too!"

Francie's smile faltered.

Alanna's eyes darkened, her smile slipped.

Ryan patted Alex's shoulder. "It's not definite, though. We'll discuss our next vacation as a family, and if it's somewhere you want to go, Alanna, we'll decide together."

"And you said Francie could go," Alex persisted.

"I said if it works out for her and it's something she wants to do."

Alex stood up from his dad's lap and hurried over to Francie. "You want to, don't you?"

"That would be very nice, Alex, and thank you for asking me. We'll have to see how it works out."

Uncomfortably Ryan hoped Francie didn't think he'd placed the notion of pressuring her into Alex's head. And he didn't want Alanna to think they'd been making plans without her. He stood, brushed the creases from his trousers and picked up as many bags as he could carry. "I'll start loading the car."

"I'll help." Alex held the door open.

A half hour later, Stuart was waiting at a table when they arrived at the selected restaurant. He glanced pointedly at his watch.

"Hi, Grandfather," Alex said. "We're gonna go to Disney World."

Stuart's white eyebrows raised. "Oh?" His attention slid from Alex to Ryan to Francie, and his gaze took in the flattering red dress. He was old, but he wasn't dead, and Ryan stifled a laugh at the unnatural expression that crossed his father's face.

Stuart cleared his throat. "You and your sister come sit beside me."

Obediently Alex took a chair.

Alanna followed a little less eagerly.

Ryan held a chair for Francie before seating himself, and the waitress immediately brought menus and coffee.

"I have a few legal matters I want to go over with

you within the next week or two,'' Stuart said to his son. ''We could do it over dinner one evening.''

''Sounds good,'' Ryan replied. ''I packed my planner, so I'll have to give you a call.''

Stuart eyed him with obvious worry, then took a sip of his coffee.

In between ordering and the meal arriving, Alex chattered about the high school play and his boat-building trophy. Stuart listened and smiled stiffly.

''Dad and I got a trophy, too,'' Alanna said. ''Didn't we, Dad?''

Ryan nodded with a smile.

Stuart eyed her as she spoke about the three-legged race. ''Do you have on *makeup*, young lady?'' he asked.

Alanna's expression flattened. ''Yes.''

Stuart looked at Ryan quizzically. ''Isn't she too—''

''Doesn't she look lovely?'' Francie interrupted before he could say the words. ''Warm colors suit her perfectly. Because of her great hair, she can wear clothing in so many shades that not all of us can wear well. Like her ivory dress there…see how it complements her skin and eyes? I would completely wash out in that dress.''

Ryan couldn't imagine Francie 'washing out' in anything, but Alanna sat a little straighter at the complimentary words.

''She has a light hand and a deft touch with a makeup brush,'' Francie continued. ''She's every bit a proper young lady. Not like some of these girls nowadays who dye those awful red streaks in their hair and look like they put on their makeup with a spray gun.'' She made a face.

''And the clothes some of them wear!'' she went on. ''Why, I don't know how their parents can let them out of the house. Alanna has exquisite taste, I'm sure you've noticed.''

''I don't see how your opinion on anything my granddaughter does makes any difference,'' Stuart said, laying his fork down.

''Dad,'' Ryan said gently, but there was a warning in the tone.

''She's—''

''Francie has been very helpful to Alanna this week, and Alanna *is* growing up,'' he said before Stuart could continue.

''However, she's not Alanna's mother, and what she thinks or doesn't think is not definitive.''

''No, she's not Alanna's mother, but I'm her father. This is my decision, Dad. My family. I'm happy. *We're* happy.''

Stuart stared at his son. ''You *have* lost your mind.''

Ryan actually smiled at that. ''Good. I hope it stays lost.''

Francie glanced back and forth from one man to the other, fearful Stuart would get up and leave. She didn't want to be the cause of a family quarrel. She knew it hadn't been her place to speak up, but she couldn't bear for Alanna to take any unwarranted criticism. At least this way the focus was drawn away from the girl and placed on Francie. She wasn't as fragile as Alanna.

Ryan defending both of them warmed Francie from the top of her head to the tips of her toes. Alanna had needed to hear that. And so, she guessed, had she.

"Perhaps you'll be replacing Mrs. Nelson, then?" Stuart said in a snide tone.

Ryan obviously had no intention of being goaded. "Mrs. Nelson is adequate as a housekeeper and cook. I see no reason to let her go. I plan to spend more time with the kids, but I don't plan to spend it cleaning and cooking."

Francie hid a grin behind her napkin.

"I meant replaced by *her*," Stuart said.

"If you mean Francie, she's *not* a housekeeper."

Stuart had been fishing as to whether or not this situation would be permanent, and Ryan hadn't answered. Francie wanted to kiss him for not feeling he needed to explain their personal relationship. Or lack of. She cast him an appreciative smile.

"Dad said Francie can go to Disney World with us," Alex announced. "It's not for sure, though," he clarified, glancing at his father as though proud he'd gotten it straight this time. "And we can share a room again. Dad said Francie's kind of messy, but it's okay. We don't mind."

Francie glanced at Ryan and found him staring at Alex with a combination of horror and confusion reddening his lean jaw and cheekbones. He'd said she was messy? Compared to his neurotic neatness, she guessed she was. She knew full well Alex had taken the statement out of context, but the laughable look on Ryan's face was worth a trip to Disney World. And definitely called for a little harassment.

"I'm messy?" she asked, deliberately raising one brow.

"I don't know why he brought that up. I never said it like that."

"How did you say it?"

"He said you take too much share in the bathroom," Alex said.

"He did, did he?"

Ryan looked as if he wanted to say something, but no words emerged.

"Yeah," Alex went on, "and I thought you guys were going to fix it up last night. You sure were in there together a *lo-ong* time."

It was Francie's turn to choke on her breakfast. She took a gulp of her orange juice and didn't look at Ryan or his father.

Lordy, what did *married* people do for privacy?

"Alex, why don't you tell your grandfather about Nana?" Ryan suggested, finally finding his voice.

Alex launched into an explanation of Nana and the wheelchair rides she gave him.

Good job, Mac. You should have thought to distract him earlier. Francie glanced at Alanna and found the girl's eyes truly twinkling with amusement. She was getting a kick out of their embarrassment! She actually grinned at Francie, and Francie couldn't help returning her smile with a wry shake of her head.

Once the subject had been changed, breakfast concluded in a lighter tone.

"Did you come in a cab?" Ryan asked as they left the restaurant.

His father nodded.

"Ride with us, then."

Francie got in back, with Alex between her and Alanna, and wondered how they'd pick up Nana and her wheelchair.

"We'll arrive at the school auditorium a little early," Ryan said, catching her eye in the rearview mirror. "You go in and get seats and I'll go back for Nana."

A guarded corner of her heart warmed toward him. That thoughtful suggestion hadn't come from only his methodic Type A mind; he was being considerate of her and her grandmother.

Of course, she realized, entering the building and seeing the first few inquisitive stares, his offer left *her* to introduce Stuart to her classmates. Had Ryan really been that generous?

Dressed in a flowing blue dress with a scarf that tied around her long neck and cascaded over her shoulder, Peyton sidled up. "Someone new," she crooned, smiling hungrily at Stuart as though she'd sniffed out his breeding and money.

"Peyton Armbruster, this is Stuart MacNair," Francie said reluctantly.

"MacNair! Oh!"

Francie held her breath.

"Francie's father-in-law," Peyton murmured and stepped closer. "What business are you in?"

Stuart didn't bat an eyelash. He didn't acknowledge the introduction, either. "Alex, come with me."

Alex took his hand, and they headed through the double doors into the auditorium, Stuart drawing questioning looks en route.

Immediately Peyton looked as if she'd bitten into a persimmon. The blue-tinged veins visible above the neck scarf stood out.

Francie flipped a hand nonchalantly. "He's senile," she said, and hurried after them, feigning an apologetic smile.

The auditorium had been spruced up with carnations dyed in Springdale High's school colors. A fringed banner numbered with the graduating year draped the podium.

They saved great seats near the stage, and Francie visited with those on either side. When Ryan wheeled Nana in, Francie sat on the aisle beside her chair and took her hand. The service began with an opening prayer by one of the local pastors. The class valedictorian gave a brief talk on continuing to follow their dreams, and the chorale group sang.

Though he had retired a few years ago and moved out of state, the past high school principal had returned to speak. The winners of all the games and contests were announced and cheered for.

And finally, the lights dimmed. A slide presentation, created from photographs from the class yearbook as well as the recent ones Francie had taken, all set to music, progressed. Francie had always been proud of her work, but never as proud as at this moment when Nana got tears in her eyes and patted her hand repeatedly.

Francie received an uncommon surprise when several shots of her were displayed in a row. Slightly off center, but capturing the concentration on both their faces, one photo showed her and Alex, heads bent together, gluing masts to their boat.

In the next one, Alex's freckled face tilted to hers, a look of adoration on his dear features, and at the vulnerability in that look, her heart caught.

For an amateur, Ryan had used light and angles to a visual advantage, pleasantly surprising her.

The next photo centered on Francie, sun glinting from her breeze-tossed hair, a smile of joy softening her features as she watched Alex receive their trophy. The look of love and pride could have belonged to…a mother.

A strange, undefinable feeling of warmth and joy blossomed in her chest. Her throat burned as if she had to cry, but she stifled the shaken-up sensation, because it was unfamiliar and it carved craters in her preconceived assumptions about her own nature.

She never saw pictures of herself. Her parents hadn't doted over her every growth process as did other mothers and fathers. They'd been taking pictures of news in the making, hell-bent on winning Pulitzers, not concerned with preserving memories of their only child growing up.

As soon as she'd been old enough, Francie had always been *behind* a camera lens.

So these photographs were special...but in more ways than one. Ryan had taken them.

And he'd taken them with as much sensitivity as an artist.

He'd taken them with love.

She had turned over the last few rolls of film to the baccalaureate committee last night, never imagining the shots he'd taken would be so moving, or that the committee would choose to use them.

Francie met his tender gaze over Alex's head in the semidarkness. The slides had affected him, too. Were her emotions as plainly visible as his?

He leaned in front of Alex. She bent to hear him whisper in her ear, "You are beautiful."

How did one reply to disturbing words like that? How had she lived so long without caring that a man had never said them to her, had never thought her beautiful? She sat back, hoping her expression didn't match the foolish fluttering in her chest.

The lights came up. Around them applause roared.

"That was you and me, huh, Francie!" Alex cried with pleasure.

She nodded and returned his hug, never taking her eyes from his father.

Finally Alanna said something to Ryan, and he turned to reply.

"I'm so proud of you, Francesca," Nana said from her other side.

Francie hugged her tearfully. "Thank you."

"Your parents would have been proud of you, too," she said, with a vigorous bob of her white-haired head.

"Maybe," Francie replied. "But you're the one who took care of me and loved me. All I really care about is what you think. And that you're happy."

"I'm happy, don't you give that a second thought. There isn't an old lady in all of Illinois who gets as good of care as I do. You've seen to that."

Francie pressed her cheek to her grandmother's, their warm tears of joy mingling.

The service had ended and people milled around them, raving over her photographs. Francie composed herself and swiped at her cheeks.

"Francie, I have all your slides," J.J. called over several heads. "Hang around."

She waved her understanding.

A light buffet lunch had been set up in the cafeteria so all the out-of-town attendees could eat before starting their trips home, as well as have a gathering place to say their final goodbyes.

The MacNairs, Alex pushing Nana, located a table, and Francie went through the food line for her grandmother and carried her plate back.

Nana had been a Springdale resident for nearly ninety years, and her presence attracted immediate attention. Friends, fellow church members, former neighbors, all stopped by to say hello.

Nana enjoyed the vigilance and the company more than the food. Every so often Francie reminded her to eat.

Distinctly out of place, Stuart ate a sandwich and nursed coffee from a foam cup. His scowl grew more fierce with each person who asked if he was Francie's father-in-law.

Finally the crowd thinned, but the core group stood nearby, spouting platitudes and promising to keep in touch better during the next ten years.

J.J. handed Francie an envelope. "Your slides."

Shari Donegan hurried to her side. "Francie, can I use those for the reunion book we're putting together? I'll send them to you as soon as it's finished. In fact, I was hoping you'd help me select the rest of the pictures."

"No problem," Francie replied.

Becka came closer, too. "Thank you for the wonderful pictures," she said with a sincere smile.

Don Armbruster walked over to Ryan's father. "I hope I get to see a Karr-Taylor exhibit soon. Have you seen all of her work?"

"I have no idea what you're talking about." Stuart's scowl turned on Francie. "Are you a professional photographer?"

Peyton caught that remark with her unerring ear. "How could you not know what she does for a living?"

"Never met her before yesterday."

Francie's heart plunged.

"You live in Chicago, don't you?" Peyton asked, her eyes narrowing.

"I do."

Peyton exchanged a haughty look with Shari, then

turned to Francie. "This whole thing with your little family has seemed fishy from the start. How come none of us met Ryan until now? If you'd caught yourself a man like this one, I'd think you'd have brought him to meet your grandmother before this. And that 'child,'" she said, indicating Alanna, "can't stand you, but you act like everything's all hunky dory. And not very good acting, by the way."

Peyton turned slightly. "Now this gentleman you say is your father-in-law says he's never met you before. You claimed to have been married six months as of Valentine's Day, though that's actually only five months, but your father-in-law, who lives in the same city, came all the way here to meet you for the first time? The whole story is more than shaky."

Francie couldn't run, as was her first inclination. She had Nana here to think of and to take home. In that moment, she realized that none of this really mattered, though. These people hadn't cared about her until she seemed to fit into their expectations. She never had to see them again if she chose not to.

And the MacNairs? They could all go home and forget this week had ever happened; they had their precious brooch…and each other.

But Nana. Nana did matter. And Nana cared whether or not Francie was married. In retrospect, would it have been better to let Nana worry over her marital state, rather than see her embarrassed and disappointed like this? The whole plan had been for her sake, to protect her from concern, but Nana wouldn't understand that.

She'd be disappointed in Francie. And rightly so. Francie had added an elaborate lie to her single status.

All that had ever mattered was Nana.

"If I'm the child you're talking about," Alanna said, coming to stand defensively beside Francie, "then you don't know kids very well. I guess I said some rotten things about Francie when I was mad that night I hid from my dad. But Francie's the best mom I ever had. I should have said I was sorry that night, but I didn't."

Alanna glanced from Francie to her dad, then looked back at Peyton. "Stepfamilies have a lot of adjusting to do," she continued, as though the woman needed a quick course in manners and family concerns. "I was mean to Francie because I was jealous of the love and attention my dad gives her. But I know my dad loves me, too. And I know Francie loves me. We're all just getting used to each other. We just need to keep communicating."

Francie didn't know whether that insight had come from Alanna's counseling sessions or an episode of "Montel," but it had sounded genuine enough and seemed to have had the desired quieting effect on Peyton.

"Francie loves me, too," Alex piped up. "And we're going to Disney World *next* time."

"My father's been out of the country," Ryan said, stepping around Alex and hugging Francie to him with one arm. "Otherwise he'd have met Francie by now. She's not exactly a wife I'd want to keep a secret now, is she?"

Ryan's quick cover up surprised Francie even more than the kids'. He'd been opposed to this from the start, and now here he was keeping her story afloat as though he was an accomplished fraud.

Stuart's expression conveyed his annoyance with the whole ridiculous scheme as well as a tinge of regret for not keeping his mouth shut and letting the others handle it.

Francie gave him a tentative smile so he'd know it had turned out okay.

From beside her, her grandmother spoke up. "You always were an uppity one, Peyton Baxter," Nana said, using Peyton's maiden name, the name that linked her to the town's furnace repairman, her father. "A body'd think you were jealous of Francie marrying a handsome rich man with such lovely children and still being able to have her photography career, while you kept Neiman Marcus in business."

"I'm not jealous," Peyton denied emphatically. "I just saw all the inconsistencies in her background stories all week. Nobody can say it wasn't odd."

"Odd is relative, you know," Francie said softly.

"Well, if there's one thing I love about Francie," Ryan said, ignoring her, "and there are many things I love about her, mind you, it's that she's full of inconsistencies. She's never boring, that's for sure." He kissed her cheek for emphasis.

Francie accepted the kiss, studied the warm assurance in his dark eyes and felt the loving support of this family to the tips of her toes. Each one of them had protected her story. Even Nana, bless her heart, who believed it to be true, and now wouldn't have to know Francie had lied to her.

Francie swallowed the lump in her throat. If only Ryan had meant those words of love.

With lowered lids, Peyton wished them goodbye, gathered her husband and son and left. The Donegans and the Richardses waved as Ryan wheeled Nana to the door and Francie, Stuart and the kids followed.

"I'll call a cab," Stuart suggested. "My flight leaves in forty-five minutes."

"I'll drop you off at the airport and come back for these guys," Ryan insisted. "We don't leave until later this afternoon."

Stuart accepted a peck on the cheek from his grandchildren, then turned to Francie. "Goodbye. It's been...unusual."

"Goodbye, Stuart." Francie waved him off.

11

WITHIN THE HOUR, they had returned Nana to the care center and settled her down to rest. "I want to speak with your nurses before I go," Francie told her.

Nana shooed her on her way. "Jim will sit with me until I fall asleep. Alanna, darling, why don't you go down and play something on the piano in the day-room? I can hear it from here."

"Okay. Come with me, Alex."

Ryan watched his children scamper off, hand in hand. "You and your granddaughter do have a good effect on those children of mine."

"They just need love. You can't love anybody too much."

"How right you are."

"You know, Ryan MacNair," she said, using his real name and narrowing her alert gaze on his face. "You have your work cut out for you in making Francesca see she's worthy of your love. It's not you she doesn't trust, it's herself. I don't know how she found you, or how you came to be here this week, but you're exactly what she needs."

Ryan stared at her in abashment.

"I think you need her, too."

He couldn't find his voice for a full minute, but finally he said, "I do."

"Then don't let her go."

She knew. She'd known all along. Her wise old eyes glistened with unshed tears.

He found his voice. "I've talked to her, Nana. But she's afraid to make a commitment."

"Because she thinks she'll let you down. But she won't. She's never let me down her whole life. Look what she did this week just to make me happy."

"You and I know that. Now I need to convince her."

Her eyes drifted shut. "You will," she said. "You will."

Ryan patted her hand and tucked the soft fringed throw around her. The lighthearted notes of a concerto drifted down the hallway. Alanna had probably drawn a crowd by now.

"She sleeping?"

He turned as Francie entered the room, and he nodded.

She gestured to the doorway, and led him out onto the shaded veranda where a few residents sat playing cards. "I spoke with her nurses about her care. Her doctors say she had a silent heart attack sometime over the past months. It's weakened her some, but she's doing as well as can be expected."

"I'd say she's doing very well." He glanced at his watch. "What do you want to do until flight time?"

She surveyed their pleasant surroundings. "Stay here?"

He agreed. "She'll probably wake up before we go, and we can say goodbye."

She nodded.

He pointed to a glider and they sat side by side. Ryan set it in gentle motion, and she watched his leg flex beneath his impeccably creased trousers.

A breeze caught her hair, and she tucked an errant strand behind her ear. They were so different, the two of them. How could anything come of this?

"You really are beautiful," he said.

Heat tinged her cheeks. She didn't look at him.

"I've learned a lot from you this week, Francie."

She looked over. "Like what?"

"Like life's too short to worry about what people think or to miss out on the things that are important."

"What kinds of things?"

"You know. Things like enjoying a day just because it's there and you'll never be able to get it back again. Things like appreciating the people who love you and seeing that spending time with them is far more important than simply providing for them."

"You already knew those things."

He nodded, a slow smile gracing his handsome features. "Maybe I knew them intellectually, but I didn't feel them. Those are two different things. I needed you to show me."

Was it possible that their differences were complementary? That they could actually be good for each other?

"I don't want our time together to end," he said. "I don't want to go back home and pretend I didn't feel anything."

"You don't have to pretend you don't feel anything." As soon as she'd said that, she followed it quickly with "What do you feel?"

"Like a different person. Like we're supposed to be a family."

He still looked the same, still wore an elegantly tailored suit and turned heads wherever he went. But he had changed. He wasn't the same buttoned-up man who had come seeking the brooch. And that amazing ability to change challenged her. Maybe he was right. Perhaps she was the one buttoned-up, the one too inflexible to alter her way of thinking. After all, hadn't she been contemplating the same things? Hadn't she been imagining herself with a family—with *this* family?

"Son, could you get an aide for me?" one of the gentleman on the veranda called.

With a rueful glance, Ryan stood and walked toward him. "What do you need, sir?"

"I'd like to go in and drain the radiator." The old fellow pointed to the doors.

"I think I can manage to push you in the right direction." Ryan steered the fellow's wheelchair into the building.

Francie got up and strolled across the lawn, rolling Ryan's words over in her mind. She questioned her motives in making the decision she'd made to remain emotionally unentangled.

She'd been living in fear. And she'd been untrusting of her own character. She'd been prepared to resent everything about family involvement. If someone had told her a month ago that bonding with a man and two children could be a rewarding and pleasurable experience, she'd have told them they were nuts.

In trying to make her grandmother happy, she'd found that the things she'd resisted with all her might really could make her happy, too: a man to love her—not that Ryan had ever said he loved her, but someone to be there for her when she needed emotional support, and children who looked up to her and defended her.

Those kids. They truly cared about her. And doggone it, she'd gone and fallen for them, too.

The irony struck her. Nana had been right all along. Oh, if she only knew the truth of it, she'd have a good laugh over the realization Francie was just now coming to.

Francie: self-reliant; risk taker; reckless. Afraid... *Alone.*

She found a spot of shade under a tree, but her skirt was too short to sit on the ground comfortably. She moved on to the fountain and perched on the concrete base.

Ryan, the man she'd called a stuffed shirt, was willing to give this alliance a shot. That took courage. And a belief in himself as well as her.

He crossed the lawn toward her now, his dark hair reflecting the sun. He'd removed his jacket, and it hung draped over his shoulder on one hooked finger. Here was the man she might just possibly love—*love?*

Her heartbeat snagged at the idea.

Had she ever said those words in her life? Had she told her parents before they left her? Surely she had. Had she ever told Nana? She hoped so.

Would saying them take anything away from her?

Just thinking them had given her something: a soul-deep gratification and joy. A new place of hope on the inside. He'd told Peyton he loved many things about her—but could he actually *love* her? Not just appreciate her, or desire her, but love her?

And in that moment, with the sun glinting from his hair, and her heart thudding as though she'd run all the way from Chicago, she knew without a doubt or a fear that she loved Ryan MacNair.

She raised her hand without thought, a half welcome, half warning. "I love you!"

Her voice carried across the lawn.

His step didn't falter. He didn't behave as though the earth had just turned on its axis and threatened to throw her off into space. He reached her within seconds and stopped, the afternoon sun at his back, shading her.

"I don't think I've ever said it before."

"I'm glad you did," he replied, "because now I can tell you I love you, too."

Her heart jumped giddily, and she grasped at words, afraid to hope. "I'm used to having my own way and doing what I please and not reporting to anyone."

"You've been considerate the entire week," he countered.

"I leave messes everywhere."

He shrugged. "I can't skate."

She smiled, daring to hope. "I don't cook."

"I have a housekeeper, but she can't kiss like you."

"You've kissed her?"

He smiled. "I plan my appointments weeks in advance and color code my calendar pertaining to the event."

"That *is* sick. What color is family time?"

"There hasn't been one until now."

"What color is romance?"

"What's *your* favorite color?"

She stood to face him, daring to believe. "You really love me?"

"I really do." He tossed his suit jacket on the cement bench and ran his hand down her arm to take her hand. "I make out all my checks at the beginning of the month and mail them five days before the due date."

"This is more serious than I thought."

"I did lay my jacket down without folding it."

"But you thought about it."

He chuckled, but then his face grew serious. "Does this mean you're giving us a chance?"

She nodded. "I'm giving myself a chance, too."

"We'll take it slow and easy," he said.

"Judging from the other night, I don't think you have a slow and easy switch."

"I just want to make you happy. And I want you to be comfortable with your decision."

"I am. On both counts. And Ryan, the very last thing I'd ever want to do is hurt Alanna and Alex. I know I'll only love them more and more as time passes, and as long as they want me for a friend or whatever they want me for, I'll be there for them."

"I know you will. Just be yourself, Francie. And

let us love you. That's all any of us wants or needs from you.''

She reached up to touch his face, her fingers skimming the strong curve of his jaw, his sensual lips, the tiny lines that fanned out beside his eye, her heart full with the wonder of this man's love. ''How do people with children manage time alone?''

He brought a hand to her waist. ''I think red would be an appropriate color.''

''For what?''

''For Alone Time on the calendar.''

He pulled her against him and she went willingly. ''What if something more…spontaneous comes up?''

''There are locks.''

''Locks? I have my own apartment.''

His lips came within inches of hers. ''I promise not to say anything about the mess.''

Their lips met then, a sensual fusion that sucked her breath away and started her heart leaping giddily.

She leaned into his embrace and lost herself to the magic of the sensations he created with his kisses and the joy of belonging.

''Dad! Francie!'' childish voices chorused.

Ryan ended the kiss, but kept her tucked snugly against his side as he turned. Alanna and Alex raced along the curving sidewalk that led to the fountain.

''Concert over?'' Ryan asked.

Alanna nodded. ''They kept asking for more and more pieces. A lady even came and served cookies for everyone.''

''She was great, Dad.'' Alex took his dad's hand and leaned against him.

"I have some news," Ryan said.

His children looked up at him expectantly.

"I think Francie will be going to Disney World with us. That is if that's where you'd like to go, Alanna."

"Sure," she said easily. "That's cool." She eyed the two of them. "Does this mean you two are going to, like, go out?"

"Yes, we're going to 'go out,'" Francie replied. "But I'm not going to get in the way of your family time together. I think you should still have that time just for the three of you."

"What if we want you along during our family time?" Alanna asked.

"Yeah," Alex said.

Francie couldn't help her surprise or her tears of pleasure. "Well, then I'll be glad to join you."

They smiled at one another.

"I'd better go see if Nana's awake yet," Francie said finally. "I have to tell her I love her before we go."

Alanna moved beside her. "I'll go with you."

Ryan watched the two of them cross the lawn, his daughter in ivory, his...*Francie* in bright red. A lot had changed in the past week. Even more in the past day.

"Do you think you and Francie might get married, Dad?" Alex asked. "Could she be our mom?"

"If it's something she wants in the future, Alex. I'm going to pray it will be."

"I'll pray, too."

Later, after saying their goodbyes to Nana, and

promising to visit over Thanksgiving break, they stood in line waiting to board their plane.

"What are you going to do with those?" Francie asked, noting the laptop and briefcase at his feet.

"Store them overhead," he replied, convincing her of his remarkable transformation.

"Dad?"

He turned.

"Can I sit by Francie?"

After promising each of the kids they could have a turn sitting by Francie, he took her hand and kissed it.

She looked up with a smile, her heart full to bursting. "Thanks for being my husband this week," she said, caressing his fingers.

"Any time."

"Really?"

"Really."

"I mean *really* really?"

"Any kind of really you'd like."

"We could stop in Vegas on the way home."

He grinned. "This flight doesn't go to Vegas."

She glanced at the monitor over his shoulder. "No, but the next flight does."

His eyes widened, and he inspected his wild, impulsive Francie's expression. She was kidding. *Wasn't she?* "You would marry me, Francie?"

"Guess you won't know unless you ask."

His expression grew serious. His fingers found the gold band she hadn't removed since he'd given it to her. "What do you say to making this the real thing?

I love every crazy impulsive thing about you and I want you to be my wife. Will you marry me?''

She looked into his somber dark eyes. ''On one condition.''

''What's that?''

''That it's forever.''

He pulled her hand to his lips and kissed her fingers. ''I promise, Francie. I do promise.''

She stood on her toes to accept a sweet soul-reaching kiss, then turned in his arms to find two sets of amused eyes watching them. ''Change of plans, kids,'' she said with a husky voice. ''We're taking the next flight to Las Vegas.''

Their whoops echoed across the concourse.

▼ SILHOUETTE®
DESIRE™ 2-IN-1

AVAILABLE FROM 16TH MAY 2003

0503/51a

PLAIN JANE & DOCTOR DAD Kate Little

Dynasties: The Connellys

Handsome doctor Doug Connelly suggested a marriage of convenience to help Maura Chambers with her unborn baby—but the hungry look in his amber eyes had her hoping for more. Until she discovered his little secret...

AND THE WINNER GETS...MARRIED! Metsy Hingle

Dynasties: The Connellys

Buying her boss, gorgeous Justin Connelly, in a bachelor auction allowed Kimberly Lindgren to have one fantasy night. But how could she give her virgin heart in the dark of night and take it back in the light of day?

HER LONE STAR PROTECTOR Peggy Moreland

Millionaire's Club

Gruff private investigator Robert Cole was smitten by lovely florist Rebecca Todman, but secrets in her past made her wary. Could he convince her of the depth of his feelings and win her trust...and her heart?

TALL, DARK...AND FRAMED? Cathleen Galitz

Millionaire's Club

Tycoon Sebastian Wescott was innocent—he certainly didn't need alluring attorney Susan Wysocki to defend him! But while she tried to prove his innocence, he found himself increasingly guilty—of falling in love...

A PRINCESS IN WAITING Carol Grace

Royally Wed: The Missing Heir

Dashing Charles Rodin *seems* to be marrying pregnant beauty Lise to right the wrongs of her ex-husband, his brother. But Charles has always loved Lise...

A PRINCE AT LAST! Cathie Linz

Royally Wed: The Missing Heir

Luc Dumont, head of palace security, is the new king—and Juliet Beaudreau is to teach him royal protocol. He's determined to sweep her into his arms, but can he convince her to be his queen?

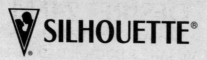

SILHOUETTE
SPECIAL EDITION

proudly presents seven more fantastic stor
from

Lindsay McKenna's

exciting series

MORGAN'S
MERCENARIES

Meet Morgan's newest team:
courageous men and women destined for
greatness — fated to fall in love!

FREE!

1 Book
and a surprise gift!

We would like to take this opportunity to thank you for reading this Silhouette® book by offering you the chance to take another specially selected title from the Desire™ series absolutely FREE! We're also making this offer to introduce you to the benefits of the Reader Service™—

- ★ FREE home delivery
- ★ FREE gifts and competitions
- ★ FREE monthly Newsletter
- ★ Books available before they're in the shops
- ★ Exclusive Reader Service discount offer

Accepting this FREE book and gift places you under no obligation to buy; you may cancel at any time, even after receiving your free shipment. Simply complete your details below and return the entire page to the address below. ***You don't even need a stamp!***

YES! Please send me 1 free Desire book and a surprise gift. I understand that unless you hear from me, I will receive 2 superb new titles every month for just £4.99 each, postage and packing free. I am under no obligation to purchase any books and may cancel my subscription at any time. The free books and gift will be mine to keep in any case.

D3ZEB

Ms/Mrs/Miss/Mr ....Initials ....
BLOCK CAPITALS PLEASE

Surname ....

Address...

....

....Postcode ....

Send this whole page to:
UK: The Reader Service, FREEPOST CN81, Croydon, CR9 3WZ
EIRE: The Reader Service, PO Box 4546, Kilcock, County Kildare (stamp required)